NO MOTIVE IN MURDOCH

J. L. Bass

Always live the story you want to be told

J L Bass

Cover Design & Illustration by Lisa Blake

Published By: J.L. Bass Books
ISBN-13: 978-0692045220
ISBN-10: 0692045228

The tragedy of an unlived life is the saddest tragedy of all.
This book is dedicated to all of those who left us before their story was complete.

Thank you to the family and friends who have championed this book for years. It wouldn't have seen the light of day, if not for your unending support, unconditional love, and consistently asking, "So, when can I read it?"
Thank you for keeping this dream alive.

CHAPTER 1

Julia's laptop sits atop her slim thighs as she hunts and pecks through her files. Scraps of old stories. Laundry lists of unused dialogue. Sifting through these folders for inspiration used to fuel her creativity. These days it feels more like meandering through an overgrown graveyard. She half-heartedly skims a short story she'd written last fall for a writing class she taught at New York University.

Uninspired, she stares at the twenty-something singing her heart out on the reality TV vocal competition and mindlessly takes another sip of wine. Suddenly, the TV flickers and then turns solid neon pink. No picture, no sound, just a pink screen.

What the hell?

Julia shuffles her computer to the side and walks to the TV to fiddle with the remote control, turning the set on and off and finally rebooting the whole system. Banging on the silver cable box, Julia gets nowhere. So she finally relents and returns to her chair.

Taking a deep breath, she exhales. Just as she does, "Boom, da-da-da-da. Boom da-da-da-da." The audible sound of music filters through her ceiling from the condo above her.

How am I supposed to concentrate when Lucas is listening to that music? Damn'it!

Julia abruptly stands again, thoughts racing as quick as her adrenaline-infused heartbeat. Anger lining every single pulse as she stomps over to the kitchen cabinet to refill her wine glass.

When did my life become this? When did I become this?

"This is so stupid!" She screams into the empty living room. Well, empty except for her fat calico cat, Mr. Pickles, who's happily perched along the back of the sofa. Not even Mr. Pickles looks up during her rants anymore, which seem to be more and more often these days.

So, this is what it's liked to be blocked. Stuck. Railroaded. Maybe I just need to get laid. Yes, I definitely need to do that. It's been too long. Frank really needs to come home.

Annoyed, Julia swiftly returns to the cable box once more seeking some distraction from her graveyard of stories and her squirrel brain full of chatter. She turns on the TV once again, still pink. She slams her hand down on the silver box, still pink.

"Boom, da-da-da-da. Boom da-da-da-da." The music continues.

"What the hell is he doing up there?" She asks Mr. Pickles, who never raises his head.

Julia plops back down into her overstuffed armchair and throws her feet onto the ottoman. After a few sips of her Chilean Merlot, her moment of rage softens into a self-deprecating chuckle. Then a full-on laugh.

"What the hell am I doing down here?" She muses.

It's a question that tumbles through her mind often. *What am I doing?* And it's usually followed with a litany of others about what's next with her career, her relationship, and her life?

The truth is, she just doesn't know.

As a child, Julia used to love playing the game Life with the neighborhood kids. They'd play for hours, usually fighting over who got to be the red car. Julia marveled at navigating through the sequence of steps, of getting married, having children, and buying a house. As a nine-year-old she was certain this was a true depiction of adulthood. What she didn't bargain for was that life came with no rule book. Sure, there were protocols of behavior and societal expectations, which she found both frustrating and comforting.

But it's at times like now when her inner nine-year-old still wishes she could just spin the wheel, draw a card, and be told how many steps, and in what direction, to take next. Instead, she just finds herself squirming, shutting down, and spontaneously bursting into raucous rants in her living room over trivial things, like cable boxes and the neighbor's music.

At forty-four, Julia Jarvis sees what she needs, more importantly wants, to see about herself and her life. The rest she leaves alone, with no intention of touching. Ever. During the rise of her success with her book *Steelhouse*, more than one reporter poked around her personal life looking for juicy, magazine-selling material. She would toss out little nuggets of personal stories here and there to keep the reporters satisfied. She had been in their shoes not long ago and knew they needed a little bait to keep the story lively.

Yet, when they'd go too far with their questioning, perhaps about Julia's late husband, Seth, or her childhood, her response was always graciously: "My life is like a book. Some chapters are meant to be read aloud, others are not."

Over the past few months, since completing her teaching job at NYU, there were days she rarely got dressed, let alone left the confines of her Manhattan condo. She thought it was hormones or maybe a mid-life crisis. Hell, maybe a little of both.

In this moment sitting in her living room sipping wine, after beating a cable box and cursing poor Lucas, all she knows is that it's not working. None of it. Not her television. Not her creativity. Not her social life. And certainly not her long-distance relationship with Frank, who conveniently always seems to be on assignment for a photo shoot in some far reach of the world.

Though lately, Frank isn't the man she's been dodging. That would be Jeff, her dear friend who calls almost daily now asking if she has any new story ideas or new material. Jeff had called and texted five times in the past two days to remind her of the meeting with Priscilla Bauer approaching next week. As Julia's publicist, it is Jeff's job to make sure she remembers her important appointments, and as her friend, he cares whether she shows up.

In the eight years Julia has known Jeff, she's always marveled at his ability to remember everything. His keen curiosity emanates from his smoky blue eyes, the kind that peer right through you. It's why she finds it so hard to lie to him. She always has this sense his eyes can read her thoughts, even when she's not looking into them. Yet, it's this sixth sense that makes Jeff so good at his job. In addition to a strong gut instinct, he has a deft ear for bullshit, which has enabled him to successfully navigate Manhattan's aggressive publishing world.

Unlike Jeff, reality isn't something Julia does well, especially during life's bumpy junctures. As a young girl, Julia daydreamed about what it would be like to be a famous writer. While her friends were fretting over which boy to date or who would be prom queen, Julia was focused on two things: getting out of Chicago and becoming a *New York Times* bestselling author.

Though by high school, her aspirations of being a novelist were put on hold. Her gift for words moved away from the narrative prose of English essays and entries in her journal to reporting for her high school newspaper and working summers at the local paper as an assistant. It was journalism that became her ticket out of Chicago and landed her a scholarship at Ball State University in Indiana. Oh, it wasn't sexy. It wasn't Harvard or Stanford or even eating Ramen noodles in a ghetto apartment in Queens trying to make it as a Broadway performer like her childhood friend Cheryl. But young Julia was thrilled to escape the suburbs of Chicago and escape the revolving door of men her mother brought home between nursing shifts.

In the midst of life's heartaches and confusion, even as a child trying to understand why she had no sisters or brothers or daddy, writing became Julia's invisible shield to keep reality at arm's length. In her land of make-believe, the world had an order of her creation. By her teens and early twenties, that sense of order fueled Julia's drive to raise the curtain of injustice. Becoming a journalist wasn't just about storytelling, it was about truth telling. That is, until the day you realize the truth doesn't set you free. The truth can turn your world inside out, upside down, and threaten your very existence. So in light of that truth, you cower backward and spiral inward to a world of your own creation once more.

Julia never imagined newspaper reporting would fit her quiet disposition and desire to blend in. At nearly five-foot-ten (which she had reached by her freshman year of high school) with a quick wit, expansive vocabulary, and wild mane of wavy auburn hair, Julia did anything but blend in.

As an only child with a small extended family, she'd always felt this nagging sense of being different, as if everywhere she went she was an outsider looking in on a world she couldn't quite comprehend. Writing provided a tether to that world she so desperately wanted to be a part of, and yet also provided her a shield to empathize, while remaining emotionally detached. Like any expert craftsman who pours her soul into the work, over time Julia had become a masterful craftsman, methodically weaving those twenty-six letters of the alphabet together as a tapestry reflecting the human experience.

So when Priscilla Bauer of Bauer & Brown Publishing called eighteen months earlier to tell Julia that *Steelhouse* had hit the *Times'* bestseller list, it wasn't anything like what she had envisioned as a little girl. It was more.

Her quiet life of freelance writing and teaching adjunct classes at the community college had steadily become a public one that thrust her into a world of attending black-tie galas, hosting book readings, judging literary awards, and making public appearances at bookstores across the country. As *Steelhouse* climbed up the bestseller's list, Julia's life climbed right out of her comfort zone.

Most writers only dream of the fame that *Steelhouse* has afforded her. "Beginner's luck," she would say when she was on the receiving end of the reporter's questions. Though she downplayed her success in the self-deprecating way she'd always shrugged her accomplishments, Julia's always been damn proud of that book. Because when a book hits the *Times*, it's one thing. When it hits number one, it's an entirely different byproduct. It was more gratifying and far more exhausting than Julia could have envisioned as a young, aspiring journalist.

Julia is keenly aware she's now held in a different esteem. That means she's to have the answers and have a wickedly brilliant stream of words flow from her every thought. It's why nights like tonight alone in her apartment with her unedited mind hashing through everything that's wrong feels so incredibly uncomfortable. Now, it's Julia who is suspended in a story of her own creation.

The hurricane of fame *Steelhouse* created left Julia realizing that the world expected, and wanted, a second act. The pressure of following that book's success has weighed on every vowel and consonant that she's tried to write since. Each time she roams her imagination for fresh ideas, she comes back empty handed. As the days creep by, Julia knows she's teetering on the verge of irrelevancy, not to mention breaching her contract for the second book.

It's why Julia avoids Jeff's calls and why she much prefers to sip Merlot and eat squares of chocolate watching twenty-something kids on reality TV. Kids who believe their musical dreams are still possible. Certainly her life, well at least her career, is a testament to the fact that some dreams do come true. Though others do not. Like her dream of a long marriage to Seth with a house full of kids, a dog, and cereal crumbs smashed in the carpet.

No, that dream came to a halt with a single shot on a cold winter's night in 1996. That dream turned into a nightmare, and one she never wished to revisit.

So now, from where she sits, Julia has distinct moments of feeling too old to be young and too young to be old. No one prepares women for this phase of life. The phase where your uterus is quickly becoming of no use and so, they think, your brain must have dried up, too.

For Julia that means an added pressure of working even harder. If women can rise to the top with a family and mountains of responsibility, then she has no room for excuses, or errors, as a (relatively) single woman. Relative in that she's still unsure of where she and Frank stand now after their last big fight about her unwillingness to commit.

Julia rubs her index finger around the edge of her glass, relieved that the searing blotches of anger are retreating from her face. She sighs deeply, sinking into her breath and realizing she needs a change of scenery, a "pattern interrupt" as one therapist had called it.

She stands emphatically. "Mr. Pickles, I'm going to the store. I'll be right back."

Mr. Pickles never stirs.

Julia adjusts her hair into a makeshift bun as she walks to the coat closet. She slips on a lightweight black sweater and locks the door behind her. Three steps down the hall toward the elevator, she feels the buzz of her cell phone in her jeans pocket.

"Shit." She mutters under her breath retrieving her phone, hoping it's not Jeff.

KATE appears on the display, and she smiles broadly for what feels like the first time in days.

Julia swipes to answer. "Kate?"

"Hey gurl!" Kate replies brightly.

Julia finds it amusing that with all the years of friendship and mounds of accomplishments between the two of them, Kate still calls Julia "gurl." For Julia, that young woman she'd been when she first met Kate in Murdoch feels like another chapter of life long forgotten. Life, and death, have a funny way of altering time.

"Oh gurl, I'm so glad I caught you…how are you?"

Julia smiles. She loves the openness of Kate's drawl and her girlish, Southern sensibilities, which Kate has somehow kept intact, even after years of rolling elbow deep as a corporate litigator and prominent figure in Atlanta's social scene.

Over the years, Julia's missed being surrounded by that unabashed sense of Southern warmth. Though she knows full well that the sugary sweet Southern bless-your-heart charm can also be a façade to distract from the unpleasant realities of life. In Kate's case, however, she makes no qualms about speaking her mind, no matter how sweet or unpleasant.

Julia glances down as she nears the elevator and sighs heavily. "Oh, you know, I'm okay…on the way to the store. I needed to get out of the house a minute after having a meltdown."

"Oh dawg. What happened? You okay?" Kate's voice turns to concern.

Julia laughs remembering her outburst. "I'm fine. My piece-of-shit television stopped in the middle of 'The Next Star.' It just blinked and turned bright pink. I don't know what happened…or why I even watch that stupid show. It's such a waste of time…"

"You watch it because that country singer coach is hotter than a dawg in heat." Kate cackles into the phone like a twelve-year-old schoolgirl.

Julia's cheeks soften as she bursts into laughter. "Yeah, he is…so what's going on? Oh and hey, I'm going into the elevator so if I lose you…I'll call you back…"

"Okay gurl…yeah, you know I'm good. Busy as usual. Jerry's in LA this week pitching a new client, so I'm just enjoying a little me time. In discovery on a big case so it's nice to have what's left of the evenings to myself."

"Aren't you always in the middle of a big case?" Julia laughs softly. Arriving at the first floor, she steps onto the marble entry way as the new doorman opens the heavy glass door. She half-smiles and mouths, "thanks," to him.

"Yeah, seems that way. But you know, this one is different because it involves a chairman of a board for a public company. They think he had his hands in the wrong pot. Well, many wrong pots. So, you know, it's just layer after layer of bullshit to wade through. More bullshit than usual."

The chilly damp air of spring in New York feels refreshing as Julia rounds the block to her favorite market. Julia stands just outside the doorway, as she never likes being on the phone in the market.

For all the rudeness and abruptness in this city (which she

participates in like a true New Yorker), she finds it disrespectful to the little old Czechoslovakian couple and their forty-something-year-old sons who own this market. The family reminds her of the Heinrichs family, who had been her and Seth's neighbors in Murdoch.

"So when am I going to see you? I miss you…" Julia kicks at a smashed cigarette butt on the ground, silently cursing whoever left their trash laying around.

"I know…I miss you too, hon." Kate's voice elevates a note. "But it's actually why I'm calling…"

"Oh? Why's that?"

"Because Marilee and I have an idea…"

"Oh Lord. Your ideas scare me." Julia laughs feeling more lighthearted.

"Well, we're thinking of going to the Johnson's cabin for a girls' weekend over Memorial Day. We wanted to see if you could come?"

"Hmmm…well, let's see…yep all clear."

"Really? Oh good! I didn't know what your schedule was like these days between writin' and teachin' and stuff. Or if you could get away a little while without Frank."

"There's not much writing or teaching right now, and Frank has been gone on assignment." Julia's voice drops. "I'm not really sure when he's coming back…or if he's coming back."

"Oh dawg, sounds like we have some catchin' up to do then."

"Yeah, we do…too much to get into now." Julia sighs.

"You okay?"

"Yeah, yeah I'm fine. I'll catch you up when we get together." Julia smiles thinking about seeing her friends.

"Okay gurl. We haven't worked out all the details yet. Just wanted to first see if you were free." Kate smiles. "I'm excited to see you!"

Julia takes a deep breath. She smiles into the phone. "I'm excited, too. It will be fun…and God knows, I could use some time away."

"You and me both, hon. Okay then, I'll touch base in the next week or so. Love you."

"Love you too, Kate."

CHAPTER 2

The barista's receding hairline extends far beyond his forehead, complimented by a tussle of chestnut hair pulled neatly into a ponytail. Yet, it's not his wire-rim glasses or salt-and-pepper goatee that catches Julia's eye. It's his camouflage overalls donned with a strand of what looks like turquoise prayer beads.

"Mornin'! What can I get ya?" He booms loudly over the counter to the petite blonde in line ahead of her.

Julia scans the coffee shop and spots a priest texting on his cell phone in the corner. Something about the sight makes her smile.

"And what will you have ma'am?" The barista now bellows in Julia's direction. He must be new because she's never seen him before now, and she comes to this particular coffee shop several times a week.

"Oh I don't know…" Feeling indecisive, her mind is already filtering through the meeting that she's to have in an hour with Priscilla and Jeff. "How about a Mondo coffee?"

"Alrighty, will that be for here?"

"Yeah, and I love your necklace by the way…" As the words tumble out of Julia's mouth, she gets a closer look at the turquoise beads and realizes what she thinks are prayer beads are really small skulls. Oh well, the compliment makes his face light up.

"Thanks. My friend made it for me." The barista smiles proudly.

"Well, I love the color and wear it a lot. Goes good with the hair, you know?" She smiles and points to her auburn hair pulled up loosely. The barista laughs as he spins back around with a massive cup of coffee. Just as she's paying him, she hears her cell phone. She lets it ring, knowing instinctively it's Jeff.

Julia finds a small table in the corner and moves toward it gingerly to keep the coffee from spilling. She finally sets the large mug down and pulls her phone from her purse. True to her gut, it was Jeff but she skips listening to the voicemail and just calls him back.

"Jules? Where are you?"

She senses the annoyance in his voice. "I stopped by Genuine Joe's to get some coffee."

"Okay, good. You're close to the office then. I just needed to make sure you weren't going to bail." His curt tone stings a little.

"Why would I bail on you?" She breathes deeply realizing that he has every reason to consider that, given the past few weeks. She softens her stance. "We still have over an hour before the meeting. It will be fine." Though she doesn't quite believe her own words.

Jeff sighs deeply in the phone, the background honks and street noise filtering through the receiver. "I know, I know. I'm just…never mind…we'll chat when I get there. I'm on my way…"

"Okay, I just sat down." Julia takes a sip of coffee.

"Great, see you soon."

Julia glances out the large window in front of her and smiles to herself. In all these years of living in New York, she still marvels that the city never stops, no matter the day, nor time, nor occasion. It's a drumbeat of life that just thumps, thumps away.

It was this steady cadence that had resonated deeply from the first moment she arrived in early 1997, just a few weeks after Seth died. She'd only come to visit her friend Cheryl, the one friend she'd made an effort to stay in touch with after leaving her hometown of Chicago.

Though Julia never intended to actually move to New York. Her plan was to take a break from Murdoch and figure out what to do next. But she quickly realized that it's impossible to know what step to take next when life has turned the only reality you know upside down in a matter of minutes. So sometimes you just act and hope for the best.

One look down onto the intersection of 50th and Park from her friend Cheryl's tiny studio apartment, with the yellow cabs dancing up and down the street like ants, and Julia was mesmerized. In that moment, she knew she was in New York to stay.

Something about the frenetic pace of Manhattan matched the turmoil swirling inside of her, having witnessed far too much death and deceit to be so young. The disillusionment Julia felt was further punctuated by the realization that even in a small Southern town, she couldn't hide from the raw, jagged edges of life. The difference was that in Chicago or New York, you could simply blend into that chaos. No one spotted your car at the pharmacy or stopped you on every aisle of the grocery store to gossip.

She quickly realized, too, that she had to change her name. If she was going to start over in a new city, then she needed to find some way to reclaim her sense of self. Within six months of living in Manhattan, she had officially returned to being Julia Jarvis, though the innocent girl she was before she married Seth Dixon was a distant memory.

Now, twenty years later, Julia similarly gazes out the window of Genuine Joe's, mesmerized and wondering what's next. The anticipation and dread of this meeting with Priscilla and Jeff had been rolling in her gut for weeks, and as much as she wanted to reschedule, she knew it was time to just face the truth. Perhaps that's why she is the one trying to reassure Jeff today.

Sure, she has read books about things like letting go, forgiving, and all that "woo woo stuff," but the art of surrender isn't something Julia has ever been able to wrap her head around, let alone her heart. Surrender felt like giving up to her, and even as down as she's been lately, she has no intention of giving up.

As Julia swallows another sip of coffee, the lump in her throat moves, too. It's an old familiar lump of choked back words, and it always seems to make its presence known when she faces tough situations. Walking into Bauer & Brown, one of the most successful publishers in the country, and admitting to being blocked is like the time she marched into her volleyball coach's office at sixteen and voluntarily admitted she *had* been at that party and drank two beers.

The coach had the team convinced he knew who was at the party, and Julia was certain her name was on that list. Rather than being caught, she willingly turned herself in, though she later realized the coach had no idea she was there. It didn't matter. She still faced the same punishment of having to run extra after practice.

Julia wonders if Priscilla will appreciate her candor the way her coach did those years ago. She's learned over time that the repercussions of telling the truth sometimes pale in comparison to the imprisonment of trying to deny what you know to be right. There's a freedom that comes in honesty, despite the consequences.

Yet, Julia also knows Priscilla Bauer isn't interested in the truth, only results. The type of results that a publisher rightfully expects on the heels of a bestseller. Julia stares into the half-empty cup of coffee, the caffeine amplifying her thoughts, which are already buzzing through the conversation that's looming. Jeff startles her as he approaches the table.

"Well, well, there you are. I almost forgot what you looked like. In fact…" He chuckles and wags a finger at her. "I think it's safe to say you've been avoiding me."

Jeff's presence always fills a space, from his jet black hair to his angled jaw line and brilliant smile, and he's always on the cusp of fashion. Today, it's a light purple button-down shirt, which perfectly tucked into pressed, skinny fit dark gray trousers. His ensemble is complemented with burnished leather shoes and a cognac-colored leather Movado watch. Jeff is the type of man even straight men secretly look at twice.

Julia stands and embraces her friend tightly. "Now, why would you think that?"

"Oh I don't know, let's see…for starters, the dozens of unreturned calls?" Jeff pulls back to look at her, his voice teeters on that fine line of playfulness and irritation.

She ducks his gaze, moving her purse and leather messenger bag so he can sit down.

"I haven't been avoiding you…I've just been busy." She sighs as she settles back into her chair.

"Bullshit. Busy doing what?" Jeff sits down, eyes still peering at her intently.

A pause of silence falls between them as he tastes his coconut milk cappuccino.

"I have nothing." Julia blurts out quickly.

Jeff looks up curiously. "What do you mean you have nothing?"

"Nothing, no material. Nothing." Julia huffs in annoyance, face intently awaiting his response.

"Umm, Jules, hello." Jeff waves his hand in front of her. "I'm not just your publicist here. I'm your friend, remember? Don't you think I've figured that out by now? It's okay, baby, we'll work through it…"

Julia looks into his blue eyes searching for reassurance, which she finds instantly, despite his gruff tone on the phone earlier.

"Thank you. I need to hear that. I really do." She swallows hard, releasing some of the pent up emotion in her throat.

For this is what Julia tends to forget. She isn't alone. It's so easy to dismiss the world around her when she's sequestered in her apartment screaming about Lucas to Mr. Pickles.

After the years of therapy following Seth's death, she became fully aware of the massive shield of armor she'd constructed around her heart. Though she's more willing to disarm now than ever before, she still finds herself wading through days shut down and tuned out, as she had in the weeks leading up to now.

"Well, I just worry about you." Jeff's sincerity is palpable. He stares out the window before turning to meet her eyes. "You won't call me back. It's like you just disappear from life, and I miss you…"

He smiles. "Plus, it's not healthy for you to sit in that apartment with that damn cat."

"Hey, now, don't bring Mr. Pickles into this." She laughs.

"You know how I feel about pussy cats and that includes yours." He winks playfully. "No offense."

She lets out a belly laugh. "None taken...but what are we going to do?" She quizzes him, feeling lighter as she finishes her coffee.

"I don't know...I mean, Priscilla isn't interested in excuses. She's going to want to hear you have something in the queue. The reality is we are closing in on this second option, and technically we have about nine months left. It's not a lot of time, but it's enough for you."

"I don't know about that at the rate I've been going." She looks down at her watch, knowing they need to wrap up.

Jeff reaches across the table, his strong fingers enfold her hand.

"Look Julia, I know you have been in a bad space lately." He peers at her intently. "I'm not exactly sure why or what's been going on...and I won't pry. All I know is you have a gift for storytelling unlike anyone I've ever known. You know me. So you know I'm not one to blow smoke up your ass...and God knows I'm not the type of queen to wave pom-poms and be your cheerleader. So I'm just going to speak as your friend, Jules. I love you, but you've got to snap out of this and get out of your own damn way. I mean, it's time to let yourself go."

Julia diverts her eyes down to her hand still wrapped in his and shifts uncomfortably in her chair. "Let myself go...in what way?" She looks back up at him curiously.

"Creatively. Even with *Steelhouse*, I sensed there was something deeper wanting to come out. It's just a feeling I have, and I've been thinking about it a lot lately. I just feel like you are holding something back. I'm just not sure what."

Jeff may not know what she's holding back, but Julia, however, is keenly aware of the Pandora's box of ghost stories that she vowed long ago never to reopen.

She pulls her hand away, looks at her watch, and abruptly stands. "We really need to get going."

"Jules, did you just hear anything I said?" Jeff remains in his chair looking up at her as she pulls on her computer bag and purse.

"Yes, I heard you, and I appreciate the compliment and the concern, but I'm fine. I'll get back into the groove. I will…I just need a little more time. But right now we need to go. You know how much Priscilla hates it when we're late."

CHAPTER 3

Bauer & Brown Publishing is like many New York book houses. It began as an idealistic vision of two Smith College friends looking to infuse the world with passion and prose. Over the years, it has morphed into a publishing machine of churn and burn to outpace the competition and avoid shrinking profit margins. Priscilla Bauer has become a masterful player in the publishing game over her nearly three decades in the business.

Under Priscilla's dyed blonde hair, always neatly pulled back in a bun, is a deft brain with sharp ideas and even quicker wit. For as bitchy and downright ruthless as Priscilla could be with, well, everyone who crossed her path, Julia had immediately connected with her. They met for the first time at a fundraising event nearly five years ago. Over the course of the evening, Julia and Priscilla had talked politics, women's pay inequality, and of course, writing. Priscilla admitted reading many of Julia's features and profile pieces through her regular rounds as a freelancer with *The New Yorker*, *GQ*, and *The Atlantic*.

Priscilla said she admired Julia's level of historical detail, woven through her words in such a way that you almost forgot that you were reading. It was more like watching a story unfold in a play, scene by scene. She specifically commented on a piece Julia had published most recently about the women behind the iconic Rosie

NO MOTIVE IN MURDOCH

the Riveter during World War II. Julia's article explored the lives of Mary Keefe, who inspired Norman Rockwell's Rosie the Riveter painting for the *Saturday Evening Post* in 1943, and Rose Will Monroe, who worked as a riveter of B-24 and B-49 bomber airplanes in Michigan.

"Superb." Priscilla shook her head in disbelief. "Simply superb."

Having had just enough wine, Julia had smiled and gracefully received the compliment. She also loved that Priscilla used a word sorely lacking in everyday conversations, *superb*.

Julia replied with a simple, "Thank you. It was a lot of fun to research and write."

It was through the course of that first conversation, and many subsequent ones over vintage Cabernets, that Priscilla planted the seed for *Steelhouse*. From the inspiration of those real, coveralls-wearing Rosie the Riveters emerged the bestselling novel about the three friends leaving their homes to work in the factories while their husbands were at war.

Priscilla had been part of the journey every step of the way, which was no doubt unusual, and really unnecessary, for a publisher given the ensemble of editors, account managers, and production assistants at Bauer & Brown. Along the way, Julia had discovered Priscilla's motivation for the book. Priscilla's great aunt had been a riveter during the war.

Julia also knew the success of her book went beyond just padding the bottom line for Bauer & Brown. As Julia's friend, it was also a personal victory for Priscilla, just as it was for the six million women who had worked in the factories during the war.

Since *Steelhouse's* rise and taper in the spotlight, Priscilla and Julia had remained friends, though life had intervened their regular brainstorms and wine therapy sessions. In fact, walking through the solid wall of glass into Bauer & Brown offices with Jeff, Julia realizes it's been months since she's seen Priscilla.

"Jeff…Julia, how are you?" Elizabeth, the front receptionist, stands and walks around the side of the chest-high modular station to hug Jeff before turning to Julia. Throughout the course of publishing *Steelhouse*, Jeff and Julia had become regular fixtures in the office, whether meeting about book edits or public appearances.

"Elizabeth, so good to see you." Julia embraces the thick brunette with a broad smile. "How are you?"

"Great, I'm great. You know, busy as usual." Elizabeth waves her arm casually behind her and smiles again. "You can go on back. Priscilla is waiting for you."

Julia and Jeff venture down the white-walled modern office suite, smiling and greeting familiar faces. Just as they head into the waiting area of Priscilla's office, Julia notices a large framed photo of herself and Priscilla, each holding a copy of *Steelhouse*, inset in a case with a hardback copy of the book. Julia remembers taking that photo at the launch party. She smiles, then feels a slight drop of sadness in her stomach, wondering if she'll ever experience that level of success again.

Jeff taps on the half-open door. Deep in a phone conversation, Priscilla looks up, smiles, and waves them in. They sit on the sleek L-shaped suede couch in the corner while Priscilla finishes her call. Jeff catches Julia's eye and winks. She sighs and forces a smiles.

"Well, it's about damn time." Priscilla stands upon ending her call, adjusting her Italian hounds-tooth Akris Punto suit as she strolls over to hug them. After the greetings and small talk, Julia knows the real questions are coming.

In the natural pause of conversation, Priscilla clears her throat and so it begins. "So Jules, how's the new material coming along?"

Julia looks at Jeff and then at Priscilla, who's peering directly at her.

"Well, I..." Julia hesitates.

"Look Priscilla, there's good news and bad news." Jeff interrupts, glancing at Julia.

"Oh?" Priscilla looks at him curiously.

"The bad news is that we're basically at square one, and the good news is, well, we are basically at square one. Clean slate."

"So you mean you have nothing?" Priscilla looks at Julia again. "If that's the case, just say it."

"Well, yes. That's the case." Julia feels the hairs along her spine stand like Mr. Pickles' when he sees the neighbor's dog. "The truth is, I've been in a hellish funk the past three months and my words just won't come. The ideas won't come."

Growing increasingly agitated, Julia stands and walks to the window overlooking the city below. She can feel their eyes peering at her intently. Julia had been in this office dozens of times before, but now it feels suffocating, like she might be smothered at any moment by an idea of some person they want her to be.

Julia had often wondered if Priscilla really cared about her, about *Steelhouse*, or if she was just the star for the minute until the next one came along. The level of expectation for producing a similar success was higher than she ever imagined it could be. But here it is, staring at her from behind.

"I've meditated. I've gone to yoga. I've journaled. I've started running again…but nothing. I have nothing, and I honestly don't know what to do anymore. I kept thinking it would be easy like before. *Steelhouse* just sort of emerged…so effortlessly. So the thing I don't really understand is how in the hell do you replicate that?" Julia turns around to their intent stares. "What do you do when it's not easy anymore?" Her voice crescendos in frustration, the questions hanging in the air between them.

Over the years she's known Priscilla, she's heard stories about authors hitting the wall, missing the mark, and writing well below Priscilla's standards. She's heard the intense passion and pressure with which Priscilla approaches every single book Bauer & Brown publishes. For Priscilla, the company began as a free-thinking, independent publisher. Now it's all about perfection, precision, and profit, not to mention the constant threat of becoming obsolete in a world where anyone can publish a book from their personal computer.

In the back of Julia's mind, she also remembers that Priscilla had once admitted to her over too many glasses of wine how burnt out she felt by what Bauer & Brown had become. How she missed the simplicity of sharing stories for the sake of knowledge and inspiration, and how deeply she feared failure with so much, and so many, riding on her to succeed.

So in this moment, Julia's unsure which Priscilla she will face. The compassionate idealist committed to the cause of creativity or the profit-hungry publisher that has no room on her bookshelf for failure.

Priscilla leans back on the couch and changes the cross of her legs. She looks at Jeff and then at Julia before smiling softly.

"Well, I can't say I'm surprised." Priscilla finally admits. "Nor can I say I'm necessarily thrilled to hear you are at…what did you say Jeff…square one?" She glances Jeff's way, then to Julia.

Julia shifts her weight and moves so she can lean against the caramel leather chair perched between them, hoping the chair will steady her growing feeling of unease.

"So that's the problem…" Priscilla looks to Jeff and then Julia. "Problems don't interest me, only solutions. So what's the solution?"

"Well, only Julia can really answer that." Jeff chimes in.

Julia glances his way angrily. *I thought he was here to help me and he just threw me under the damn bus.*

Instinctively Jeff realizes what he's done. He smiles at Julia apologetically and quickly continues. "But I do know this…whatever she comes up with will be great. As I told her earlier over coffee, she's one of the best writers around. I feel like there's something big emerging with this next book." Jeff looks at Priscilla. "But to get to it, she's going to have to dig deeper."

"Deeper how?" Priscilla looks to Julia.

"That was my same response." Julia shrugs and shifts her weight, still standing behind the chair. "Look, I know you are both big supporters of my work. Clearly I have done this once, but I'm just honestly not sure it's in me again…"

"Julia, stop." Priscilla interrupts. "You are one of the smartest writers...and hell for that matter people...I know. But you are being so damn stupid. You're missing the point. Writing a second book isn't about replicating something that's already happened. Books are like children. It doesn't matter if they are sequels or trilogies. They are independent creations, and they may share similar DNA, but in the end it's about the original unfolding of an idea...a story. You know this. So the only real question here...to Jeff's point...is what will it take for you to get out of this hole you've put yourself in? You've done this to yourself, you know..."

Julia stiffens at what feels like an accusation, though the truth is unavoidable. She had put herself here, and only she could get herself out. She says nothing but moves back to her spot at the window where the air feels cooler and the large window provides some sense of spaciousness to what feels like an increasingly claustrophobic conversation.

Julia's moving away does nothing to deter Priscilla.

"Jules, what's it going to take for you to get out of your head and get back to your heart and write from there? That's why *Steelhouse* was so successful, you know...because your passion came through so clearly. Readers can feel that passion. So, I think Jeff's right...you have to ask yourself what's the story that wants to be told? Start there. Because the only way to overcoming a block isn't to avoid it. Sometimes you just have to plow *through* it."

Julia's relieved that they cannot see all the color has instantly drained out of her cheeks, quickly followed by a flash of fiery heat. She knows they are right. There is a story to tell. A twisted, complicated, and incredibly painful story, but it's not just any story. It's the story of two murders that shook a sleepy little one red-light town in Mississippi to its very core. Above all, it's the story of losing the love of her life, and that's a story she swore she would never tell.

CHAPTER 4

Over the few weeks since meeting at Bauer & Brown, Julia's brain has replayed the conversation with Jeff and Priscilla like a game of mental Ping-Pong. On one side of the table, she sees the intent behind their pushing and prodding. She knows there's great material to uncover in those memory banks.

The turn of events that happened in Murdoch, Mississippi are the kind of true stories that create bestsellers and movies. They are the kind of stories you simply cannot make up, especially not about a town of three thousand people, most of whom were born and raised there. These stories are too unbelievable, too surreal, too sad, and far too confusing.

So she understands Jeff and Priscilla's role and their stakes in the game. Though Julia knows her friends and colleagues have absolutely no idea what they are talking about when they're asking her to "dig deeper." Sure, throughout their years of friendship and over late happy hours, Jeff and Priscilla had each peppered Julia with questions about her past in Murdoch, quizzing intently about her marriage to Seth. Julia always managed to answer with just enough to keep them satisfied. As far as they knew, Seth's death was an accident on the job as a police officer. That wasn't the full truth, but it's all they needed to know. On the other side of the Ping-Pong table, there's the reality that the stories lining Julia's memory bank aren't about fictitious people. There are consequences for poking around the past. Bringing to light all that happened wouldn't just implicate the little Southern town where she began her career and her adult, married life with Seth.

Unearthing this story of Murdoch and the deaths that forever changed the fabric of people she had come to love there also means coming face to face with a past that she's desperately tried to forget. Most of all, it means facing the ghosts of unanswered questions. Questions she'd spent thousands and thousands of dollars in therapy trying to answer. Like why did those two women have to die? More importantly, why did Seth die, too?

On this cool, rainy spring morning, Julia stares into her coffee cup gulping back the caffeine, while simultaneously trying to swallow back the tears. One tear escapes, rolls down her cheek, and plops onto the lined page of her journal, smearing the blue ink. Julia always writes in blue ink.

She hasn't written in her journal in over a week but something stirred in her this morning, leading her to these pages almost an hour ago. She places the heavy ceramic mug on her coffee table and then sits further back into the stone-colored sofa, freeing up space so she can cross her long legs underneath her.

Julia wipes her eyes and peers down at the entry and rereads it, as she usually does at the conclusion of each journaling session.

Thursday, May 19

What am I going to do? This is the question that's been swirling through my mind since the day I left the meeting with Jeff and Priscilla. I've considered it from every possible angle, and I still don't really have a conclusive answer. Of course, when I look objectively at it all, I see there is a really good story to tell about Murdoch and the murders. But what happens if I do write it? What are the consequences to the town? To Nelda and Marilee? Hell, to me?

I really, honestly don't know. I don't know...

I have been wrestling with the conversation I had with Jeff and Priscilla, and each time I come back to the same place. Something in me has always wanted to write this story to let the voices of Betty Ann and Allison come to light. They never had a chance to tell their stories, not to mention Seth. They all died before they even had a chance to fully live their lives, and that has haunted me for years. The tragedy of an unlived life, I think, is the saddest tragedy of all.

I see all the reasons not to write it. I see, and certainly feel, all the fear. I think that's what's stopping me the most, knowing that once I start digging into the past there's no turning back, and there's no guarantee about what I'll really find. I've spent so much time trying to put Murdoch behind me. So why is this coming up now?

If I'm honest with myself, however, my creativity isn't the only thing that feels stuck. It's my whole damn life, most especially my relationship with Frank. It's as if after the success with Steelhouse, the roller coaster just as quickly plummeted, and now I'm just here hanging out at the bottom of the ride exhausted and wondering how to gain that momentum to make that climb once again.

Over the past week, however, when I've forced myself to sit still and stay open, I notice there's a little space in me that's curious. Honestly, part of me feels excited about the prospect of trying to answer all the questions I had back then covering the murders for the newspaper. I was so young and afraid, and I had so many questions that I never asked, and certainly, never got answered. Then again, I'm not sure anyone could answer them.

But what if I did know? What if I'm the one to share Betty Ann and Allison's stories? What if I could do it in such a way that's respectable and honors their memories, while also finding some sense of justice...and peace? What if writing this book about Murdoch helps me find some semblance of closure to it all?

Maybe writing this book about their deaths is the one thing that can help bring me back to life...

Now the tears stream unabashedly and quickly become full sobs. Sobs that had been pent up for days, weeks, and months, possibly even years. Julia covers her face with her slender fingers, breathes deep, and lets go. The heave of emotion ripples through her from her belly to her head, shaking her body like a leaf.

"I have to do this. I have to…I don't know why or how…but I do…" She cries harder into her hands, feeling the usual flutter of her belly as a full-on, lined-up feeling of YES!

She breathes deep into the moment of certainty, one that leaves little question or doubt. "This is my book to write…" She whispers quietly, wiping her face, sighing again heavily and also more lightheartedly. The tears of emotion have unlatched the heaviness she has been feeling for so long. Now there's only an emptiness, an opening.

Julia peels herself off the couch and goes in search of more coffee. She hears the ding of her phone and finds an email has just come through from Kate about the girls' weekend over Memorial Day. Julia is looking forward to the weekend with her friends, though panic tingles in her stomach.

It's one thing to write in her journal about writing a fictitious book for readers. It's another to begin to vocalize this new project to those whom she had come to know and love in Murdoch, including her two best friends, Kate and Marilee.

CHAPTER 5

Julia settles into the seat next to the window. She always sits near the window. Something about the view across the vast sky calms her. It's ironic, really, given how much she seeks to control the minutiae in her daily life. Yet, when it comes to flying she's had to learn to just breathe and let go. Oh, it hasn't been easy.

In fact, when she was younger, she'd teeter on the verge of panic attacks at the thought of this huge mass of metal flying at thirty thousand feet through the sky and at the hands of a pilot she was never quite sure was there. It's why she'd sit and wait for the pilot to come over the loudspeaker after takeoff. Hearing his voice assured her that he really was there, and that perhaps it would be okay. I mean, he had friends and family he wanted to get home safely to, right?

Flying all over the country for *Steelhouse*, however, Julia had grown accustomed to airplanes. Sure, there had been bumpy flights and ones that stressed her out. But then there were times like now, moments where Julia welcomes any mode of transportation to carry her out of New York and out of her life into a different world.

As she settles into her seat and pulls out her e-book reader, she smiles at the thought of spending the weekend with two of her favorite people. Julia, Kate, and Marilee had become inseparable living in Murdoch in their twenties. Like Julia, who moved to Murdoch for Seth's new job in the police department, Kate had also been transplanted into the sleepy town by way of her husband Mike's football coaching career. Marilee, on the other hand, was born and raised in Murdoch.

Marilee knew everything about everyone. Yet, unlike many in the community, she loved welcoming newcomers to her hometown. Marilee had known the Dixon family her whole life, and while she was a few years ahead of Seth in school, she knew who he was. But then, who didn't know Seth Dixon? He was the star quarterback for the Murdoch Mustangs and the most charming boy in school, with that tall frame, chiseled jaw, and perfectly parted chestnut hair.

"Oh God, I hate this airline."

Julia's reminiscing is suddenly halted by a sixty-something woman with graying hair and a broad forehead.

"They always screw things up. I had a terrible time trying to get my seat changed…" The woman takes a quick gasp of air between labored breaths. "They had me all the way to the back next to the toilet. Now why would I want to sit next to the toilet?"

The woman shuffles her carry-on as she settles into her seat, still breathing heavily.

"I'm Phyllis, by the way." The woman huffs, struggling to wrap the seatbelt across her round midsection.

"I'm Julia."

"Nice to meet you." Phyllis smiles and the subtle wrinkles around her eyes become more pronounced.

"You too." Julia smiles back as politely as she can. Though she has no interest in making small talk with strangers on airplanes, something about Phyllis' brassy demeanor reminds Julia of her former mother-in-law, Nelda.

"So now Julia, where are you headed?" Phyllis peers over at her. "Atlanta? Or somewhere else?"

"Yeah, Atlanta." Julia nods and adds nothing more.

"So what takes you there? Family?"

Julia sighs and smiles realizing her little snippets of answers aren't going to satisfy this strange woman. "No, I'm going to visit some very dear friends. Actually, we aren't staying in Atlanta. We're heading to my friend's family's cabin up near Lake Burton."

"Oh how wonderful! That sounds like fun." Phyllis smiles broadly.

"Yeah I'm excited to see them. We haven't all been together in nearly five years."

"Oh yes…there's nothing like being with old friends." Phyllis shuffles the magazines in her lap, which keep sliding off in the small space between her midsection and the seatback in front of her. "Yeah, I live in Connecticut, but my daughter and her family live outside of Atlanta. My grandson completes the first grade this week so I'm excited to see him. He's so precious!" Phyllis beams with grandmotherly pride.

A twinge of envy flashes through Julia as she returns a forced smile. She will never know that feeling of children or grandchildren. She and Seth had talked of having a baby in the months before he died. After his death, Julia resigned herself to the fact that children were not part of her life's picture.

"I'm sure he will be excited to see you, too." Julia responds sincerely.

"Oh yes, only because I spoil him rotten." Phyllis lets out a laugh. "So your friends…they live in Atlanta?"

"Well, my one friend Kate lives there. My other friend is traveling in for the weekend like me."

"You've known each other a long time then?" Phyllis' questions are relentless, and Julia's growing weary of the chatter.

She sighs heavily. "Yeah I met them in my early twenties when I moved to this very small town in Mississippi."

"Oh, which one?" Phyllis sips the red wine the flight attendant had just delivered to each of them. "I mean which town?"

"Murdoch, it's near Natchez. It's very small, only about three thousand people…one red light." Julia smiles.

"Murdoch? Oh my, yes, I know Murdoch. My sister-in-law had family there but I haven't been there in years."

"Really? You're kidding? I didn't think anyone knew of Murdoch." Astonished at the coincidence, Julia takes a big gulp of her Cabernet and peers out the window. The brilliant blue sky is dotted with shaving cream white clouds. *I guess I'll have to return to Murdoch soon. Am I am really ready to face that town after all these years? I wonder who is still there I would even know?*

Julia's thoughts are once again interrupted by Phyllis who is still rambling about Murdoch and her grandson as she flips mindlessly through her magazine.

Julia nods and smiles. "I think I'm going to rest a bit now." She pulls out her headphones from her carry-on, hoping to relax a little before arrival.

"Oh okay. I'm sure you want to rest up for your friends." Phyllis looks up from her magazine and smiles.

As Julia closes her eyes, however, her mind moves into full throttle, sorting, shuffling, and wondering how Marilee and Kate will react to this book. She sighs heavily with uncertainty and tries to center her breath, but instead her mind centers on a memory that's always made her smile: the night she met her two crazy friends for the first time.

CHAPTER 6

September 8, 1995

"How'bout them Mustangs!" Mike Woods hoists his red plastic cup of beer overhead to commemorate the Murdoch Mustangs' first home win. At only twenty-eight, Mike is the head football coach, and anyone who knows anything about Southern towns knows that every victory is like winning a national championship. It's momentous and it matters, especially if you want to keep your job the next season.

High school football and the rituals that take place under those Friday night lights are a religion all their own. In a state like Mississippi with no professional sports teams, the stakes are even higher and victories matter more.

As for Julia, it could have been Englishmen playing cricket on that large green field for all she knows or cares. Julia's days as an athlete were short lived, spending a few years on the volleyball team in junior high and high school before quitting after her sophomore year to join the yearbook staff.

"What? You mean you don't like sports?" Seth was shocked and somewhat bewildered on one of their first dates three years earlier when she expressed her ambivalence. He lived and breathed football, perhaps because he depended on his scholarship as Ball State University's backup quarterback. But for Seth, it was also about the simple fact that he loved the game: lacing up his cleats, smelling the damp grass under foot, and the camaraderie of being part of a team.

Now, with one look at Mike Woods, his red cup brimming with keg beer, and the flocks of people gathered around him like a celebrity, Julia realizes football is about something very different among this crowd.

"Come on, let's get a beer…" Seth yells to Julia, grabs her hand, and begins leading her across the crowded living room.

Having only been in Murdoch about six weeks, Julia knows very few people still, except for Seth's family and the two other staff at the newspaper. For Seth on the other hand, it's a homecoming as he greets old friends and siblings of friends, like Paul Johnson, who's now flagging Seth down on the way to the kitchen. Seth had played football with Paul's brother at Murdoch High, though Paul was a few years ahead of him, he'd always treated Seth like a little brother, too.

"Well, if it isn't Seth Dixon. I'd heard you were back in town!" Paul beams at his old friend, leaning in to give Seth a handshake and then pulls him in for a man hug.

"Yup, here I am. Never thought I'd be back." Seth's face crinkles into a smile revealing a perfect dimple in his left cheek. He looks at Julia and winks. "But with dad being sick and all, well it's how it goes, I guess." Seth shrugs and then points toward Julia. "Paul, this is my wife, Julia." Seth's voice carries over the noisy room and he places his large palm on the small of Julia's back. She smiles. Something about his hands always comfort her.

"Nice to meet you." Julia looks up at Paul, who's taller than Seth but not as handsome.

Paul hunches over to greet her with a smile like a lanky schoolboy. "You too, Julia. It's good to meet anyone brave enough to try and settle Seth Dixon down."

The three laugh just as Paul's wife approaches. "And this is my wife, Marilee."

"Well, yes I know Miss Marilee." Seth hugs the beautiful brunette. Her wavy hair frames her face, setting off her greenish brown eyes.

Not quite as tall as Julia, Marilee reaches up and hugs Seth smiling broadly at seeing her old friend.

Seth pulls back and introduces Julia, who reaches out to shake Marilee's hand. Marilee skips right over the gesture and leans over to hug Julia. Julia's taken aback by the kindness but gingerly gives this strange, beautiful woman a half-hearted hug.

"Oh, it's so good to meet you, Julia. Come on, let's leave these boys to talk football. Looks like you need a drink."

Seth nods and smiles, happy to be home and have Julia by his side. Always willing to take a risk on the football field, Seth exudes the same feisty confidence off of it. Since falling in love with Julia, many had commented that something had shifted in him. He's calmer, more settled into his skin.

Like most of this crowd of high school friends now gathered in Marilee and Paul's house, Seth swore he'd never return to Murdoch. But when his mother, Nelda, called six months ago and asked him to consider moving back after his dad, Richard "Doc" Dixon, had become ill, Seth knew he had no choice. The Dixons had nearly a hundred acres of land with cows and chickens that Nelda couldn't manage alone, and selling was out of the question.

While Seth had butted heads with Nelda often, perhaps because they were so much alike, he always felt a sense of duty when it came to Doc. Though Seth had no interest in saving dogs and birthing calves as a veterinarian like his dad, he was absolutely committed to doing the right thing by Doc. Really, the timing was perfect as Seth had recently completed his police academy training in Indianapolis and was looking for a full-time position. Julia worked as a reporter at a community newspaper. When Seth broached the topic of returning home with Julia, she'd been less than thrilled about the idea of moving to Murdoch, though she certainly understood why Seth needed to be here.

So as Seth smiles at Julia now, his look is equally one of love and relief that she's meeting Marilee. Marilee was a senior when he was a lanky freshman, but they'd gone to church together growing up. He'd always admired Marilee like an older sister. Seth smiles and waves as the two walk off and returns to his conversation with Paul and a few other guys who have now gathered around.

Marilee leads Julia by the arm toward the kitchen where Mike Woods continues talking wildly about each play of the game. Mike is an unlikely football coach by appearances alone, at only five-foot-nine with a stocky frame he looks more like a wrestler than football player. Yet, with his buzz haircut, tanned face, and square jaw, Julia notices he certainly has the passion, or rather, arrogance that's necessary for the job.

Marilee squeezes her way through the crowd smiling and waving at folks along the way like a beauty queen flanking a runway. Finally, they arrive at the almond-colored Formica counter in Marilee and Paul's kitchen, which is lined with large bottles of gin, vodka, and wine.

"This okay with you?" She yells at Julia holding up a bottle of red wine. Julia nods and welcomes the elixir to help numb this very loud, very uncomfortable situation. As Marilee pours their glasses, Julia scans the room for Seth. She finds him gathered near the fireplace among a group of guys, laughing and talking with big gestures.

For as uncertain as Julia is about living in this town, she knows that Murdoch is Seth's world, a world that's familiar to him. And in that familiarity comes a sense of warmth, connection, and belonging, which is something she's yet to fully understand coming from a single-parent household in the suburbs of Chicago. Knowing how homesick Seth had been at times in Indiana, however, she now watches his face illuminated in laughter, and her heart is equally engulfed. Marilee interrupts Julia's gaze as she hands her a plastic cup of wine.

"Sorry we don't use real glasses 'round these parties. They'll just get broken. " Marilee smiles apologetically.

"This is perfect." Julia smiles back.

"Come on let's walk outside where we can actually hear ourselves think." Marilee leads Julia out the side door near the laundry room.

The air is thick and warm but luckily about ten decibels quieter. Marilee wanders up to a circle of people talking in the yard, tapping a petite blonde on the shoulder.

"Gurl, there you are!" The blonde hugs Marilee tightly and catches Julia's eye. Julia smiles, slightly embarrassed. Social situations like this make her either want to spontaneously disappear or consume inappropriate amounts of alcohol. Since she hasn't yet developed a superpower for vanishing, she's working toward the latter, as she takes a large gulp of her wine.

"Yes ma'am, here I am!" Marilee playfully holds up her glass and the blonde lifts her white wine to toast. "And this is Julia Dixon, Seth's wife." Marilee gently pushes Julia forward, and Julia sticks out her hand.

"Hi! Kate Woods...I'm Mike's wife." This explains why she's all dolled up in a bright red Mustangs polo shirt tucked into her high-wasted black slacks matched by red ballet flats and huge silver hoop earrings.

"Nice to meet you." Julia responds.

"So how are you getting settled into Murdoch?" Kate takes a sip of her wine.

"Oh okay, finally got the house unpacked. But it's definitely an adjustment for me to be new here. Still getting to know everyone."

"Well, that won't take long...just gotta hang with Marilee." Kate laughs. "She knows everyone in town and then some."

"Yawl just consider me president of the welcome wagon." Marilee laughs with a playful curtsy.

Julia laughs at their banter. Immediately feeling more relaxed around these two, she leans into the small circle she, Marilee, and Kate had formed. "Well, there is something I've been wondering..."

"What's that?" Marilee asks.

"Are we always introduced as our husbands' wives?" Just as the words fly from her mouth, she feels a pang of regret for having said it. Maybe they liked being known as so-and-so's wife. Not Julia. While she loves Seth and finds it flattering to be married to

Murdoch's football star who's now come home to protect and serve the community on the police force, Julia wants to be known on her own merit, as her own person. She blushes and nervously takes the last sip of her wine.

Kate looks at Marilee and the two burst into a chorus of laughter.

"Oh gurl..." Kate laughs and pats Julia on the arm. "You're gonna fit in with us just fine."

CHAPTER 7

"Oh gurl, it's sooo good to see you!" Kate steps around the back of her car parked along the curbside pickup outside Atlanta's Hartsfield-Jackson International Airport. Kate beams and throws her arms around Julia, who softens into Kate's bear hug of an embrace.

Affection is something Julia has been sorely lacking lately. Aside from Jeff's little pat-pat-on-the-back fabulous gay man hugs and Mr. Pickles' random nuzzles on her legs, Julia has not been touched by anyone in the many weeks since Frank left on assignment.

"It's good to see you, too." Julia smiles through the apprehension, which appeared again somewhere between the pilot's final call to prepare to land and the baggage claim. For Julia knows that within a few hot breaths the conversation will turn to Murdoch. It always does when the three of them get together. Usually, it's reminiscing about the old days in their twenties, the parties, and good times. Every now and then, their conversation turns to what happened, but then it always circles back to Marilee's update to fill Kate and Julia in on who's still in Murdoch, who's returned, and who's now having an affair or divorced.

Unlike their typical reunions, however, Julia is the one with the zinger to toss into the wine-induced ring of conversation. She's just not sure it will be met with the same jovial 'Oh my Gawds' and 'Can you believes…' She's honestly not quite sure how the news of her possible book based on what happened to Allison Mercer and Betty Ann Stark will be received.

The last thing she wants is to upset her friends. Though deep down Julia knows that something about this book is quickly becoming larger than herself, larger than Kate or Marilee. It's quickly becoming her soul's mission.

Having been down this path with *Steelhouse*, however, she knows what it takes to execute a book of this magnitude. It's a fully immersive experience, and one that requires Julia to delve headfirst into another world. The difference now is that the world she constructs in this novel won't be based on other people's lives, it's based on hers. That's what worries her the most.

How can she distance herself from the pangs of sadness she still feels over the untimely deaths of Allison and Betty Ann? Most of all, how in the hell can she possibly be objective when she's always believed that something about those two murders is what ultimately led to Seth's death, too?

Over the years, Julia's remembered that old wives' tale her grandma used to say: "What ails you is also what heals you." Lately, it's been rolling around her head more often, and perhaps that's true? All Julia knows is she's tired of dragging around the mounds of baggage from her past. She's tired of sitting in therapists' chairs and at dinner parties hearing the same sentiment from her friends, which is something to the tune of: "Julia, it's been twenty years. When are you going to move on?"

Through the fog of her depression and after the last huge fight with Frank, she has been in denial that she'd been hanging on to the past. Actually, not just hanging on, but white-knuckled, clamped down like a dog with a bone. In the past few weeks, Julia's knuckles have softened a little. Now she feels the flickers of curiosity urging her forward, despite her uncertainty and fear. So, she reminds herself, this weekend is less about securing permission from her friends and more about regaining that sense of balance within herself.

Kate's joy emanates as bright as the sun. "How was your flight? I hope you didn't have to wait on me too long. I was gonna go to the cell phone lot but those things just seem like a damn waste of time to me. So I just drove around in circles."

Julia laughs at Kate's inability to sit still. That hasn't changed. Kate Schaub is one of the sassiest, classiest women Julia has ever known. They met when Kate was twenty-four, just a year older than Julia, and yet even back then Kate carried herself through life with this uncanny sense of wisdom and a richness that Julia secretly envied. Not rich in the way of old Southern money like Marilee.

Kate's richness stems from her quick wit, hearty laugh, and crystal blue eyes that peer straight into you. What's impressed Julia over all these years is Kate's ability to simultaneously be compassionate and unflinchingly candid all at the same time. Unlike many lawyers, she has no act, no gimmicks, no game.

"I'm a WYSIWYG." Kate once told Julia over a cold beer, sitting in her favorite patio chair with her legs crossed like a man. It was a scorching summer day.

"A what? What the hell is a WYSIWYG?" Julia peered at her friend.

"What You See Is What You Get, gurl. A WYSIWYG."

Julia laughed. "What makes you think you're a WYSIWYG?"

"Unlike many people in this town, I have no need to pretend. It's not that I think I'm better than them. It's that my Mama raised me to respect myself."

"You mean like R-E-S-P-E-C-T..." Julia belted the words to the song.

Kate cracked up in laughter and threw her bottle cap across at Julia.

"Yeah, gurl, just like that."

Whether it was the effect of the beers or just the simple joy of the moment, they laughed so hard Kate nearly peed her pants.

Now well into her forties, Kate still carries herself with that same sensibility as she did back then, though it's now matched by the type of wisdom only time can impart. In some ways, Julia has always envied Kate's confidence. Like Marilee, Julia was devastated when Kate moved away from Murdoch around Thanksgiving of 1996, just shortly before Seth died. Kate had separated from, and later divorced, her husband, Mike Woods, and returned to the Atlanta area to live with her family while working and studying for the LSAT so she could apply to law school. It was in graduate school that Kate met her second husband, Jerry Schaub.

Kate still looks the same to Julia, with better clothes and age-appropriate blond hair. Yet, in the eighteen months since they'd last seen one another, Julia notices life's twists and turns have left more subtle traces along Kate's eyes and mouth. She excitedly grabs Julia's suitcase and stuffs it in the back of her black Mercedes SUV.

"Yeah, so the flight was good. You know, thought a little, read a little, got into a conversation with a woman…and get this. She has family that lives in Murdoch. Isn't that crazy?"

"Gurl, when it comes to Murdoch, nothing seems crazy to me anymore. That town is like a vortex of crazy."

"I know, right?" Julia buckles her seatbelt and looks up to find Kate staring at her.

"I do know one thing…" Kate flashes that huge smile, blue eyes dancing. "It's about damn time I see you. I have missed you so much."

Julia smiles at the kindness in Kate's voice. Kate had been that way since day one with Julia, assuming the role of overprotective, adoring big sister. In the past two decades, no matter how many months or years pass between visits, they pick right back up where they left off the last time. In her years of living, Julia has come to know these types of friendships are rare.

Feeling a surge of warmth, which eases the butterflies in her stomach, Julia reaches over and squeezes her dear friend's hand. "It's so great to see you too, Kate. I have really needed this weekend, more than you could possibly know…"

"Yeah, I had a feelin' you might..." Kate's expression turns lawyer-like, questioning Julia without actually asking a question.

"Oh really? How?"

"I don't know. I just have this way of knowing when things aren't right with you. Lately I've just had the sense they weren't, but I wasn't going to push. I know how you are. So I knew you'd talk when you were ready. But now you're here, so spill it gurl...what's been going on...?"

"Oh I'm fine. It's just life..."

"Liar!" Kate yells sarcastically as she enters I-85 heading north toward Lake Burton.

Julia laughs feeling a little more at ease, remembering this is the friend who called her every single night at precisely nine o'clock for an entire year after Seth's death, just to check on her. The friend who cheered her on and sent care packages with gourmet dark chocolate bars and Mad Libs when she had a short bout of writer's block working on *Steelhouse*. The friend who flew to New York to surprise her for her fortieth birthday and actually arranged the whole party, all the way from Atlanta.

"You're right. I'm not fine. Actually things have been pretty crappy..."

"Frank?"

"No...well, yes...but he's the least of my worries. He's always just sort of on the back burner."

"I don't know how you do it with him gone so much. That fine of a man. Aren't you ever worried he's messin' around?"

Julia laughs. "Well, no, I don't really worry about that. I mean from what he tells me the only living things he sees most of the time are endangered animals."

"Well, men get desperate sometimes..." Kate explodes in laughter at the thought.

Julia laughs deep from her belly. "That's disgusting!"

"So then what? What's goin' on?" Kate's tone remains light, though lined with sternness to refocus Julia back to the conversation.

"Well, it's a lot of things, or at least it's felt that way. Mostly, it's my career." Julia sighs deeply. "I'm in jeopardy of breaching my contract with Bauer & Brown if I don't crank out another book…and soon. The problem is every single idea I've had has been crap. Complete crap."

"Well you know, crap is subjective, Jules."

Julia laughs. "Yeah, I guess it is."

"So how much time do you have?"

"It was a two-year deal with an option for an extension." Julia sighs heavily. "Basically, I have about eight months to get the first draft to them to stay within the terms."

"Damn gurl, so what are you gonna do?"

"I have an idea. Actually, it was Jeff's idea…"

"Ohhh, how is Jeff? I just love him." Kate changes gears momentarily.

"He's great. Still being a pain in my ass and still seeing Sam off and on."

"Gawd he's fine. It's a damn shame all those good lookin' men are gay. I mean, they actually care about how they look and dress, especially as they age. Straight men don't care. I'm sorry, I may be old but I'm not into that round-belly Dad-bod. I'm always on Jerry to actually use his gym membership…"

Julia ignores the interruption and bursts into laughter before taking a deep sigh to restock her courage. Kate chimes in with a laugh before bringing them right back to point.

"So…you were sayin'…about the book idea…" Kate looks over at Julia. Julia shifts nervously in her leather seat.

"Yeah…so Jeff and I met Priscilla Bauer, my publisher, a few weeks ago. I was terrified to go in there with no material. I mean when you put out a book like *Steelhouse* that goes number one so quickly, it's a pretty high bar to produce the next book. I mean, I don't have any magic formula to writing, no cookie-cutter…"

"Of course you don't." Kate interjects with a laugh. "You're too damn idealistic."

"You're one to talk!" Julia counters.

Kate laughs again before growing quiet. Her look turns to one of concern. "Why didn't you call me, Jules? I don't know a thing about publishin' but I could listen…"

"I don't know…"

"Too proud, that's why."

"I know, I know…it was just easy with *Steelhouse*. It just sort of flowed. Beginner's luck, I guess."

"Gurl, please. You're an amazin' writer. You just have to find your mojo again."

Julia laughs. "Mojo? Really?"

Kate flashes that wide grin. "Yeah, you know…your flow…your sass."

Julia laughs harder. God, she needs this weekend. She needs her friend to remind her not to take everything so seriously. Although out of nowhere, the flutter of nerves kick up again in her stomach as she looks out the window onto the billboard-lined interstate leading them through suburban Atlanta.

She feels Kate's stare.

"So what is it? What's the idea?"

Julia sighs heavily, exhaling her nervous thoughts. "Okay, I will tell you but I really need you to hear me out before you say a thing."

"Sure…I mean, I can try." Kate smiles again.

"At first I thought it was insane and there was no way I could pursue it. Although the more I've thought about it, the more I know it's my next book to write."

Julia pauses and looks at Kate.

"Well…" Kate raises her eyebrows and circles her manicured right hand for Julia to get on with it.

Julia breathes deep again, the flutters moving into her throat forcing her words out faster.

"Murdoch. I've decided to write a book about what happened to Allison and Betty Ann. Honestly, I don't know how many of the facts I'll actually use yet, but the basis of their stories are the backdrop for the book. I mean, their deaths have always haunted me, not only because they happened right in the middle of Murdoch....but mostly because no plausible motive was ever established. Ever! How is that possible? It wasn't fair that they died such cruel deaths." Julia looks out the window, thinking of Seth as part of this equation as well. She clears her throat and swallows hard before continuing.

"I remember when I was reporting for the *Messenger*, I had this nagging sense that there were so many lies and so much deceit covering up what really happened but I was too young and too naïve to know what to do. Now, I feel like maybe in some way through this book I could vindicate their deaths by bringing their story to light. Maybe I can give them a voice to finally tell their stories...I don't know..." Julia finally draws in a breath. "So that's it...that's the idea..." She pauses and looks to Kate who has been eerily quiet. "What do you think?"

Kate continues driving, staring ahead silently before finally looking to Julia and breaking into a broad smile.

"Yes! I. Love. It. Love it!"

"You do?" Julia's not fully convinced.

Kate's blue eyes are aglow with excitement as she peers over at Julia before back at the interstate. "Yeah gurl, I mean I'd often wondered why you didn't write a book about that. Hell, when I was in law school I wondered why I didn't write one. I've never passed a July that I didn't think about Allison Mercer or an October that I didn't think about Betty Ann Stark. But gurl, seriously, what happened in that town...you just can't make that shit up."

"I know, it's just insane..."

Kate grows quiet for a moment in thought. "Are you sure you're ready? I mean, what about Seth? Are you telling his story, too?"

Julia's face darkens, brow furrowing behind her sunglasses, which she no longer really needs as the sun is setting deeper in the sky, casting brilliant orange and pink hues over Kate's shoulder.

"I don't know yet what I will reveal about Seth. I don't really know what I will write about any of it. I don't have an outline...just my memories right now." Julia's mind tumbles through the uncertainty and wonder, much like that feeling of staring at a three-thousand-piece jigsaw puzzle. When looking at the pieces packed in the box, it seems easy. Then you dump out them out on the table, and quickly feel overwhelmed about how all these seemingly unconnected pieces will snap into place to make a complete picture.

Julia gazes out the window, sighs heavily, and then turns back to look at her friend. "But I've tried hard to forget everything that happened, so some of those memories are a bit hazy. I'm going to have to spend time trying to remember..."

"What about Dan? Couldn't he help?" Kate asks the question that had been rolling around in Julia's mind for days now. Could her former editor be the crux in unbinding the web of rumors, theories, and truths about Allison's and Betty Ann's deaths? And maybe Seth's too?

"Yeah, I've thought about that. Honestly, I don't know where he is these days. The last time I heard from him was right after my first big feature ran in *The New Yorker*. He emailed to congratulate me, but God, that was years ago. He was still in Murdoch then."

"Gurl, I think we're the only people who's left Murdoch that hasn't been in a pine box." Kate laughs at her own joke.

Julia quietly gazes out the window again, doubt creeping in the recesses of her mind. "I'm not sure..." She murmurs aloud, though drops the thought in mid-sentence.

"Sure 'bout what?"

Julia sighs heavily. "I'm not sure about who I should really involve in this yet..."

Kate nods quietly in understanding. "Yeah, that's just it, Jules. You gotta be really sure you're ready to stir that hornet's nest. We both know that town swept everything under the rug years ago and hasn't looked back."

"I know. That's what I'm afraid of. I don't know how willing anyone will be to talk to me. I'm not even sure who's there anymore…and honestly, it's all so overwhelming I don't even know where to begin…"

"Well, what about your old stories? You still have them?"

"Nope."

"Why not?'

"I burned them."

"Burned them, really? Why in the hell would you burn them?" Kate laughs disbelievingly.

"I don't know…it was Cheryl's idea, you know all her woo-woo stuff. Something about fire being transformative energy. She thought it was weighing me down to carry around the past, and I agreed. So we had a big bonfire a few years after I got to New York." Julia does remember that night clearly. The real reason she didn't want to keep any of her *Murdoch Messenger* clips was because they reminded her of Seth and how in love they had been before everything happened.

Kate grows contemplative, as she focuses on the road.

"Wait a minute. Gurl, you know my memory isn't what it used to be, but for some reason I am thinkin' Nelda has them."

"Has what?" Julia's confused.

"Has all the old articles!"

"Hmmm…maybe…but why would she still have them?" Julia's doubtful.

"No gurl, I think she does…or well, she did…" Kate's voice crescendos with excitement. "Because I remember one night we all went over for dinner and you had been reportin' on that big school bond election George Stark was tryin' to push through. She showed me your story. She was so proud of you standin' up to him."

"I didn't stand up to him. I was doing my job as a reporter." Julia laughs envisioning her former mother-in-law. Of course Nelda Dixon would be proud of Julia for reporting on that story. Nelda is the other breed of Southern woman. She's strong, feisty, loyal, and stitched together by a thread of honesty that's unflinching. Even if it means hurting your feelings, Nelda's going to say it like she sees it.

Kate laughs. She'd always loved Nelda, too. How could you not love a woman who could wear overalls better than any farmer and make the best peach cobbler east of the Mississippi River?

"Well, according to Nelda you did stand up to him. You should call her."

"Oh, I don't know. I think it would upset her…" Julia shakes her head.

"When's the last time you talked?"

Julia flips through her mental calendar, landing on the last conversation.

"Year before last….on Seth's birthday."

"Call her, Jules. If she has those articles, it would be a gold mine, and the perfect place to start."

"Yeah and save me a trip to the microfiche machine at the *Messenger.*"

"Microfiche machine?" Kate bursts out laughing. "Oh Gawd, I hated those things. Haven't seen one since law school. Surely they've archived everything online by now."

Julia laughs thinking about the old newsroom with the two massive desktop computers perched atop heavy wooden desks that had been there, she guessed, since the mid-1960s. "You'd think but if it's anything like it was when I was there, then no. Consume too many resources." She imitates her former editor's voice.

Kate laughs. "Well, we are twenty minutes from the cabin and we have a bigger issue than microfiche machines…" Kate looks over at Julia and smiles.

Julia instinctively reads Kate's mind. "I know, but I can't tell her yet."

"What? What do you mean you can't tell her? It's Marilee."

"Exactly. Marilee who still lives in Murdoch and Marilee whose husband is on his second term as mayor. It's too big a risk right now."

"Risk? Hell, Jules everything 'bout this book is a risk. How in the world do you think you can show up in that one red-light town and Marilee Johnson not know?"

Julia sighs heavily. "I know, I know. I mean she will find out, but I'm not sure this weekend is the right time to tell her."

"She will be devastated if she hears about this from someone else. Or what if you run into her when you're in Murdoch?"

"Yeah, I've thought about that. I guess I'm just trying to take this one step at a time. I mean, I didn't arrive at this decision lightly."

"Well I'm not saying you have to parade through Main Street announcing you're there. But Marilee is your friend, and she's gonna find out sooner or later. Let's face it, you've already been to hell and back, Jules. So whatever ghosts are still there, you can face them. Besides, we both know you need Marilee and Paul on your side."

"Yeah, I know. But that's exactly why I'm not sure how deep to involve Marilee. She has a lot more at stake than we do. We're not there anymore. We're outsiders now."

Kate laughs. "Gurl, we've always been outsiders in that town."

"Yeah, I guess we have…" Julia laughs and changes the subject to quiz Kate about her husband Jerry and their daughter, Jennifer. The sixteen-year-old is a spitting image of Kate and just completed her sophomore year at a prestigious boarding school in Connecticut in hopes of attending Yale after graduation.

After ten minutes of playfully bickering over the directions, Kate finally turns onto the gravel road leading to the cabin. Julia glances over at Kate who's intently focused on the road though wears a broad smile. The sight of her old friend makes Julia smile in nostalgia and gratitude.

For every success Julia's achieved or all the money she's made, the time she spends with Kate and Marilee always brings her back to what truly matters: spending time with the people you love and who love you, too.

CHAPTER 8

"You can slow down a little…" Julia laughs as Kate hauls down the dirt road, dust flying up around the black Mercedes in big cloudy puffs. "You've been in the city too long."

Kate cackles as she steers down the long dirt road leading up to Marilee's family's cabin. With the sun now plummeted deep below the horizon, the car's headlights reveal only the edges of the huge birch and pine trees lining the narrow road.

"Gurl, speak for yourself. Do you even know how to drive anymore?" Kate smiles over at her playfully.

"I do, but driving in Manhattan is a life-and-death situation, and I choose to live."

"I don't remember the cabin being this far back in the woods." Kate leans over the steering wheel looking from left to right at the canopy of trees, wondering what's lurking in the shadows. "This is sorta creepy."

Julia stares intently at the road with deep grooves where the rain has washed the gravel out over time. Then she lets out a laugh thinking about similar dirt roads they'd traveled together years ago. "Do you remember that piece-of-shit car I had in Murdoch?…"

"Yeah and you'd drive that thing like a bat outta hell. I don't think I ever saw it clean." Kate laughs.

Julia chimes in, recalling the boxy 1988 silver Toyota Corolla she had back then.

"Or how 'bout when Marilee threw up in the back floorboard after that New Year's Eve party at the KC hall?" Kate cackles louder as she slowly navigates the big grooves in the gravel.

"Oh God…that's right." In the pause between her laughs comes the realization of just how long it's been since Julia has laughed. Really laughed. She's laughed more in this hour-and-fifteen-minute car ride with Kate than she has in months.

"Oh there it is!" Julia points at the bright glow produced by the cabin's front porch light.

"Thank Gawd," Kate sighs. "It's definitely wine-thirty."

Marilee barrels out of the cabin's front door waving wildly at her two friends. Even now, just a few years shy of fifty, her porcelain skin echoes few traces of aging and shines even brighter set against the darker hair color she now uses to hide the gray.

Marilee Johnson had always been the mother hen to Kate and Julia. It's strange, really, that the three of them got along the way they did. On the surface, it appeared they had little in common, but then there are times in life when people just inexplicably connect.

"Sisters from another mister!" Marilee used to say, wine in hand, over long conversations with Kate and Julia on her back porch, while their husbands watched whatever flavor of sports was on television. Even now as the years have ticked by and their lives have gone separate, and very different ways, the three could pick right back up in a heartbeat. While Julia and Kate had remained close on their own, Marilee had been the glue that kept the trio together, organizing weekends like this every few years.

But that's Marilee's way. Even in Murdoch years ago, she played the role of connector. Since that first Friday night post-game party, Marilee took it as her personal mission to ensure Kate and Julia got to know all the right people in town. For having grown up in Murdoch, Marilee has always had an adventurous spirit. Some in Murdoch found the arrival of outsiders threatening to their quiet way of things, but not Marilee. She's always loved meeting new people and hearing of their adventures, especially what brought them to her tiny town. Yet to this day, Marilee's very much an insider, and in a town like Murdoch, it matters who's an insider and who's not.

That's not to say Marilee never had aspirations beyond the city limit sign. She'd always wanted go away, far away. As the most beautiful, popular, and smartest girl in the Mustangs' Class of 1987, she felt limitless. Having starred in the drama club, her dream was to go to Hollywood to be in commercials until she landed her big break for the silver screen.

Everyone told her she looked like Brooke Shields. Marilee felt that was one of the highest compliments, though she secretly wanted people to think of her as pretty on the inside, too. It was that internal drive to do the right thing that enabled Marilee to get along with every circle in high school, whether the jocks, the geeks, the potheads, or the regular kids.

For as big as Marilee's dreams were, the reality of life only landed her further east at Mississippi State. Though she came from old Southern money, her parents were determined to teach Marilee and her younger brother about the importance of personal responsibility and finding their own way. They would pay for four years of college and nothing else. Plus, it wasn't the worst proposition. Her high school boyfriend, Paul, was already at State a year ahead of her. Soon after their wedding, they found themselves back in Murdoch, agreeing it was the best place to raise children, of which they would later have two.

While Marilee's life hadn't produced a star on the Hollywood Walk of Fame, she is in many ways the most content of the three. Perhaps it's because over the years she has become masterful at tucking away life's unpleasant things, like hidden dreams, old scars, and ugly secrets. Marilee's always lived the motto of her grandmother, "you just gotta pull up your bootstraps and keep moving."

"Ohhh girls, you're finally here!" Marilee waves and rushes to meet Kate and Julia, hugging them each tightly. "I hope you found the place okay."

"I just don't remember it being so damn far back in the woods." Kate throws her arms out to greet her old friend.

"Well, you're here now." Marilee's voice goes higher in excitement embracing Kate. "Yawl want some wine? I just opened a bottle of Cab."

"It's always time for wine." Julia takes her turn at the hugs.

Marilee pulls back and looks at Julia, cracks in laughter, and then hugs her again. "It's just so good to see yawl. I really needed this weekend." Marilee sighs. "Plus, you two already got a head start in the car, so I need a full recap." Marilee straightens and grabs one of Julia's bags, which she had deposited on the porch.

Kate looks over at Julia with a partial smile, partial smirk. "Oh, yeah gurl, there's a lot to catch up on."

Julia shoots Kate a don't-you-dare look. "But first let's unload the rest of this stuff and change. I hear my yoga pants calling me."

After unloading the car and exchanging their designer clothes for cotton stretchy ones, the three settle around the long bar top in the kitchen. The cabin had been renovated since the last time Julia had visited more than a decade ago. It still held traces of that rugged lodge feel she loved then, with the hardwood floors and mounts of deer and other wild game dotting the paneled walls. The cabin had been in Paul's family for two generations, originally a hunting cabin for his grandfather. Over the years, Marilee and Paul had taken primary ownership, and knowing Marilee's taste for finer things, the cabin had been gradually transformed.

Whether it was the long day of travel, the heavy wooded cabin full of animals, or suddenly coming face to face with the two women who epitomized her life in Murdoch, Julia suddenly finds herself wanting to shrink back, go silent, and just observe. Either that or get really drunk. Pangs of regret in telling Kate about the book swirl through her, underscored by that journalist's curiosity in wanting to pepper

Marilee with questions about the latest Murdoch gossip. Suspended in the middle, she finds it safer to stay quiet while Kate and Marilee catch up.

"Yeah, Jerry's always gone pitchin' some new account, and I'm always in court or preparin' for the next case." Kate explains. "Honestly, I'm not sure how we would have ever given Jennifer the time and attention she deserves, and I feel so guilty about that."

"Well, you don't have to feel guilty. She's still at boardin' school, right?" Marilee sips her wine.

"Yeah, I know. She'll be home next week for summer break and hopin' we can spend some time together. I just want her to have a normal childhood." Kate sighs and picks at the spread of cheese and crackers before her.

"I know you want that for her, but Kate, let's face it...nothing about you is normal." Julia cracks the heaviness.

Kate wads her paper napkin and playfully throws it across the granite countertop at Julia, who dodges and laughs.

"Well, my kids had a 'normal' childhood..." Marilee flashes her red tipped nails in the air mimicking quote marks. "And they're still ungrateful as a summer day is long."

"It's just their age." Kate replies.

"Hell, they're twenty-six and twenty-two. You'd think they'd have outgrown that hate-your-parents phase by now." Wine sometimes makes Marilee feisty, and Julia loves to see the departure from her usual candy-coated demeanor.

"I'm still not sure I like my parents, and I'm almost forty-six." Kate laughs as do Julia and Marilee. The wine is flowing freely now through their glasses and their veins.

"I think it's the curse of life that kids just blame their parents for everything..." Julia chimes in. "I'm glad I don't have any of my own to hate me. Just Mr. Pickles...and he loves me." She smiles satisfactorily.

"Oh, that damn cat. How's Mr. Pickles?" Kate laughs. She hates cats.

"Forget Mr. Pickles. How's that fine man?" Marilee winks.

"Honestly? Who knows. It's complicated." Julia shrugs.

"What could be complicated 'bout havin' a hot boyfriend?" Marilee laughs and looks at Kate, who shrugs.

"Yeah Jules, I'll gladly trade him for Jerry…even just for a night." Kate winks.

"Or for Paul…" Marilee laughs harder to the point she snorts loudly.

"The snort!" For Kate, no get-together with Julia and Marilee is complete without a good Marilee snort.

Julia and Kate are now hysterically laughing, too.

"I can't breathe…" Kate laughs harder.

Julia wipes her eyes from the laughter-evoked tears. "Damn I've missed you two. I haven't laughed like this since…well…I can't even remember."

Marilee hoists her wine glass in the air. "Sisters from another mister!"

"Hell yeah!" Kate chimes in.

"Sisters!" Julia shouts emphatically as the three clink their wine glasses and another wave of laughter ensues. When the hysterics pass, Kate picks right back up where they'd left off.

"Ahhem, now where were we?" Kate says in her best lawyer tone.

"We're at the hot man."

"Ahh, yes, the hot man." Kate and Marilee both look at Julia.

Julia smiles sheepishly. "What? What do you want to know?"

"Oh come on Jules, you two have been datin' for years. When you gonna finally marry him?" Marilee pries.

"Well, he wants to…" Julia shoves a chip into her mouth packed with a hearty scoop of Marilee's famous seven-layer party dip.

"What? He does? Did he propose?" Kate asks excitedly and somewhat offended that she hadn't heard this news yet.

"That would be the next step here." Marilee abandons her diet to shovel another chip drenched in dip in her mouth, too. "I mean, why not? You're gettin' old. What could you possibly be waitin' for?"

"Oh, but you'll always be older." Julia teases. "He hasn't proposed. We've just talked about it and just end up going in circles. It's not like I'm waiting for anything...I do love him. I just..."

"Just don't think you can marry again?" Marilee's voice grows softer, sweeter referring to Seth.

"Well, yes, there's that...but really the truth is, I like my life, and with our careers, we never see each other. We've spent most of our relationship apart. He doesn't seem to understand that we've never really been in the same place very long. We've never lived together, except for a few week stretches here and there. So how would we know a marriage would really work?" The wine flowing through Julia has now unlocked her words...and those unspoken questions.

"You never really know if a marriage is going to work." Kate chimes in first. "I certainly think it depends on your partner, but it's also about you. I mean look at Mike. He was a complete asshole, and I couldn't see it. Then Jerry came along and actually treated me right."

"Yeah but you were, what, all of twenty when you met Mike?" A hopeless romantic, Marilee defends her friend. "We all do stupid things for love at that age."

"Oh dawg, don't we though?" Kate laughs then looks at Julia. "But Jules, you know exactly who you are...and you know Frank well enough after how many years?"

"Six...six years..." Julia sighs in resignation.

"Look gurl, I'm just sayin' that deep down you already know whether it would work or not."

Julia takes a sip of wine. Kate's right. It's what she's never wanted to admit. Frank is a wonderful man...a kind, loving, and good-hearted man. He was the man that took her by complete surprise when they met at the Howard Scripps Awards gala years ago. She was being honored for the article that eventually led to *Steelhouse*. Standing in line for another drink during the cocktail reception, she had turned abruptly at the sound of her name, uttered in a deep smoker's voice.

"Is it *the* Julia Jarvis?" Frank had asked playfully.

"Yes…" Julia had spun around to see if she knew the voice but was so startled by the man standing behind her, she nearly spilled her glass of wine on his starched white shirt tucked behind the tailored suit jacket.

Frank Jackson defies the stereotype of most photographers. He doesn't actually smoke, voice all his own. He's tall and trim, with a perfectly tanned, angled face and broad smile that looks like it belongs on a stage entertaining crowds. And he knows his way around fashion when he needs to.

That first night, Julia found Frank charming and a bit mysterious as he spoke of his travels with *National Geographic*. Yet, there was also something ruggedly handsome about him, reminding her of the Robert Kincaid character, the wandering, charming photographer, in the book *Bridges of Madison County*. And much like Francesca in the book, Julia also waited for her lover's return.

But Julia cannot wait any more. She's waited far too long for Frank to set her heart on fire like Seth, far too long to actually build a substantial relationship with him. At first, their fire was purely physical, connected by a common adventurous spirit and a passion for great sex. Over time, Frank and Julia's fire simmered, punctuated now only by an occasional spark when he returns. Those reunions are certainly welcome and pleasurable for Julia in the right ways, but she knows they are simply not enough.

Julia's passion runs far too deep. It's the one common denominator in her life, whether in work, love, or even with her food. If something doesn't make her come alive and set her heart on fire, she knows it. And there's very little gray space in between. Oh sure, she will hang out in the gray and try to pretend she doesn't know what she knows. But the truth is, the fire with Frank is long gone. Now, it's a relationship of convenience.

"I know…you're right. I do need to be honest with him, but it's just not a good time. I've just been trying to hold off the marriage conversation. I mean, he's gone again anyway, and I need time to focus on my book."

Heat rises in Julia's cheeks just as the words regretfully fly out of her mouth. *Oh shit. The book.*

"Oh? Are you working on another book?" Marilee looks over curiously as she opens another bottle of wine. They are now on number three, but who's counting?

Kate also peers at Julia wondering how she will work her way out of this one. A masterful orator, she feels certain Julia can, though under the influence of many rounds of Cabernet, maybe not.

"I have some ideas I'm exploring but nothing definite yet." Julia's face grows hotter, but relaxes a bit knowing she can blame it on a wine-flash, if needed.

"Well, I just loved *Steelhouse*. I mean I read it three times, and every time I loved it more. Mostly I would just sit there in amazement that my friend who started at the little 'ol *Murdoch Messenger* had actually gone off and written a book. No...not just a book. A *New York Times* bestseller." Marilee smiles proudly over at Julia as she pops open the cork. "So what's the new one about?"

"Oh, I don't know...nothing I'm ready to talk about..."

"Why not? You know we're secretly your muses." Marilee smiles, sets the bottle down, and waves her hands around her face like a fairy.

Julia and Kate laugh and glance at each other.

"Wait a minute!" Even in her tippy state, Marilee is keenly aware of the look just exchanged. "Kate, do you know?"

"Know what?"

"Don't play the dumb blondie with me. I know that look. You DO!" Marilee slurs slightly on the last word.

Kate looks down at her glass before taking a sip of the wine Marilee had just poured, hoping to swallow her words as well. Julia, on the other hand, has suddenly found hers.

"Murdoch." Julia blurts out nervously. "The new book is about Murdoch."

Kate coughs on her wine, looking up half amazed at Julia's ballsy confession and half in horror waiting for Marilee's response.

"Murdoch? What do you mean the book is about Murdoch?" Marilee looks confused through her wine fog. Silence hangs in the air for what feels like minutes before the ah-ha comes.

"Noooooo. Jules you can't." Marilee shakes her head slowly.

"I have to."

"What do you mean you *have* to? You can't…and that's it." Marilee looks at Julia, brow furrowed in thought.

Silence hangs in the air with Kate peering at Julia, who's swirling her wine glass. Marilee also peers at Julia intently.

"I mean, why can't you just let it be?" Marilee's voice rises as she abruptly stands. She's clearly irritated as she begins putting away the food. The party's over.

Julia clears her throat hoping to also clear her head from the wine haze. "Because you just can't make up what happened in Murdoch…it's the perfect backdrop for a book."

"It's not just material for a book, Julia. People *died.*"

"I know that. I mean, remember…my husband? Seth?" Julia's voice elevates matching Marilee's, though with a shield of defense in her tone.

Marilee glares at Julia sternly before silently returning to tidy the kitchen. She turns her back to Julia and Kate who are still sitting around the bar silently. Kate shifts uncomfortably in her chair, unsure whether to interject.

When Marilee spins around, the anger pours off her like steam from an overheated radiator. "And what do you think about this?" She stares at Kate. "I assume you already knew…"

"Just today…Jules just told me in the car on the way over…" Kate looks at Marilee as she leans back in her chair and runs her hand through her blonde waves of hair in a sweeping motion. "Honestly? I think it's a damn good idea. I've always thought about digging into those cases myself, but just never had the time. I mean, come'on Marilee. Hasn't it haunted you that those women died? And for what? It doesn't make any damn sense."

"Exactly, and that's why I am doing it." Julia's interrupts, her voice calmer, though the butterflies in her belly have turned into flames of conviction. "Allison and Betty Ann died in vain. I have always believed that, even when I was writing those stories for the *Messenger*. The more time has passed, the crazier it all seems. I mean…it's absolutely ridiculous that no one has ever been arrested…let alone convicted for Allison Mercer's death. How can that be? Those women have a story that needs to be told, and it's time for someone to tell it."

Marilee is now standing over the bar, collecting her thoughts with the dish towel draped over her shoulder. "Come'on Julia, don't you think I know that? Betty Ann was my very dear friend and mentor. I have never understood why she died or Allison for that matter. It's just never…never made sense…"

Marilee's voice dips deeper to a guttural tone that Julia has only heard once before from her friend, and that was the night George Stark was arrested for murdering Betty Ann. "But how…how in the hell…do you think writin' this book is gonna give Allison and Betty Ann a voice? They're dead, and nothin'…nothin' can bring them back."

Marilee quickly moves her hands to cover her face, choking back the sob daring to escape. "All that book's gonna do is stir up trouble. No one talks about what happened back then…and no one needs to now." She breathes deeply fighting back the tears before slowly lowering her hands in resignation, tears streaming down her blushed cheeks. "You know what? I can't do this…I'm goin' to bed."

Marilee tosses the dishtowel on the granite bar and squeezes Kate's shoulder as she heads through the open room. As she passes by the heavy wooden dining table, she grazes her fingers lightly over the top to steady herself as the wine has taken full effect.

"Marilee, wait…please don't…" Julia stands abruptly. "I'm so sorry. I didn't mean to upset you." As she watches her friend walk toward the staircase, Julia sinks back into the chair realizing she needs to let it go for now.

Marilee pauses at the third step, turns to Julia and Kate and wipes her eyes again. She stares blankly across the room at them. "I just need to go bed. I think I'm drunk."

"Oh honey, don't worry. I think we're all drunk." Kate raises her glass. Marilee half smiles before turning to continue her march up the staircase.

Julia rests her elbows on the edge of the bar. Even through her drunkenness, a flash of awareness jars her like a lighting bolt cracking and illuminating a pitch-black sky. Writing this book isn't just about having conviction to redeem Allison and Betty Ann.

In this moment, it occurs to Julia that writing this book will also require compassion. It's the compassion she's often failed to extend to others for the sake of the story, and the compassion she most especially forgets to show herself.

In the years after Murdoch, Julia lived suspended between two parallel universes. In one she was unable to fully forgive and forget what happened in Murdoch, and yet in the other, she did everything possible to never think about or mention it all.

Now Julia can't quite determine if the run-in with Marilee has sobered her up or spiraled her downward. All she knows is that it's left her dizzy. Elbows still down on the bar, head in her hands in thought, Julia traces the edge of her face with her slender fingers.

"That didn't go the way I wanted." She finally says quietly to Kate, who has been silently loading the rest of the dishes in the dishwasher and putting away the cheeses and dips.

"Well Jules, how'd you think it'd go? We both knew that'd be her reaction. You know Marilee doesn't like things to be messy, and nothing could be messier than what happened in that town."

Julia interrupts, irritation lining her words. "I know. I just really didn't want to upset her...and now I feel terrible."

"Like I said earlier, it's better comin' from you now than findin' out through someone gossipin' in Murdoch...or worse you runnin' into her when you go visit."

"Yeah…I guess…" Julia's own drunkenness now amplifies the guilt.

"Look gurl, there's nothing you can do 'bout it tonight. Let's just all sleep it off and she'll come around in the morning."

Julia sighs heavily as she stands to head upstairs. "Yeah, I sure hope you're right."

CHAPTER 9

The next morning Julia is the first to awaken and she's glad to have the time alone for her usual ritual of brewing a strong pot of coffee, settling into a comfy spot, and writing in her journal. It's what she calls her "Zen time."

Julia nestles into a big wicker chair on the wraparound porch, coffee steaming in the damp morning air. Cascading in front of her is a thicket of large trees, shimmering in the light of the swiftly rising sun. Reeling from the wine fog and replays of last night's conversation, Julia stares into the trees looking at nothing in particular. Then her eye catches a glimpse of a red cardinal. Even though she abhors birds, she's always enjoyed seeing cardinals.

She'd once read that cardinals are symbolic of lost loved ones. They are also thought to represent hope, love, renewal, and pride, not ego pride, but that natural pride that stems from your soul in being who you've come here to be. Julia liked that explanation and every time she sees one, she reminds herself to stand a little taller.

After last night's encounter with Marilee, she went to bed with her confidence shaken, questioning whether she should really move forward with the book. Seeing the cardinal flitting between branches in the morning sun, she smiles. Perhaps it's the confirmation that she so desperately seeks.

As her gaze softens, Julia realizes Marilee is the first person to truly be upset by the idea of her book, and she won't be the last. This is the consequence of being a journalist, a storyteller. Sometimes in telling the story, you have to say what no one else is willing to say. She had received her fair share of nasty letters, calls, and emails in response to her stories over the years. It hadn't phased her and certainly hadn't slowed her down from doing her job.

Unlike years ago as that unsure reporter for the *Murdoch Messenger*, however, Julia's writing is no longer just a job. For in the years that have passed, it's become clear that writing is not just her passion, it's her life's purpose and it's personal. Somewhere over the last few months, she'd lost touch with that sense of herself. Slipping into a world of self-doubt, and then sinking deeper into anxiety and fear, Julia had felt completely disconnected from that purpose. But over the last few weeks, as she's tiptoed out of that fear and returned to her heart, she's been gradually rekindling that sense of determination. That's why last night's spat with Marilee felt so jarring.

Now in the light of morning, caffeine gradually clearing the wine-induced cobwebs and nature's canvas providing lightness of heart, she closes her eyes and breathes deeply. A flicker of joy in her chest rises into a smile. For in the stillness of the morning, she leans back into that sense of purpose and realizes exactly what she must do next. Call Nelda and find those old articles.

"Mornin'!" The sliding glass door jolts open, yanking Julia back to reality. She jumps, coffee spilling on the edge of the chair and drips onto the wooden planked floor.

"Holy shit, you scared me!" Julia's heart pounds in her chest.

"Sorry." Kate giggles. "Whatcha doing?" She pulls up a wicker chair beside Julia and settles in with her coffee.

"Just journaling a little."

"You mean stewin' 'bout last night? Your notebook isn't even open." Kate laughs and points at the unopened leather book laying in Julia's lap. "Did you get any sleep? Or didja worry all night?" Kate takes a sip of her steaming coffee and winks at Julia.

"Oh yeah, I passed out. Think I drank too much." Julia laughs.

The sliding door opens again, and Marilee emerges silently, coffee in hand.

"Mornin'..." Marilee bids quietly and slowly pulls up a third chair.

"Good mornin!" Kate replies in the same chipper tone.

"How'd you sleep?" Julia smiles up to Marilee.

"Well, I passed out and then woke up about four and felt awful." Marilee frowns. "Headache and indigestion. Gawd...I'm not used to drinking that much. Did one of you come into my room and stab my forehead with a screwdriver?"

Julia laughs. "No, but I swear someone stabbed mine also." She and Marilee look at Kate.

"Don't blame me. I didn't pour the wine down your throats!" Kate says loudly.

Marilee's smile brightens her bare face, which now reveals the fine lines of age and the dark circles of worry.

Kate laughs. "You two are just out of shape 'cause I feel fine."

"What we need is some grease." Marilee blows on her coffee. "Yawl hungry? I bought all kinds of stuff for breakfast."

Even with her horrendous hangover, Marilee manages to produce a huge spread of an egg-and-spinach quiche, bacon, toast, and fruit. Julia's relieved the conversation hasn't yet turned to the previous night or to Murdoch. Instead, the three dance around both topics until Kate can no longer stand it. The lawyer in her prevents any conversation she deems relevant from sitting too long untouched.

"So how's Paul doing as mayor? Isn't he on...what...his second term now?"

"Yes, second term and going for the third this fall." Marilee nods.

"There aren't term limits?"

"Yeah, it's capped at four, and he's determined to go for all four."

"So then does he still have his insurance business, too?" Julia asks sipping her coffee across the table. Marilee cuts her eyes trying to overlook the elephant still sitting between them.

"Oh yeah, he's never letting that go. He loves it. It keeps him busy."

"It's funny to think of anyone being too busy in Murdoch." Kate teases.

Marilee lets out a half laugh. Whether the hangover or the unspoken tension, there's a heaviness around Marilee this morning that Kate senses and looks for every attempt to lighten.

"So then is he already in campaign mode?"

"Not yet, but will be by the end of the summer. Right now he's trying to keep the new newspaper editor in check. He's been stirrin' up trouble."

"Oh? Who's that?" Julia's curiosity piques around talk of the paper.

"His name is Matt Case. His family actually bought the paper a few years ago and Matt came in early last year to run it and be the editor. He's a nice enough guy but lately he's been a thorn in Paul's side at the council meetings...digging 'round old records and stuff."

"What's he looking for?" Julia quizzes.

"Who knows. He used to be editor at the New Orleans paper, so I just think he's bored in Murdoch and looking to make up stories that aren't there." Marilee turns to Julia. "But he certainly knows who you are."

"Me? How does he know me?" Flustered, Julia quickly scans her memory bank for a Matt Case and it turns up empty.

"Oh, from the paper and from *Steelhouse*. He was at Nine Ed's Cafe the other morning, and I went in with a few friends from church. He overheard me sayin' I was comin' on this trip with you. So he asked about you. Plus, I mean what other writers from the *Messenger* do you know that have written a book, let alone a *New York Times* bestseller? Come on Jules, you're a living legend." Marilee smiles.

Julia laughs, grateful for her friend's teasing. "I'm not sure about that...but when I was there, I'm not sure anyone even knew what a bestseller's list was."

Marilee's face darkens, brow furrowing in thought. "There's somethin' else you should know...if you are really gonna write that damn book." The edge returns to her voice.

"What's that?" Julia asks quietly.

"I'm not sure if it's true or not, but rumor has it that Matt has also been investigating Allison's death."

"Really?" Now Kate perks up. "Why?"

"I'm not really sure…and don't even know if it's true." Marilee shrugs.

"Well, I wonder if he's found out anything? Or better yet, what's he looking for?" Kate quizzes.

Julia sits quietly listening and calculating. If this Matt Case has been digging into Allison's case, then maybe he could provide some new insight? All she has to go on right now is those articles at Nelda's, and she's not even sure whether Nelda still has them.

It's this juncture in the research process that Julia finds the most uncomfortable and the most exciting. It's the point of not knowing. She doesn't know what she will uncover in those articles, through this Matt Case, or in Murdoch. All she knows in the light of day, sitting around this table with her old friends is that nothing, and no one, is stopping her from writing this book.

"All I'm sayin' is that he might be a good place to start…" Marilee scoots the remaining bite of quiche around her plate, and then looks up at Julia. "But you didn't hear that from me."

"I appreciate any help I can get, and honestly I don't really know where this is going to all go." Julia sighs heavily. "Marilee…I'm really sorry about last night. I never wanted to upset you because I know how close you were to Betty Ann."

"I know…" Marilee clears her throat as if making way for the tangled thoughts that haven't fully become words. "I still don't agree with this book. I think you'd be playing with fire to walk back into that town and expect anyone to offer any information to help you write it." Marilee's irritation bubbles back to the surface. She sighs heavily.

Kate studies Marilee, her lawyer brain working overtime to observe not just what Marilee says but also her expressions and tone.

It's this sixth sense Kate has cultivated over the years and why she's one of Atlanta's most sought-after lawyers. There's something about the irritation, verging on anger, in Marilee's voice that Kate picks up on but says nothing. She wonders what Marilee isn't saying.

Julia tries to keep the irritation at bay. "I know, Marilee. I don't expect anyone to be particularly happy about me writing this book, but I don't plan to announce it from Main Street, either. I don't even know who's still in Murdoch or what I will find there. I realize this has the potential to surface a lot of stuff for a lot of people, including me." Julia swallows hard, collecting her words. "But I've walked around for almost twenty years carrying the baggage of what happened there…and what happened to Seth. So this wasn't a decision I arrived at lightly. I just have this gut feeling it's my book to write."

"Well, I hope it all works out for you. I really do. And maybe I'm just a dumb Southern woman, but I am smart enough to know when to leave things alone." Marilee abruptly stands and starts bussing the table, uncomfortable quiet hanging in the air. Julia sips her coffee to avoid replying with anything she'll regret.

Kate jumps in and changes the subject. "So what do yawl wanna do today?"

Silence hovers as Marilee scrapes a plate in the sink. After a few moments, she stops, looks up, and gently smiles at Julia. "I'm sorry, Jules. I know you…and that means I know when you set your mind to somethin', it'd take a freight train to stop you. So I know I won't be able to sway you on writin' this book. But I just want you to promise me one thing…"

"What's that?"

"Watch your back and be careful who you trust."

Julia stands and walks to her friend and hugs her in an unspoken apology. "Okay I will…"

The final day and a half of their girls' weekend is full of more wine and laughter, which is typical of their reunions. Julia usually leaves these weekends feeling massively hungover and in need of a full detox. This time, however, she also needs an emotional detox. As always, it's been wonderful to laugh and catch up with her friends, but in the aftermath of her run-in with Marilee, she still feels unsettled. Although nothing more is said about the book, Marilee makes Julia promise to call if she comes into town.

The trip home does little to soothe Julia's nerves, as the flight home to New York is a turbulent one, both literally because of a major storm line crossing the East Coast and figuratively because of the swirl of emotion and doubt still tumbling through Julia.

When she finally does make it home, she makes a direct line to her bed. The heaviness finally lifts and a delicious ten hours of sleep ensues.

CHAPTER 10

"Oh honey, I don't have road rage. I have stupidity rage. Course 'round here there's not much can be done 'bout that." Nelda Dixon sits at the long rectangular table in the dining room cradling the phone in her weathered hand, the same way she has for years when friends or family call. This table has been the heart of the Dixon household for three generations. Julia remembers the heavy walnut table, as it had been the gathering spot for quiet dinners, large Christmas feasts, and vicious games of spades.

Julia laughs into the receiver picturing Nelda at the table in the old farmhouse. "Nelda, you've always had a way of putting things…"

"Just gotta say it like I see it, honey. But you know these days I don't get on the road that much anymore, at least I'm not supposed to. Doc Stephens says I'm not safe behind the wheel with my eyesight. I keep askin' him, who am I gonna hit in this small town? I swear the farmers on their combines are still more dangerous than me…"

Nelda pauses and draws a quick breath. Julia senses the nervous curiosity in her voice beyond the small talk.

Why call now, after so long?

Seth was like her in that way. He could use humor to distract from the depth of emotion that lay underneath. For all the witty one-liners and jovial teasing, both Nelda and Seth shared a curiosity and a longing for deeper meaning. Unlike many in Murdoch who turned to religion for that, the Dixons turned to each other. Sure, the Dixons believed in God and went to the Methodist church on most Sundays. For the Dixon family, however, that sense of meaning also came in the form of shared ideas. Julia had found it both odd and refreshing that a retired veterinarian and his retired schoolteacher wife would instigate conversations about everything from race and religion to homosexuality and politics. Behind closed doors, Nelda and Doc invited their kids and select visitors (the ones they trusted) to wholeheartedly discuss the things that mattered.

Beyond the edge of the Dixon's farm, however, those conversations were hushed. That's because Nelda and Doc long understood that in Murdoch you talk about how much rain you've gotten, who the Mustangs play on Friday night, who's died, or who's had a baby. Yet rarely do you wade into the deep end of the pool to talk about things like how you really feel, what you dream of, or anything else that dips into that unpredictable well of vulnerability.

In the nearly five years Julia had been with Seth, she'd only seen him cry twice. The first was at their wedding and the other when Doc died. Although Seth would often share his vivid memories of life in Murdoch with Julia, from family Christmases to their cross-country vacations packed in Nelda's salmon-colored Ford Fairmont station wagon. While this notion of family was completely foreign to her, Julia had been hungry for this sense of belonging growing up. So, she inhaled the memories as quickly as Seth would share them.

The first time Seth brought her home to meet his parents and older sister Pam, Julia instantly fell in love with the Dixons and the Norman Rockwell idealism that went along with living in a small town. For Julia, Murdoch was a quintessential sleepy Southern town of farmers, teachers, and hard-working people who were completely and utterly devoted to three things: God, family, and Mustang football (in that order).

Upon moving to Murdoch, Julia had quickly picked up on this unspoken agreement to skate along life's edges. She learned that to survive in Murdoch, you'd better check your quest for deeper meaning, your incessant curiosity, and your need to challenge the status quo at the county line. Seth was masterful at this game, quietly observing all the goings on and then responding with judicious grace.

It was a prescription for living that Julia had never quite grasped, professionally as a reporter, nor personally as someone who married into the town. Oh, she wanted to understand and to fit in. Most of all, she wanted to be embraced as an insider. Every time she was asked, "Now, who were you before you were married?" Julia realized she wasn't one of them. As an outsider, particularly a passionate, open-minded one with idealistic views on things like equality, acceptance, and justice, some considered Julia a threat to the Murdoch way of life.

Julia knew that then, and she certainly knows it now that she's about to excavate the past. That's why she needs Nelda's help. In this moment, Julia is grateful for Nelda's small talk about her eyesight and the family that moved into the farm down the road to fill in the gaps of space that time has etched between them.

Julia's relationship with her mother-in-law hadn't been perfect by any means. They'd had their share of spats over the years, as any two strong-willed women would who both deeply love the same man. Early in their relationship, Julia often worried whether in Nelda's eyes she was good enough for Seth, but that's when she'd retreat into the world she knew: writing. Yet, for all her doubts, Julia could see in Nelda's expressions that she respected her, especially when Julia was willing to speak up and stand up for herself.

It's why on some level she now seeks Nelda's permission. There had been few people in Julia's life that she sought approval from, but Nelda has always been one of them. In many ways over the years, Julia had grown closer to Nelda than she felt to her own mother. She used to sit with Nelda for hours at the wooden table, asking questions about Nelda's life growing up, what Seth was like as a boy, or her thoughts on life in the South as a woman. Nelda welcomed the conversation. Julia savored the connection.

Julia's own mother never had much time or interest in chit-chat, which is why as a child Julia's incessant questioning of "why" and "what's that?" visibly grated her mother's nerves. Her mother used to say that from the time she was born, Julia had thousands of words bottled up inside her, and she'd talk or write as long as she needed to every day to use them all up.

Yet, there are moments like now in the middle of a conversation, when Julia knows that words sometimes fall short. For words can't touch the depth of hurt or answer the many questions she and Nelda both still carry about Seth.

Over the years, Julia called Nelda here and there to say, "Hello" and check-in, but two rituals had been the same. Calling Nelda on Seth's birthday and sending a Christmas card with a handwritten note. In the beginning this connection to Nelda was Julia's lifeline back to her husband, back to a time that gave her life a sense of grounding she hadn't ever found again.

After every conversation with Nelda, a volcano of memories erupted whether Julia wanted them to or not. The memories would linger in the back of her mind and in the middle of her dreams for days, weeks, and sometimes months. For some reason, the last conversation with Nelda had been particularly difficult, and Julia hung up realizing she couldn't bear to keep scraping off the scab on that old wound. Even after all the passing years, it still hurt too much. So she stopped calling, and she missed Seth's birthday call earlier this year. The guilt now hangs over Julia's words.

After the long ramble, Nelda clears her throat. "So…enough 'bout me. How are you, honey? Everything going okay? I haven't heard from you in awhile and was starting to worry."

Now pushing eighty, Nelda coughs between sentences. Even though she'll never say it, Julia knows Nelda's health is declining, which makes her feel even more guilty that she hasn't called in so long.

Julia swallows hard and stares down at the circles she's been nervously doodling on the notepad perched on her desk. "Nelda, I feel like I owe you an apology. After that last phone call, I just couldn't bear to…"

"Now listen here, Julia." Nelda stops Julia from finishing. "You have no need to apologize for anything. I could've just as easily picked up the phone and called you. Honey, you need to hear me when I say this…I don't blame you, and I never did. As much as I appreciated you calling so often, and I've missed our chats, sometimes talking to you just made it all the harder. Nothing either of us said was ever gonna bring him back. At some point, you just gotta let go of the past…"

"I know Nelda. I do…" Tears well in Julia's eyes and the wave of emotion crawls up her chest uninvited, in the way it had for so long. No matter how much she's spent on yoga, flying to exotic places to hike or run new trails, partaken of wine therapy or the regular kind in the therapist's chair, nothing has fully removed the guilt, the questions, or the grief.

That son-of-a-bitch grief. In the beginning, the grief was like a heavy blanket that threatened to suffocate her and on some days Julia was quite certain it would. She'd wear sunglasses everywhere to cover her swollen eyes. Over the years, that grief had shrunk little by little. Time does have a way of stitching the heart back together, one piece at a time.

Now instead of a blanket, Julia's grief is more like a handkerchief, like the kind a grandpa might carry in the pocket of his trousers. Sometimes Julia forgets that handkerchief of grief is there. Then a song, a scene in a movie, or a bird singing in the morning can spontaneously cause Julia to reach in her pocket and touch that grief. Sometimes she even clutches that handkerchief of grief for a little while and holds it close.

It's that familiar handkerchief of grief, however, that Julia's clung to like a child clings to her favorite blanket. The truth is, she doesn't know who she will really be if she lets go of the grief completely. In many ways, the grief has defined her life, serving as the barometer by which she measures just how happy she allows herself to be.

There's a saying that, "God throws a pebble and then God throws a brick." Julia had certainly seen and felt the little pebbles after Seth, but lately that brick has been whacking her full force reminding her of the words Nelda just shared.

It's time to let go.

For a while Julia held on because she loved Seth so much, then because she was so blasted angry, and now because…well, now, she doesn't know. Hell, now she's just annoyed. Annoyed with herself that she still carries that handkerchief of grief. Annoyed that she's aware enough to know now when she shuts down and shuts Frank out. Annoyed that she can write stories with twists and turns and grand endings and still can't seem to solve the mystery of what really happened in Murdoch that led to the deaths of Betty Ann Stark, Allison Mercer, and her own husband.

Call it a mid-life or whatever you will, but Julia knows deep down, in that place you just *know*, that until she immerses herself in the remainder of this grief. Until she invites that grief to show her what she most needs to know, there will always be a shadow of a doubt. There will always be a place in her heart that joy just cannot reach.

It's why she's so tired of running, hiding, and partitioning off her heart in fear, and it's why she's ready for the truth. A truth that she believes still lurks behind the manicured smiles, uneasy laughs, and under-the-table handshakes in Murdoch. A truth that may very well be buried in all those newspaper articles she hopes Nelda still has stored away.

Julia clears her throat. "I know, Nelda. I know Seth loved me, and I know I don't owe you anything, but thank you for saying that. Honestly, that's partly why I'm calling…"

"Whaddya mean, honey?"

Julia exhales nervously. "Well, I'm wondering if you still have all the newspaper articles I wrote back when I was at the *Messenger*?"

"Hmm, I think so. Think they're in the attic but I haven't been up there in years so can't say for sure." Nelda coughs again. "Why?"

Julia briefly hesitates whether to tell Nelda the truth after what happened with Marilee but then remembers the truth is the only way forward. "Well…I'm working on a new book and am basing some of the events on what happened to Allison Mercer and Betty Ann Stark. I reported on both of those deaths for the paper and want to use those articles as the place to start my research."

Silence. So much silence Julia wonders if she's lost the connection. "Nelda? You there?"

"Yeah, honey, I know I can't hear nuthin' and know my mouth travels loud sometimes but I haven't gone completely deaf yet. I just…I just don't understand why you'd wanna do that?"

"Do what?"

"Go and stir all that mess up again. Some things are better left alone, especially 'round here. You may have been gone a long time but you know how this town is…and there are a whole lotta people who don't want to see that all brought back out in the open."

"I know Nelda. I know there's some risk involved, but this story needs to be told. Now that I've been gone for so long, I realize what happened there wasn't normal. It wasn't just some random acts of crime. I really believe those deaths were connected, and I feel like I owe those women a voice. Plus, I mean it's all the makings of a bestseller." Julia laughs nervously, realizing that she may have said too much, too emphatically.

"I just don't know…don't think it's a good idea." Nelda's voice turns motherly. "That man, George Stark, may still be in prison, and I'm sure others need to be there right alongside him. But diggin' all that up again isn't just the makings of some fiction book, it's our life. It's what happened. I know you also want to get to the bottom of why Seth died. Hell, I still wonder about that, too. I'm an old woman, honey, and may not know much anymore. But I know one thing for sure…no amount of poking 'round here is going to change what happened."

"I know…" Something about Nelda's words open a keyhole to Julia's heart and the cool tears slide down her high cheekbones. She sighs in resignation. "I have done everything I know to do to resolve this grief and move on with my life, and I have come a long, long way. I think writing this book, in giving those two women a voice, maybe I could heal some of the anger and grief. Maybe I could answer some of the unresolved questions…maybe I could really…"

"Or maybe this one can't be solved." Nelda interrupts softly. "You can't rewrite the past, Julia. You just have to keep your feet pointin' forward."

"I know, I know…" Julia wipes the edges of her eyes. "I know I can't bring any of them back, but I can try to make sense of why they died. I can try to share their story…I have to try, Nelda…I have to try."

Nelda pauses before replying. "Well, you are a grown woman, and I can't tell you what to do. If you do come to town, honey, be sure and come on by the house. You're free to dig through that mess of an attic all you want for those papers. I'd love to see you."

"Okay Nelda, thank you, and I apologize if I upset you. I would love to see you too. I will call and let you know when I'll be in town."

"That sounds good, honey. You do that. I'll be here."

As Julia hangs up the phone, she recalls the hurt, confused look on Marilee's face from last week at the cabin. She feels a pang of anxious energy well up from her stomach sending a flash of heat through her head and adrenaline down her legs. Those ghosts from Murdoch may not want to be unearthed, but she reminds herself, nothing she might face in that town could be as scary as the last twenty years have been.

CHAPTER 11

Julia rolls down the front windows of her small rental car and inhales that palatable smell of the Mississippi summer, infused with a potpourri of dry grass, asphalt baking under a radiant sun, and crisp blue skies. Her auburn hair whips wildly about, with an occasional piece covering her Gucci sunglasses. She yanks the loose strands of hair away before returning both hands to the steering wheel, navigating down the narrow two-lane country road leading her toward Murdoch.

Whether it's the drunken aroma of summer, the winding stretch of road dotted with cows grazing in green pastures, or the fact she's not actually driven a car in months, there's a sense of possibility simmering within her that she hasn't felt in quite sometime.

She's always loved this drive to Murdoch. Even when she and Seth would travel from Jackson, she'd beg him to take this route as opposed to the interstate, even though it was far less efficient, and Seth was all about efficiency. Something about this stretch of countryside led to a well of contentment within her. Contentment that comes naturally like the way a good stretch and a yawn signal that it's a lazy Sunday morning. Inhaling that deep breath what follows is spaciousness and ease.

Arriving into neighboring Pleasant Ridge, she slows the midnight blue sedan to the designated thirty-five mile-per-hour speed limit and glances around on either side of the highway. She smiles realizing that little has changed from when she used to travel here to cover a council meeting or election. Pleasant Ridge was one of the smaller communities surrounding Murdoch on her beat as a reporter, so she knew it well. Driving along the main stretch, she notices one of those large illuminated arrow signs with black plastic letters reading, "Pleasant Ridge Needs a Doctor," with a phone number to call on the line below it.

She laughs hysterically. God, how she's missed small town life, and Kate's right. You can't make this shit up.

◆ ◆ ◆

Somewhere in the twelve miles from Pleasant Ridge to the Winding River Cottage, which Julia had rented sight unseen online, her rays of sunshine abruptly shift. The nostalgia rolls in, much like the thick dark clouds that suddenly appear out of nowhere and produce a rain shower on a hot summer's day.

Though she's tried hard to erase that memory of leaving Murdoch, it's been one of those deeply entrenched episodic memories buried way down deep. It was an usually cold Mississippi day in early 1997, just weeks after she buried Seth. Anything Julia cared to keep from her shattered life, which wasn't much, was packed into her car as it pointed east to New York. Once she crossed the Mississippi state line, it was as if an iron curtain fell over that chapter in her life.

As she nears the edge of Murdoch, it's as if that curtain has parted and the memories come flooding in, with a kaleidoscope of colors, smells, textures. Like the memory of her first house, the little bungalow she and Seth bought with Doc's help for a down payment. Memories of parties and lively card games at Marilee and Kate's houses. And finally, those memories permanently emblazoned in her brain of what she was wearing and where she was standing when she got the news that Allison Mercer had died, and then Betty Ann Stark, and then about her own husband.

A lump wells in Julia's throat. *What the hell, I don't know if I can do this.* She rubs her thumb along her temple and index finger along her forehead in the way she always does when nerves set in. *Just breathe*, she reminds herself. As she allows the wave of emotion to pass, another crucial piece of information filters into her memory. Murdoch is dry, or at least it was back then.

So in lieu of going straight to the cottage, she steers her rental down the farm-to-market shortcut to Salty's Liquors. The gas station-liquor store, perched all alone among two large fields right along county line, welcomes a rotating door of locals. That is, of course, except the closeted Baptist drinkers like Marilee who only drink at home and always send friends to make the beer runs. It's why even though Julia cannot recall what she ate last week, she somehow remembers the shortest route to Salty's. Inside the place looks the same, small and lined with bottles starting with whiskey closest to the door and the wines toward the back next to the beer coolers.

"Can I hulpya find somethin'?" The graying fifty-something man stands from the stool from behind the counter, plaid shirt untucked with a white tank top underneath.

Julia stiffens and scans his face. Nope, she doesn't know him. "No thanks, just looking for some red wine."

"Alright then, just hollar if I can help ya." He sits back on the stool and picks up his magazine.

"Thanks."

Julia browses the dusty bottles of cheap whites and reds and finally comes across a few California varieties that will do. Just as she turns to check out, she spots the beer she used to drink with Kate and Marilee on hot summer nights like this one. She smiles and grabs a six-pack from the large refrigerated cooler.

As she settles back into the car, she reaches for her phone to text Kate.

Well, I'm here! Nervous as hell so stopped at Salty's to get some wine. Found our beer so I'll drink one for you tonight. Miss you!!

Julia had just dropped her phone back into her purse when she hears the ding of Kate's text reply.

Oh damn, I wish I was there! Definitely drink a beer for me. You okay??

Julia smiles and replies:

Yeah, I'm good. It's a little weird being back but just getting into town. Headed to the cottage now. Wish you were here too! I could use some moral support.

Kate immediately responds:

Have to run to a meeting right now, but call me later okay?! XOXO

◆◆◆

As Julia pulls onto the dirt road leading up to the cottage, she's relieved there's still daylight. The lush trees lining the road create a canopy, with only small swaths of sunlight dancing through. It's a sight she finds beautifully haunting, reminiscent of the drive to the Johnson's cabin. She thinks of Marilee and quickly dismisses the pang of guilt. She's not ready to see Marilee yet. Rather, she's focused on visiting Nelda to find the articles.

She pulls her car up to the white-washed cottage with an aging brown shingled roof. The front door and windows stand in bright contrast with their pumpkin-colored paint. Centuries old trees line all the sides of the house, which displays minimal landscaping out front, though a black wrought iron fence provides a quaint frame for the perimeter. She guesses it's to keep out the cows roaming through the rest of the acreage. The house is a colorful and quirky sight, really, to be tucked at the back of a farm in Mississippi.

Julia's relieved the space she'll occupy for the next week is actually livable. With little time to plan and so few options for short-term rentals, she wasn't exactly sure what she'd find when she searched online. All she knew was that she didn't want to stay at the Murdoch Inn. She wants, and needs, some distance, and at five miles north of town nestled off the beaten path, this place is small, but perfect.

One step into the narrow living room lined with huge windows and she understands why the old farmhouse is called the Winding River Cottage. Through the bay of windows and down about a hundred yards from the back porch is, indeed, a winding river. She smiles at the sight of water, something she's missed in New York. Sure, she's surrounded by water in Manhattan but something about it isn't quite the same as this splay of grass, trees, and river gently reflecting the quickly setting sun.

After lugging in her suitcase, briefcase, and purchases from Salty's, Julia realizes she has forgotten about food. With her tall frame and healthy curves, she's never been one to worry much about her weight or missing a meal here or there. Though, she could certainly eat. She's looking forward to her fair share of good Southern cooking while she's in town, starting tomorrow at Nelda's. They'd spoken several days ago and arranged the late morning get-together. Nelda was adamant she cook for Julia, much to Julia's attempt to convince her to just go to Nine Ed's Cafe.

She relinquishes the evening meal and opts to open a bottle of wine, sit on the back porch, and then take a hot bath in that delicious claw-foot tub she spotted earlier in the bathroom. With the sun now setting, she sips her wine from the back porch soaking in the view and sounds of the tree frogs, crickets, and what she guesses are mockingbirds.

She'd never understood how a six-foot-three-inch man could love birds so much, but Seth tried to no avail to teach her the different calls of birds. He loved birds. With the exception of cardinals, all other birds still creep her out, especially those damned pigeons all over New York.

In this moment now, something about the birds is appropriate. By the end of her first glass of wine, however, she looks around at the almost completely dark landscape half expecting a cab to whiz by or a random stranger to yell a profanity. Realizing just how quiet, how dark, and how alone she is out here in the middle of this farm, she shudders, jumps up, and practically runs inside, ensuring every door and window is locked tight.

She stands at the rustic wooden farm table in the kitchen and laughs in spite of herself. She pours another glass of wine and takes a deep breath to relax. Just as she exhales, her phone rings, jolting her wine glass in her hand, a hearty sip spilling onto the table.

"KATE" reads the display.

"Hello?"

"Hey gurl."

"Damn'it, you scared me!" Julia feels her racing heart slowly subsiding in her chest.

"Why? Where are you?"

"At the cottage. I was sitting out back enjoying the evening and then suddenly it was dark and I got freaked out."

Kate belts out a laugh. "Gurl, you're just sissified living in the city so long. You've forgotten what it's like being out in the country with nature."

"I'm not sissified." Julia stands a little taller and sips her wine. "I just need to get adjusted."

"So how's the place? Have you run into anyone yet?"

Julia hears the excitement in Kate's voice. Always afraid she's going to miss something, Kate can't stand it that Julia's here without her.

"The cottage is actually really cute. It's off that farm-to-market cut-across from Salty's, just north of Murdoch."

"Oh yeah, I know where you're talkin' about. So didja go into town?"

"No, not yet. Just got some wine and came straight here. I'm going to Nelda's tomorrow around eleven."

"That'll be good. I know she'll be thrilled to see you. I sure hope you find those articles." Julia can hear the ding of Kate's car door in the background. She must be leaving work. "So when are you gonna see Marilee?"

"I'm not sure. I haven't talked to her yet." Julia moves from the kitchen to sink into the sofa in the living room.

"What? You mean she doesn't know you're there?" Kate gasps.

Julia pauses. "Nope." The pang of guilt filters through her again.

"Julia Jarvis. You're plum crazy. You better call her tomorrow." Kate sounds far too much like a scolding mother.

Julia sighs heavily. "I will, I will. I just needed some time to get here, get squared away, and figure out my game plan before I see her."

"Well, okay. I can understand that, but please call her tomorrow. For me. She'll be heartbroken if you don't." Kate sighs.

"I will, promise."

"Okay, I need to run gurl, but call me if you need me. Oh and hey…"

"What?"

"Don't let the bedbugs bite." Kate belts out a laugh.

Julia echoes the laugh. "And if they do, I'm moving to the Murdoch Inn."

Kate cackles louder into the phone. "Bye gurl, call me tomorrow. Love you."

"Love you, too."

CHAPTER 12

It's only a ten-minute drive from the Winding River Cottage to the Dixon farm but it might as well have been ten hours because everything's in slow motion for Julia. Everything, that is, except her heart which is beating like a hummingbird. She's also quite attuned to the well of emotion stuck somewhere between her throat and her left lung, leaving her unsure whether she's about to laugh, cry, or throw up.

She'd awakened at four this morning fretting about what lurked in the dark woods outside the cottage. With no lights or city noise, the pitch black unnerved her. There were only a few nightlights sprinkled throughout the seven-hundred-square-foot, one-bedroom cottage.

She finally got up around midnight and turned on the bathroom light. That comforted her a little. It wasn't so much the dark that kept her restless. It was also the hamster wheel of thought worrying about returning to the Dixon's house after so many years, what she might find in the articles, and most of all, the looming question of whether she's ready to face what lurks in Murdoch? Julia also laid awake, she realized, because her stomach was knotted in hunger and producing deep growls.

Fortunately, now there's not enough time left to hash over how this meeting will go because before Julia knows it, she's pulled up in front of the old Dixon farmhouse. Time has taken its toll on the two-story house built in the late 1920s by the family who had originally owned this land before Doc and Nelda moved here in 1967. Chipped white paint lines the roof's edge, and the flooring of the porch looks even worse, with slats of exposed wood where the teal-blue paint has been stripped completely.

This porch was once a gathering spot to sit on summer evenings to sip lemonade and cold beers in the pair of wooden rocking chairs, which were flanked by Nelda's collection of plants. Now, the porch holds only a few empty clay pots and a stack of newspapers in a cardboard box by the front door. The sight makes Julia's heart sink and leaves her wondering if Seth's older sister, Pamela, ever stops by. The last Christmas letter she'd gotten from Pamela several years back indicated she and her family were still in Natchez.

Like clockwork to Julia shutting the car door, Nelda yanks open the screen door beaming as any mother would whose prodigal daughter has returned home. Joy emanates from Nelda's wrinkled face, which looks so much like Seth's, with those big inset eyes, curious eyebrows, button nose, and a mouth that's always eager to break into a wide smile. Julia sucks in a deep breath at the sight of her.

Death and time do have a way of taking a toll on a person, and in Nelda's case, the evidence is in her hair. As a school teacher, Nelda has never been one to keep up with fashion trends but once a week she would go to the Cut 'n Curl downtown to ensure her chestnut locks were always pristine. Though one time, Nelda confessed to Julia she really went each week to relax, visit with her friends, and catch up on the latest Murdoch gossip.

Now Nelda's white hair frames her head with the kind of curls produced from those big pink plastic rollers. Another of Nelda's signature looks is also gone. She used to wear overalls around the house and occasionally on a quick trip to the supermarket. Today, they have been traded for a pair of navy crop pants, white sneakers, and a white buttoned-down shirt with small embroidered flowers in hues of pink and blue.

"Oh, Julia! You're here!" Nelda smiles and waves as she moves to the front steps, so she can make her way down to meet Julia. But Julia rushes up the wooden planks to avoid Nelda from having to travel the five steps down to the concrete walkway. Just at the top of the steps, Julia embraces Nelda, her long arms engulfing Nelda's back. Julia's forgotten how small Nelda really is because her personality always made her seem ten times bigger.

"Oh Nelda, it's so good to see you." Julia hugs her tighter as if in this moment hugging Nelda also means embracing Seth. She feels Nelda's arms clasp around her tighter, too.

"Oh my sweet, sweet girl. You're home."

With those words the lump in Julia's heart melts into a mixture of tears, some sad, some happy, some just grateful for this moment to be enfolded in the arms of the woman who has been more like a mother to her than any woman she's ever known. Nelda's tears cannot be contained either, and she lets out an audible sob. She pulls away slightly to look at Julia, her soft hands now clutching Julia's long slender fingers. "And it's about damn time, too."

Julia laughs at Nelda's playful scolding and gently pulls her hands away to wipe away the river of mascara under her eyes. "Yes, you're right, Nelda. It's about damn time."

◆ ◆ ◆

At eleven in the morning, Julia's fully expecting brunch but Nelda has prepared what looks like a post-church meal of pot roast, roasted red potatoes, green bean casserole (the kind with the little onion strings on top), and the most delicious sweet tea Julia's had in twenty years. While the meal is heavier than what Julia's accustomed to at this hour, the conversation over lunch has been surprisingly light. Nelda catches Julia up on friends and relatives in town, who Julia vaguely remembers, and on Pamela and her family, who are still in Natchez, and come to see her every Sunday afternoon.

"Oh my God, I'm full." Julia places her hand over her stomach completely and utterly content.

"Well, good. Looks like you could use some more hot meals." Nelda winks. She'd been trying to feed Julia since the day she first arrived here with Seth. Food has always been how Nelda's shown love, whether simple snacks of homemade bread and cheese, fresh-baked pies and Bundt cakes (Doc's favorite), or full-on meals like the one she's prepared for Julia today.

"Oh don't worry, I eat plenty. I just walk all the time living in the city."

"I don't know how you do that. I'd like the walking, or would have before this knee gave out. I mean the city life…I couldn't do it." Nelda shakes her head. "Not sure how you even hear yourself think."

"I have to admit the older I get, the more it loses its charm. Everyone's just so self-consumed, rushing here and there. It can be overwhelming at times, but the city is all I know now. I don't know where else I'd go." Julia shrugs slightly.

"Well, if it makes you happy then by all means stay there. I'm not sure I ever told you but I went to New York once."

"Oh really? When?"

"Let's see…guess it was summer of seventy-six and Doc's sister, Sally, decided we needed to have our own women's liberation. So we ran away on vacation. Sally…you remember her? Lived in Jackson? She died a few years ago."

Julia thinks for a minute and envisions the chubby blonde with a thick Southern twang and hilarious one-liners. "Oh right, Sally."

"Yeah, so we just up and decided one day to leave the kids with Doc and Smitty and go on an adventure. Oh now, Doc didn't like it that we took off but he knew better than to tryin' talk us outta it. We just went a few days." Nelda chuckles at the memory.

Julia laughs picturing Sally and Nelda loose in the streets of Manhattan. "Did you like it?"

"Oh, it scared the bejesus outta me, with all those people and cars and craziness. But we had a bawl. Saw "A Chorus Line," toured the Empire State Building, and the Statue of Liberty. Oh, I loved seeing that!"

"Yeah, I don't go to shows much anymore and only do the touristy stuff when people come to visit. The whole thing is just sort of lost on me now, I guess."

"So you got a fella up there keepin' you there?" Nelda peers over at Julia.

Taken aback by the sudden topic change and the question that sounds more like a statement, Julia isn't quite sure how to respond. Somehow saying "yes" feels wrong considering she was once married to Nelda's son, and yet denying it isn't right, either. So she takes the safe route.

"Sort of."

"Whaddya mean, sort of?"

Julia blushes knowing she isn't getting out from under Nelda's scope. She'd always had a way of zeroing in on a subject and firing off rounds of questions until she got a satisfactory answer.

"Well, yes, I've been seeing someone for a few years. His name is Frank."

"A few years? So it's not serious then? You don't want to marry him?"

"No, I am not marrying him, though we've talked about it. He's a photographer and gone a lot on assignment and..."

"And you haven't moved on." Nelda interrupts softly.

Julia swallows hard. "No, I guess I haven't."

Nelda reaches across the old table, smiles, and squeezes Julia's hand. Just as quickly, she changes the topic once again. She may be getting old, but Nelda Dixon is a wise, compassionate woman with a keen intuition. She knows when to let something be. It doesn't mean she always will, but she always knows.

"You want some dessert, honey?"

"Maybe in a bit. I'm so full right now, I don't think I have room for it."

"Well, then I guess we can get on to whatchya came to look for."

Julia looks up with interest. The articles.

"So you don't mind if I go look for them?"

"Well, honey there's no need. When Pamela's family was here the other day, I sent Josh...you know her oldest boy...well he went up to look for 'em in the attic. Sure enough, I still had 'em. Gawd knows, Doc never threw anything away. Hang on a sec."

Nelda stands and pads her way across the hardwood floors to a closet in the hallway next to Seth's old room, which is now Nelda's sewing room. With the exception of a few photos of Seth as a boy on family vacation, from football, and their wedding, Julia's relieved to find few ghosts of him in the house.

Julia scans through her phone waiting for Nelda. She sees Kate's already texted wanting to know how it's going and missed a text from Jeff to let her know Mr. Pickles is okay. She can hear Nelda wrestling with something in the closet.

"Need any help?"

"No, no I'm fine."

Julia's engrossed in her social media account when Nelda walks in proudly holding the box of stories. Yet, as Julia looks up she's completely confused. There in front of her is a baby blue accordion box with a fold over lid and plastic handle on top. On the front of the box is a huge red heart with a cartoon of a smiling Jesus, standing with outstretched arms. In big green letters above Jesus' head reads, "Vacation Bible School 1994." As Nelda plops the box on the dining table with a satisfied grin, Julia sees the words, "Julia's Articles - Murder Trial," scribbled in black marker in the top right corner.

"See! I knew I had 'em!" Nelda proudly points at the box.

Open mouthed, Julia looks at the box, then at Nelda, and bursts into laughter.

"What?" Nelda sits back in her chair confused.

"Nelda, really? A Vacation Bible School box? Why on earth would you put articles about murders in a Jesus box?" Julia's now doubled over unable to contain her laughter.

Nelda catches the irony and Julia's contagious laughter sets Nelda off, too. The two laugh for what feels like minutes, tears once again streaming down their faces.

Nelda finally catches her breath. "Well, seemed like as good a box as any. It was the right size and with the mess that happened in this town, I guess maybe I thought they could all use a little Jesus."

With that Julia laughs again. "Oh Nelda, I've missed you. You always make me laugh."

Nelda smiles. "I'll give you those articles on one condition, honey."

"Anything…"

"You gotta come back and see me 'cause I can't wait twenty more years. I'll be in a pine box six feet under by then."

Julia laughs, heart full of love for this amazing woman across from her, and squeezes Nelda's hand. "Deal."

CHAPTER 13

Bidding Nelda good-bye and leaving the Dixon farm this time is far easier than Julia imagined, perhaps because she knows she'll be back and the thought of seeing Nelda again makes her smile. She's relieved that the lump in her chest has given way to a rhythm of deep ease, like the liberating feeling after being buried to the neck in sand at the beach. That claustrophobia of being covered up becomes one of liberation as the caked sand crumbles off and the sunlight once again shines warmly on the parts of you once hidden.

Through the shared tears with Nelda, Julia feels that same sense of warmth and freedom, and not just because the high afternoon sun has made it clear that it is, indeed, summer. In Murdoch that means you never stop sweating. You wake up sweating, step out of the shower sweating, and go to sleep sweating. It was something Julia had never grown accustomed to her in her two-and-a-half years in the South. After her first summer living in Murdoch, she stopped wearing makeup from May until October because she'd just sweat it off.

As the sun pummels her blue sedan, Julia flips down the visor to shield the bright light bouncing up from the pavement. She heads down Highway 29, the main road that passes through Murdoch from east to west. It's the one the high school kids used to call "the drag," driving up and down on Saturday nights drinking Dr. Peppers and waving to friends. It's also how curious travelers seeking a back roads adventure from Natchez to Jackson stumble upon Murdoch. Otherwise, you might never know Murdoch is there, it's tucked so far back in the pine trees.

Indigenous Native American tribes had occupied the lands surrounding Natchez for hundreds of years. Murdoch was settled nearly thirty miles to the north and east from Natchez, along the Natchez Trace, during the reconstruction era after the Civil War. The area was largely unharmed in the war, making it easier for farmers to move outward from Natchez and settle land.

Over the years, Murdoch became a hub for cotton, grain, and timber, as the railroad passed through the downtown square. Before World War II, in the 1930s, the Stark family established Murdoch's hospital, making it the first hospital in the county. While Murdoch wasn't the county seat, the small town enjoyed its share of visitors who frequented the Main Street district of shops.

In the years Julia had lived in Murdoch with Seth, the Main Street area remained a hub of activity, with the Cut 'n Curl, Winyard's Five & Dime, Floyd's Barber Shop, the Blossom Bouquet florist, and of course, Nine Ed's Cafe on the corner of Main and Washington Streets.

As Julia navigates slowly down Main Street now, she is astonished by the revitalization of the four-street area. Many of the red-brick shops have been restored with updated signs and gleaming windows. The square now boasts several artists' galleries, boutique clothing and gift shops, and a bed and breakfast. New streetlamps dot the town's sidewalks, displaying large red-and-white banners, alternating between "Welcome to Murdoch" and "Home of the 2007 State Football Champs." About the only familiar business is Nine Ed's, which still looks much the same except for an updated sign.

Julia slows her car even more as she passes the *Murdoch Messenger* office, which still displays the same gold and black lettering on the frosted glass panes. She smiles thinking of all the days she went buzzing in and out through that heavy glass door.

"HONK!"

Julia jumps, startled by the driver in the car behind her, who isn't interested in her trip down memory lane. The car's horn jolts Julia back to reality, and she pulls over to the side of the street. As she glances at the office again, she thinks again about Dan and then remembers Marilee's comment about the new editor, Matt Case. She wonders if it would be awkward to just stop in to talk to Matt, and then realizes, yes, it would. Besides, what would she say to him? She needs to read the articles first.

As Julia pulls away, nostalgia fully engulfs her remembering the days she'd drive away from the office and travel the few short blocks home to Seth. *I wonder if our house is still there?* Julia swallows hard and instinctively navigates the car toward the old neighborhood. With each house she passes, it's evident that twenty years and two recessions have left an undeniable mark on the small town since she was last here.

Doc had once told her and Seth that their neighborhood sprang up in the 1920s before the Depression and World War II took its toll on the South. Then, after the war and into the 1950s, many of the homes had been updated, including the bungalow at 1015 West 11th Street that she and Seth purchased.

Of all the places Julia's ever lived, she has always loved that house the most. It was only two bedrooms but had a spacious feel, with deep walnut floors and a wide set of French doors leading from the living to dining room. The swing on the large front porch was often where she and Seth gathered to rehash their days, muse over heartfelt dreams, and share a bottle of wine.

As she turns onto West 11th Street, she smiles remembering the first time she and Seth pulled up to the house with the realtor. It was a sweltering July day, much like now, and in places yet unspoken she was doubtful about this move to the South, let alone her husband's small hometown. But when she saw that seafoam green bungalow with the broad white trim and white front porch swing, her face lit up like a kid on Christmas morning.

"Isn't it perfect?" Seth had beamed at Julia before pecking her on the lips and tearing out of the car to go inspect it. In the few short years they owned the home, they'd invested in small projects to update it. Above all, they loved welcoming others into their home with impromptu potlucks and barbecues with the Woods and Johnsons, as well as Seth's larger circle of friends, which had become Julia's friends, too.

Now the houses along the street appear as if the color has been drained out of them with muted paint and chipped, weathered trim. She parks along the front curb and leaves the car running but rolls down the window to take a closer look.

Her heart sinks at the sight. The house is still light green and in decent shape but the front porch swing is gone. In its place is a stack of rusty bicycles leaning up against the side of the house. The yard is a smattering of weeds and grass framed by flower beds, which have been neglected for some time.

As she surveys the scene, her eyes rest on the front door. Despite the weathered condition of the home, the rich mahogany door with the three small window panes at the top still beckons. Tears well in Julia's eyes and her brain scans trying to remember the last time she and Seth came home through that door. What were they talking about? Where had they been?

That's the thing about memories. Sometimes the ordinary moments of life become etched into memories and sometimes they just fall away. And sometimes the moments you would rather forget become emblazoned forever, like her last day in Murdoch years ago.

Waves of grief had thrashed through her as she studied the house for the last time, grappling with how her life could dismantle so abruptly. That was the day she vowed to leave Murdoch behind and never return.

"Hi!" A little boy screams from the neighbor's front yard, waving at Julia. She jumps at the interruption. "You goin' in?"

"What?" Julia wipes her eyes and tries to focus on the boy, who looks to be seven or eight. "No, no...I'm not going in. I used to live here." She forces a half-smile.

"Oh, cool. Okay." The boy seems satisfied. "Have a good day!" With that he runs around the side of the house to retrieve his bicycle. Sitting here in front of their old house certainly produces a whirlwind of bittersweet memories for Julia, but it also conjures the question she's been trying to keep at bay for weeks since she knew she was making this trip. *Am I ready to visit Seth?*

She shudders at the thought as she had on the handful of other occasions the question had emerged. Over the years, she'd always loathed those dramatic cemetery scenes in movies, though once contemplated writing such a scene into a short story. Something about standing in a field of bones staring at a cold marble tombstone unnerved Julia to her very core.

She rolls up her window and glances in the rearview mirror to inspect her face before making her way to the grocery store to pick up the essentials for her stay. Fortunately, the trip is uneventful and no one recognizes her among the shelves of bread and boxes of cereal.

Julia heads out the old river highway, which is a narrow two-lane road that provides a shortcut across town. The old Murdoch bridge, a hulking iron structure built in the early nineteen hundreds, connects the north side of Murdoch to the land south of the riverbanks where the football stadium sits.

Sure enough, Murdoch's landmark is still there. She smiles thinking about how excited Seth would get to take her over the precarious bridge, barely wide enough for one car. Sometimes when the truck windows were down, they'd hear the bridge sigh a loud creak. Julia would cringe and tell Seth to hurry up and cross it. He'd laugh and slow down even more. It was always a game of chicken, never knowing if there was another car coming from the other direction.

Not a quarter-mile from the bridge still looms the Murdoch Mustangs stadium. Although, there's a new high school that's emerged in the field between the old high school and the football stadium. It appears the old high school is now the middle school. She drives slowly along the road near the school peering over at the football complex.

The Mustangs stadium served as the center of excitement on Fridays every fall and the backdrop of anguish one unforgettable July night.

CHAPTER 14

Julia unloads the plastic bags of groceries from the car, realizing she never looked to see the extent of the pots and pans available at the Winding River Cottage. Fortunately, her salad ingredients, fruit, and cereal don't need much prep.

The last item she unloads is the Jesus box full of articles. She carries it to the kitchen table gingerly, afraid of what might pop out. As Julia sets it down, she laughs again at the sight. She flips open the lid and thumbs through the stack of papers tucked neatly inside but stops herself from retrieving one. First, she needs to change clothes and retrieve a hefty glass of wine.

She returns to the kitchen in her favorite black yoga pants, oversized white tee-shirt, and pulls her hair up into a loose bun. Just as she's unearthed the cork to the Cabernet, her phone rings. She realizes she never called Jeff back earlier, but smiles seeing who's on the other end of the line.

"Hello?"

"Hey gurl." Kate smiles into the phone. "How are you?"

"Hey! I'm good. What are you up to?" Julia places the phone on her shoulder to finish pouring.

"Oh I'm just headed home from the office and thought I'd check on you. How'd it go today?"

"It went well." Julia smiles thinking about seeing Nelda. "It was a little hard at first. We shed a few tears, laughed, and caught up. It was a bit depressing seeing the house…and she's aged a lot."

"Well, I'm sure she has, it's been a long time. So what did you talk about? Did you find the articles?"

"So many questions!" Julia laughs. "Yeah, I did." She looks over at Jesus sitting on her table and laughs harder.

"What? What's so funny?"

"Well, Nelda had the articles in her attic, and get this…" Julia takes a sip of wine and looks over at the box.

"What?"

"They're in a Jesus box."

"A what?" Kate laughs. "What in the world is a Jesus box?"

"I'm sitting there at the old table and out walks Nelda with a Vacation Bible School box from 1994. On the side, it has this caricature of Jesus in a white robe. He's smiling and his arms are outstretched with a huge red heart drawn behind him. In the corner of the box, she had scribbled a note about my articles on the murders." Julia laughs repeating the story.

Kate's hysterically laughing on the other end of the phone. "Why would she put articles about people dyin' in there? That seems a little sacrilegious." She gasps for a breath through her laughter. "See, gurl, I told you…you can't make this shit up. You gotta use that in your book."

Julia laughs again and shrugs. "I don't know about that, but I asked Nelda and she said it was the right size and thought those articles could use a little Jesus. I'm just glad she still has them."

Kate's laughter starts up again. "I just love that woman. How is she?"

"She's good, I think. She won't admit it, but I don't think she's in that great of health." Julia sighs heavily.

"So, what's going on with her?"

"I don't really know. She's not driving any more and she seems to cough a lot. I know how private she can be. She doesn't want anyone worrying about her, so I didn't really ask. It just made me sad seeing her looking so old."

"Yeah, it's hard watchin' the people you love age right in front of your eyes." Kate's voice drops thinking of her own mother whose health had been declining after the loss of her daddy last year. Unwilling to go down that trail of conversation right now, Kate refocuses back on Murdoch. "So what else did you do? Who did you see? Have you called Marilee yet?" Kate's voice grows more excited with each question. "Gawd, I wish I were there!"

"Again with all the questions…slow down and take a breath." Julia laughs. "I didn't do much, just went by the grocery store and drove around a little. I'd forgotten what a cute little town Murdoch is, but it's just surreal being here. Actually, not a lot has changed except…" Julia's voice trails in thought.

"Except what?" Kate interjects curiously.

"I drove past our old house."

"It's still there?"

"Yeah, it is but a little run down and the porch swing is gone." Julia swallows hard.

"Oh man, that swing made the whole house."

"I know…it did…" Julia takes a deep breath. "I also drove past the football field."

"Oh?" Kate's voice drops.

"Yeah, there's a new high school but the field is in the same spot. It's been updated some but it was bittersweet seeing it. Made me think about the Friday nights we spent there and…"

"Allison…"

"Yeah."

"So have you started reading the articles yet? Are they all there?" Kate asks quietly.

"I don't know. I just got back a little bit ago and just poured some wine. I was just about to start reading when you called."

"Well, you have to let me know what you find out, gurl…"

"You're really loving this, aren't you?" Julia smiles.

"Hell yes, I'm loving it. I mean it's time someone bring this back to life and try to make some sense out of it. Or at the very least try to figure out what possible motive someone had for killing them."

"I know. That's the question that replays over and over again in my head. What did Allison and Betty Ann know that got them killed?" Julia rubs her forehead in thought.

Kate's silent on the other end of the phone, and in a more hushed tone she finally responds. "Honestly, between us, I've always wondered what Marilee knows."

Taken aback, Julia pauses. "What do you mean? You think she knows something we don't?"

"I don't know. I've been thinkin' about it since we were at the cabin a few weeks ago. Thinkin' about her reaction to your book. There was somethin' about it that just didn't add up to me."

Julia's mind flips back to the girls' weekend quickly trying to recall anything out of the ordinary. "Really? I didn't notice anything…"

"Well, you know, this is my job…readin' people to figure out what they're sayin' without sayin' it. It was in her reaction…her body language. I mean, I understand she'd get upset because she and Betty Ann were good friends. Plus, now Paul is mayor and we both know…God-love-her…Marilee is all about lookin' good. But there was somethin' I picked up on at breakfast that morning we were sittin' around the table."

"Like what?" Julia's voice rises in curiosity.

"I don't know, gurl. I can't quite put my finger on it, but I do know you need her, Jules. If you are gonna stir that town up again, you need Marilee and Paul in your corner."

Julia sighs. "I know, you're right…but with Marilee, sometimes it's just easier to ask for forgiveness rather than permission."

Kate chuckles in agreement. "That's true, but she's your dear friend and you need to call her."

"Okay, okay, I will."

"Well I better get going...just pulled in the driveway...but call or text me later if you come across anything juicy."

"I will for sure..." Julia smiles.

As they hang up the phone, Julia knows Kate's right. She does need Marilee and Paul on her side. Now her curiosity is also piqued. What does Marilee know that she hasn't shared? Is that why she got so upset?

Julia vows to call Marilee the next day, but first, she has a date with Jesus.

CHAPTER 15

October 13, 1995

The crisp autumn air reverberates through the stadium along with the trumpets and tubas blowing the notes of Murdoch High's fight song. Julia's relieved to see there's still nearly ten minutes to go in the second quarter so she has time to get settled before the homecoming court makes its way onto the field.

Never in journalism school did she envision being here, at a Friday night football game in Murdoch, Mississippi, covering the crowning of a homecoming court. She has been stewing about the assignment all week. She's ready for more advanced stories but her editor, Dan, has yet to give her anything exciting like house fires, car accidents, or anything involving city council. She's not sure if he's just unwilling to share the tougher assignments or if it's because she's the only woman on the staff of three.

"It's just stupid…" She'd told Seth earlier that morning over breakfast.

"It's not stupid to those girls. Homecoming is a big deal around here." Seth smiled.

"I guess but I don't see why I have to cover it. I mean it's not really news." Exasperation lined Julia's words.

"Have you never been to a homecoming football game?"

Julia paused before biting into her peanut butter toast. "Hmm…nope."

"Seriously? Not even in high school?" Seth could not comprehend this.

"Nope."

Seth had laughed as he stood, picked up his cereal bowl, and took a final sip of his coffee. "Well, my love, you are in for a real treat." He kissed her forehead as he walked over to put his dishes in the dishwasher.

Her irritation had softened into a smile. "So I'll just see you there tonight then?"

"Yeah, I may run out to the farm and check on things before the game but I'm not sure. So I'll just plan to meet you there."

Now twelve hours later, Julia scans the crowd looking for Seth, unsure if he'll be in his police uniform or street clothes. A Murdoch resident for all of a few months, Julia's still getting to know the locals.

Wherever she goes, she's mostly met with a sea of unfamiliar faces. Every now and then, however, she recognizes someone she had interviewed for a story or met in the grocery store with Seth. Though as a Dixon (even one who's married into the family), far more people know who Julia is than she realizes.

As Julia navigates her way through the stadium, the sight is unlike anything she's ever witnessed at a sporting event. Granted, she hasn't been to many. With each step, the frenzy of energy makes her pulse quicken. Crowds of small children are gathered alongside the bleachers playing catch with little red-and-white plastic footballs. Moms of players, cheerleaders, and band members are donned in red tee-shirts with huge photo buttons proudly displaying their kids' faces. Throngs of junior high boys stand around awkwardly near the concession stand with their dates, who are proudly showing off their massive mums.

Beyond this foreign scene of high school football, the mum situation is something else Julia cannot wrap her mind around. Seth had tried to explain it but she still doesn't see the purpose of the huge fake flowers the size of a dessert plate decorated with streamers, glitter, and cowbells.

"Julia!" She swears she hears her name coming from the stands but with all the chaos she's not totally sure from where. Standing down below the bleachers, she peers up and scans the crowd of spectators.

"JULIA!" This time, it's a louder chorus, which pierces through the noise. She searches the crowd once more to find Kate and Marilee on their feet waving their arms wildly near the top of the bleachers.

Julia laughs and waves back. She holds up her index finger to signal she'll be there in a minute. She wants to say hello to Seth before she gets carried away with her friends. Turning back toward the scoreboard, she spots him standing along the fence with two men whose faces and names she does know by now. That would be George Stark and Ricky Watson.

Julia walks toward them and upon spotting her, Seth's face lights up from ear to ear.

"Hey babe, there you are!" He hugs her and then pecks her on the lips. "I've been looking for you. You're just in time for the naming of the court." He pokes her side teasingly.

"Shut up." She responds with a playful smile.

"Hey Julia." Ricky leans over from the fence to greet her. Ricky Watson is a few years older than Seth and at least a foot shorter. He has a thick build and square head, made even squarer by his flattop haircut. When he's in uniform, like now, Ricky looks even stockier, with tanned arms poking out of his short sleeves like stuffed sausages.

By most every account, Ricky is the epitome of a Southern redneck. Given his lot in life, what other option was there? His mother was only seventeen when he was born. She skipped town by the time Ricky was two, following after another junkie boyfriend and leaving little Ricky behind to be raised by his grandparents. Ricky never knew his father, and when he'd ask, his grandad would simply reply that Ricky was better off not knowing him.

Ricky's grandparents did their best to keep him in line. But after his grandad passed away in junior high, Ricky became a force that couldn't be contained, especially his anger. He was often wearing a black eye from an after-school fight or bruised butt from the licks he had received from the principal for mouthing off to teachers, stealing money from the school store, or relentlessly bullying another kid.

Ricky stormed through life with only a handful of friends back then, and their only mission was to obtain cigarettes, beer, and pot. It wasn't until he nearly died at sixteen that anyone or anything got his attention. Very little scared Ricky Watson, and although he would never admit it aloud, wrapping his grandad's 1978 Chevy pick-up around a tree on the outskirts of town shook him to the core.

Ricky straightened up and scraped by to finish high school with a high C average, which was barely enough to get him into Southwest Mississippi Community College. Ironically, he decided to become a cop. Ricky struggled to put himself through two years of school, working full time as a mechanic and studying at night. It took him three attempts to get into the police academy but he was finally accepted and graduated in fall of 1989.

By the time Seth joined the Murdoch police force, Ricky had several years of experience on him. Seth had known Ricky all through grade school and high school. However, they ran in vastly different social circles and had never been what you'd call "friends."

Seth was surprised to find Ricky on the panel interviewing him for the open position on the Murdoch police force. Seth had even commented to Julia afterward that he never imaged Ricky would be the kind of man to follow the law, let alone uphold it as a cop. Nevertheless, Ricky was technically Seth's superior, and Seth was dutiful when it came to rank.

Peering over at Ricky now, Julia studies his face, with his thick brown eyebrows knotted slightly and bottom lip fat from the freshly packed dip. His face is deeply tanned and cleanly shaven. Julia's not sure she's ever seen Ricky without his aviator sunglasses, though they have only met a few times before now. It's a surprise to see his face, which is attractive enough, almost handsome. Based on their brief interactions so far, it's clear Ricky thinks more highly of himself than he should, especially in uniform.

"Hi Ricky." Julia returns a smile his direction. Ricky nods before returning to the game.

George Stark spins around on the heels of his leather cowboy boots. She's yet to meet him in person but she knows exactly who he is. In the short time she's been in town, Julia has been briefed about the Starks by her editor and, of course, Kate and Marilee. Kate's known George a few years since taking a job as a clerical assistant for the city, while Marilee's family has known the Starks for decades.

George's father and namesake, the late George Stark Sr. hailed from generations of old Southern money. George Sr. had provided the endowment to establish the Stark Hospital Foundation. After his father's passing, George Jr. had taken over and now serves as the hospital's chairman. Julia doesn't understand how he could also be mayor, but apparently in a town of this size, the mayor is an elected official that serves more as a figurehead. Though with the Stark name and inheritance behind him, George has the power to go with the title as well.

"Well, hello Julia." George smiles. Unlike Ricky, George does have the kind of looks that make women blush. He's about Seth's height, with broad shoulders under a red Murdoch Mustangs polo shirt, and thick, jet black hair parted neatly to the right. As Julia leans in to shake his hand, she spots a few strands of gray around his temples and guesses he's somewhere in his early forties.

"It's nice to finally meet you, George." She's a little shocked he knows who she is, but her voice turns professional, as she quickly shifts her reporter's steno notebook to shake his hand.

"You too, Julia. I'm surprised our paths haven't crossed yet over at city hall. I hear you're quite the reporter…at least that's what Kate tells me."

Julia laughs nervously. "Well, I don't know about that. I'm here tonight to cover homecoming and that doesn't seem like earth-shattering news to me."

George and Seth both let out hearty laughs, while Ricky is seemingly paying no attention to them. He's leaning over the fence watching the game, occasionally spitting a stream of black produced from the snuf.

"I tried to explain it to her." Seth shrugs.

"She'll just have to see for herself." George smiles. "Speaking of…it's almost that time." He points to the convertibles carrying the high school girls, with their colorful dresses and anxious smiles, now slowly making their way around the earth-toned cinder track.

"I guess I better go. I'm going to sit with Kate and Marilee up in the stands, so I can take notes." Julia turns to Seth. "I'll just meet you after the game."

"Okay, babe." He smiles and kisses her.

"It was nice to meet you, George."

"You too, and I'll look forward to reading your article Wednesday."

"Thanks. I'm sure it will win a Peabody Award." Julia retorts sarcastically before breaking into a smile.

George and Seth both laugh, as she turns to find Kate and Marilee. Ricky pays no attention to Julia's departure, as he's silently eyeing the girls on the cars.

Much to her annoyance, Seth's right. Julia actually enjoys the homecoming festivities and watching the girls line up with their fathers and dates mid-field to hear their names called. It's a ritual that she's completely unfamiliar with but something about the innocent excitement of youth rekindles in Julia that feeling of hope. The hope you feel at sixteen when life is spread out like a banquet before you.

In the end, it's high school junior Allison Mercer who is named the 1995 Homecoming Queen. After halftime, Julia makes her way down to the field to catch up with the newly crowned queen. She finds the petite blonde wearing a shimmering blue strapless gown standing at the end of the football field, near the old bell tower. She's greeting classmates as they stop by to congratulate her.

Julia snaps a few photos of Allison, but given how distracted Allison is with her friends, the two agree to meet the next morning at Nine Ed's Cafe to conduct a more in-depth interview over brunch.

◆ ◆ ◆

The next morning at Nine Eds, Julia's pleasantly surprised to find depth and ambition behind Allison's youthful beauty. Allison has a sweet disposition and huge blue eyes that Julia finds equally engaging and playful. At sixteen, she is president of her class, a member of the National Honor Society, and lobbying her government teacher to start a debate team. Of course, she's also a varsity cheerleader.

"Oh, so you know my friend, Marilee…Mrs. Johnson?" Julia corrects herself and smiles.

"Yes, I just love Mrs. Johnson. She's worked with most of us on the squad since we were in junior high."

"So what do you like about being a cheerleader?" Julia smiles across the table.

"The friendships. Really, we're more like sisters. But don't get me wrong…" Allison leans across the table as if she's about to reveal a secret. "Sometimes we can be so mean to each other. I guess it's just what girls do." Allison shrugs and sits back in her chair.

Julia laughs at the wisdom in the statement thinking about her days as a teenager. "You're right about that."

"So you're married to Seth Dixon, right?"

"Yes, I am."

Allison blushes. "He's so handsome, and much nicer than Ricky Watson."

"Oh? How do you know Ricky?"

"I worked at city hall over the summer, and actually last summer, too. I helped out making copies, filing cases…you know, that kinda stuff. He used to come in all the time saying he needed this or that. He's okay, I guess. He just…" Allison's voice drops off as the waitress interrupts the conversation to deliver their orders of food.

As they dig into their pancakes and bacon, Julia's curious about what Allison was going to say about Ricky. Julia hasn't quite gotten a pulse on him yet after only a few short exchanges. But seeing Ricky again last night confirmed that there's something about him that makes her uneasy.

"So, what were you saying about Ricky?"

"Oh I don't remember…" Allison looks down and nervously shifts the scrambled eggs around her plate. "But I did love working there…at city hall…especially with Missus Kate. She is *so* funny!"

Julia laughs thinking about her new friend. Kate is just one of those warm, open people who make you feel like you've known them forever. "Yeah…she is that."

Allison goes on to tell Julia about the reason she worked at city hall, rather than babysitting or lifeguarding at the pool with her friends, is because she dreams of going to law school. She admits she isn't sure what type of law she wants to practice yet, but she knows she's fascinated with the law and ideals of justice. Julia agrees and explains that sense of justice is why she went into journalism school.

Upon wrapping up their brunch and heading out to their cars, Allison hugs Julia goodbye, and Julia finds herself surprisingly enamored with the young girl, perhaps because Julia sees a little of herself in young Allison. When the article comes out the following Wednesday, it isn't material for a Peabody Award, but it certainly makes Allison Mercer's year.

CHAPTER 16

July 8, 1996

"We found her." Seth says from the other end of the Motorola bag cell phone in his cop car.

Julia can hear muffled voices in the background behind him.

"And? She's okay?" Julia's voice rises in hope, though in her gut she knows hope may be futile.

"No, Jules." Seth's tone is lower, softer. He pauses as if in thought. "No baby, we found her body near the football stadium. She's dead, Jules. Allison's dead."

Stunned Julia stares blankly at the TV, which she had muted when their home phone rang. She'd put the cordless phone right beside her on the couch waiting anxiously for either Dan or Seth to call with an update. Like most everyone in Murdoch, she had been on high alert the past twenty-four hours. All day at the news desk, she and Dan had speculated on theories about where Allison could be, both secretly hoping she'd just had an irrational teenage moment and ran away for attention.

While Allison received plenty of attention for her looks, smarts, and genuine charm, Julia couldn't imagine Allison needing to create a scene just for more. Besides, Julia wondered, why would her car be left at the pool where she was supposed to meet her friends? Wouldn't she have run away in her car?

None of it added up, not then, and certainly not now that Seth has revealed the truth.

"Oh my God..." The hot tears line the edge of Julia's eyes and her voice catches. "Are you serious? I don't understand...why? How?"

"I can't get into anything right now. I just wanted to call and let you know."

"I can't believe it. I just...I just don't understand..."

"I know, I can't either. I'm so sorry, baby...and I hate to do this, but I really need to run. We have a lot on our hands tonight. I probably won't even be home until morning. I'm going to stay and help out."

"Okay." Julia blinks quickly still trying to comprehend this news. "Are you okay?"

Seth sighs heavily. "Well, no, not really. But unfortunately tonight this is my job, so I have to be okay."

"I know. Please be careful." Julia's voice cracks. "I love you so much."

"I love you, too."

Julia hangs up the phone and the tears grow hotter. Since their interview last fall for homecoming, Julia and Allison had continued their conversations about politics, current events, and Allison's dream of law school.

Whether at the Lion's Club pancake supper, sporting events, or just bumping into each other at the grocery store, each interaction had a similar rhythm of Allison greeting Julia with a huge smile and a hug. The more Julia got to know Allison, the more she liked her, and each time Julia walked away with this sense that Allison would do something great one day.

The last time she saw Allison was a week ago, when Julia went into city hall to grab Kate for lunch at Nine Ed's. Allison had talked about the latest book she was reading and how she was already starting to study to take the SAT in September, so she could apply early to college.

"I've already got senioritis and school hasn't even started." Allison had said with a laugh.

Julia cannot imagine how the light in Allison's beautiful face could go out. At only seventeen, she emanated life, hope, possibility. Julia buries her face in her hands as the sobs rise from her chest. After a few moments, the waves of emotion pass, and she climbs heavily off the couch to find a tissue. Walking back to the living room, the phone rings again.

"Hello?"

"Hey Julia, it's Dan." His voice is quiet. "Have you heard about Allison Mercer?"

"Yeah, Seth just called. I can't believe it."

"I know, it's so sad. I'm going to need you to come down and help me cover this."

"Really? Tonight?"

"Yeah, tonight. Can you be at the stadium in twenty minutes?"

Julia looks down at her black cotton shorts and Mustangs football tee-shirt.

"Yeah, just let me change clothes and I'll be right there."

"Okay. See ya."

As Julia hangs up the phone, a rush of fear pulses through her. She'd never covered a death before. About the toughest assignment she'd had thus far was for the community paper in Indiana, writing about a Gulf War soldier who'd died in combat. She'd written a profile about him and the family he left behind. It wound up being one of her favorite clips, though was by far the most emotional to write, and emotion is something Julia would prefer to leave out of the story. In her mind, reporting the news was about reporting the facts, not feelings.

So until this moment, it hadn't fully occurred to Julia that Dan would need her to actually work this as a story. They hadn't talked about it as an assignment yet, because until they knew more about Allison's whereabouts, there was no point. Now, like Seth, she has to try to find some way to put her emotion aside and go to work.

◆ ◆ ◆

Julia's relieved the drive from their house is only a few minutes to the stadium. Any more time than that and her brain might have exploded with questions. *How did Allison die? Was she murdered? Who did it? Why did they do it? How are her parents going to get through this?*

Julia's hands are now visibly shaking as she loosely grasps the steering wheel. She pulls her car into the dusty gravel lot circling the stadium, driving around to where the other cars are parked on the west side. Just as she parks her car, she wipes a bead of sweat from her forehead, whether produced by nerves or the fact that it's just after eight o'clock at night and it's easily still a hundred degrees outside.

A red and blue stream of lights produced from the police cars, fire truck, and ambulance illuminate the area. The stadium lights are also on, even though the sun hasn't made its final descent. About a dozen other cars are there, too. She finds Dan on the outside of the fence by the bell tower.

"Hey Julia." Dan waves casually though his shoulders are slumped more than usual.

"Hey…"

"You alright?" He peers over at her.

Julia's face is now ashen white and the twinge in her stomach, which feels like nausea, sends a wave of panic through her.

"Yeah. I'm okay."

"You sure? You look like a ghost."

"I'm fine." She wipes her forehead, hair pulled back in a tight ponytail. "What do you need me to do?"

"I was thinking it would be better for me to be with the family since I know them." Dan points to the Mercers who are standing near a cop car talking to the Chief of Police Dave Smith. "Thought you could stick with the cops and the JP to see what you can find out."

"So what happened?"

Dan studies her face and sighs heavily before glancing over Julia's shoulder at the scene. "Seth didn't tell you?"

Julia stomach churns again. "No...he didn't have time to give me any details."

"She was murdered." Dan says quietly. "Peterson hasn't officially confirmed the exact cause of death yet, but he will soon, and I need you there to get his quote. I'm gonna go over and see if I can talk to her parents to see what else I can find out." He sighs again heavily as he brushes away the beads of sweat from his forehead.

"Okay." Julia swallows hard, forcing back the tears and wishing she had some water.

Dan studies Julia through his wire-rimmed glasses in concern, his graying brown hair matted along his temples from sweat. "You sure you're okay?"

"Yeah...yeah, I'm fine." Julia tries to sound convincing. "I'll catch up with you in a bit."

She turns to walk toward where Seth and the other cops are congregated at the far edge of the parking lot closest to the woods. Julia takes a deep breath, her mind unable to fully comprehend that someone could possibly murder sweet Allison Mercer.

The cop cars and fire truck create a barricade of sorts, with a dozen or so people gathered around. Fortunately, no one notices as she draws closer. She's still a good twenty yards away as she comes into view of the stretcher behind the ambulance with a black body bag laying atop.

This time the wave of nausea forces her to double over, notepad and recorder flying beside her onto the gravel. Julia squares her hands over her kneecaps trying to steady her stance, but the nausea wins. She vomits right there in the middle of the parking lot. After a few heaves, she stands and wipes the tears and sweat from her face. Julia retrieves her notebook and recorder, grateful that she didn't puke on them and even more so that no one saw. At least, she hopes not.

Dan had walked ahead of her and now stands with the Mercers nodding his head in understanding. He's scribbling on his notepad while talking to Doug Mercer. Doug's arm is draped around the slumped shoulders of his wife, Shirley, who's now visibly shaking through the sobs.

As Julia slowly travels the remaining distance to the scene, she realizes maybe throwing up helped cleanse her. Rounding the front of a cop car, Julia spots Seth who halts his conversation and rushes to her, visibly startled by her appearance, with brow furrowed and jaw tight.

Julia's relieved to see him and smiles as she approaches. She reaches up to hug him. He stiffens and pulls away quickly.

"Julia, what are you doing here?" His voice isn't sweet like earlier. It's tense, verging on anger.

"Well, hello to you, too."

"I'm sorry, babe, but you can't be here. You need to go back home."

"Yes, I can be here. Dan needs me to help him cover the story."

"No, Julia, you can't be here. You don't want to see all this." Seth says again more sternly, waving his hand in the direction of the ambulance.

Incensed by his tone, she straightens to her full height so she can look him in the eye, though he's still a good three inches taller.

"No, I don't want to see this, but I'm a reporter. And tonight this is my job." She looks him squarely in the eye, the fire rising in her belly lining her words with decisiveness. "You have a job to do. So do I...and I won't get in your way but I do have questions. Now are you the one to answer them?"

Seth sighs heavily. Knowing Julia, he won't dissuade her, but he also knows she isn't ready to start digging into the details of this girl's murder. The irritation in his face softens to a look of concern.

"Jules, seriously." He says quietly, eyes glistening in the light. "I really wish you would go home and let Dan handle this. It's a bad scene."

"I know but I have to do my job..." Julia hates that the words come out sounding far more like a question than a statement of truth. She starts moving around him.

Seth knows he's lost the fight and moves to the side as Julia walks past him toward Chief Smith and Justice of the Peace Alan Peterson. She turns on her recorder and the questions begin.

◆ ◆ ◆

It's nearly eleven o'clock before Julia returns home. Whether from exhaustion, adrenaline, or sadness, her body feels completely numb, weighing far more than her hundred and fifty pounds.

It was grueling enough to stand there and ask questions about the cause of Allison's death, even more so to know she had been sexually assaulted before she died of suffocation. No amount of reasoning and none of the replies she received had satisfied her laundry list of questions. The cops didn't know much of anything except Allison's beaten body was found in the woods on the west side of the stadium around seven-thirty Monday night.

After showering off the dust, sweat, and regurgitation of emotion, Julia makes a cup of hot tea and returns to the place on the sofa where just hours before she still had hope of Allison's safe return.

The singular thought creeps back. *Why? Why did she die?*

Knowing Seth wouldn't be home until morning, Julia realizes the other person she needs to talk to most right now. Even though it's late, far past the usual time she'd call, she feels sure Kate is awake, and she's relieved it's Kate who answers the phone.

"Hello?"

"Kate, it's Julia."

"Oh gurl, I have been trying to call your house all night." Kate's voice is raspy and heavy. "I guess you heard about Allison?" She audibly cries into the phone.

Julia's heart sinks even further hearing her friend cry. "Yeah, I just got home from the stadium."

"What? Why were you at the stadium?"

"Because I had to work. Seth called me a little before eight and told me she'd died and that's all I knew because he couldn't talk long. Then Dan called a few minutes later saying he needed me to help him gather information. I didn't know until I got to the stadium that she'd been murdered."

Kate cries harder. "I just can't believe it. Why in the hell would anyone want to hurt that sweet girl?"

"I don't know…" Julia wipes her eyes.

"So what did you find out? Do they have any leads?"

"No, they don't know much at this point, all speculation. I'm sorry I didn't call right after Seth called me. I was so overwhelmed, I wasn't thinking right. So how did you find out?"

"It's okay…I think we're all overwhelmed. Betty Ann called me. George wanted to let me know and he needed to be down at the stadium. So she called me about eight-thirty, I guess. She was really upset."

"I know…I think everyone's in shock. Does Marilee know?"

"Yeah, I talked to her earlier. Everyone knows by now. I mean the way news travels around here, a lizard could pee on a line in Natchez and they know about it in Murdoch before it hits the ground."

Julia laughs for the first time all day. "You always have a way of putting things."

"I just don't understand what happened. Why did she die? Who did it? And how in the hell did she end up at the stadium when her car was left two miles away at the pool?" Kate's voice rises in anger as she rattles off the questions faster than Julia can compute them.

Julia's brain is foggy from the sheer volume of information she's also tried to absorb over the past few hours. "I don't know, Kate." Julia says quietly. "I wish I did, and I'm going to do everything I can to find out. For now, I need to get some rest. I have to be back at the paper early in the morning to meet Dan."

"I'm sorry, gurl. I just…I just don't understand…" Kate's voice breaks again through the tears.

"I don't either and sorry if I woke you. I know it's late…but I just had to call."

"No, we're still up. I'm glad you did…I've been wantin' to talk to you all night. I know you're exhausted…so get some rest and we can catch up tomorrow."

"Okay sounds good…"

"And Julia?…" Kate's tone rises.

"Yes?"

"I hope you know I love you, gurl."

Julia smiles through the phone. "I love you, too, Kate. Goodnight."

CHAPTER 17

July 9, 1996

The next morning, it takes an extra cup of coffee for Julia to feel halfway normal. It had been a restless night of sleep, especially without Seth in bed next to her. With each sip, Julia tries to erase the mental cobwebs, though her mind cannot shake the scenes from last night.

Even her attempt to write in her journal is futile. Her body feels as though someone squeezed it like a sponge, emotion still raw and laced with an underlying feeling of deep exhaustion. Julia sets her journal to the side and leans her head against the back of the overstuffed armchair they'd found at a second-hand store in Natchez. Her legs rest on the wide chambray-and-white-striped ottoman.

The unanswered questions play mental pinball, as Julia keeps pinging back into the same fundamental question of why. *Why Allison Mercer? Who could have killed her? Did anyone see her at the pool? Did she get in a car with someone or did they grab her against her will?*

Ten minutes later Seth's key rattles in the lock of their small, two-bedroom home. Julia smiles, eager to see her husband. It feels like it's been days.

"Good morning." Julia smiles sleepily as he walks in.

"Oh hey, I wasn't sure you'd be up. It's still early…" Seth drops his keys in the ceramic bowl sitting atop a small wooden table near the front door. He heads straight to the couch where he plops down heavily.

"I know...I couldn't sleep so I got up. Have to meet Dan at the paper in a bit. He wants to go over our notes from last night and figure out if we can get the stories in tomorrow's paper. It's going to be a tight turnaround..." Julia deposits her half-empty coffee mug on the small table next to the armchair and joins Seth on the couch.

Perched on her knees next to him, she hugs him close. He turns to enfold her in his arms, buries his head in the crook of her neck, and sighs heavily.

"Sorry about last night..." His words are muffled in Julia's mane of hair, as he breathes deeply. He's always loved how her hair smells. In moments like now, he finds it comforting like when you pull your favorite blanket out of the dryer, draw it to your face and inhale the warmth.

"It's okay. I know it was a rough night for you."

"Yeah, it was..." He slowly pulls back to look into Julia's face, relieved to see her green eyes are somewhat brighter this morning. He traces the edge of her cheek with his fingertips. "I was just worried it'd be too much. You know I worry about you, even though you're tough as nails." He laughs and then kisses her softly on the lips.

Julia smiles. "Well, I wasn't tough last night."

"Umm...you made it clear you had a job to do, remember?" He studies her face with a tired smile.

"I remember...but that was after I threw up in the parking lot."

"You did? Oh baby, I'm sorry." His smile turns to a soft, sympathetic chuckle. "I didn't see you."

"Thank God...I was hoping no one noticed. So how'd it go after I left?"

"Okay, I guess. We don't have any new information...still trying to figure out what happened." He sighs again heavily and she can see the weight of it all in his face.

"I just still can't believe it. I mean, it just doesn't make sense. Why would someone kill Allison?" Julia's voice grows louder, the caffeine now doing its job.

"I don't know…and honestly that's what had me so rattled last night." Seth admits as he rubs his large hands over his bloodshot eyes.

"What do you mean?" Julia quizzes.

"Well, I've never seen…or known…of anything like this happening in Murdoch. Things like this don't just happen here…and…" Seth stops short.

"And…?"

"And what?" Seth looks at her.

"You were about to say something else." Julia knows there are more words in his mouth but Seth won't let them out.

"No, I wasn't…" He leans in and rests his head gently on her chest. "I'm so tired I think I'm delirious. I'm gonna take a shower and go to sleep. I have to be back at the station this evening to cover the night shift again. What are you up to today?"

Julia rubs the back of his hair, just at the nape of his neck, wondering what other information is rolling around in his thick head. They walk a fine line of staying in integrity with her being a reporter and Seth a cop. As much as she wants to pepper him with questions, she knows when he's off duty, he's also off limits as a source.

"I'm just heading to work and then coming home after that…" Julia glances at the clock. She still has forty-five minutes, plenty of time. Everything in Murdoch is five minutes away, and the only time there's ever traffic is after a football game or there's an especially long train that causes cars to back up. "I'll probably just rent a movie or something tonight. I'm really tired, too."

Arms wrapped around Seth's broad back, Julia kisses the top of his head, which is growing heavier. "You asleep?"

"Huh?" Seth stirs and then sits up slowly.

"Why don't you go shower...want me to make you some eggs?"

"Oh yeah, that'd be great." He smiles sleepily and kisses her on the lips.

After breakfast, Seth heads to bed and Julia heads to the paper. The cobwebs have fully dissipated and she's eager to start working on this story. She may not have much influence or power as an outsider in this town, but the newspaper is the one place where she is beginning to have a voice. And she has every intention of using it.

◆ ◆ ◆

The energy is palpable in the *Messenger* office, which on most days, has a steady, but simple, cadence. On this steamy summer morning, there is a feeling of purpose.

Dan hovers over his desk listening to the interviews he recorded on his cassette tape, while the photographer works on photos in the darkroom. It's a small office lining Main Street with frosted front window panes that still reflect the gold stenciled words, "The Murdoch Messenger: Est. 1895." Inside, the heavy wooden desks and brown paneled walls perfectly match the hint of stale cigarette smoke, which still hangs in the air like tattered curtains.

"Hey Julia." Dan removes his headphones and drops them on the desk. He peers curiously over the top of his white desktop computer, as she stands at her desk pulling the tape recorder and notebook out of her backpack purse. "How you feelin'?"

"I'm okay." She looks up and smiles, her coloring and confidence restored.

"That's good. I was worried 'bout you last night." Dan studies her.

Julia's cheeks turn a shade of cranberry. "Yeah, I was worried about me, too."

"Part of being a rookie...happened to me, too." He smiles sadly.

"What did?"

"Puking when I saw the body bag. It was my first murder also. I think it's a reporter's rite of passage."

Julia's cheeks flush deeper. "You saw me?"

"Yeah, well only as you were pickin' up your things. So I assumed that's what happened."

"Oh Jesus…I'm sorry. It was just a little much to take in at once."

"It's okay. I know it's hard, especially when you know the person who died. I don't think anyone else saw. But hell, I'm an old crusty reporter…so I have eyes on every side of my head, so I'm always on alert." He laughs softly at his own joke.

"So you've covered murders before?" Julia regrets the question. Of course he had. Dan had shared a few of his stories from working at papers around the South, with his largest being on the news desks in Jackson and New Orleans. Dan and his wife had moved to Murdoch about ten years ago to raise their two kids. His son Jake is in the same age as Allison, so he knows the Mercers well.

"Yeah, I've covered too many deaths over the years. That first one though stays with you though. Mine was a black boy in Shreveport and was only fifteen. Gunshot…just got caught at the wrong place at the wrong time. Damn shame, too. He was a good kid."

"So was Allison." Julia's heart sinks thinking about the bright future Allison had planned ahead of her, a future that will never be realized.

Dan rubs his face in his hands in thought. "Yeah, this kinda thing is the hardest of all because it just doesn't make any sense. It wasn't an accident, you know. This was intentional."

And that's precisely what has everyone thrown. Murdoch isn't the kind of town where people just walk out of their house one day, get abducted, sexually assaulted, and left dead in the woods. It isn't like Julia's hometown of Chicago, where murders happen every day.

No, random things just don't happen in a town like Murdoch, a town that has such a predictable rhythm of life. It's this steady cadence that Julia secretly loves most, as life in Murdoch revolves around the academic year, Mustang sports, and the annual traditions and festivals.

In Murdoch, people wave from their cars to everyone, even if they don't know you. They greet you on the aisles of the grocery store, and the one Julia really still can't get over, is they regularly leave their cars and houses unlocked. Nelda and Doc even leave their keys inside their unlocked cars every night.

"So we can remember where they are," Doc once told Julia when she'd first asked if he was afraid anyone would steal his big white Chevy truck. He laughed. "I leave 'em in there or else I'd lose those damn keys every day. That means Nelda would have my ass in a sling every day."

Julia scans her notes about Allison's scratched and scuffed body. She shakes her head sadly. "I never imagined this would happen here...but what I don't get is why? Why Allison?" She looks squarely at Dan. "What possible motive would someone have for killing her?"

"I don't know. Maybe redemption...maybe just a power play. The rumor mill is already churnin.' Had five phone calls just this morning."

"Really? What kind of rumors?"

"None worth repeatin'. Besides, I don't want to distract you from the facts. You need to focus on your story."

"Yeah, but there are hardly any facts to go on." Julia sighs and she flips through her notes from last night.

"Right. But in these types of situations, you just gotta use what details you can. There's no room to make shit up, especially not in a murder when there's no motive, no weapon, and no suspects. So I need you to focus on straight reportin' of what happened...and what Smith and Peterson said."

"How do you know there's no motive or suspects? I mean it just happened!" Julia's tone grows agitated, as she's never had to write a story with so little information.

Dan looks at her sternly and sighs heavily in frustration. "Julia, look…you just gotta trust me on this."

Julia stares at him intently, realizing there's more going on with this case than anyone is letting on. She's just about to put on her headphones to listen to her cassette tape of last night's interviews when Dan looks up again.

"Oh, and in the piece, you need to mention a reward fund is being set up at First National Bank. Fifteen thousand dollars. People can donate to it over at the bank."

"Fifteen thousand dollars? Dang, that's a lot of money. Who set it up?"

"Just write that it's anonymous."

"No really…who set it up? The Mercers don't have that kind of money, do they?"

Julia's questions are hitting a nerve for Dan this morning, so he ignores them. "Just write that they're hoping the fund will spur some leads."

Julia glares at him in frustration but scribbles the note in her steno pad. Dan leans back in his chair and scratches his head as he stares out the window. Even with the frosted panes, the large window provides a clear lens directly into downtown Murdoch.

After a minute or so, Dan stands and walks over to the coffee pot to refill his brown mug with #1 Dad in red letters on the side. He looks Julia's direction, though she is now intently transcribing the tape from last night to string together the details.

"You know, I did get one call that's making me wonder…" Dan's words cut over the voices coming through her headphones.

Julia stops the tape. "Huh? Did you say something?"

"I was just sayin' I got one call that bothered me. Can't stop thinkin' bout it."

"From who?"

"I don't know. They wouldn't give me their name…" Dan takes

a sip of the stale coffee. Much to Julia's amazement, Dan will drink the oldest, stalest, blackest, coldest coffee all day long. Not Julia. One cup and she's functional. Two cups and she thinks life is magical. Any more than that, and the coffee somehow has a reverse effect, and she wants to fall asleep.

Dan stands at the end of her desk. "So did you notice anything suspicious from the cops last night?"

"Like what?" Julia thinks back trying to recall anything out of the ordinary.

"Any comments or shiftiness when you started asking questions?"

"No…not really, but I only talked to Smith and Peterson. Why?"

"Well, this caller said he'd heard there was a police car spotted around the football field Sunday afternoon about the time Allison went missing."

A bolt of adrenaline pulsates from the top of Julia's head to her feet. *Is that what Seth was going to tell her this morning? Was he there? Did he see something or someone?* She swallows hard, trying not to reveal her panic.

"Did they say which cop it was?"

"No." Dan looks over at her again, seeing the worry splayed across her face. "But it wasn't Seth. Yawl were gone out of town, right?"

Julia pauses and scans her mental timeline. "Yeah, we didn't get back from Lake Burton until nearly seven Sunday night." She lets out a nervous laugh, heart slowly returning to its normal cadence.

Of course it wasn't Seth's car. How could she forget their drunken, laughter-filled Fourth of July weekend with Kate and Marilee and their husbands. "I just seem to have lost all sense of time lately. Feels like my brain is in a fog."

"I know whatcha mean." Dan sips his coffee again, still peering over at her but lost in thought.

Julia leans back in her chair. "So do you think there's anything to this rumor? Anything we should look into?"

"Not right now. I think we just need to report on the facts as we know 'em. So you focus on the story of her body being found. I'm working on more of a short profile piece. We also need to figure out which photos to use."

"Okay." This time, Julia doesn't question Dan's orders. She realizes finally has a chance to write something of substance, and she wants to prove she can handle the assignment before he changes his mind.

◆ ◆ ◆

Julia arrives home to an empty house. Well, empty except for the note Seth left on the kitchen table indicating he's going out to Nelda's before his shift. She also discovers a blinking message on her answering machine from Kate inviting her over for drinks and dinner.

Julia plops down heavily on the couch and dials Kate's number.

"Hello…" Kate answers on the second ring.

"Hey…it's Julia."

"Oh hey gurl, whatcha up to?"

"Not much, just got home from the paper…had to write the story."

"Oh yeah…" Kate's voice drops. "You okay?"

"Yeah, I managed to avoid any ugly cries and just left the piece with Dan. He was too busy fielding phone calls to edit it. So he told me to come on home."

"Really? What kinda calls?"

"All sorts, really. Mostly people wanting to know what happened." Julia refrains from sharing anything more, at least over the phone.

"Ahh, gotcha. Well, Mike went to open the field house for some of the football kids who wanted to hang out and lift weights. They are all pretty upset about Allison, so he wasn't sure what time he'd be home. What about you? Whatcha up to tonight?"

"Nothing really, Seth is working night shift again."

"Wanna come over? Paul's watchin' the kids, so Marilee will be here 'round six."

"Yeah sure that sounds good. What can I bring?"

"I've got food covered but feel free to bring the usual order from Salty's. You know Marilee won't be seen there...so I can't ask her to stop." Kate laughs at their friend, the good Southern Baptist teetotaler in public who can drink both of them under the table behind closed doors.

"Sounds good. I'm just going to rest a bit, and then I'll be over."

The short power nap refreshes Julia and she's looking forward to seeing her friends. No matter what's happening, they always make her laugh. After stopping by Salty's for their usual order (a six-pack of Lazy Magnolia beer and two bottles of any kind of inexpensive red wine), Julia arrives at Kate and Mike's house, a few blocks from the high school.

"Hey gurl..." Kate opens the door snacking on a raw carrot, blonde hair pulled up in a loose ponytail in her favorite blue-jean shorts and purple tee-shirt with matching purple and pink Keds sneakers. She hugs Julia tightly.

Julia's arms are of full of spirits so it's hard to reciprocate the hug. Marilee appears from around the corner and plucks the two bottles of wine out of Julia's arms. Even with little makeup and a simple white tee-shirt and yellow-and-green plaid shorts revealing her long, muscular legs, Marilee looks like a supermodel. Her gray-green eyes, framed perfectly by manicured eyebrows, light up with joy seeing Julia at the door.

"Julia Dixon...did you ever know you're my hero?" Marilee laughs holding up the bottles and then leans in to hug Julia.

Kate looks at Marilee seriously. "I think that's more like your bootlegger."

"Shut up." Marilee touts playfully and then turns to head to the kitchen.

Kate cackles with laughter. "Come on in, we're just talkin' and snackin' and now that you're here…drinkin'!"

Julia laughs and follows her friends to the kitchen. "Yeah, I could use a drink. It's been a long day."

"I know…it's crazy that we just got back and now all of this." Marilee lifts the wine bottle to Julia in a question.

"Yes, wine please."

Kate pops open a beer. "Yeah…where should we even begin? I mean…I just still can't believe it."

"I can't, either." Julia welcomes the full glass of wine from Marilee. "Thanks."

"You're welcome darlin'…glad you came over." Marilee smiles at Julia, though her eyes remain hazy from the sadness.

There are moments like now when Julia feels completely at ease around her two friends. Then, there are other moments when they're together, she's aware that she's the youngest of the three. Not having grown up or competed with siblings, Julia often catches herself comparing how she feels on the inside (sometimes uncertain in her own skin) to how her two friends appear on the outside (feisty and beautiful).

"So let's start with last night…" Kate looks over at Julia. "What happened at the stadium?"

The three gather around the end of the long cabinet in Kate's galley kitchen. Bowls of ranch dip and salsa compliment the tray of raw veggies and tortilla chips. Julia grabs a chip and then takes a large drink of wine. Just as the question emerges from Kate, Julia feels a growing agitation. She doesn't want to rehash last night again.

Really, what she doesn't want to face again is the truth of life's unpredictability. At twenty-four, Julia certainly knows life isn't wrapped in bubble gum, bows, and happy endings. Her childhood was a testament to that, but in some ways that's why she agreed to move to Murdoch.

Perhaps it's why she enjoyed this quaint life in her husband's hometown, as it finally cultivated in her a sense of belonging, of security. Now the veil has been lifted, and Julia realizes that maybe there is no inoculation for life's ugly, hard edges, regardless of how seemingly perfect it may all appear on the surface.

"What do you want to know?" Julia asks flatly.

"I want to know what really happened..." Kate retorts.

"When I got there, they had just recovered her body. I interviewed Chief Smith and Alan Peterson. She had been sexually assaulted and suffocated. It was definitely murder but they don't have any suspects. The Mercers...or someone...has set up a fifteen-thousand-dollar reward fund hoping it will bring forward some leads." Julia sighs heavily and takes another drink of wine. "I don't know much else..."

Marilee quietly interrupts. "It just makes me so sad. I can't believe she's gone." The tears well in Marilee's eyes. "Allison was one of the sweetest kids I ever taught. Why on earth would someone kill her?"

"I don't know..." Julia reaches over and gently rubs Marilee's shoulder. Her own irritation melting into sadness. "It's the question I keep playing over and over in my mind."

A rare moment of quiet falls over the three as they each try to wrap their minds around how this could happen, especially here in Murdoch, to an innocent seventeen-year-old kid. Kate grabs her drink and silently moves to the living room. The two follow.

"So this is interesting..." Julia breaks the silence once they have settled into their respective seats. Marilee and Julia on the peach-colored sofa, while Kate sits cross-legged in Mike's brown recliner near the brick fireplace.

"What?" Kate peers over at her.

"Dan got at least a dozen calls at the paper today."

"What kinda calls?" Marilee wipes her eyes.

"Mostly people wanting to know what happened to Allison, but there was one that came in before I got there, and I think it shook Dan up a bit..." Julia chomps on a chip. "Someone called anonymously and said they'd heard a police car was seen at the football stadium Sunday afternoon. Dan wasn't sure if it was true, but he wanted to know if the cops were acting weird when I was talking to them at the stadium last night."

"Seriously?" Marilee's mouth is half open.

"Yeah, I don't even know if it's true..." Julia shrugs.

"Well, who could it have been?" Kate leaves the question hanging as she finishes her beer and stands to grab another. "Yawl need anything?"

Julia hoists her near-empty glass in the air. Kate retrieves it and walks to the kitchen.

"I don't know..." Julia says a little louder so Kate can hear her from the other room. "I do know it wasn't Seth's."

"Yeah, he was nursin' his hangover in Paul's truck and endurin' Mike's endless stories on the way back from the lake." Kate says with a laugh and returns with their refreshed drinks. The three girls had caravanned separately in Marilee's suburban.

Marilee's deep in thought before quietly speaking, as if someone could hear her who wasn't supposed to. "Well, I hadn't heard that but I did hear she had a diary the cops were tryin' to find."

"Really? Who told you that?" Julia quizzes.

"Betty Ann."

"When?" Kate chimes in.

"This mornin'. We had the cheer squad come over to the Starks' for a prayer circle...and you know just try to support them. It was really hard. They are all so upset." Marilee wipes another straggling tear from the corner of her eye.

"They're just kids...I can't even imagine what they must be going through." Julia gently shakes her head and sets her wine glass down on the side table so she can put her hair up in the hair tie she's been wearing around her wrist. It's that time of day when the hair always goes up.

"So what did Betty Ann say?" Kate's zeroed in on the diary.

"Not much, just that Chief Smith apparently called George early this mornin' askin' if Allison ever talked about writin' in a diary. So George asked Betty Ann if she knew anything about it. She didn't recall so Betty Ann asked me if I did..."

"And...have you?" Kate peppers Marilee, while Julia listens intently.

"No, but Allison was always somewhat reserved around the other girls. She was definitely the leader but never brassy like some of the others." Marilee wipes her eyes again. "I just...I just still can't believe it...I mean this is Murdoch for goodness sakes!" Her voice grows louder in frustration, unable to comprehend how this could happen.

"So what do the cops think they'll find with this diary?" Julia's wheels are turning.

"I don't know." Marilee shrugs and then fetches her wine glass on the side table by the couch. "I guess they want to see if it leads to any information. I mean why was her car left at the pool? And then her body was a few miles away at the stadium? She had to know whoever she got in that car with..." Marilee shudders faintly. "And here's something else I haven't told anyone. So you gotta swear you won't say a word."

"What?" Kate leans in from the recliner. Julia looks over at Marilee intently.

Marilee swirls the wine gently in her glass. "Our babysitter Dana called me this afternoon..." She pauses recalling the conversation. "She told me that she saw Allison leanin' against the back of her car at the pool Sunday. They were drivin' by after leaving the park. Dana said she waved and Allison waved back."

"Oh my Gawd, seriously? So she was at the pool!" Whether it's the new bit of information in this unsolved mystery or the effects of the second beer, Kate's excitement grows. "So did Dana tell the cops this?"

"Yeah, Dana went in for questionin' this morning." Marilee takes another sip of her wine.

Julia's quiet, calculating the order of what she knows thus far. "But I thought her friends at the pool said she never showed up."

"Or maybe they just didn't see her? Maybe she was in the parking lot and never went inside?" Kate chimes in.

"I don't know. I'm just goin' on what Dana told me and it's not like I can ask Paul Jr. He's only four."

"Wait, why was Dana babysitting? I thought Paul Jr. was stayin' with your parents when we were at Lake Burton." Kate's completely confused.

"Well, my folks were watchin' him for us, but mama has her quiltin' circle on Sunday afternoons at the church and she didn't want to miss it. So I told her to have Dana watch him a few hours, and they went to the park. She has permission to take him to the park and then back home."

"Ohhhh okay." Kate seems satisfied with this arrangement.

"So why did the police question Dana? Did she see something else?" Julia's concern isn't with the child care logistics, but rather with what Dana might have seen.

"I don't know but there are so many pieces to this that just don't add up." Marilee shakes her head.

"Yeah, my head is spinnin' and not from the beer." Kate agrees. "So we have the cop car at the stadium, Dana at the pool, and this diary."

"What the hell..." Julia's about to explode trying to make it all fit together, like when she got her first Rubix Cube at twelve. She got so mad trying to solve it, she threw it across the room. "This just doesn't make sense...I mean, Allison must have been meeting someone at the pool to just be sitting there in the parking lot like that...and she never went inside? I don't get it..."

"Yeah, that's just not like her." Kate says quietly.

Silence falls over the room again as Marilee stands and heads to the kitchen. She returns with the bottle of wine.

"I'm starting to wonder if we're ever going to make sense of this…but I'm sure as hell going to try." Julia lifts her glass for a refill.

"Well, then we are going to need a lot more bottles of this." Marilee smiles and winks at Julia.

CHAPTER 18

The Murdoch Messenger – July 10, 1996

Recent Murder of Murdoch Teen Remains a Mystery
$15,000 Reward Fund Established to Spur Leads

By Julia Dixon

Every crime produces a series of questions, and in the case of Allison Mercer's recent death, those questions continue.

Mercer was reported missing the evening of Sunday, July 7 by her parents, Doug and Shirley Mercer. Allison Mercer was last seen leaving her home around 3 p.m. Sunday afternoon. An honors student and Murdoch's 1995 Homecoming Queen, Mercer would have been a senior at Murdoch High School in the fall.

According to Mrs. Mercer, her daughter reported that she was going to the city pool that afternoon and then later to the track at the football stadium to run, as she did most evenings. However, accounts from classmates indicate that Mercer never arrived at the pool as planned, though Mercer's car had been parked there on Sunday afternoon.

After a search by Murdoch Police, the Mercer family and concerned citizens, Mercer's body was discovered in the woods on the west side of Murdoch's football stadium the night of Monday, July 8. According to preliminary autopsy reports, Mercer died due to suffocation. The report indicated she had also been sexually assaulted.

Justice of the Peace Alan Peterson pronounced Mercer dead at 8:45 p.m. on Monday, July 8, 1996. According to Peterson's report, Mercer's body also had lacerations and scuff marks on it.

According to the Murdoch Police Department, there are no new leads in the 17-year-old Murdoch High School student's abduction and subsequent murder.

"Our investigation in the murder continues," explained Murdoch Police Chief Dave Smith. "So, if anyone has information on this case, we want to know, no matter how small or insignificant it might seem."

Chief Smith asks that anyone who may have seen Mercer on the afternoon of Sunday, July 7, or who may have seen suspicious persons around the city pool, to please contact the Murdoch Police Department immediately.

A reward fund of $15,000 has been established at First National Bank for those who help police arrest and indict a suspect (or suspects) in the case. Donations may be made to the fund at First National Bank in Mercer's name.

CHAPTER 19

The Murdoch Messenger – July 17, 1996

Mayor Denies Police Involved in Recent Murder

Rumors Could Slow Investigation of Murdoch Teen's Death

By Julia Dixon

Every small town has a rumor mill, and with the recent abduction and murder of local teen Allison Mercer, that mill has been working overtime in Murdoch.

Murdoch Mayor George Stark is looking to put an end to these rumors circulating throughout the community since the abduction and murder of Murdoch High School student Allison Mercer. Mercer's body was found on Monday, July 8, 1996 after being reported missing the day before by her parents Doug and Shirley Mercer.

The most notable rumor is that a Murdoch police officer was involved in Mercer's abduction and murder. Stark said Monday that immediately after the rumor of the police officer's involvement circulated, the sources of information being used to investigate have ceased. Thus, police are at a standstill in their investigation.

"The rumors allege a Murdoch police officer's car had been impounded and searched, and objects used in this terrible crime were allegedly found in the officer's car," said Mayor Stark. "The rumor also claimed that a Murdoch officer had been arrested for the murder of Allison Mercer. These rumors are simply not true. They are completely false."

Stark continued in his commentary urging local residents, "Let me also state that I have complete faith in our police department to carry through with this investigation. We are doing everything possible to find out who killed Allison. Certainly, every possibility and lead is being taken seriously and being examined."

Stark concluded by encouraging local citizens to have faith in the efforts of the police department and to continue providing any tips or leads that may be of assistance in the case.

CHAPTER 20

Julia stares blankly at the newspaper clippings spread out in front of her. She's only two articles into the Jesus box, and the questions are already percolating. She's been sitting so long, the cottage is now illuminated only by the couch lamp, as the bright summer sun has dipped well below the horizon.

She picks up her wine, takes a sip, and then returns the stemmed glass to the coffee table in front of her. She retrieves more of the yellowing pieces of newsprint, digging for more articles on Allison. She finds none. The rest are about the death of Betty Ann Stark, which would take place just months later in October.

Julia's tempted to keep reading on, but given the litany of unanswered questions about Allison, she realizes she needs to focus on one murder at a time. She scans the few articles on Allison again, searching and scanning the recesses of her memory. Exhausted and confused, articles placed on her lap, Julia leans her heavy head against the floral tapestry of the sofa with eyes softly closed.

She'd spent nearly two decades trying to erase all recollection of what happened in Murdoch. So coaxing these memories back to the surface is like when her swim instructor used to stand in waist-deep water bartering with four-year-old Julia to leave the side of the pool. It's scary and exhausting.

She takes a deep breath, her brain still sorting and shuffling. Then, like a cascading fall of slick ivory dominoes, her memory gives way and reveals why there are only three articles about Allison's death in this large box of paper.

Several days after the article came out about the rumor mill, George Stark appeared at the *Messenger* office with his polished black dress shoes, pressed black slacks, and baby blue shirt with a white pencil stripe. On most occasions, Julia found him strikingly handsome but on that day what stood out was his clouded facial expression, dark eyebrows furrowed and his thin lips pursed tight.

To this day, she doesn't know the context of the conversation that went on behind closed doors in the back conference room between Dan and George. All she remembers is hearing several rises of their muffled voices, and then shortly after George's departure, Dan appeared at her desk saying they had to halt their investigation on Allison's death.

"What? That's ridiculous. Why would we do that?" Julia had quizzed emphatically.

"Because we just are." Dan replied flatly.

"But Dan...that's crazy...no one has even been arrested!"

"I don't want to be asked about it anymore." He barked back angrily. "So just drop it." With that, he turned and walked right out the door. Julia sat stunned, face reddening in anger.

Why did I just let it drop? She sits straight up on the sofa in the cottage. *Why didn't I press to keep going, especially when no one had been arrested? What did George Stark say to Dan that day to make him stop our investigation?*

Julia returns the newspapers to the Jesus box and rests her elbows on her knees, blankly staring into the empty living room. *Because I was a twenty-four-year-old reporter who did what I was told, that's why. I didn't know any better.*

Julia's thoughts snap back to the present with the realization her stomach is growling vehemently, and it's somehow nearly nine o'clock. Darkness has fallen throughout the small cottage, and she turns on every light possible on her way to the kitchen to make a salad.

Just as she's cutting her tomato, lost in a thunderstorm of thought, a loud rustle comes from outside the back window, followed by scurrying.

What the hell...she jumps, adrenaline pouring through her veins, and instinctively rushes to the sliding glass door. She quickly flips on the light, only to find a fat raccoon padding his way from the porch across the dried grass toward the river.

"See...it's just a raccoon, crazy." Julia laughs and mumbles to herself. Something about seeing the fluffy raccoon makes her think of Mr. Pickles. Jostled by the commotion, Julia once again checks all the locks, finishes her salad, and heads for a bubble bath in the claw foot tub.

◆ ◆ ◆

Julia rises early, the sun beaming through the large window in the bedroom. She's amazed at how hard she slept given the roller coaster of emotion from yesterday's visit with Nelda, drive through Murdoch, and rehashing of Allison's death.

Julia engages in her usual time of coffee and journaling and then heads out for a short run down the farm-to-market road. Drenched in sweat from the thick summer morning, she returns to the cottage full of energy and with a host of new questions.

She glances at the clock and hopes eight-thirty isn't too early to call Marilee.

"Julia?" Marilee answers on the third ring.

"Hey Marilee...how are you?"

"Well, I'm good. You sure are callin' early. Everything okay?"

"Yeah, things are good. I'm here...in town and wanted to see you guys." Julia swallows nervously.

"Here? In Murdoch?" Marilee sounds completely dumbfounded. "Why?"

"Yeah, here to start working on things."

"Oh, right..." Marilee's voice drops as she remembers the heated dialogue at the cabin last month. "So, where are you stayin'?"

"At a vacation rental...the Winding River Cottage just outside of town."

"Ohhh...the Peterson's old place."

"The Peterson's?"

"Yeah, you remember Alan Peterson...he was the JP when you were here."

"Oh, yes, of course I remember him. I didn't realize this is his place?" Julia asks the question as if she would have even known this piece of information. She'd only had a few brief conversations with the man.

"Well, it's not really his anymore. It was in the Peterson family, and after he died, his daughter fixed it up a few years ago and started renting it out."

"Oh, I see. Well, it's really cute but way back here in the sticks. So he's died? Alan?" Julia realizes that's another person she can't talk to about what happened.

"Yeah, he died last year. So...how long you stayin'?" Marilee quizzes.

"I'm not sure. I rented the cottage for a week, and I may stay longer. It just depends on how things go."

"Oh I see..." Marilee repeats herself. Clearly, she doesn't have a stream of caffeine and endorphins running through her bloodstream like Julia.

"So I wanted to see if you guys were around. Maybe for dinner this evening?" Julia feels the wave of nerves kicking up. Since their last get-together over Memorial Day, Julia's teetered on how deeply to involve Marilee and Paul.

"Yes, we'd loved to see you but we already have plans. What

about dinner tomorrow night? You could just come over to the house. I'd love for you to see it." Marilee and Paul had built a new home on two acres on the west side of Murdoch last year, of course, and Marilee's always ready to play host.

"Yeah, that works perfect." Julia rests the phone on her shoulder as she makes another pot of coffee.

"Great, I'll text you our new address. Maybe seven?"

"Sure, that's great. Need me to bring anything?"

"Just the usual. A bottle of wine." Marilee laughs.

"You got it." Julia laughs, relaxing a little, remembering Marilee isn't just another source she has to subtly pump for information. This is one of her oldest friends. She smiles. "Miss Marilee, you know I'll always be your bootlegger."

Marilee laughs harder. "Well, good. See you tomorrow."

"I'm looking forward to it." Julia smiles again. She'd always had this feeling Marilee disapproved of her, kind of like the older sister whose approval you seek but never feel like you'll get.

Julia leans her elbows on the kitchen table and looks around the room. She has no set agenda today, and now that Marilee and Paul are unavailable, she's not quite sure what to do. Just as she places her empty coffee mug in the sink, however, she knows her next move.

She pulls her laptop out. After responding to a few emails and engaging with fans on her social media accounts, she brings up *The Murdoch Messenger* online.

The paper's masthead still renders the same block letters and she smiles scanning the web page. The stories are a familiar smattering of a city council meeting recap, obituaries, and promotion of the upcoming county fair. She remembers how slow the summertime news cycle can be given that school is out for summer break.

She clicks through the miscellaneous articles, recognizing a few names here and there. Then she lands on Matt Case's email address. Next to his contact information is a two-inch square headshot, which reveals a rugged, yet symmetrical jawline framed by a crop of wavy brown hair. It's his mischievous half-smile that stands out to her, like the boy who just got caught doing something he's not supposed to.

She jots down his email address on the yellow legal pad next to her computer. If Marilee's right, and he is investigating Allison's case, then he could very well be the person she needs in her corner. Yet, until she's certain she can trust him, she knows she must keep her distance.

Julia hesitates about what to say, the blank email screen staring back at her. Don't overthink it, she reminds herself. *Keep it simple, just throw out a hook.* With that, she pecks at her keyboard to produce the note.

Hi Matt,
My name is Julia (Dixon) Jarvis, and I'm a former reporter at The Murdoch Messenger. I was on staff back in the mid-1990s and am in town a few days on business. I have a few questions that I understand you may be able to answer.

Would you have time to meet today or tomorrow?

Thank you,
Julia Jarvis

Julia reads the email again. It's definitely evasive, and it works. Not more than thirty minutes after hitting send, her cell phone rings. Matt must have retrieved her number from her email signature. She recognizes the six-zero-one area code.

"Hello?" Julia answers on the third ring.

"Julia?"

"Yes, this is Julia…"

"Oh hey, it's Matt Case…from the paper. I got your email…" His voice is deeper than she anticipated.

"Oh yes…thank you for calling so quickly. How are you today?" Julia's voice stiffens to hide the twinge of doubt in whether it's such a good idea to engage this stranger so soon, especially after Marilee's caution about him.

"I'm good. A little surprised to receive such a cryptic email from the likes of Julia Jarvis." He laughs heartily into the phone. "But how can I help?"

"Well, I'm here working on some research and don't want to get into it over the phone. I was hoping we could meet in the next few days." Julia stares down at the flowers and letters she's doodled on her notepad.

"Research, huh? What kind of research would that be?" Matt scoffs slightly.

"Yeah…" Julia clears her throat. "I'm looking into a new book."

"Well, I have to say that I loved the last one. It's not every day a *Messenger* reporter goes off and hits it big. You made our little 'ol paper proud." Matt's slow articulation, blended with that distinct Southern drawl, sounds like thick molasses.

Julia blushes in the phone. "Thank you. It was a fun book to write."

"So, is this one going to be fun, too?" Matt quizzes curiously.

Julia sucks in a quick breath. "Fun? I wouldn't say that. This one hits a little closer to home."

Matt's quiet for a moment, reading between her words. "Right. I understand. Well, listen, I'm happy to meet with you but I'm slammed this morning and have to be in Natchez this afternoon."

"What time will you be done in Natchez?" Julia decides she doesn't want to wait. She wants to find a way to meet him today.

"Around five."

"Would you be free for a drink around five-thirty or six?"

"Hmm…" Matt scans his mental calendar. "Yep, I could do six."

"Great, well I haven't been to Natchez in years, so I'll let you pick the place." Julia smiles in anticipation.

"Okay, I'll text you a place a little later."

CHAPTER 21

Matt and Julia arrange to meet at six o'clock at McCain's Cafe in the historic district of Natchez, which is the area locals refer to as "Under the Hill." As Julia waits at the thick oak table, she takes in the charm of the exposed brick walls lined with an expansive wine cabinet along the large main wall. The others are framed by an eclectic mix of old newspaper clippings of memorable Natchez events, vintage wooden wine barrels, and Rise and Shine Coffee tins. White lights twinkle overhead adding to the quaintness of the place.

A hum of murmurs and occasional laughter fill the space, which clearly serves as a cafe in the daylight and bar and grill by evening. She's glad to see that this area of Natchez has been preserved over the years, unlike so many small Southern towns whose own version of sprawl has pushed locally owned places like McCain's out of business in favor of the large chains popping up along the main highways and interstate routes.

Julia is relieved to have a few minutes before Matt arrives to gather her thoughts. For some reason, she's nervous. She glances down to adjust the long silver necklace laying against her black tank top. She didn't know what to wear, so went with her staple choice of black paired with her favorite dark jeans, cuffed at the ankle, and black strappy sandals, the ones with the shorter heel. Given how tall she is without any help, she's always aware of overpowering people, well men, upon first introduction. So she opts tonight for her lower heels. She also broke her old Murdoch rule of no makeup in the summertime and had applied just enough to subtly highlight her high cheekbones, green eyes, and full lips.

Running her right hand through the ends of her auburn mane, she picks up the happy hour menu with her left to study the wine list. Just as she scans the list of Merlots, her eye catches a tall, brawny man in blue jeans and a white linen buttoned-down shirt who appears, at least from afar, to be in his late thirties, maybe close to forty.

She recognizes him immediately and sucks in another nervous gasp as he casually strides over to her table. The headshot picture she saw online earlier this morning did little justice to depict the handsome man standing before her now.

In person, Matt's brown wavy hair is a bit longer and at one time today had been combed back but now a few waves fall forward over his forehead. The one thing she recognizes from the picture is that mischievous half-smile, which now reveals perfectly straight white teeth and illuminates his steel-blue eyes.

"Julia, nice to meet you…" He sticks out his large hand, still smiling at her, as she stands and meets it with her own.

"You too, Matt…thanks for coming." She smiles back and hangs onto his hand a moment longer than necessary. They stand awkwardly smiling at each other.

She's never believed in magnetic encounters, like in those terrible romantic comedies. She's far too cynical for that. Yet, in this moment, as she's looking at Matt, there's an undeniable energy, like when you feel that little jolt of static electricity zap you as you turn on a light switch in the winter. It startles you awake. She places her left hand on the table to steady herself as she sits back down.

"Thanks for the suggestion. This is a great place." She looks around the room and spots the waitress heading their way.

"Yeah, I guess it's new since you were probably last in Natchez. I can't imagine Natchez would be a place you'd just come visit, you know voluntarily." He winks and bellows a throaty deep laugh. His tanned face stands in contrast to his white shirt, with the cuffs rolled loosely revealing his bronzed forearms.

"No, not exactly but I've always loved the history of Natchez. It's as if you can feel the ghosts of the past everywhere you go." She smiles, grateful for the waitress's arrival.

After placing her order for a glass of the Napa Merlot and his local microbrew beer, a moment of quiet hangs between them like that uncertain silence of a first date. Though she keeps reminding herself, this isn't a date. It's a business meeting.

"So how's your visit goin'?" Matt breaks the pregnant pause.

"It's good, but I have to say it's a little strange being back after so long."

"Yeah...how long's it been?"

"Nearly twenty years." She takes a sip of water to relieve her dry throat, watching as Matt casually shifts in his chair.

"Wow yeah, so it's been awhile...but can't imagine much has changed." He smiles and studies her face.

His gaze makes her uncomfortable so Julia looks down and adjusts her clear water glass atop the paper coaster. She can feel his gaze upon her. When Julia finally looks up, they lock eyes again.

"What about you? Are you from the area?" She quizzes.

"Sorta. I grew up in Jackson and then went to Ole Miss. After college, I hopped around at papers between Louisiana and here. I've been in Murdoch...let's see...I guess goin' on just over two years."

"So how are things at the *Messenger?*" Julia looks at him curiously.

"Okay, I guess. It's kinda hard to remain relevant as a weekly paper these days. So I've been looking for more interesting things to cover...speakin' of...your message caught me a little off guard. I don't usually get such cryptic emails from bestselling authors. I have to say though, you certainly know how to write a good hook to leave a man intrigued." Matt laughs. "So I can't help but wonder what kinda 'business' brings you to town?" He tilts his head to the side and playfully smiles over at Julia.

She glances around the room nervously, collecting her thoughts.

Matt quickly catches on and leans forward to reply in a hushed tone. "Don't worry. People 'round here don't read many books so they don't know who you are." He winks and laughs at his own jest, noticing the mix of fluster and amusement on Julia's face. "Oh, I'm just teasin' but you can be candid, here."

"I know…" The waitress interrupts Julia, and she's relieved for the glass of wine. She smiles and thanks the waitress before returning to study Matt's face trying to determine what exactly she should reveal. She takes a long sip of wine before opting for the straightforward response.

"Well, I am starting to work on a new book inspired by the murders of Allison Mercer and Betty Ann Stark. So I came back to track down all the articles I wrote for the paper." Julia pauses and locks eyes with him again.

"I see…yeah you were at the paper right in the middle of all that." Matt shakes his head in disbelief. "Crazy shit…"

"Yeah, it was, but when you're living in the middle of it, you don't realize just how crazy it really is." Julia gently swirls her wine in the glass.

"I know what you mean. I covered a lot of murders in New Orleans and Jackson, but none of them were like what happened in Murdoch."

"What do you mean?" Julia's curiosity is piqued.

"Well, for starters they were both prominent white women who were murdered right in the middle of a town of only three thousand people…and for no apparent reason." Matt rests his arm on the table and leans forward slightly before continuing.

"I read your articles too, and the thing I can't figure out is why there are so few about Allison. Were more written?"

Julia shakes her head. "Nope."

"Really? Why not?" Matt's voice rises slightly.

"Because they shut me down." The few sips of wine have begun to ease Julia's nerves and she leans back in her chair.

"Who did?" Matt looks at her curiously.

"Dan Murphy." Julia offers nothing more.

"Why?" Matt's brow is furrowed in thought.

Julia shrugs. "I'm not sure, really. One day after the story about the police rumors ran, George Stark barged into the office. He and Dan got into it and then George left in a huff. Dan told me we needed to move on to other things."

"What? Are you serious? That's crazy!" Matt laughs disbelievingly. "Why would an editor stop reporting the news, especially about a young girl's unsolved murder?"

"Great questions, but I still have no idea." Julia responds flatly.

"Have you talked to Dan since you've been back?"

"No…" Julia shakes her head. "I've wondered if he was still around. We kept up for awhile after I left but then I lost touch with him. Do you know him?" Julia quizzes.

Matt takes a sip of beer before locking eyes with her. "No, not really. I mean, I know who he is and he knows me, but he's kept a pretty low profile since he tried to reopen Allison's case…"

"Wait…I thought you were trying to reopen it?" Julia looks at him confused.

"No, no. I was just curious and started poking around but I stopped pretty quick."

"Why's that?" Julia wonders.

"Because as a newcomer in town, folks don't think too kindly of you diggin' into their dirty laundry." Matt smiles.

"So then what happened with Dan? What did he find out?"

Matt hesitates. "I don't know exactly, but I do know he went and interviewed George in prison."

"Oh really? When?" Julia's curiosity grows.

"Oh I guess, it was about ten years ago...Dan released a series in the paper about his interview with George. I can't say for sure but I think he was fishin' to find out what George knew about Allison's death."

"Oh I didn't know that. I'd love to read the series. Do you have them archived somewhere?" Julia takes a sip of her wine, which is now almost empty.

"Sure, I can get you copies." Matt smiles again.

"So wait, Dan is still around town then?"

"Yeah, he is. He's retired now and not doing well from what I hear." Matt rubs the condensation on the outside of his pint glass with his index finger.

"What's wrong with him?"

"I'm not really sure exactly, but from what I've heard I don't think he's in great health."

"Oh no..." Julia pauses, concerned about her former mentor and then realizing maybe Dan won't be a viable source for her. She pushes the thought aside for now.

Matt leans in again and crosses his thick forearms on the table. "So can I ask you somethin'?"

Julia nods. "Sure."

"Why don't you think anyone's ever been arrested for Allison Stark's murder?"

"I honestly don't know. I've had so many theories over the years...but that's all they are...theories. I will say that it was strange when Betty Ann died and George was arrested. Once his trial moved into the spotlight, everything about Allison was dropped. It was like everyone forgot about her."

Matt nods thoughtfully. "That makes sense."

"Why?"

"Because it seems George ran every part of that town back then...so naturally the focus would turn to him."

Julia silently studies Matt's face. It's one of those ruggedly handsome, All-American male faces, the kind of face you'd want advertising trucks or cologne. Yet, it isn't just his looks that make Matt attractive. She finds his open, playful disposition easy to engage in conversation.

Matt breaks the silence. "It seems your husband knew him well…"

Julia flinches. "What? Who…Seth?"

"Yeah, didn't he play poker with George?"

"Poker? Seth didn't play poker with George Stark. Who told you that?" Julia laughs disbelievingly. She doesn't know where Matt retrieved that piece of information but he's clearly mistaken.

For starters, Seth was far too animated to ever keep a straight face playing poker. Not to mention, if he was out gallivanting in town, she would have known. He would have told her, and being as perceptive as she is, she would have picked up on it.

Matt looks at his beer and then up at Julia, reading her puzzled face and realizing she clearly doesn't know about Seth's poker playing. "George…George told me."

"George Stark?" Julia asks almost laughing. "How could he tell you that…isn't he still in prison?"

"Yeah, he is…" Matt nods slowly. "Actually, I went to see him, too."

Julia's words drop into her stomach. She swallows hard, the heat rising in her face. She takes a sip of wine to try and fetch her voice.

"Seth never told me about any poker games." She looks into Matt's eyes and then quickly breaks his gaze, angry that this stranger just revealed something to her that she should have known years ago.

"Well, I'm not sure many people knew 'bout them so don't feel bad. Apparently, they were all underground. Well, as under the radar as you can be in the back room of Floyd's. According to George, the games were by invitation only."

Julia racks her brain trying to remember Seth giving any indication he'd played poker, like discrepancies in their bank account or nights of coming in drunk or late. She doesn't recall anything out of the ordinary, although her memories are sometimes unreliable.

That's the thing Julia has learned about trying to recall the past after so long. It's as if her mind zeroes in on some moments and freezes them forever, making it easy to recall the sights, sounds, and smells so acutely. In other times, she swears her mind plays tricks on her, and those memories are tucked away in soft focus with no discernible edges. So it's easy to fill in the gaps with how she wants to remember the experience.

As far as she knew, Seth's time off duty was spent tending to the cattle and doing odd jobs at the Dixon farm. He also ran and worked out at the field house with Mike, and he'd occasionally take trips to Natchez to have beers with the guys. But poker in a smoky back room of Floyd's Barber Shop with George Stark? That just wasn't Seth.

"So when were these games?" Julia stares at Matt intently. "Who was there?"

"George says they happened on most Thursdays, but Seth only played occasionally. He wasn't a regular." Matt tosses in this piece of information, as he can see the irritation evident on Julia's face.

"So who were the regulars?" She presses harder.

"Well, let's see…Dave Smith, Alan Peterson, Ricky Watson, and a few other guys like Paul Johnson and Seth would rotate in and out."

After a few more focused breaths trying to calm that rush of adrenaline, Julia's pang of betrayal subsides. So she's able to absorb the information Matt just shared judiciously, and not just as Seth's widow, but as a writer.

How interesting that the mayor, justice of the peace, and more or less half the police department played secret poker games in downtown Murdoch. God, she would have loved to have been a fly on the wall in that backroom to hear those conversations.

Suddenly, the other tidbit Matt just shared fully registers. He went to see George Stark in prison.

"So back up a minute. What in the hell possessed you to go see George Stark?" Julia finishes her wine. "When?"

"Last year. I had some questions for him and the thing about guys in prison is, well, they're usually always up for visitors." Matt chuckles at his own joke.

Julia smiles. "Weren't you worried?"

"Worried about what?"

"Going to a prison to visit a convicted murderer for starters." Julia laughs softly. "Pissing off the people in town. I mean, there are still people in Murdoch who know what really happened." Julia looks away from Matt's gaze to find the waitress. Matt's just polished off his beer, and this conversation clearly calls for more drinks.

"Oh, I know there are. Murdoch is like so many small towns…where people like to keep things clean and pretty. They'd rather walk around with a mouth full of saccharin and pretend it's really sweet rather than swallow the bitterness of reality." Matt smiles slowly, revealing a dimple on the right side that Julia hasn't noticed before now.

She laughs in agreement at his assessment, interrupted by the waitress who's noticed their empty glasses. They order another round of drinks, and upon Matt's insistence, also order appetizers of fried pickles with ranch dressing and McCain's famous bayou egg rolls stuffed with sausage jambalaya and tasso ham. As soon as the waitress retreats toward the kitchen, Julia returns to conversation.
"So why did you go see George?"

"Well, my dad and George went to college together at Ole Miss. So I'd met him a few times as a kid. I was just curious more than anything."

"So your family has a history with the Starks?" Julia's taken aback, but then again, everyone knows everyone around here.

"Well, I wouldn't say we have a history. George is more of an acquaintance to me. I was just curious what he would be willing to share." Matt shrugs.

"So what did you ask him?"

"We just talked about my dad and their days at Ole Miss and then I asked him a few questions about what all happened with Allison and Betty Ann…"

"And?" Julia motions with her hand to keep going.

"I don't know. One minute I sensed he was tellin' the truth and the next he'd be sittin' eyeball deep in a heap of his own bullshit. I think he's been in prison so long he's mixed up on what's fact and what's fiction. But do I think he pulled the trigger on his wife?" Matt shakes his head. "No…I don't."

Julia pauses in thought before replying. "Honestly, I never thought so either…pull the trigger, I mean. I think he was there…and definitely involved in some way…but I don't think he had it in him to kill Betty Ann."

"Well, we aren't just talkin' Betty Ann, here." Matt leans back and pushes his hand through his hair.

"You think he had something to do with Allison's death?" Julia's always wondered about George's connection to Allison. Certainly, the girl was close with Betty Ann through the cheerleading squad and knew George through her summers working at city hall. But what possible motive would George have to kill Allison Mercer?

Matt pauses in thought. "I'm not sure but I think the people in Murdoch must think they are."

"Why do you say that? Why…" Julia's questions are interrupted by the young smiling waitress delivering their drinks, and Julia hopes the appetizers soon follow. Her stomach is knotted in a mix of hunger and nerves.

Matt smiles and thanks the waitress for his beer. He takes a sip and picks right back up. "Because the husband always takes the fall. Once George was arrested, indicted, and then convicted for Betty Ann's death, there was no need to go back and find Allison's killer. I honestly think once George was in prison, people convinced themselves they were safe again. They were satisfied."

Silence hangs in the air and Julia's mind flashes to that hot July night, the vision of Allison's black body bag on the stretcher at the football stadium. Her quiet thought morphs into indignation at the injustice of Allison's death.

"What's wrong?" Matt reads the look on Julia's face.

"I've just never understood why either of them died…and why no one was ever convicted for Allison's death. That girl was so sweet and so full of life." After reading the articles last night, the memories of Allison are fresh under the surface. She feels the tears threaten, so abruptly sits up straighter hoping to push the emotion aside. "It's why I am doing this book. I have been haunted by their deaths for years."

"And what about your husband's? Are you including his also?"

Julia's quiet for a moment. "It's a valid question…but no. I'm focused on Betty Ann and Allison right now."

"But why? His death didn't add up, either. You don't really think it was a suicide, do you?" As soon as the words tumble from his mouth, Matt wishes he could reel them back inside. He takes a big gulp of beer.

"Of course it doesn't add up. Don't you think I know that? No one leaves a party and then just randomly decides to kill himself…at least not Seth." The heat rises from Julia's belly and crawls up her chest, creating blotches of strawberry colored spots on her neck and jawline. "But let me ask you something…has anyone you've known or loved died like that? So suddenly? Just there one minute…and then POOF! they're gone?" Her raised voice evokes a few curious eyebrows from the tables around them.

The anger pouring through her is the kind that shoots emotional black ink through your veins. *Who in the hell does this guy think he is?* She's just about to gather her purse when Matt leans in to respond.

Realizing he's pushed too far, Matt's thick voice is quietly apologetic when the words finally emerge. "No, I haven't." He shakes his head slowly and then stops like a pendulum, right in the middle, those steel eyes locking on hers. "Julia, I'm so sorry. I just get carried away in the moment, sometimes…"

Julia stares back then takes a deep breath. Awkward quiet hovers over them. As the anger recoils and her defiance softens, she smiles. "Clearly, I do, too…"

"Well, you have every right to put me in my place on that one. I honestly didn't mean to upset you." His tone is still reserved, as he nervously runs his hand through the brown waves of hair falling over his forehead. "I know you didn't come here to talk about your husband."

"I don't have a husband anymore." She says flatly, partly referring to Seth, partly referring to Frank. She secretly smiles at his choice of words, *put me in my place*. Seth used to say that to her, too.

"I don't, either." Matt responds, then realizes what he's said. "I mean…a wife…I don't have a wife." His face clouds in nervous confusion.

Julia bursts into laughter. "Well, I don't mind if you do have a husband…or a wife."

Matt laughs in spite of himself. "Thanks…I guess…" He looks over at her.

Julia meets his gaze again, trying to read between his words, his energy, and his face. She's uncertain about whether she can really trust him, but something in this moment reminds her she just doesn't care anymore. She lost everything the day Seth died and now, there's nothing anyone can say or do to hurt her. As she sees the curiosity in his eyes and the way he's once again playfully smiling at her, she realizes Matt's questions weren't lined with malicious intent.

She realizes she has nothing to hide from him. "You know…honestly, I'm not investigating Seth's death right now because it would just be too much. It's hard enough coming back here as it is. Part of me wants to…has always wanted to understand what really happened. I have spent so many years wrestling with all those unanswered questions. Hell, they were more like demons…and

I've never understood why he died. After awhile, I realized I may not ever understand, so I just did the best I could to move on. I just wanted so desperately to forget what happened here..."

"But now you're back...trying to remember..." Matt says quietly.

"Yeah, I am, and it's not easy. It's like all these memories start bubbling from this deep place where I tried to lock them away years ago. The reason I became a journalist in the first place was because I was convinced the world was very black and white. I was so young and idealistic that I thought I could somehow expose those shadows to bring more justice to those who needed it."

Julia glances down and smiles remembering that young version of herself. She pauses and then meets Matt's eyes before continuing.

"Seth was like that, too. It's why he became a cop. I think he felt responsible...and by the end really guilty...that he couldn't fix what happened to Allison and Betty Ann. He loved Murdoch and everyone there. He was so distraught by Allison's death and then to have Betty Ann's murder so quickly after, and George be arrested for it, well...it nearly crushed him. Seth's family was friends with the Starks and he'd known them for years. I've never thought Seth would have taken his own life over it all, but then again, there were clearly things about him I guess I didn't know."

She looks at Matt, referring to the poker games. "Or maybe I just didn't want to know...I was only twenty-four when he died. I was so in love with him...maybe I just saw what I wanted to." Julia looks down at her wine glass and swirls the red liquid around like the thoughts churning in her head.

Matt nods slowly trying to register all that she's revealed to him. Julia's now quiet, too, wondering if she shared too much.

"Well, I admire you for comin' back. It takes a lot of courage to go diggin' into the past sometimes. I can't even imagine how hard it was to lose your husband like that. I know it's not the same...but I lost the love of my life in my twenties too. Not to death but to the son-of-a-bitch who slept with her and then stole her heart. We were engaged to get married, but she left me six weeks before the wedding. It was sheer hell gettin' over that…so I can't even imagine what you went through."

"Well, lost love is lost love…however it happens. It robs a part of your soul and you're never the same afterward. No matter how hard you try to regain that sense of yourself, it's just not there anymore." Julia looks up at him.

"See…and it's statements like that why you're the bestselling writer and I'm the hack of an editor in Murdoch, Mississippi." Matt winks. Julia blushes. And the two get lost in another hour of conversation and laughter over fried pickles and egg rolls, swapping the kind of war stories amassed by two veteran journalists.

Turns out, it's the best business meeting Julia's had in years.

CHAPTER 22

Julia's nestled in the crisp white sheets atop the cottage's antique double bed. Stretching heartily, her feet knock the black wrought iron footboard. The sun is beginning to make its morning debut through the canopy of trees, sending gentle beams of light through the cozy bedroom. Though the sun shines brighter by the minute, Julia's head is hazy after a restless night of sleep and vivid dreams. She peers up at the ceiling, mind scanning and recalling one of the dreams was about Seth.

In the years after his death, Seth had appeared in her dreams frequently. Sometimes he spoke to her and sometimes he was just there as a silent presence. The common thread of the dreams was that they were always in color and she always awoke the next day overwhelmed by sadness. She would have given anything to talk to him once more, touch him once more. Most of all, she wanted to ask him why? Why did he die?

If he had committed suicide, which she'd never fully believed, then what was causing him to suffer? How could she have missed the signs of that suffering? He had left no note or explanation. And if it was foul play, who on earth would have killed her husband? Was his death related to Allison and Betty Ann's?

Over the years, as she navigated through the grief and anger and her heart began to mend, Julia dreamt of Seth less and less. It was as if their souls had found some solace. So it's unusual to her now that he would appear again in her dreams. Though, is it?

After all, she has returned to Seth's hometown where they created their first real home as a married couple. Then last night, Matt really hit a nerve when he'd asked about researching Seth's death. She'd fielded that question before, so she isn't sure why she reacted with such anger. Perhaps it's because she's tired of people asking about investigating Seth's death, as if the thought hadn't occurred to her before now.

Julia rolls to her side and the cottage bed lets out a squeak. She grabs a pillow and hugs it close. That familiar shudder of grief suddenly ripples through her, and the tears well in her eyes. She knew coming to Murdoch would do this, would open those old wounds, especially the ones produced by all of her unanswered questions. She sighs heavily and then, as she's done so many mornings over the years, she closes her eyes and envisions putting those sad thoughts into beautiful hot air balloons and visualizes them floating away. It's one of the many little tricks a therapist had given her to practice detachment.

Julia inhales another deep breath and redirects her mind to the day ahead of her. Then, a gentle smile creeps across her lips thinking about Matt. For as angry as he had made her last night, she also laughed a lot, that kind of guttural laughter that lights up your insides like a firefly. She'd enjoyed listening to Matt's vivid tales as a reporter, and he was equally intrigued by her journey in writing *Steelhouse* and the fame afterward. They'd parted ways with an awkward handshake and ear-to-ear smiles on each of their faces.

Julia finally sits on the edge of the bed and thumps her feet onto the cool hardwood floor. She pulls down the white tank top and then yanks on the legs of the blue-striped cotton men's boxers, which had gotten bunched during her tossing and turning through the night.

It's why she never sleeps in gowns or those fancy camisoles. She's too restless of a sleeper and she loves the simplicity of men's underwear, or "man panties" as she's often called them. It's what she's slept in since college. She reaches for her tortoise shell glasses and hair tie on the nightstand table, knotting her hair into a loose bun.

As Julia stands, she sleepily looks down at her phone and sees that she's missed a series of texts from Frank. It's the first she's heard from him in weeks, and she hasn't reached out, either. She's had a feeling he would surface soon, and of course, it would be now when she's in Murdoch.

She rubs her face with her left hand, cell phone in her right and yawns again as she reads Frank's messages.

Hi Jules, how are you?
I miss you, baby. I'll be in New York tomorrow. Can we have dinner? I will be flying all day but so ready to be home. I can't wait to see you. Call you when I land. I love you.

Julia stares at Frank's message blankly and the heavy sigh she exhales is laced with both a twinge of sadness missing him and guilt in thinking about how much fun she'd had with Matt last night. She hasn't felt that lighthearted around a man in…well…she can't even remember.

Even though it wasn't a date, all she could think about on the drive back to Murdoch was she hoped she could see Matt again soon. That realization left her feeling guilty.

After brewing a strong pot of coffee, Julia settles into the overstuffed arm chair in the cottage's living room. She's tempted to go sit outside on the porch but between the sun, which is growing hotter by the minute, and the quarter-sized mosquitoes, she opts for the air conditioning.

She laughs to herself thinking about Kate's comment the other night about her being a sissy. Maybe she isn't as tough as she used to be wandering through the back roads of Mississippi in her twenties, but she's sure as hell a lot smarter.

Julia takes a sip of her steaming coffee before placing it on the whitewashed end table and plopping a puffy pillow onto her knees as a makeshift lap desk for her leather-bound journal. She taps the end of her blue ballpoint pen against her chin, thoughts beginning to rumble.

Friday, June 24

Well, it's only been a few days in Murdoch and already my head is swimming with memories and overloaded with questions. I saw Nelda, and she's aged so much. God, how I've missed that woman. I'm going to see if she wants to have lunch later today. I feel like I should see her as much as I can while I'm here.

Whether it was seeing Nelda or from the conversation I had with the new editor, Matt Case, I dreamt of Seth last night for the first time in months. He was wearing jeans and a red shirt, sitting on the tailgate of his pickup with Doc, and they were laughing at something. We didn't speak but he was there and so happy. Then I woke up. I tried going back to sleep to keep dreaming of him but I just laid there staring at the ceiling.

Part of me wonders if I haven't gone too far? I mean, the deeper I get, the harder this becomes. Well, no, not hard, as much as it is overwhelming. I haven't even begun researching Betty Ann's murder yet, and just barely started on Allison's. As I reread all that happened, it's just leading me down new paths of questioning. Most of all, it makes me wonder if it's even appropriate to continue?

This is all harder than I imagined it would be. I woke up so sad this morning thinking of Seth. I keep wondering what he would say about the book, but deep down I already know that answer. He would hate it.

After the grief passed, then came the pang of guilt in thinking about Matt Case, the handsome new editor of the Messenger. We met in Natchez for drinks last night, and I feel like he could be a big help in all of this. But then again, I'm not sure. How much do I involve the people here? Sometimes I wonder if they are assets or liabilities.

Being back here is like walking into the middle of a tornado with memories hurdling at you faster than you can blink. It's no wonder I woke up feeling stirred up and a little confused this morning. I was dreaming about Seth, started thinking about my evening with Matt, and then had texts from Frank.

It did make me a little sad to see the messages from Frank. I love him, I do. I just know it's over.

The reality is it's been over for a long time, and neither of us has had the courage to just call a thing, a thing (as Jeff always says). It's unfair to keep him hanging on. What frustrates me more is that I haven't trusted myself to just tell Frank the truth. It's been easier to pretend that everything's fine, easier to avoid the conversations about marriage, easier to not rock the boat.

In some ways, coming face to face with so many old people and memories from my past reminds me that no matter how hard I am on myself, I have grown and changed so much over the years. And maybe just like the relationship with Seth, maybe the relationship with Frank fulfilled a distinct purpose in my life. For in his own way, Frank helped me to love again.

Yet, after meeting Matt and observing the ease of our interaction, I drove away with this realization that Frank hasn't ever really understood me. He has carried some idea of me in his head and would go away for weeks and months at a time with that fantasy. I think over the years he simply came to love that idealized version of me that he constructed more than the reality of me in everyday life.

God, this is so hard. I don't want to hurt Frank, but I know it's time. I hate having that conversation over the phone, but I'm not ready to go back to New York. I'm committed to this book and committed to myself, no matter how uncomfortable or overwhelming it feels at times.

We shall see how it all unfolds...until next time...

In typical fashion, Julia scans back through her entry, and sits quietly ruminating over the insights that have just emerged. Over all the years and dollars spent on therapies, remedies, and classes to mend her broken heart, nothing has ever produced more insight or healing as journaling. Not the journaling she did as a girl about what the weather was like, who was dating whom, or the news headline of the day. Rather, Julia's journaling sessions had morphed into the type of writing that evokes the inner voice of wisdom inside us all, but we rarely hear because we're too distracted through our days.

Julia's never considered herself religious. Spiritual, perhaps, but not religious. However, on days like today it's as if God is speaking directly through her hand, channeling all the unspoken whispers of her heart onto the page so she can see them in plain sight.

Reading through her lined pages now, her thoughts merry-go-round between Allison, Betty Ann, Seth, Frank, and Matt. Just as she feels that sense of overwhelm hovering, trying to calculate every next step, she stops. Julia closes her journal, and leans her head back against the chair.

All she has to do, she reminds herself, is take the next step. For now, that's getting ready for her day. Julia rises from her chair, stretches, and then takes another sip of lukewarm coffee. She heads to the kitchen to retrieve her phone. After a call to Nelda, Julia finally coaxes her into lunch at Nine Ed's at noon. Julia promised to be at the Dixon's a little beforehand to pick her up.

Before heading to the shower, Julia stops by her laptop sitting atop the farm table to check a few emails. There's one email that immediately catches her eye with its simple subject line: "Hello." She grins and opens it first.

Good morning Julia,
I just wanted to say how much I enjoyed meeting you last night. I don't have the chance to meet women like you around here (you know, ones with all their teeth). So I really appreciated the conversation and fried pickles. If you'd like to get together to talk more about your book, I'm happy to help. I'm around most of tomorrow, so just let me know.

Matt

Julia laughs reading the email and wonders if he meant anything else by the phrase, "women like you." *Women like what? Is that a bad thing?* Her mind begins firing off questions before she stops herself.

Love is the one area where Julia's analytical, imaginative mind does her little good. Because no matter how hard she's tried, she's never outsmarted love. Not that Julia's allowing herself to get that far ahead with Matt after one dinner. It's more that feeling of nervous curiosity bordering on schoolgirl crush.

Of course she wants to see him again. She replies but opts to text him instead of email. It's less formal. Though she freezes momentarily before sending her reply wondering, is this another meeting or is it a date?

Hi Matt. Thanks for the email. I had a great time last night, too. My dentist will be happy to hear the compliment! I'm free to connect tomorrow, so just let me know what you had in mind.

As soon as she hits "send," a flash of regret follows. She really needs to talk to Frank…and soon. For now, she needs to get moving if she's going to pick up Nelda on time. If there's one thing she knows about Nelda, it's that she hates being late.

CHAPTER 23

There's something about Nine Ed's Cafe that's always tugged at Julia in that iconic way Norman Rockwell paintings always tugged at her grandma. Maybe it's the idea of a simpler time. A time when life is really lived face to face, not in a phone, and stories are really shared, not over social media, but in the way Julia believes the best stories have always been told. Over fifty-cent cups of coffee with all the free refills you could handle.

Nine Ed's has been the hub of Murdoch since Nine Ed Botnick opened the doors in 1958. Everyone knows Nine Ed (and yes, that's her given birth name because she was ninth child of Ed's). She has always been the real mayor of Murdoch.

Nine Ed knows all and sees all. Every farmer who lost a calf, every baby born at the Stark Hospital, and every funeral taking place that week at Dobb's Funeral Home. Not to mention, that even with only a seventh-grade education, Nine Ed could rattle off customers' names faster than the winner of the state spelling bee could spell M-i-s-s-i-s-s-i-p-p-i.

As Julia opens the door for Nelda, she scans the place for Nine Ed, not expecting to see her given that she should be well into her early eighties by now.

Sure enough, Nine Ed assumes a post on a stool at the cash register smiling through her cherry red lipstick and hair in her signature up-do, which is now ash white. The register still sits in the same spot in the center of the long bar covered in classic 1950s tropical green Formica.

Locals are casually perched atop the same chrome-and-opal padded barstools laughing and trading jokes, while waitresses scurry through the quaint space delivering plate-sized chicken fried steaks and baskets of burgers and fries.

A thirty-something brunette approaches them, tucking her pen behind her ear so she can shake Nelda's hand.

"Hi Mrs. Dixon, it's so good to see you!" The woman shouts over the cafe's noise, leaning into Nelda slightly. The black plastic name tag against her white buttoned-down shirt indicates her name is Heather. "What brings you out today?"

Nelda smiles broadly. "Oh, my daughter-in-law convinced me." Nelda skips the introduction and Julia's relieved. "Now tell me who you belong to again, honey."

"Charles Rawls is my daddy." Heather smiles. "But I had you for a teacher many years ago."

"Oh yes, yes of course!" Nelda smiles and wags her index finger at Heather in agreement. Julia's not sure Nelda actually remembers the woman or if she's just being polite. "Well, good to see you. We'd like to sit down now but I'd prefer a table. Can't scoot in a booth with these damn knees."

"Of course, Mrs. Dixon, right over here." Heather walks toward table, covered in the same tropical green Formica with the same padded chairs Julia sat in years ago with Seth, Kate, and Marilee.

Julia smiles, glad to see some things really do stay the same. She helps Nelda into her chair, and the two chit-chat while Nelda fields occasional greetings from locals from the beauty shop and church. With only a glance at the menu, Julia knows immediately what she wants. She proceeds to order a cheeseburger, fries, and sweet iced tea but holds the side of guilt. She might gain a pound or two while she's in Murdoch, but she doesn't care because Nine Ed's has the best burgers around.

"So didja find what you need in those articles?" Nelda quizzes Julia curiously.

"Yeah, they were all there. I started reading them but haven't finished."

Nelda shakes her head from side to side. "Still don't see why you need to do all that, honey. Just not sure how dredgin' up the past is gonna help anybody. You gotta point your feet forward and keep goin' no matter what." Nelda smiles. "But you know I said my piece...and you can do what you want."

Julia smiles. "I know, Nelda. I'm not even sure if any of this will come together in a book. But if it does, I promise you one thing...I wouldn't write anything to disgrace Seth...or you or Doc for that matter."

"Oh honey, I ain't worried 'bout that." Nelda waves her hand casually dismissing the thought. She sighs in resignation. "I just worry about you...just worry it'll be too stressful."

"I'm doing really well, actually." Julia smiles. "Coming here has been really good for me..."

Nelda smiles. "Good. I'm glad to hear it..." She reaches over and pats Julia's hands, which have been fidgeting with her paper straw wrapper. She's trying to distract herself because she really wants to check her phone to see if Matt has replied to her text. Nelda continues in an unexpected direction. "So how's it goin' with that fella...what's his name again?"

Julia drops her gaze to her hands and her voice drops as well. "Frank. His name is Frank. Things are fine. I heard from him this morning."

"You don't sound too happy 'bout that."

Julia sighs heavily thinking about to her journaling session from this morning. "If I'm honest with myself, I just realize it's not working. I know deep down it's time to end things with him. Actually, our relationship hasn't worked in a long time…but I didn't want to hurt him so I just kept hanging on." Julia sighs thinking about how hard that conversation will be. "He gets back into New York tonight, so hoping we talk soon."

"Well, I'll tell ya, if I've learned anything in all these years, it's that you can spend your whole life fixin' to do something…waitin' for some magical moment to be happy. You gotta be happy now because life is short and unpredictable. You never know if the moment you've got in front of you will be your last one. So you gotta make it count. If this Frank fella isn't the one to bring you happiness, then you gotta let him go. Find the man who you can be happy with. For all his faults…and God knows we fought like the dickens sometimes…Doc was the one man who could always make me laugh." Nelda's eyes briefly cloud thinking about her late husband, who she still misses terribly.

Julia smiles at Nelda's wisdom. "I know…you're right." Her words dip into her stomach, into that well of guilt she's carried for so long about living on after Seth.

She had carried that survivor's guilt everywhere, from the European vacations to the bestseller's list to laughing in the bed with Frank in the wee hours of the morning. While she had eventually grown accustomed to life without Seth, life as a widow, dragging around the guilt often left her exhausted.

So that feeling of happiness Nelda speaks of hasn't truly existed for Julia. Any time she would allow herself to momentarily forget, to really laugh, to be in the moment, and to truly enjoy life, it was as if a little voice would pop up unexpectedly and remind her that Seth was gone.

Studying Nelda now, she wonders if perhaps Nelda is right. Perhaps holding onto that guilt had just become a safety measure to keep life at arm's length away. She's not sure but she is relieved that their food comes quickly. They eat in silence for a bit, Nelda catching glances of Julia's face, searching her as if she's reading her thoughts. For as much as she's aged physically, Nelda is still mentally sharp as a tack. Finally, Nelda breaks the quiet.

"You know, honey, I know you don't need me to say this but you know I will anyway...and probably should've a long time ago." She looks squarely at Julia. "You've got my permission to find that happiness again." Nelda smiles and squeezes Julia's hand.

Julia returns the smile, enjoying the sweet exchange amidst the raucous lunch conversations and rattling plates. Neither of them notices the stocky man in the police uniform approaching the table.

"Well...hello Mrs. Dixon." Ricky Watson's booming voice startles both women. Julia looks up to see a man slightly resembling the cocky young officer she remembered. About the only thing the same about Ricky is his metal name badge and his blue Murdoch Police Department uniform.

The rest of Ricky's body looks as though it was put into a steamer and puffed up a good fifty pounds, which at five-foot-ten, bloats his already thick frame. The bottom buttons of his uniform strain to stay in place over his round belly and his arms bulge even more, with a black sports watch and gold wedding band creating indentations in his skin. Ricky's square head still sports a flattop haircut, though his brown hair has been nearly completely outpaced by sprigs of gray. His eyes crinkle at the edges as he smiles at Nelda, his curled lips revealing yellowish teeth from all the snuff he's dipped over the years.

Julia stiffens at the sight of him, a pang of anxiety underlies the hamburger in the pit of her stomach. Ricky is the one person Julia hoped to avoid while in town. She made it clear years ago to Seth she didn't respect Ricky.

Back then, he was a stereotypical meathead cop, the kind who just loved to throw his badge around because he could. Every now and then, Seth would chime in and complain about Ricky, too, especially at how much Ricky was favored by Chief Smith and

George Stark. The rest of the time Seth remained neutral.

As the days ticked by after Allison and Betty Ann's deaths, the cord of dissention in Seth and Julia's conversations deepened when it came to Ricky and the murders. Julia had been shut down by Dan in investigating any further who killed Allison and the town was convinced George killed his wife.

Yet, it didn't Julia her from peppering her husband with questions, usually at random times Seth wasn't suspecting, like on a random drive to Natchez for dinner or over coffee in the morning as he read the paper.

It wasn't that Julia wanted to catch Seth off guard. It was more that she just couldn't bury what happened to Allison and Betty Ann like everyone else. For Julia, witnessing their untimely deaths had been like watching a movie with no ending, and the questions didn't go away over time, they simply simmered underneath the rhythm of her life.

Seth deflected most of Julia's questions easily, but when it came to Ricky, Julia always noticed that Seth's body language changed. He squirmed like a kid on the front-row pew at church, becoming shifty and uneasy and always wondering if he was being watched.

"Why do you always defend him?" Julia had demanded one night over a steaming plate of spaghetti. It was during the middle of George's trial, and she was pressing Seth again as to why no one was questioning Ricky and George's connection.

Seth hardened at the accusation. "I don't defend him."

"Well, you certainly don't seem willing to push to get answers…and we both know that Ricky is as dirty as they come." Julia retorted.

"What the hell do you expect me to do?" Seth barked back. "My hands are tied. Ricky has seniority over me and he's Smith's golden boy. George is on trial for his life, and I'm just trying to stay out of it all and do my job. But God knows, you don't make that any easier. You know damn well I cannot sit here with you every night and talk to you about all this shit. So just drop it!"

They finished their meal in silence and didn't really speak until the next morning. Julia had glared intently at him that night over dinner, trying to read his thoughts and piece together what Seth really knew and wasn't telling her. In the days after, she softened her approach, though it led her nowhere. In fact, the more time passed, the more Seth withdrew.

After Seth died, Julia spent endless nights pacing and sobbing in her studio apartment wondering what he knew, especially about Ricky. What was really going on at the police department? What was so dark, so oppressive that it could have forced Seth to kill himself? Or did he also find out something he wasn't supposed to, and like Allison and Betty Ann, it got him killed? Was Ricky Watson at the center of all three deaths?

Between the cloak of grief, profound regret, and litany of unanswered questions, there were times after Julia moved to New York, she swore she was losing her mind. There were a few brief moments in the midst of that grief that she was convinced she couldn't even go on living, for that grief was strangling her ability to see or think or feel anything other than guilt.

Over time, however, and with the right therapist, she began to emerge from the depths of her grief and slowly tip-toe back into the land of the living.

Now on this sweltering summer day as Ricky looms over her table at Nine Ed's Cafe, Julia's body swiftly recalls that anguish and nausea washes over her.

"And who's your pretty lunch date?" Ricky looks over at Julia with a wide grin and gleaning eyes, slightly leaning over the table with his puffy hand outstretched.

"Oh you remember Seth's wife, Julia?" Nelda responds before Julia can say a word.

Ricky stiffens and awkwardly drops his hand as if he's encountered a ghost. Julia breathes a sigh of a relief at not having to actually touch him.

"Yeah, of course, how could I forget Miss Julia." His pudgy, confused face forces a smile.

Julia swallows hard to steady her voice. "Hi Ricky…"

"So what brings you to town? Just here visitin'?"

"You know she's a famous writer now." Nelda never misses a beat, smiling proudly. "So she's here workin' on her new book."

Julia's hamburger once again threatens in her gut. She shoots Nelda a look but Nelda doesn't catch it because she's looking up at Ricky.

"A book, huh? What kinda book?"

"Oh, she's writin' about all that mess that happened here." Nelda clearly isn't getting the glares Julia's shooting across the table. Julia turns ashen white. *Well, there it is. Damn'it Nelda.* She swallows hard and freezes again without saying a word.

"And what mess is that?" Ricky asks curiously.

"Why, those two murders and all that business." Nelda waves her hand dismissively as if shooing a fly hovering the table.

Ricky's face flushes red behind his tanned skin, weathered from too many days spent in the sun.

"Ahh…I see." Ricky responds slowly, then squares his fat head Julia's direction, squinting his beady eyes even narrower. "Now why'd you want to go and do that? That was a long time-go."

Julia's face feels like it might burn off, it's grown so hot. *What in the hell would possess Nelda to just blurt that out? And to Ricky Watson of all people? Maybe she really is senile?*

Julia swallows again, glances at Nelda, and then opts for the brush off. "Well, I don't exactly know if I'm writing a book about it."

Ricky grazes the back of his hand across his upper lip, wiping away the beads of sweat, never taking his eyes off Julia. He grunts lowly before responding. "Well, I'd be careful, if I were you. I reckon most of the people 'round here would rather let that lie. Those were some tough days for Murdoch."

"Oh I remember." Julia looks at him, a surge of adrenaline shifting her fear into a fight. "It was tough for us, too. Seth probably hardest of all."

Ricky glares at her but stops himself from saying anything more. Instead, he glances down at his watch. "Well, I'd best be gettin' back to it. Good to see you Mrs. Dixon…and you too Julia." Ricky half smirks, spins, and leaves their table before Julia and Nelda can properly bid him farewell.

"That was a surprise." Nelda looks at Julia as Ricky heads out the door.

Julia collects herself before responding. "Yeah, I haven't seen him in years. I didn't recognize him…but Nelda, I wasn't really planning on telling the whole town I'm working on this book. You just said you worried about me writing it. So why would you tell Ricky about it?"

Nelda chuckles. "Well, honey, you know in this town everyone's gonna find out your business whether you want them to or not. So I made it a policy a long time ago to just tell the truth. Then they hear it straight from the horse's mouth."

"Yeah but Ricky is probably the last person in this town who needs to know about this book."

"Oh, why's that?" Nelda looks at her curiously.

Julia leans across the table and lowers her voice. "Because I've never trusted him."

Nelda takes another bite of her chicken wrap, apparently deep in thought. Julia's not sure Nelda heard her.

Finally, Nelda nods her head slowly. "Yeah, I understand that. I gotta say, there's always been a little something off about him. I just never figured out what."

"Me either." Julia looks toward the door. "I can't believe he's still on the police force."

"Oh well, you know he's the chief now…and honestly everyone wonders how he got that job."

"He's the chief?" Julia looks at Nelda stunned. *That snake Ricky Watson is now the chief of police?*

"Yeah, he's been chief goin' on…let's see…" Nelda looks up to the ceiling in thought. "Guess three or four years or so now."

Julia can't believe Marilee didn't share this with her before. "I didn't realize that. Well, I've just never liked him. I mean…he certainly didn't make Seth's life any easier on the force."

Nelda scoffs. "Ain't that the truth. Ricky bullied Seth when they were kids. I always thought it was because he was just jealous of Seth, but I taught my boy to turn the other cheek. No sense gettin' all in a twit about someone like Ricky Watson, especially because I knew years ago that poor boy never had a chance in life."

Julia's lost her appetite. She pushes her plate away and changes the subject. After their lunch, Julia takes Nelda home where they continue their visit over a cup of coffee, though Julia's mind wanders back to the conversation with Ricky earlier. As much as she wants to visit with Nelda, she cannot stay focused, so she finally excuses herself.

Like with their last meeting, Julia promises to see Nelda again soon. This time, however, Nelda also adds an, "I love you, honey" as they hug good-bye.

CHAPTER 24

Before Julia even pulls out of the Dixon's farm, the date with Matt is confirmed. He had responded soon after she texted him earlier this morning wanting to know if she's interested in going to the Natchez Food & Wine Festival. He had added that it's one of his favorite events, which Julia finds a bit surprising. She had taken him for more of a crawfish boil kind-of-guy. They planned to meet at the *Messenger* office at four o'clock tomorrow.

Between the lunch with Nelda and the thought of seeing Matt, Julia smiles and sings at the top of her lungs to the classic rock station along her drive back to the cottage. She laughs remembering how she, Kate, and Marilee used to tear through the back roads listening to what Julia considers the true classic rock, that of the 1970s. Now, it's a bit depressing to realize all the songs that were actually popular when she was in college and lived in Murdoch in the nineties are now considered "classic rock."

Just as Julia turns on the dirt road leading up to the Winding River Cottage, her phone rings.

"Hello…" Julia smiles.

"Hey gurl! Whatcha doin'?" Kate's voice is bright as usual.

"Hey! Just getting back to the cottage…had lunch with Nelda at Nine Ed's."

"Nine Ed's...that place is still open?" Kate laughs.

"Oh yeah, and Nine Ed was there working the cash register. God, she has to be close to eighty now."

"Hell, she was eighty when we were there, wasn't she?" Kate laughs harder. "So what's been happenin'?"

"Well, I ran into Ricky Watson at the diner. He didn't even recognize me." Julia unlocks the front door of the cottage and tosses her purse on the table as she passes by. She heads straight to the sofa, kicks off her black flip flops, and then drops onto the couch. "He's probably gained forty or fifty pounds. He's so gross...he's always creeped me out."

"Oh dawg, I know. I hated it when he used to come into city hall all the time."

"Yeah, tell me more about that...I'm not remembering why he was always there. He didn't really need to be."

"Honestly, I don't really know...he was just always sorta snakin' around. He'd wander off to George's office...and then come out and make sure we all knew he was there. He used to eye Allison when she worked there in the summers. Honestly, he's always been a little pedophile-like, if you ask me."

Julia laughs at Kate's description. "It's interesting you say that...do you remember that there were rumors of a police car being seen around the pool the day Allison went missing?" Julia rests the phone on her shoulder and ties her hair up in a loose bun. The sun is blazing today and her hair feels like a blanket on the back of her neck. As she sweeps up her mane, a few damp, loose strands curl slightly at the base of her neck. Julia can hear Kate thinking on the other end of the line.

"Hmm...yeah, I do remember that. But nothing ever came of it, right?"

"Nope. In fact, I'd forgotten...but there were only a few articles about Allison's death and then George shut us down."

"Oh, that's right! I remember how pissed you were about that! I

187

also remember right after that article came out about the police rumors, Ricky came by to see George one afternoon. They got in a big fight, and I don't know what happened but one of them musta slammed something because this loud racket came from George's office. Ricky came stormin' outta there mad as a hatter."

Julia pauses, absorbing this information, passing it through her brain to see if it dings another memory. She doesn't remember Kate ever telling her about Ricky's visit that day, and she wouldn't forget a piece of information like that.

"I wonder what they were meeting about? Could you hear what they were saying?" Julia quizzes.

"No, we just all sorta kept on workin' but it was definitely tense in that office. George was pissed for a good while afterwards."

Julia pauses, thoughts rolling around. She recalls the startled look on Ricky's face when Nelda mentioned the book. She repeats the question aloud she and Kate have both wondered for years.

"So tell me…as a lawyer…do you think Ricky did it? Do you think he killed Allison?" She leans back heavily, feeling the tiredness encroach after her restless night of sleep and the heaviness of Nine Ed's cheeseburger. She glances at the white clock on the wall. It's just after three, and she's relieved that she'll have a little time to nap before heading to Marilee's for dinner.

"I don't know gurl. I really don't. They never produced any motive or evidence linking him…or anyone…to the murder."

"Yeah, but did they even look for evidence? They stopped that investigation before it even began. That's the thing I still don't get. Was it premeditated? And if so, why? How could Allison Mercer possibly be a threat? And why did everyone just let it go and never push to arrest anyone?" Julia's swirl of unanswered questions come tumbling out.

Julia pulls the overstuffed throw pillow onto her lap and rests her elbows on it, brain gnawing on all the tidbits of information trying to formulate some semblance of order. There isn't any.

Kate must be doing the same because there's a long silence. "Maybe she did find out something about George or maybe about Ricky? Maybe George was in some sort of trouble? But how would Allison have known about it?"

"Hmmm...." Julia rubs the side of her forehead with her index finger in thought. "Maybe...I don't know."

"I think you just have to keep diggin' gurl. Have you started looking into Betty Ann's case?"

"No...not yet. It was too overwhelming so I just focused on one at a time. But I think I may start reading the articles tomorrow." Julia glances over at the Jesus box sitting on the table.

"Look, gurl, I know you want to figure this all out. I know as well as anyone that having all these little minute details of a case, with no clear path to a solution, can just make you plum crazy. But if I've learned anything in all these years of practicing law, it's that sometimes things just don't snap together like a jigsaw puzzle. You have to learn to make associations and at the same time be okay in the ambiguity. Somehow, taking that approach has always led me to the next piece of information I need. I've always thought about it like seeing at night with your car headlights...like when we used to drive down the Natchez Trace through the fog. The car's headlights would only light up the next hundred yards. So you just have to keep trustin' that the next hundred will reveal itself...and then the next. So maybe for you, it's not so much about figuring out how it all fits together. Maybe it's just about finding the kernel of the story you wanna tell and then create the rest. Just tell a good story, gurl. You clearly know how to do that."

Kate's words sink in, but Julia still isn't satisfied with that answer. "Thanks...and I guess you're right. It just feels like it should all make sense..." She sighs heavily in resignation. "I thought coming back here after so many years would give me more clarity...and make it easier to see how it all connects."

"Yeah...I know...but sometimes things just don't fall together in the way we think they should." Kate pauses, then shifts gears. "So what'd Ricky say when you saw him?"

"Well, Nelda piped off and told him I was there writing a book. He's the last person I wanted to know I was in town, let alone working on this book."

Kate gasps. "Shut up...she didn't!"

"Yeah, you know Nelda. She said everyone was going to find out anyway, so they might as well hear it from the source."

Kate laughs. "Well, I guess...but still...that's not something you want to go parading around town. So what'd Ricky say?"

"He just stood there with this dumb look on his face and warned me I should leave it alone. Then he turned and left...and that was about it. I wish she hadn't said anything. You know how I feel about him."

"Well, I wouldn't worry. We both know he's not the sharpest tool in the shed, and I'm sure he gets dumber by the day, too. I just can't believe he's still there...and he's still a cop?"

"Oh, he's not just a cop, Miss Kate." Julia deepens her voice and fakes a Southern accent like Ricky's. "He's the chief 'o po-leece."

"What?! You're kiddin' me." Kate laughs in disbelief.

"Nope, I'm serious."

"Damn gurl. That's crazy. So what about that editor...you talk to him? What'd he have to say about all this?"

"You mean Matt Case? Yeah, I met him last night for drinks in Natchez...and seeing him again tomorrow for the food and wine festival." Julia giggles like a schoolgirl.

"What a minute, gurl. That doesn't sound like work...that sounds like a DATE!" Kate's voice billows as she howls with laughter. "How could you not tell me this first? Screw Ricky Watson...tell me about Matt Case. Who is he? Where's he from? What's he know?"

Julia laughs at Kate's playful interrogation. "It's not a date...I don't think. He's just helping me with my research..."

"Oh, I'm sure he is, gurl…" Kate cackles.

"He's been in Murdoch a few years and has been a reporter at multiple papers between Mississippi and Louisiana. You know, his dad bought the *Messenger*."

Kate interrupts again with a laugh. "I don't want his resume…what's he look like?"

"Somewhere between Jude Law and Matthew McConaughey."

"Day-um, gurl. And he's single?"

"Yeah, based on what he said, he is. I'm not sure how someone so good looking could be at his age." Julia pictures Matt's wavy hair and those eyes. She smiles.

"Is he gay?"

"Noooo, he's not gay." Julia laughs.

"Well, I'm sure those women 'round there probably stick to him like flypaper."

Julia laughs harder at Kate's analogy. "Yeah, I was a little nervous during our meeting last night. I mean, he is gorgeous…but we just had this energy. I can't explain it. But it was really nice…he seems like a good guy."

"Gurl, it's called sexual tension." Kate teases.

"Well, I don't even remember what that is." Julia says half teasing, half truthful.

"So you're seeing him again tomorrow? How's Frank feel about that?"

Julia grows quiet. "Yeah, I am. Actually, Frank doesn't even know I'm here. He texted me this morning that he gets into New York later tonight."

"Well, what are you gonna tell him? I mean, are you gonna tell him you're in Murdoch?"

"Yeah, I will." Julia's voice drops again, uncomfortable at the thought of having that conversation with Frank. She sighs heavily.

"I know I need to talk to him. I mean, this relationship is over, and we need to go our separate ways. I realized this morning as I was writing in my journal that I've just been sitting here all this time waiting for another outcome, a different way to end things…an easier way. But all I'm doing is wasting time."

"Oh now, no relationship is a waste of time. Frank is a good man. Maybe it's just more that the relationship has served its purpose…and it may be over for you, Jules, but is it over for him?"

"No…I don't know…surely he knows this isn't working. We haven't communicated more than a few random emails and texts for almost eight weeks. We never see each other…barely have sex. I love him, and I know he means well. But it's just ridiculous to even call whatever this is a relationship. He says he wants to marry me, but deep down clearly he doesn't want anything more either or he wouldn't jump at the next assignment that takes him right out of New York. The truth is, I'm just *done*." The heat in Julia's body matches the rising crescendo of anger in her voice, which catches her by surprise.

Sure, she's tapped into the disappointment and frustration over Frank, but she hadn't fully dipped into the well of anger. As the honesty emerges with Kate, and Julia expresses what's been stirring within her, she realizes that it's been the anger that she's tried to keep at bay. For how long, she's not sure, but a good while.

Anger about the half-hearted relationship with a man who's been completely absent. Anger at herself for blindly playing along for over six years of her life, thinking it was somehow okay to never be with or sleep with the man you've committed to. Anger at not giving voice sooner to the nudges and whispers she'd felt stirring within her but shrugged off and ignored.

It all sat in stark contrast to the open feeling evoked when she saw Matt or even thinks of him. After only one meeting, she's not naïve enough to assign any real meaning to their exchange or pending get-together.

Maybe Kate's right. Maybe it's just sexual tension and that's why it feels so exciting. But there was also something effortless in their interaction last night, this openness and ease that she'd only ever felt with Seth. She's not sure what that means.

What's clear is that the illusion has been dismantled about Frank, and when that happens, it's not only disturbing, it's infuriating to see the aftermath of your denial.

"Sounds to me like you know exactly what to do about Frank." Kate says quietly. "It's time to tell him what you just told me. I mean, I've always thought some love is like a big fireworks finale and other love is like Crock-Pot love...it's low and slow. Sounds like you are done with the slow-cooker and ready for some fireworks, gurl."

Julia's bubble of anger bursts into laughter. Kate always knows what to say to bring Julia back to herself.

"Yeah, maybe I am. We'll see...but first I have to get through dinner with Marilee and Paul tonight." Whether from the wave of anger or the fluffy pillow on her lap, Julia's now sweating and tosses the pillow on the couch.

"Oh good, you're gonna see them. Wish I could be there! Yawl goin' over to Natchez?"

"No, just doing dinner at their new house. Haven't seen since I've been here, so it will be interesting."

"Well gurl, tell them I said 'Hi.' I better run finish up so I can get outta here. Jennifer's home for the summer so we're doing family dinner tonight."

"Okay, sounds good...hug her for me. And thanks for calling...I always feel better after talking to you." Julia smiles.

"Anytime...and promise me you will call tomorrow after your hot DATE." Kate says loudly followed by a laugh.

"I promise. Love you."

"Love you too, gurl."

CHAPTER 25

Refreshed from her nap, Julia follows her phone's navigation to Marilee and Paul's new house, which sits a few acres west of Murdoch toward Natchez at the top of County Road 1411.

She's lost in a merry-go-round of thought wondeing how this evening will go with Paul and Marilee. She hasn't seen Paul in years, and the exchange with Marilee at the cabin last month didn't go quite as she planned. More than anything, she's unsure how deep to dig with Paul and Marilee, given Paul is mayor and Marilee's allegiance has always been to Betty Ann Stark. As she turns down the narrow road leading up to the Johnson's house, she opts to just see where the evening goes.

Julia pulls up to a massive two-story brick home edged with mocha-colored wood trim and a beautiful stained glass front door. The wrap-around porch overlooks a large thicket of trees cascading down the hill and two welcoming rocking chairs await visitors on the front porch. It's exactly the type of home Julia envisions Marilee and Paul would build.

Before she can even gather her purse and bottle of wine, a squatty basset hound lumbers off the porch and greets her at the car door barking in a low muffled tone.

"Charlie!" Marilee yells as she heads out the front door then smiles and waves at Julia. "Charlie stop it! Get over here." Marilee motions wildly as if Charlie were a kid.

Charlie doesn't budge. "Rar-rar-rar-ruf-ruf. Ruf. Ruf." His bark makes Julia laugh. He's like an old lawn mower that's not quite sure it wants to start.

"Damn'it get over here!" Marilee yells again, as she walks down the steps in her white shirt with a long colorful turquoise-and-silver necklace and denim capris pants. Of course, her outfit is complete with shimmering aqua-and-white rhinestone-studded flip flops. Marilee always sparkles. Her black hair looks even bigger than before. But like they say in the South, "the bigger the hair, the closer to God," and let's just say Marilee's always been real close.

Julia finally squeezes out of the car door but Charlie still isn't having it. She's pinned now between her rental and Charlie. "It's okay Charlie." She says in a sweet tone, all the while muttering to herself, *Damn dog. I hate dogs. Mr. Pickles would never do that to a guest.*

Of course, Mr. Pickles rarely leaves his post on the sofa except to eat and use the litter box. Julia hopes Jeff's been cleaning it regularly. She knows she needs to call him but just hasn't had the time. She's a little surprised she hasn't heard from him, either, but assumes he's busy. That's always been their way, going days and weeks without talking and then picking right up and talking every day. It's a rhythm of friendship that suits them.

"Haaay Julia!" Marilee waves again.

"Hey! Some watchdog you have here." Julia laughs as Charlie finally relents and saunters back to the porch, ears flopping with each stride, and occasionally producing a singular, "Ruf," just to remind Julia he's still watching her.

"That blasted dog. He's a pain in the butt but Paul loves him." Marilee laughs and hugs Julia tight. She pulls away and glances at Julia's skinny jeans, black strappy sandals, and purple tank top. Despite the heat, her hair spills over her slender shoulders, and the shimmering evening sun sets her auburn mane aglow. "You look great, gurl."

"Thanks." Julia smiles. "So do you."

"Come'on in. I see you brought my favorite." Marilee points to the bottle of Merlot in Julia's hand.

Julia laughs. "Why of course. I know you're supposed to drink white in the summer months, but every time I drink white wine, it feels like someone stabs the corkscrew in my forehead."

Marilee laughs. "I know whatcha mean. Though in the summer I do add a cube of ice to my glass of red. I know that'd make the wine snobs in Napa cringe but I don't care."

"I love your house. It's beautiful…" Julia glances around the large open kitchen with stainless steel appliances, beige-and-charcoal granite countertops, and coffee-toned hardwood floors. The kitchen spills into the dining area and great room, which of course, has a massive flat-screened TV for Paul to watch his football games. He and Seth never missed a game, college or pro.

"Thanks, yeah we are finally settled in. You know we'd lived in that same house for over fifteen years and amassed so much stuff. I got rid of tons."

"Yeah, I've been in my condo for nearly ten and cannot imagine trying to pack and move." Though glancing around this spacious home, with no Lucas living upstairs playing his horrible music, makes Julia a bit envious. Not to mention she probably paid quadruple for her eleven-hundred-square-foot, two-bedroom condo in Manhattan for what Paul and Marilee paid for this plot of land and custom-built, four bedroom home.

"Well, looky who's here!" Paul appears from the back of the house. He looks much the same to Julia, still tall and handsome though his midsection is a little rounder and his brown hair is graying at the temples. Julia can smell his aftershave as he envelopes her in a bear hug.

"Good gracious, I haven't seen you in what…four or five

years?" Paul booms as he pulls away and looks at Julia. "Still beautiful as always."

"Awww...thanks." Julia smiles at her old friend. "Yeah, I guess it's been since that summer we all met at your cabin."

"You mean that *one* summer yawl let me, Jerry, and Frank come along on your secret girls' trip." Paul lets out a hearty laugh. "Well, sure is good to see you." He walks around to the other side of the bar top, where Marilee is still uncorking the wine, and pecks his wife on the lips. She smiles up at him.

"Want some?" She asks about the wine. He shakes his head and heads to the fridge for a cold beer.

"You know I can't drink wine in the summer. It just makes me even hotter." He playfully fans himself and winks at Marilee.

"Why if you got any hotter Paul Johnson, you might just catch on fire." She laughs as does Julia.

Paul and Marilee have always been Julia's Southern version of Ken and Barbie. Not only are they both strikingly attractive as all power couples seem to be. With Paul and Marilee, however, there's something more. It's something about the easy way they interact and respect each other, which is evident in their exchanges.

Julia had asked Marilee years ago if they ever fought, and Marilee admitted that they'd had a few yelling matches and a rough patch after Paul's father died. After so many years together, however, they'd come to a general sense of agreement. They knew when to press issues and when to let up and go to their respective corners. "Even though we're both stubborn as the dickens, we know when to compromise." Marilee had added with a laugh.

Seeing them together now, Julia can't help but wonder if she and Seth would have been that way. If they would have mastered the dance of marriage to the same degree...or would they even still be together? She looks down and smiles wistfully, as she'd never considered until this moment that they might not even be together if he were alive.

Over the next hour, Julia's relieved the conversation is light. Paul wants to know all about Frank, their pending split, and what it's like to be a famous author living in New York. Of course, Julia and Marilee spend a little time catching up on Kate, reminiscing, and laughing. They're casually gathered around the large mahogany table simply adorned with a fresh bouquet of chipper sunflowers, all standing happily at attention, and surrounded by an assortment of votive candles.

Their delicious meal of grilled salmon on brown rice and spinach salad topped with walnuts, pears, and goat cheese is long gone. Marilee adds with a laugh that the healthy meal would be completely negated by the peach cobbler and vanilla ice cream she'd made for dessert.

But before Marilee can even serve it, Paul looks squarely at Julia and draws a sip of his third beer. "So tell me 'bout this new book..."

And here we go, Julia sighs as she pushes back her chair and crosses her long legs under the table. She had known it was only a matter of time, and after splitting a bottle of wine with Marilee and heading into their second, Julia finds no need to mince words.

"Well, there's not much of a book right now. I'm just here gathering some research." She matches Paul's inquisitive gaze before pushing the throttle wide open. "Actually, I'm still trying to figure out how Allison and Betty Ann's murders were connected."

"So you think they were?" Paul raises an eyebrow, his tone somewhere between a question and an accusation.

Marilee says nothing and looks over at Julia.

Julia glances at Marilee and then back over to Paul sitting at the head of the table, with Julia and Marilee on either side. "Yes...I think so. I'm just not quite sure how. The only thing I do know is that there was no motive established for either death." Julia's intonation on the word death echoes slightly in vast room with its fourteen-foot-vaulted ceiling.

"You know, the Mercers tried to reopen the case about ten years after Allison died." Paul responds matter-of-factly.

"Yeah, I'd heard that...is that when Dan did the series in the paper with George?" Julia curiously peers back at him.

Paul looks confused wondering how Julia would have known about Dan's interviews. "Yeah, I believe it was about that same time. Have you seen those newer articles?"

"No...not yet. So whatever happened to the Mercers?"

"I'd heard they moved somewhere in the Midwest..." Marilee chimes in.

Julia studies her friend, trying to gauge Marilee's wine barometer. Marilee's always been a bit of a dicey drunk. Sometimes she's hilariously happy and others she's downright angry. Julia quickly realizes she also needs to slow down so she can make it back to the cottage safely. The last thing she needs is a DWI hand delivered by chief 'o po-leece Ricky Watson.

"So, no one's heard from them? The Mercers?" Julia quizzes again.

"Nope." Paul replies. "Truth be told...no one seemed to care about bringing justice for that girl's death once George Stark went to prison. They just let it go."

Julia scoffs. "Yeah, and that's what bothers me the most. I was a reporter trying to cover news in a town that would rather pretend bad things could never happen here. They weren't really interested in the truth."

Paul laughs. "Well, and that hasn't changed."

A pause hangs over the conversation and Marilee stands uncomfortably. "Yawl want dessert now?"

"Sure honey, that'd be great." Paul smiles and Marilee squeezes his broad shoulder as she walks by.

Julia takes the time out in the conversation to visit the half-bath down the hall. The wine has snuck up on her so she's glad to see the mound of hot cobbler with a hefty scoop of melting ice cream on top when she returns to the table. Maybe it will soak up some of the alcohol.

After she and Paul take turns complimenting Marilee's peach cobbler, Julia moves right back into the conversation. It's the question that she's been wanting to ask Paul all night. "So Paul, tell me what happened at those secret, backroom poker games? Seth never told me he played poker…"

Paul coughs as he's trying to swallow his cobbler. "Guess they weren't so secret…"

Julia darts her eyes at Marilee. "Did you know about them…or was I the only one left out?"

"Yeah, Paul told me, but not until after he stopped playing." Marilee nods and shoots a displeased look Paul's direction.

"So what was happening at those games that you couldn't tell your own wives?" Julia returns her heated gaze back to Paul, as a wine-induced flash of annoyance crawls up the back of her neck making her face flush.

"Nuthin'…I don't know…" Paul shrugs his broad shoulders. "The usual stuff that happens at poker games. You know…talkin' trash…smokin' cigars…drinkin' whiskey…that kinda stuff.'" Paul shifts in his chair and takes a swig of beer. "Honestly Julia, back then Seth and I were just two kids doing what we thought we were supposed to if we wanted to be considered leaders in this town. There was a lot of shit happen' back then, and you wanted to be on the right side of things. We just subbed in here and there at those games. We weren't regulars, and we knew to keep our heads down."

Julia absorbs his explanation and zeros in on one phrase. She wants to know more. "What kind of shit are you referring to?"

"Well, the drugs for starters." Marilee surprisingly interjects before Paul can respond. He looks over at his wife, eyes narrowing to see where she's going with her words.

"So that was true?" Julia interrupts from across the table. "I'd heard rumors about the drug ring but could never find a source willing to come forward and talk to us at the paper...especially when all that came out about the stolen cash during George's trial. And how he kept the cash in case high school kids needed a loan. I mean...seriously? He had to be involved in all of that, right?"

"This whole thing is like peeling an onion. Just makes you want to cry before you can slice the damn thing to get to the heart of what's true." Marilee somehow avoids slandering George or verifying the rumor. Julia knows her friend well enough to know that when Marilee changes the subject with one of her Southern sayings, she's usually covering up something. So she makes a mental note to ask Matt about the drugs and George's involvement tomorrow and lets that thread of questioning go.

Julia stirs the melted ice cream in her nearly empty bowl. "I know...it's hard to even know what's true between all the rumors and vague memories. Hell, half the people I would need to interview for this book are dead."

Paul looks at Julia pensively. "Well, now Julia there's plenty of folks 'round here who are alive and kickin' and know what really happened...more than they'd ever care to admit. The rest have their theories..."

"And which camp are you in? Do you know what really happened or do you just have theories?" Julia smiles at Paul. He doesn't smile back. His brown button eyes look hazy, perhaps from all the food, the beers, the conversation, or maybe from the heaviness of all three combined. He quietly stands to retrieve another beer.

Paul spins around from the refrigerator and tosses the beer cap on the granite counter, returning to the table with his Lazy Magnolia and the open bottle of wine. He places it on the table halfway between the women.

After taking a long, slow sip of beer, Paul finally answers. "Well, if you ask me, I think the wrong person is sittin' in prison. I think whoever killed those women is still runnin' free. Sure, George Stark could be the biggest son-of-a-bitch in town if you caught him on the wrong day. But I've known George my whole life. I'd known him as a deacon at church prayin' with some poor farmer who'd lost his wife. I'd seen him have one too many Jack and Cokes and want to start up with someone. And God knows, I'd seen him try to cheat at poker. But I have to say, never in all my years would I ever think George Stark had it in him to kill someone…especially his own damn wife."

"Oh come on…" Marilee bristles. "George Stark isn't lily white and never has been. He's the biggest liar and cheat I ever saw. I think 'bout the only time that man could keep his zipper shut was sittin' at church on Sundays. Any other day of the week, he'd stick that thing into anyone with a hole and a pulse."

Julia bursts into laughter and Paul follows. Marilee picks up their contagious amusement and soon all three are doubled over in their chairs.

"Oh my God, Marilee, you summed him up alright." Julia finally wipes the tears of laughter from her eyes.

"I don't know about you, but George has always made my skin crawl. His good looks were always lost on me…and don't think he didn't flirt. Sometimes right in front of Betty Ann!" Marilee shakes her head in disgust.

Paul finally composes himself, too. "Well, Julia I don't know which direction you will go with this book but I'll say one thing…watch who you trust 'round here especially that Matt Case."

A jolt runs down Julia's spine. "What makes you say that?"

"He's an outsider and doesn't care about the truth. He just wants to stir shit up to sell newspapers. He's always sniffin' around city hall."

Julia's just about to respond that she'd met Matt and seeing him again tomorrow, but quickly reels those words back in. "So you don't like him?"

"Oh, it's not that I don't like him. He's a nice enough guy. I just think he's askin' for trouble, and so are you, if you're not careful. I'd be cautious who you talk to about this book." Paul looks at her concerned.

"That's a little too late..." Julia scoffs.

"Whaddya mean?" Marilee's eyebrows raise.

"I had lunch with Nelda at Nine Ed's today, and Ricky Watson stopped by our table. After Nelda reminded him who I am, she went on to explain I'm in town working on this book."

"Oh shit. What'd he say?" Paul quizzes.

"He was pretty flustered about it, actually. He said I should be careful because people don't want me poking around their 'bidness.'" Julia jokingly adds an extra twang to emphasize the word.

Paul responds quietly. "You do need to be careful, Julia..." Paul's jaw tenses in thought. "Especially when it comes to Ricky."

"Why do you say that?" Julia tenses.

On one hand, Julia considers Ricky just a dumb redneck and on the other, she knows he's always carried some unspoken influence in town. It's why everyone has always steered clear of him, including Seth. At one police department Christmas party, they'd nearly come to blows. But Seth always played it off as just a rivalry among officers, and yet Seth's shifty body language around Ricky always told another story. She'd push and push questioning what was happening with Ricky, but Seth would just get defensive and Julia would finally relent. In the years since Seth's death, Julia had wondered if it was perhaps because Seth was afraid of Ricky or if it was because Seth was smart enough to keep a safe distance from Ricky, too.

She also couldn't help but wonder if Ricky was in some way responsible for Seth's death. The thought of it, and the image of him standing there today, makes her nauseous.

"Ricky's more than a just a schoolyard bully..." Paul picks at his beer label. "He's connected Julia, and he's far more cunning than his ignorant, good 'ol boy demeanor would have you believe."

"Connected how? To whom?"

"For the sake of all our safety...and my job as mayor...I can't say anything more. Just trust me on this. Ricky isn't somone you wanna pick a fight with. You'll lose every time."

Julia studies Paul, frustrated at his unwillingness to say anything more. She has so many more questions, like what Ricky knows...or has done.

"So why don't you do something about him?" Julia retorts in anger.

"Like what? We both know I don't have that kinda power in this town. Ricky stepped right in after George went to prison. He certainly doesn't have the financial influence George did, but he knows how to keep everyone in check."

"So is that why Allison's case just...POOF!...went away?" Julia's voice grows louder as she motions with her hands.

Paul silently glares at Julia before a heavy sigh of resignation.

"Julia...I just..." Paul begins.

Marilee interrupts the exchange before Paul can go any further. "You know, Jules, I've thought a lot about this book since we were at the cabin." She briefly hesitates. "And I feel like I owe you an apology..."

"No, please Marilee. You don't owe me anything." Julia's voice has returned to normal. Paul silently observes them still stewing over Ricky.

"No, no...I do." Marilee cuts in. "I want you to understand why I got so upset..." She pauses and looks down at her hands which are loosely resting on the table around the base of her wine glass. She swallows hard in thought. "You see, what I haven't said...and feel like you oughta know is...well is...well, I was the last person to talk to Betty Ann."

Julia looks at her friend, arched eyebrows knitted together in confusion. "What do you mean?"

"I mean, she called me the night before she died."

"She did? What did she say?" Julia's heart pounds in her chest, mind turning over how Marilee could have kept this from her all these years. Kate was right. Marilee had been holding something back, but Julia never imaged it would be this.

Marilee takes a sip of wine. "You gotta swear you will keep this between us."

"I will...I swear. So what happened?"

Paul continues to watch Marilee and Julia on either side of him, much like a tennis match, eyes jumping from one woman to the next, saying nothing.

"Well, it was 'bout quarter to ten or so that Sunday night when the phone rang. I could tell she was upset but we just chit-chatted at first about the women's guild meeting at church. I thought it was unusual for her to call so late, especially on a school night. Finally, I asked was something wrong. At first she said, no, she was fine. Then, she broke down cryin'. She said that she and George had just gotten off the phone and had a big fight. You know, he was at that conference in Jackson. So, I asked what was the fight about and she wouldn't say. She asked if she could come over Monday after school to talk confidentially. But then she was found dead that Monday morning. I don't know...I don't know what happened or what she was gonna talk to me about. But I feel sure it had something to do with George." Marilee inhales a deep breath and studies Julia.

"Oh my God..." Julia says quietly. "I never knew that." She looks across the table at her friend and then at Paul.

"Yeah, it really messed us up for a long time." Paul breaks his silence, slurring ever so slightly.

"So she didn't say anything else?" Julia quizzes.

"No, that's it. But there was just somethin' not right in her voice. I knew she and George had fought before about his runnin' around and drinkin' but she sounded different. Almost panicked. I asked if she needed me to come over...or if she wanted to come our house. She said no. Said that she just needed to sleep it off and things would be better in the morning. But that's it. The whole call didn't last but five minutes. I'd do anything..." Marilee's voice breaks through her tears. "Anything to go back and insist she come over. She might still be alive."

Julia's eyes dot with tears of empathy for her friend, knowing all too well that it's one of the most indescribable, heart-wrenching feelings in the world to think you could have said something or done something differently and perhaps the person you love could still be alive. It leaves you utterly and completely paralyzed with regret.

"Oh Marilee, I'm so sorry you went through that. Why didn't you ever tell us?"

"Because I just couldn't. At first, it was just too horrible to talk about. I felt so incredibly guilty, and then over time, I just wanted to forget...tried to forget. But the sound of her voice has haunted me for years. I used to have dreams she was calling, and I was trying to get to her and I couldn't."

"It was a rough time." Paul adds, reaching for Marilee's hand and covering it with his. "She did go to the cops."

"Well, I went to Ricky and Dave Smith...Paul came with me." Marilee clarifies.

"Did Seth know?" Julia interrupts.

"I never told him, but yeah I'm sure he found out."

"Or maybe not..." Paul adds.

"Why do you say that?" Julia looks over at him.

Marilee jumps in first. "Because they did nothing 'bout it. We went to the police the day after Betty Ann was found dead, and they never even brought me in for questioning."

"That's crazy! Why wouldn't they want to know about that? I mean, I wonder what the fight was about?" Julia asks rhetorically.

"Because they already had George Stark pegged as guilty in the first fifteen minutes on the scene. So they didn't need anything else to interfere with that." Paul's voice grows louder. "That whole investigation was a joke."

"So you think he was framed?" Julia quizzes.

Paul stares at her with glassy eyes. "I don't know, Julia. I really don't. After we went to the police about the phone call from Betty Ann, and they did nothing, I decided right then it was safest for us to just lay low. I mean, we had nothing to hide…and still don't. But we were close family friends with George and Betty Ann. So partly it was shock, and partly we were just scared shitless that this was happening again after Allison."

"Yeah, I know…" Julia agrees. "It was difficult for me, and I had only known Allison and Betty Ann for a few years. So I can't imagine how hard it must have been for you."

Marilee stands abruptly and begins picking up the dessert bowls. "It was a nightmare…but I know you understand how hard it is to lose someone so suddenly. It's why I still don't understand why you would write this book when it hits so close to home." Marilee looks at Julia, bowls in hand.

Julia returns Marilee's gaze and opts for the truth, as much as a reminder for herself as an explanation for her friend. "Because I've been stuck…I mean, really stuck for years. I've never had a healthy relationship and even with the success of my career, I always felt like the other shoe was about to drop. It was like I couldn't really allow myself to enjoy life because I felt guilty…and because I was afraid that if I enjoyed it too much, I'd wake up one morning and it would all just be gone." Julia swallows hard to keep the tears at bay. "I need to move on with my life, and the only way I know to do that is to write…to get it all out. For twenty years, I've been trying to forget everything that happened in Murdoch. But I'm starting to believe that maybe uncovering all of this again is actually the very thing I need to finally let it all go."

Paul looks over at Julia and softly pats her hand resting on the table. "I can understand that…and certainly respect you for it. But I'm speaking for my best friend Seth here, when I say I just want you to really watch who you trust. And if you need anything…anything at all, you better let me know."

After wrapping their conversation and helping Marilee load the dishwasher, Julia bids Paul and Marilee farewell. Marilee hugs her tight and whispers, "I love you, Jules. Be careful." The love wells into a smile on Julia's face as she waves her friends good-bye. On the drive back to the cottage, Julia's heart and mind are in a see-saw of nostalgia and questions.

Why is Paul so afraid of Ricky? How has Ricky managed to never even be questioned about Allison's death? Why is this town so willing to just forget everything that happened? And what could Betty Ann have been trying to tell Marilee? Was she calling for help?

By the time Julia arrives at the cottage, she's thoroughly mentally and emotionally exhausted. It's not until she retrieves her phone that she realizes she's missed two calls and three texts from Frank wondering where she is and is she okay. She glances at the clock and with the hour time difference it's nearly midnight in New York. She sighs again heavily, pondering what to do, but quickly realizes she doesn't have the energy to deal with Frank tonight.

However, there's one more text that produces a smile.

Looking forward to seeing you tomorrow!

"I am excited to see you, too, Matt." She mumbles aloud. "And I hope you're ready because I do have more questions for you."

Julia heads to the bathroom to begin her nightly ritual, and just as she splashes the first pool of warm water onto her face …VRRRRING….VRRRRRING…

She visibly jumps at the sound of the cottage's phone ringing. She never even noticed the white push-button landline phone plugged into the wall in the kitchen next to the refrigerator.

"What the…" Heart racing, she grabs the hand towel and wanders into the kitchen and stares at the ringing phone before answering on the fourth ring.

"Hello?" Julia asks hesitantly.

"This Julia?" A man's voice asks huskily on the other end.

Julia's heart races faster trying to figure out who would have known she was here. "Who's this?" She asks forcefully.

"Oh you don't need to know who I am. You need to be more concerned with what I know...and what I can do." He hisses.

Julia stays quiet trying to recognize the voice, which sounds like a mixture of bourbon and venom. Her mind jumps to the only person she can think of who would call her out here.

"Ricky? Is that you?"

"No, this ain't Ricky. This is just a friendly warnin' that you best pack your shit and take that pretty little Yankee ass right back to Nu'York. You don't belong here and never did." He coughs heavily as if he'd just smoked an entire pack of Winston's. "You sure as hell got no bidness writin' a book 'bout a place you don't belong. And you never did. This ain't a suggestion. It's a warnin'."

CLICK.

Before Julia can fully absorb what happened, the call is over. She inhales deeply realizing she had been clenching her breath. *Who was that? How in the hell does anyone here know me? Better yet, how would anyone know I'm out here?*

Hands visibly shaking, Julia hangs up the receiver and checks all the doors again. Laying in bed, the conversation with Paul and Marilee replays in her head. Then, with this phone call, Julia's even more restless. Sleep feels very far away as she contemplates her next move. *Should I really pack up and go home?*

Somewhere in that hazy space between slumber and fully awake, Julia thinks back to her meeting a few weeks ago, peering over the city in the Bauer & Brown offices. She remembers standing there as Jeff and Priscilla encouraged her to write the story that wants to be told.

So, no. She isn't going home. She's just getting started, and she has more work to do, which will resume in the morning with piecing together the death of Betty Ann Stark.

CHAPTER 26

October 21, 1996

BEEP, BEEP, BEEP. The alarm clock is unforgiving as it blares its chorus through Julia and Seth's bedroom. Seth bangs the snooze button, which now reads 6:01 A.M.

The cool air in the room contrasts the warmth produced by Seth's presence. Julia rolls into him and wraps her arms around his bare, muscular chest. "No...don't get up yet." She mumbles sleepily. Seth turns to his side and enfolds her, kissing her forehead.

"I have to, baby." His voice sounds even deeper upon waking. "Need to be at the station early today for a meeting."

"Ugggghhhh...I hate Mondays." Julia groans. "Guess I should get up, too."

"No, why don't you sleep a little longer. I'll get you up after I'm dressed." Seth kisses Julia's nose and she drifts back to sleep.

Seth returns an hour later, fully alert from two cups of coffee, a hot shower, and a dose of the morning news. He now stands over the bed dressed in his police uniform.

"Rise and shine!" He booms over the bed.

Julia's already half awake, laying in the queen-sized bed looking up at the ceiling going through her mental to-do list. Mondays are always hectic at the paper, between meetings and wrapping final edits to the weekly edition. The paper has to be at the printer in Natchez promptly at noon every Tuesday so the Natchez printer can set, print, and deliver the papers back to Murdoch by five in the morning on Wednesday. It's certainly not a quick news cycle but the *Messenger* lags behind on technology, and with such a small staff, Dan and Julia handle everything from ad sales to tracking down school board and city council minutes.

Julia turns her attention to Seth. "Please don't sing…it's too early…" She smiles up at him.

Seth ignores her plea. "Rise…and SHINE…and give God the glory, glory…" His large hands clap as he bellows the old church-school song he sang as a kid. He loves to randomly sing in the mornings to get a stir out of Julia, who can't stand how chipper Seth is every single day.

It doesn't matter if he's downed an entire twelve-pack of beer until three in the morning, quietly sipped hot tea at home on the couch, or pulled an all-nighter at the station, Seth wakes each day with a smile on his face. "It's because I get to wake up next to you." He'd once told Julia. Her heart melted right there in the bed and then they'd made love for the next two hours.

Seth laughs and finally relents his song. "Oh now, Miss Julia, I know you secretly love my singing."

He perches on the edge of the bed, arms on either side of Julia, coffee-lined breath close to her face. He stares into her eyes and kisses her gently on the lips. "Even if you hate my singing, I still love you." He whispers and then leans back slightly, his face still close to hers. "I gotta run but I should be home around five this evening. Mama asked if we wanted to come out to dinner later."

Julia traces his handsome, freshly shaven face with her hand and smiles. It's these simple moments of life that she's come to appreciate the most living in Murdoch. It's a pace that surprisingly suits her. A life of leaving work at five in the afternoon and being home a few minutes later. One of knowing the first name of everyone you pass in

211

the grocery store. And one of gathering on a random Monday night to eat home-cooked meals with your widowed mother-in-law, just to talk and keep her company.

"Dinner with Nelda sounds great. I'll just meet you here around five." Julia leans up and kisses him again.

"Okay baby, have a great day." Seth smiles broadly, eyes twinkling. "I love you."

"Love you too."

Julia rises and ticks through her predictable routine of a cup of coffee, a quick journaling session, and a shower. Over her scrambled eggs and toast, she scans the highlights of the *Jackson Clarion-Ledger* to see what's happenings around the state. Twenty minutes later as she steps outside onto the broad front porch, she's greeted by a crisp, sunny day. She smiles grateful at the first signs of fall.

Just to the right of the front door, a passel of birds in the Crepe Myrtle sing with wild abandon. For as much as she's grown to love the small town way of life in Mississippi, one thing she's still not grasped is how anyone survives the summers. The oppressive heat and humidity make her insides cook and her already fiery disposition even more volatile.

If there's one thing Julia abhors, it's being hot. Her mom used to laugh at how she'd stamp, scream, and throw a temper-tantrum being placed in a hot car as a little girl. Julia's convinced she must have died in a fire in a past life. Seth just laughs and says it's because she's "high maintenance." So on days like today, when the heat gives way, Julia can't help but feel a deep sense of relief.

At eight-fifteen, the small bells on the *Messenger* door jingle as Julia passes through. Dan hung the bells there years ago because he wanted to know when someone entered the office, especially when he's in one of the back workrooms. This morning, however, he's already sitting at his desk staring blankly into the room as Julia enters.

"Morning!" Julia barrels into the room. "God, it's gorgeous outside. I'm so glad fall is coming and hope it stays cool for

Halloween…" She sets her purse on her desk and looks over at Dan who's staring at her white as a ghost, saying nothing.

Julia freezes in confusion because it's usually Dan who's full of vigor from the pot of coffee he's consumed by the time she rolls in the door. "Dan, are you okay? What's wrong?"

Dan blinks and coughs, but it still sounds as if someone's stuffed wads of cotton down his throat when he finally speaks. "Betty Ann was found dead this morning."

"Wait…what? Betty Ann…Betty Ann Stark?" Julia stammers. "I don't understand…how?"

"I don't have all the details yet but I just got a call from Sam Shepherd…you know the high school AP…"

Julia nods conveying she knows the assistant high school principal, but her mind reels trying to compute what Dan just said. Finally, she gasps for a breath, as she's not sure she's exhaled in the past minute. *Betty Ann Stark is dead?*

"So what did Sam say?" Julia finally asks quietly.

"He said Rick got concerned because the first bell rang at seven-twenty and Betty Ann hadn't called for a substitute or shown up…and that's not like her. Apparently, the school tried to call the house about ten different times. Finally, Rick went to the Stark's house and banged on the door and she didn't answer. So he went 'round to the back door. It was unlocked, so he went in. He found her dead in the kitchen." Dan stops and rubs his face with both hands before dropping them heavily into his lap. "Apparently, it was a bloodbath." He adds quietly.

Julia sucks in another breath, brain reeling even faster trying to absorb these facts and piece them together into some coherent thought. "You mean she was killed?" Julia plops down in her chair to keep from falling down. Tears threaten along the corner of her eyes. She blinks to hold them in, while trying to compute how this could be happening again. *Not a heart attack, no aneurysm. Murdered?*

"Murdered? ..." Julia repeats dumbfounded. "What in the hell is going in this town? Who would want to kill Betty Ann Stark?" That same wave of fear and sudden onset of grief she'd experienced a few months ago with Allison rush back, and once again, her emotions betray her. The tears now fall, as she quickly brushes them away. "I don't understand...why? Why would someone kill her?"

"I don't know." Dan shakes his head despondently. "I just...I just can't believe it. It doesn't make any sense why anyone would hurt that sweet woman...but we need to head over there."

"Now?" A flash of panic courses Julia's veins.

"Yeah, I mean I just got off the phone with Sam not five minutes before you walked in."

Julia doesn't budge. She blinks again several times still trying to register that this is the second murder in Murdoch in only four months' time. *Oh my God, George.*

"Where's George? Why wasn't he home?" Julia looks over at Dan. "God, I feel terrible for him..." She adds softly.

"I know, poor guy was out of town at a conference in Jackson. It started yesterday. He's apparently on his way back now." Dan stands and gathers his notebook and recorder. "You okay to go over there with me?"

Julia flushes as she recalls the scene at the football field a few months earlier covering Allison Mercer's death.

"Yeah...yeah...I'm good." She fibs, swallowing hard as she stands. In this moment, she's anything but good. She was good a few hours ago laughing at Seth. This feeling of dread feels anything but good, especially as she realizes that once again Seth has to sort through the aftermath. Neither of them bargained they would come back to his hometown to face so much death. First Doc from the cancer and then Allison and now Betty Ann, both at the hands of someone else.

It's a short, silent car ride from the office downtown out to the Pine Forest subdivision on the southern edge of Murdoch where the

Starks had lived for more than a decade. For as much money and influence as the Stark family has in town, George and Betty Ann's brick, ranch-style house is understated in stature. The yard, however, is immaculate with an array of blooming Gardenias and Hydrangeas, which are perfectly placed in front of the healthy Boxwood shrubs. Betty Ann loved to garden.

All of that life, punctuated by a crisp blue sky and glistening fall sun, abruptly contrast the darkness that lurks inside the house. Julia shudders at the thought as Dan pulls the car up behind the police cars, ambulance, and assortment of other vehicles snaking down Pinehill Acres Drive. Seth stands in a huddle of men talking near the large Florida Maple tree in the front yard.

As Julia crosses over the rich green grass and draws closer, she can see Seth is talking to Ricky, Chief Smith, and Rick Burgess, the high school principal who discovered Betty Ann. Alan Peterson stands a bit outside the huddle taking long drags on a freshly lit cigarette.

Julia hangs back as Dan approaches the men first, each greeting him with a solemn handshake. They nod over at Julia, except for Seth who walks over and hugs her tight.

Seth pulls back slightly and removes his aviator sunglasses, searching Julia's face for some sense of the joy and normalcy they'd shared a few hours ago. "Hey…you okay?" He whispers.

"Yeah….I guess. Betty Ann is dead." Julia's stomach turns at the thought of her friend's lifeless body covered in blood.

"Never in my wildest dreams did I think we'd be back here again." Seth shakes his head.

"I know…it just doesn't make any sense. Who on earth would want to kill Betty Ann?" Julia repeats the question quietly. "Do you have any leads?"

"No…not yet. We're waiting on George to get here."

"Waiting on George for what?" Julia's not tracking.

"To search the house…"

"Why wouldn't you start the investigation now? Why does he need to be here?"

"I don't know...Smith just told us we had to wait. That's about all I know. I guess I need to get back to the guys." Seth gestures to the group of men still chatting, occasionally taking sips of coffee from white Styrofoam cups. "You gonna be okay?"

"I think so...hopefully I won't throw up this time." Julia smiles sadly in spite of herself.

Seth smiles back at her and then his face flashes dark. "Julia, I'd rather you not go inside."

"Why?" Julia's actually relieved to hear him say it. For the past twenty minutes, she's been trying to figure out a way to tell Dan that she cannot stomach seeing blood, especially the blood of someone she knows.

"Because it's a really, really bad scene. Whoever shot her was a sick son-of-a-bitch." Seth's face pales recalling the sight of Betty Ann's body lying on the cold linoleum floor. He'd only walked in briefly before having to turn and leave. No amount of training in the academy or watching horror movies on a Friday night with your buddies can prepare you for the sight of a murder at close range.

"Trust me, I have no interest in going in, but I need to do my job. So I'll do whatever Dan tells me."

Seth nods in understanding. "Just take care of yourself."

"I will."

With that, Seth returns to the huddle and a minute or so later Dan heads back over to Julia, pointing toward the curb. Julia follows her boss back to the street, curious about what information he's procured.

"So what'd you find out?" Julia asks quietly.

Dan shakes his head. "Not much of anything...but this isn't adding up."

"What do you mean?"

"Well, typically they begin the investigation immediately while the evidence is still fresh and untouched." Dan looks over at the group of men. "But they're acting like they can't do anything until George arrives."

Julia looks confused. She's not well-versed on the sequence of a murder investigation but it's the frustration and concern on Dan's face that lets her know something is amiss. "Why would they wait for George?"

"I don't know…" Dan shakes his head and lowers his voice. "I asked if they already had a search warrant and they all just ignored me." Dan looks over and notices Alan Peterson and Chief Smith wandering in through the open front door. "From the homicides I've covered, they aren't following protocol."

Julia doesn't know what protocol is for this type of situation, and based on the annoyed look on Dan's face, she opts not to ask. The only thing she's wanted to know since they arrived on the scene is whether Betty Ann's body is still in the house. It's as if Dan reads her mind.

"They haven't moved the body. I do know that much. They're waiting for the investigators from the Sheriff's Department to get here."

"So what are we going to do?"

"I guess we're just gonna wait until we can get some more information. No one will give a statement yet."

The Adams County Sheriff's Department investigators show up soon after and the men continue to wander in and out of the house, occasionally gathering in their semblance of a football huddle with Seth and the Murdoch police. Finally, around ten o'clock Alan Peterson makes the pronouncement of death, creating some sense of motion, but then Dan and Julia resume the wait over near his car. Every twenty minutes or so Dan wanders over and asks for more information.

Seth occasionally glances her way and smiles or waves, and for some reason today, that's enough. That sense of defiance Julia had with Allison's death isn't present this morning. In its place sits a reservoir of sadness. She cannot wrap her heart or mind around this second murder. She and Betty Ann have never been what you'd call "close" but Julia has always held reverence for her.

While George has the looks and charm in the relationship, Betty Ann brings the integrity and resignation. With her short chestnut brown bob and emerald green eyes, Betty Ann emanates the kind of quiet grace that warms you like sunshine. Standing only five-foot-three, Betty Ann has been a pillar in Murdoch for years.

From the women's circle and activities at First Baptist to working with the hospital auxiliary and cheerleaders, Betty Ann always shows up at the right time, with the perfectly baked pie or casserole. Of course, being George Stark's wife also brings its own sense of admiration from onlookers given his family's lineage and influence in the community.

Julia's main connection to Betty Ann is through Marilee. Often, when she and Kate stop by Marilee's, Betty Ann is there. The four sip wine, laugh, and share stories. Years older, Betty Ann always offers the sage advice, a broad smile, and a genuine hug. Julia had often secretly wondered why Betty Ann and George never had children of their own, given Betty Ann's love for the kids at school.

Thinking of Betty Ann and Marilee's cheerleading squad and all the kids impacted by this unfathomable loss, another piece of Julia's heart breaks. And for what? It's not like a car accident or illness. No, here Julia stands again witnessing the murder of another woman who died an unthinkable, calculated death. With a deep sigh, Julia's sadness morphs into frustration as she looks around the scene. She and Dan have been standing around in silence for what feels like hours.

"Shouldn't George be here?" She asks glancing at her watch. It's nearly noon by now, and the crisp morning has given way to a warm day. She wipes the bead of sweat from her brow, stomach growling. Her breakfast is long gone.

"You'd think." Dan replies disgruntled. "I mean it's only an hour-and-a-half drive from Jackson dependin' on how fast you drive. He should've easily been here by now. I mean, they called him before eight o'clock this morning." Dan looks at Julia through his tinted sunglasses and then back at the assortment of police still standing around. "This is ridiculous." He mutters under his breath.

Julia checks her watch again. Dan's mentioned there being a protocol for how all of this should be going, but he never mentioned if there's a standard order on lunch. Her stomach has been rumbling for the past half-hour.

Over time, Julia's grown more comfortable around Dan, who's not a big guy by any means. His buttoned-down, short-sleeved shirts reveal slender arms. Sometimes he sports a checked or lined pattern, but more often than not, it's a solid shirt neatly tucked into khaki pants or dark blue jeans. Lately, she's noticed the bottom few buttons of his shirts are a little more strained around his belly.

Like most veteran newspaper editors, Dan wears a gruff demeanor most of the time. Underneath that rough exterior, however, Julia's come to discover a kind man who's been a great teacher and mentor, helping her sharpen her writing skills and bolstering her confidence. Yet today, that sense of purpose as a reporter wanes under the heaviness of death. Julia opts to remain silent and follow Dan's lead despite her gnawing stomach.

"Damn, I'm hungry." Dan finally admits twenty minutes later, clearly irritated that nothing is moving forward on this investigation and that there's still no sign of George.

Of all the uncertainty this morning has produced, that's what bothers Julia most. If you'd received a call that you're wife had been murdered, wouldn't you drive like a bat out of hell to get home? She shudders at the thought of being on the receiving end of that phone. She looks around to find Seth, who is talking to Ricky on the front porch.

"Why don't you go over to Dairy Queen and get us somethin' to eat?" Dan pulls out his wallet and hands her a twenty dollar bill. "We could be here awhile."

After Julia takes Dan's order, she heads to Murdoch's only fast food joint in search of a few hamburgers and fries. She's concerned about whether Seth will eat, but decides to just leave him to his job, and hopefully soon she can do hers. It seems a waste of time to just stand around for so long. This is obviously the headline story of the week, so there's nothing she can do on the paper, anyway. Everything they had prepared for this week's edition will have to shift. She wishes she could talk to Marilee and Kate, but they are both at work. She's tempted to stop by city hall but knows Dan wouldn't approve, and she is driving his car.

Upon arriving back at the Stark's, Julia's unnerved all over again that George still hasn't shown. "I just don't understand…where in the world is he?" She asks Dan.

"I don't know but somethin' just isn't right 'bout all this. They did finally remove her body right after you left, and I tried asking Smith a few more questions but they don't seem to know anything. Either that or they are just stayin' tight lipped…and they still don't have a search warrant." Dan shakes his head as he gladly takes his hamburger from Julia.

Julia's relieved that she didn't have to witness another body bag.

A few bites into their hamburgers, George's car pulls up in the middle of the street. It's now been well over five hours since he was notified about Betty Ann. Dan and Julia simply observe from their post by the car, and Julia's taken aback by the sight.

George saunters across the green lawn as gingerly as someone heading to a church picnic. His chiseled, cleanly shaven face reveals no emotion, with his crisp white shirt tucked neatly into dark slacks. He smiles and shakes the hands of the few police standing in the yard, before heading into the house.

Your wife has just been brutally murdered, so how in the hell could you be smiling? Julia bristles in indignation.

"Glad he could make it." Sarcasm drips from Dan's words. "This whole thing is just a big clusterfuck." Dan's lost in thought, clearly confused and now angry by the sight of George as well.

Dan sets down the last of his hamburger on the hood of the car and wipes his mouth. Julia says nothing.

"I'm sorry…" Dan says with a muffled tone, before swallowing his bite of food. "I just don't understand how he can stroll in here like that…like nothing happened. If that were my wife, I'd be a train wreck."

"I know…" Between the emotion, heat, and now the food sitting on her stomach, Julia's exhausted and ready to be back in the quiet confines of the *Messenger* office to finish this day.

"Let's wait for him to come back out, and we'll get a statement. They already have enough people crawlin' in and out of the house."

About fifteen minutes later, George returns to the front yard. Dan makes a beeline to him and Julia follows in tow.

"I'm so sorry about Betty Ann." Dan sticks his hand out to shake George's.

"Thanks, Dan. I just can't believe it." George rubs the side of his face with his large hand, lost in thought.

It's the first semblance of emotion Julia detects. All she wants to know is where George has been but defers to Dan to keep asking the questions. She says nothing.

"So do they have any leads?" Dan gently quizzes George.

"No, nothing yet. Whoever did this really wanted her to die though." George says quietly.

"Why's that?"

"Because the kitchen is covered in blood." George swallows hard, the color draining from his face. "Listen, I'm sorry I don't know anything more…but I need to go…" George looks over Dan's shoulder toward the driveway where his in-laws are walking up to the house. Julia guesses they must have driven straight from Beaumont this morning.

"Sure, sure…" Dan nods as George walks away.

"What do we do now?" Julia asks quietly.

"I think we just have to report on what we know for now." Dan looks over toward George, who is hugging Betty Ann's sobbing mother. "But I'll tell you one thing…this story is far from over."

CHAPTER 27

The Murdoch Messenger – October 23, 1996

Second Murder in Four Months Shocks Murdoch

High School Librarian Found Dead in Home after Multiple Gunshots

By Julia Dixon

Still reeling from the unsolved murder of Murdoch High School student Allison Mercer, Murdoch citizens were shocked once again upon hearing of the brutal murder of high school teacher Betty Ann Stark, 42, wife of George Stark, Jr., Mayor of Murdoch.

Mrs. Stark was pronounced dead on Monday, Oct. 21, 1996 at 10:04 a.m. by Justice of Peace Alan Peterson. Her body was found in the kitchen of their home early in the morning of Oct. 21 by high school principal Rick Burgess. Burgess went to the Stark's home to check on Mrs. Stark, when she had failed to report to school at her usual time. Her husband, George, was in Jackson at a conference for the state's municipal leaders.

According to Peterson, Mrs. Stark had been shot multiple times at close range with two shots to her head and one to her abdomen. She is suspected to have died sometime between 9:30 p.m. Sunday night and 5:30 a.m. Monday morning. The gun is estimated to be a large caliber gun similar to the one the Starks' kept in a safe in their home. The gun from the Stark home is missing and has yet to be found.

Murdoch Chief of Police Dave Smith said the shooting is being handled as a burglary-homicide. There were valuables missing from the Stark home, including money from a safe estimated at approximately $5,000 that was kept in the master bedroom closet.

According to Police Deputy Ricky Watson, who was the first investigator on the scene, there was no sign of forced entry into the home and none of the neighbors heard anything out of the ordinary. The back door was unlocked when Mrs. Stark's body was discovered. Several fingerprints were lifted from the home, and they are currently being evaluated.

Even though there are no solid suspects in the attack, Murdoch police are investigating thoroughly to determine what happened to Mrs. Stark, according to Chief Smith. "We're looking at several leads," said Smith but provided no further comment.

This is the second murder of a Murdoch resident this year. Murdoch High School student Allison Mercer was found dead on July 8, 1996. Smith did not indicate whether the two murders are linked. Upon initial investigation, he does not believe they are, but added, "it hasn't been ruled out completely."

Mrs. Stark was born in 1954 in Beaumont, Texas. She graduated from Forest Park High School in 1972 and received a bachelor's in education from Mississippi State University. She had been a teacher for 13 years and the Murdoch High School librarian for the past seven years.

CHAPTER 28

The Murdoch Messenger – October 30, 1996

Mayor's Arrest Baffles Murdoch Community

By Julia Dixon

Adding another twist to the already incomprehensible murder of Murdoch High School Librarian, Betty Ann Stark, was the arrest of her husband Murdoch Mayor George Stark, Jr.

Stark, 44, was arrested Saturday, Oct. 26 at his mother's home in Natchez and charged with murder in the slaying of his wife, Betty Ann Stark, who was found dead of gunshot wounds on Oct. 21. The Starks had been married 18 years.

In addition to serving his third term as Murdoch's mayor, Stark also serves as the chairman of the Stark Hospital Foundation established by his father, the late George Stark.

The arrest left Murdoch residents trying to cope with the second blow to hit the town in a matter of weeks. "You just get over one shock and then another one hits," said a shaken teacher at Murdoch High School. "It just doesn't make any sense."

Stark was released from the Jefferson County Jail Saturday

after posting a $50,000 bond.

Mrs. Stark, 42, was discovered by Murdoch High School Principal Rick Burgess, who went to the Stark home to check on her after she failed to report to work at Murdoch High School on Monday, Oct. 21.

According to autopsy reports, Mrs. Stark had been shot three times and investigators believe the shooting occurred several hours before she was found.

Funeral services for Mrs. Stark were held on Friday, Oct. 25 at the Murdoch High School auditorium, with more than 500 Murdoch students and residents attending.

Authorities would not comment on a motive for the shooting of Mrs. Stark, and Peterson said if any marital problems existed between the couple, "they weren't public knowledge."

Stark, who was reported to have been at a conference for Mississippi municipal leaders in Jackson was arrested on evidence from forensic test results, said Jefferson County District Attorney John Wrenn Saturday.

"We believe the evidence is pretty strong indicating George Stark is culpable," said Murdoch Police Chief Dave Smith, who declined to be more specific as to what evidence indicated Stark would be responsible for his wife's death.

Smith said Murdoch residents have had a hard time accepting the news of Stark's arrest. "It's been a really tough shock for everyone," he added.

Smith said some residents called him in disbelief that it could be Stark. Other Murdoch residents, he said, told him the police department has done a "real good job" in making an arrest.

"I think when the shock wears off, everyone will come around and be real relieved that the person wasn't somebody coming around from out of town," said Smith.

Smith said authorities have not recovered the gun used to kill Mrs. Stark, which they believe belonged to the Starks.

Vicksburg Mayor B.J. Riley, who was with Stark at the conference in Jackson on Oct. 20, said he was "really surprised" of the news of Stark's arrest. "We were all in sympathy with him and horrified that his wife's murder could happen," said Riley. "He (Stark) had a typical grief reaction at the news. So it's surprising now to know he's been arrested."

The possible suspect is in jail, Smith said, but "because of circumstances beyond our control," Stark's case cannot be investigated for another two weeks. Smith declined to comment on where Stark is being held.

CHAPTER 29

The Murdoch Messenger – April 9, 1997

Former Murdoch Mayor George Stark Convicted of Murder

By Dan Murphy

NATCHEZ—The trial of former Murdoch Mayor George J. Stark, Jr. concluded Friday, April 4 at the Adams County Courthouse resulting in the conviction of Stark for the brutal murder of his wife, Betty Ann, 42, a former high school librarian.

Stark, now 45, who also served as the former chairman of the Stark Hospital Foundation in Murdoch, was sentenced to 99 years in prison and fined $45,000 by the jury after more than an hour of deliberation. He could be eligible for parole after 30 years.

Stark had been free on $50,000 bond since his Oct. 31, 1996 arrest and was immediately taken to the Adams County Jail. He will soon be transferred into the custody of the Mississippi Department of Corrections.

Stark showed no emotion when the verdict was read Friday and appeared composed when testifying during the punishment phase of the trial. "By witness to my Lord and Savior Jesus, I did not kill my wife," Stark pled to jurors for leniency. "She was my rock, and I love her."

"Mr. Stark when are you going to quit lying and tell everyone the truth? It's appalling and embarrassing to everyone the lies that have been spread throughout this trial," said special prosecutor Greg Thaxton who countered Stark's plea. Thaxton was hired privately by Mrs. Stark's family to lead the prosecution team.

The jury of six men and five women returned the conviction after six days of testimony. Throughout the trial, the courtroom was filled with spectators, but there was complete silence following the announcement of the guilty verdict.

A juror, who wished to remain anonymous, later said the jury believed all the circumstantial evidence and testimony considered together pointed to Stark's guilt.

"There was nothing we were presented that pointed us in another direction," he said. "All of us agreed he was guilty." The juror followed by saying the jury found "no degree of guilt," indicating that because Stark was found guilty of murder, they could not lessen the sentence.

Defense Attorney Jim Ledbetter said he was "disappointed" in the sentence and plans to appeal the conviction. "I don't think the State of Mississippi has come close to proving George Stark's guilt beyond a reasonable doubt," Ledbetter said. "Stark hasn't shown anything but love for his wife."

In the prosecution's case, Thaxton argued that Stark's private life did not match his public one, which was described by more than a dozen character witnesses as "an upstanding, honest Christian man."

Stark had been suspended from his role as Murdoch's mayor upon his arrest and was placed on leave with pay as chairman of the Stark Hospital Foundation. In the case, Thaxton pointed to discrepancies in Stark's character in private, painting him as a sometimes volatile man with known infidelities during his marriage to Mrs. Stark.

The prosecution team was not required to prove a motive in

the slaying of Stark's wife, Betty Ann, who was the librarian at Murdoch High School and co-sponsor of the Murdoch cheerleading squads. Mrs. Stark was shot three times at close range on the morning of Oct. 21, 1996 in the kitchen of her Murdoch home. The murder weapon was never found but investigators believe she was killed with Stark's .38-caliber pistol, which he said was kept loaded in the bed stand for protection.

The prosecution team also pointed out that both Stark and his wife had each taken out $500,000 life insurance policies in early 1996, roughly eight months before Mrs. Stark died.

Another central piece of evidence used against Stark was the prosecutors' convincing arguments that Stark could not account for his whereabouts on the night and morning following Mrs. Stark's murder. According to Stark's testimony, he was at a conference in Jackson for the state's municipal leaders and was in his hotel room at the Hilton Garden Inn hotel the night of Sunday, Oct. 20 and morning of Oct. 21. However, prosecutors called several witnesses from the conference to testify.

According to testimony by Vicksburg Mayor B.J. Riley, who said he's known Stark for several years, Stark was last seen at approximately 9 p.m. on the night of Oct. 20. Riley recounted that he, Stark and three other acquaintances had planned an early dinner upon arriving at the conference. They returned from dinner to the hotel bar around 8 p.m.

"Soon after we arrived at the bar, George began talking to a woman who introduced herself as Sheila," said Riley. When pressed about the nature of this interaction, Riley said Stark and the woman were "definitely flirting."

Riley reported that Stark left the hotel bar with the woman around 9 p.m., and he never spoke to Stark again until approximately 8 a.m. on Monday, Oct. 21 when Stark was notified about his wife's death.

The defense could not locate the woman named Sheila to corroborate Stark's alibi as a witness. Prosecutors argued the woman was "another one of George's lies," and that Stark could have easily made the 70-mile drive to Murdoch, murdered his wife and returned to Jackson unnoticed.

"He's trapped himself with inconsistencies and lies," said special prosecutor Thaxton.

Prosecutors also apparently convinced jurors that Stark lied on several other occasions in an attempt to cover up the crime. During his final argument, Adams County District Attorney Brad Cheatum recounted Stark's "huge lies," including money Stark said he found in the trunk of his car, unaware that investigators had searched his trunk and found no money.

In his testimony, Stark said he and his wife usually kept around $5,000 cash in a safe in their bedroom closet. "The kids at the high school sometimes needed loans," Stark testified. "So we kept petty cash around to help them out."

The money was missing at the time of the murder, and then according to Stark, he found the money in the car several days after Mrs. Stark's death and deposited it in the bank. Stark said he never told authorities he found the money.

Special prosecutor Thaxton argued that Stark planned to make his wife's death look like a suicide by shooting her once in the head but the plan went awry when she did not die immediately and he shot her two more times.

The last point made during the prosecution's final argument, which had not surfaced previously, was that Stark's car could be proven at the murder scene. A lab expert testified that a drop of blood was found on a pair of plastic gloves in a box in the trunk of Stark's car.

Thaxton broached the theory during his final argument—the last thing jurors heard before beginning their deliberations and leaving the defense attorneys unable to respond.

"The moral of the story here is that even a smart man can screw up," Thaxton said in his closing statement. "And George Stark screwed up by thinking he could get away with this vicious murder."

CHAPTER 30

Julia places the article about George Stark's conviction atop the thick coffee table and sighs heavily. She shuffles through the dozens of other newspaper articles spread across the couch and coffee table. Seeing them all now, she understands why she's had to consume these old stories in small nibbles. Because trying to devour all of this information in one sitting would have made her nauseous.

She blinks and gazes across the small living room of the cottage, sun tumbling through the large bay of windows. She's keenly aware of the churn of nostalgia and emotion, twisted together like those swirled chocolate-and-vanilla ice cream cones her grandfather used to buy her in the summer.

Mostly, in reading the articles about George Stark, she realizes how much she'd selectively chosen to remember and far more of what she conveniently chose to forget. She folds the newspapers neatly and places them back in the Jesus box, thumbing across a half-dozen others about the Stark trial (far more than was ever written about Allison Mercer). Her brain is already too full to absorb more right now. Three is enough. She leans her head back on the couch and closes her eyes.

Maybe Paul is right...maybe everyone was satisfied with George going to prison so they never felt a need to investigate further. But why didn't the jury have to establish a motive in Betty Ann's murder? Who was that woman Sheila…and did he sleep with her the night before the murder? Maybe that's what the fight was about with Betty Ann right before she died? Maybe Betty Ann had enough of his gallivanting and called him on it. Could that have been George's motive for killing her? But that doesn't seem like a reason to kill someone…or maybe Betty Ann found out about the drugs? Or maybe Allison did? Maybe George was pushing them through the high school? What if George had his sidekick Ricky Watson kill Allison and Betty Ann found out? So then George had to shut her up by killing her, too?

"Zzzz…zzzz…zzzz…" The vibrating buzz of Julia's cell phone rattles on the wooden coffee table underneath a few of the newspaper clippings. Startled back to the moment from her tornado of thought, she moves the papers aside to pick up her phone.

She briefly panics. *What time is it?*

As she retrieves her phone, she sees that it's nearly eleven o'clock. Good, she still has plenty of time before she meets Matt at four. It's no wonder her stomach is growling relentlessly. She's been so engrossed reading the articles sipping coffee, she'd forgotten to eat breakfast.

As she scans her phone, she sees the missed call isn't from Kate or Matt. It's from Frank. *Shit, I never called or texted him back yesterday.* Julia takes a deep breath and listens to his voicemail.

"Julia…hey, it's me. Umm…I'm starting to get a little worried that I haven't heard from you. Are you okay? I'm back in the city and would love to see you later, if you're around. I love you, baby. Call me, okay? Bye."

She notices that faint, familiar feeling of guilt wanting to creep in but she halts its presence. Instead, a deep sigh of frustration follows. She deletes Frank's voicemail. *He's gone for months with hardly any communication, and now the moment he steps into town, he thinks I need to be sitting at home waiting for him to call.*

Julia frees herself from the heap of papers, knees creaking as she stands and carries her empty mug to the sink. She looks at nothing in particular out the kitchen window for a moment before her eyes zero in on a black Dodge pickup, kicking up clouds of thick dust as it heads down the dirt road, away from the cottage toward the farm-to-market road. She momentarily panics after last night's phone call. *It's probably just someone checking on the cows…but what if it's someone checking on me?*

Julia takes another deep breath to try to calm that fearful thought and glances around the kitchen. Her eyes land upon the white landline phone. If there's a phone, then there must be a phone book around here somewhere. She digs through three drawers before stumbling across the old familiar Murdoch phone book. Buried in the back of the drawer, under a matchbook and several extra garbage bags rolled loosely, she extracts the thin, yellowed book dating to 2003.

Julia smiles remembering when the new edition of the phone book came out shortly after she and Seth moved to town. She'd giggled and pointed at their names listed right under Doc and Nelda's. Before moving to Murdoch, Julia had never given much thought to phone books, probably because in Chicago, and even in college, they were only good to order a pizza from the yellow pages. Yet, something about being included in the quaint collection of names and numbers of Murdoch's annual phone book felt right.

Now, Julia smiles as she scans through the pages before settling on Dan's number. *I wonder if he's still around?*

Julia lingers a moment longer remembering her conversation with Matt a few days earlier and realizing that this one call could unleash a whole other trove of information. She presses the keypad's soft buttons, and before she knows it, a woman abruptly responds.

A pulse of confusion courses through Julia as she realizes she's forgotten Dan's wife's name. They'd only met a handful of times because Dan tried to keep his work and family life separate. Well, as separate as you can in such a small town.

"Yello." A woman answers on the second ring.

"Hello...yes...umm...I'm looking for Dan Murphy...is this still the Murphy residence?" Julia swallows to calm her voice. She's never thought twice about calling complete strangers, celebrity journalists, or really anyone. Something about reconnecting with her former editor conjures up another reality that she's stepping into.

Not only had she far surpassed her mentor professionally, which is always a bit awkward for any apprentice, but she also knows Dan is keenly tuned into Murdoch's underbelly. While Dan never admitted it years ago, she's always suspected that he knew what really happened. On top of all that, Julia knows Dan is ill, though she's not sure of what or how serious that illness may be.

"Who's this?" The woman sounds skeptical.

"Julia Jarvis...Julia Dixon. I used to live here in Murdoch in the mid-nineties. I was married to Seth Dixon and worked with Dan at the paper."

The woman clears her throat in thought and responds in a milder tone. "Oh...Julia...yes Dan's talked 'bout you. Lemme see if he feels like talkin.'"

"Great...thank you."

Julia can hear murmuring and shuffling in the background before a raspy, strained voice emerges. "Julia?"

"Hi Dan. Yes, it's Julia." She smiles through the line.

"Why this is a nice surprise...how are you?"

"Good...I'm good. How are you, Dan? It's been a long time." With the phone receiver cradled on her shoulder, Julia winds the long white phone cord around her left hand.

"Well, I've been better but hangin' in. So what do I owe this honor?" Dan chuckles before barking a deep throaty cough. "Sorry..." He murmurs after the coughing subsides.

Julia's tone drops. Hearing him cough so laboriously she regrets calling. "It's okay...so yeah...I'm in town for a few days and just wondering if I could stop by and see you before I leave?"

"Oh...what brings you to town after all these years?" Dan quizzes.

She hesitates briefly before drawing a deep breath. "Well, I'm starting to research a new book and wanted to see if I could talk with you. But if you're busy or not up for it, it's okay..."

Dan pauses in thought before finally answering. "A book, huh? What about...or do I even need to ask?" He chuckles, which sets off another round of coughing.

Julia laughs softly. "Well, I'd rather chat more in person, if that's okay?"

"Sure, sure...that'd be fine. It would be good to see you."

"Okay great. I won't keep you long. I'll stop by tomorrow around three o'clock."

After gathering Dan's address and bidding farewell, Julia hangs up the phone with nervous excitement.

Though the moment she turns around, her cell phone taunts from the counter where she'd left it. Julia sighs in resignation about the other call she needs to make. She quickly locates Frank's name in her list of favorites and presses his number before she has time to change her mind.

"Jules?"

"Hi Frank..."

"Hey baby, how are you? I was starting to worry..."

Despite her initial apprehension in calling him, she smiles hearing Frank's familiar rasp on the other end of the line.

"I'm fine. How are you? How was your flight?" She asks with genuine concern.

"It was good...but you know, no matter how many times I make that trip the jet lag still kicks my ass. It's good to be home though." Frank clears his throat. "When can I see you? I've missed you."

"I know..." Julia opts for noncommittal in the exchange of

sentiments. "I'm really glad you're home, too, but I'm not there."

"What do you mean? Where are you?" Confusion creeps into his voice.

"Murdoch. I came down to Murdoch…"

"Murdoch as in Murdoch, Mississippi? Why in the hell are you in Murdoch? Are you okay? Did something happen to Marilee?"

"No, no, everything's fine. It's just that a lot has happened since you left. In a nutshell, I had a come-to-Jesus meeting with Priscilla and Jeff about my second book. After a lot of thought, I've decided to use everything that happened here as inspiration for a new project. So I've been gathering my old newspaper articles and visiting with Nelda and Marilee."

Julia's been pacing around the small cottage like Mr. Pickles sometimes wanders around her apartment. She finally moves back to the sofa and crosses her long legs underneath her.

Frank says nothing.

"Frank? You still there?" Julia wonders if she lost the connection.

"Yeah…yeah I'm here…" He responds quietly. "I guess I just don't understand why you would do that…"

"Do what?"

"Look, I don't know everything that happened down there but from what you've said, it seems it was all really tough on you. So I don't understand why you'd go back, let alone write about it all."

By now, she's well-rehearsed on the response to this sentiment, which she's heard countless times. She sighs heavily before responding in a matter-of-fact tone. "Because it's a story that needs to be told, and I am the one to tell it."

Frank smiles. Julia's confidence and conviction are the two things he loves about her most. "Well, and knowing you, no one could change your mind, huh?" He chuckles softly. "So how long are you staying?"

"I'll probably be back early next week. "

"Okay good…" Frank interrupts her before she has the chance to say there's an option to stay longer. "I can't wait to see you, baby. I've really missed you…"

Julia tenses this time, the irritation bubbling to the surface. "So if you've missed me, then why haven't I heard from you?"

"Baby, we've been through this…you know it's difficult for me to communicate when I'm remote like that."

Julia sighs. It's the same excuse he's given for years. He can somehow upload his photos to his editor from all over the world, but he can't seem to pop her an email or call?

"Right, I know…" The frustration pools in her throat and she breathes deep in an attempt to clear it.

"Look, I'm home for two weeks. Let me make it up to you. Maybe we can take a quick trip somewhere to catch up?"

Of course you are…two whole weeks. Just enough time for a few good lays and a few loads of laundry. The frustration has now simmered into a full boil that she's trying desperately to contain.

"I'm not sure we'll have time for that…" She sucks in a quick breath.

"Well, okay then we'll do something else…"

She pauses and contemplates whether to schedule time with him when she's back in New York or just say what she needs to say. A break up is a break up, no matter how it happens.

"Jules? What is it?" Frank detects her frustration.

"I really didn't want to talk to you over the phone about this…" She looks down at the floor between the sofa and the coffee table, elbows resting on her knees, one hand cradling the phone and the other rubbing her forehead in thought. Frank says nothing.

"But Frank…look, I've been doing a lot of soul searching the past few months and not just about this book. The thing that's really become clear is that I just have to tell the truth. For so many years, I wasn't willing to do that. I was in denial about so many things…" Julia swallows hard. "So what we had was enough…"

"What we had?" Frank interrupts defensively before she can say more. "So you've already made up your mind then? Don't I have a say in all of this?"

"Well, you've certainly given me plenty of time to think..." Julia sighs trying to exhale her anger. She rises and paces around the small cottage trying to carefully pick her words. She doesn't want to say anything she'll regret. Her voice is quieter when she finds her words again. "Frank, no matter how many times we have this conversation, nothing changes. You fly out for months and I never hear from you. Then, you come back for few weeks or a month and expect me to be waiting at home for you like no time has passed. Then you fly right back out."

Frank interrupts. "But you did the same thing when you were touring with the book. So what's the difference? We are both focused on our careers, what's new about that?"

"Frank, the difference now is that I realize I want something more. I want a relationship that actually *feels* like a relationship, not a convenient layover between assignments." The heat from Julia's throat has now plunged into her belly and the red splotches produced by nerves and frustration dot her face.

"I offered marriage to you the last time we saw each other, remember? And you turned me down."

Julia discerns that the defensiveness and frustration in Frank's voice have now morphed to sadness. She realizes maybe it was his bruised ego that kept him from contacting her while he was away this time. When they saw each other before he left, he had made it clear that he wanted marriage and she didn't.

Now, she realizes she's confessing the same desire, if not for marriage then at least for a truly committed relationship. However, the unspoken difference is that in Frank's absence, she's arrived at the harsh realization, or perhaps finally admitted to herself, of what she's known deep down. Frank isn't the man she wants to marry.

"I know that you love me, Frank, and I love you, too. It's just that sometimes love isn't enough to fill the gulf that grows between us when you're gone. I just feel exhausted from all this back and forth...and for so many years. I mean we are in the same spot we've always been. The truth is, I just can't do this anymore."

Frank is quiet again and Julia braces herself for pushback, for a fight like last time. Much like Julia, Frank's never been shy about voicing his opinions. Born and raised in New Jersey, he's always ready to defend his post.

"I get it..." He says quietly with no intonation. "I mean, I understand. Part of me wants to fight you on this and fight for you..."

"There's nothing left to fight for, Frank." Julia rises from the couch in one motion and paces around the small room.

"I know...and hard as it is to hear you say that...I know this hasn't been easy on you. I think for a while this worked for us. You were busy with your career and mine clearly hasn't slowed down."

"Mine hasn't either." Now, it's Julia who retorts defensively.

"No, I didn't mean it that way. I just mean your career has natural starts and stops, and well, mine never seems to stop. I love my work and I love you. I never wanted to have to choose..." He pauses in thought. "So I guess I just kept you hanging on even though I know that's selfish of me. It's selfish of me to expect you to always be here waiting for me to come home. You are so beautiful...so smart...and have so much going for you. You don't need to waste your time waiting on me to come home. I want you to be happy, Jules. I truly do. I just wanted to be the one to make you happy."

Julia makes her way to the small table and sits down heavily into the wooden chair. Though she had mentally prepared herself for this conversation, she hadn't prepared her heart.

How can you ever fully prepare your heart for the end?

Tears frame her green eyes, and she swallows to keep the emotion in check.

"I know you do, Frank. And I love you…and loved our time together. It's just that now I realize I want and need something more than just my work. Being back in Murdoch makes me realize that I want a life, too."

"Have you met someone else?" She knows Frank's question is fair, but it still catches her off guard.

"No…I haven't."

She realizes there's no need to bring up Matt because in her mind there's nothing to explain. Besides, she regularly has drinks with reporters, editors, and other networking connections. The lace of guilt, however, is that she's never been this excited to see an editor for the second time.

After another few minutes, Frank and Julia conclude their conversation. He presses her to have dinner when she returns to New York, though she's non-committal. She knows seeing Frank again will just make things that much harder but she promises to call when she's back.

After she hangs up, Julia places her phone gently on the table. The wave of emotion that had been rattling under the surface rises in one complete motion. The heavy sobs shake her shoulders and she leans her head down onto her bare forearms crossed on the table. The waves of grief engulf her, so much grief that she gasps to catch her breath.

That's the thing about grief, it's latent and sneaky, until out of nowhere it suddenly sparks and then in one fell swoop can completely overtake you. It's as if in this moment all the buried grief she had been carrying is unleashed. Grief over Frank…over Allison…over Betty Ann…over Seth…over everyone she had loved and lost.

After all, grief is just love with nowhere to go.

Now, as the realization of another ending fully registers, Julia's pent-up grief is like an angry bull in a shoot. Once that beast is turned loose, you just have to let him buck and thrash until he stops.

It's the all-too familiar beast of grief that naturally comes when another chapter of your life is complete and you aren't quite sure what's next.

After the heaves of emotion pass, Julia finally sits up in the chair, shoulders still slumped. She wipes her eyes though tears silently stream down her damp cheeks. She inhales deeply, down into the pockets of her soul that had been tucked behind that great wall of denial.

For it's in that little sliver of her heart's surrender where Julia touches what it feels like to finally stand in the midst of her truth.

CHAPTER 31

Lunch and a hot shower restore Julia's energy after the emotional breakthrough earlier. Nearly an hour later, she expects to still be carrying some remnants of sadness, but instead it's more like that calm parting of the clouds that takes place after a sudden rain storm. There's nothing you need to do to alter the situation, rather you find yourself simply observing and marveling at how an hour earlier the bottom dropped out. Now in its wake, there's simply a feeling of deep peace.

Wearing only pink panties and beige bra, Julia paces between the bathroom and closet trying to decide what to wear. It's the same wardrobe dilemma she endured during the scorching Mississippi summers when she lived here before. Finally, she settles on the casual route with a pair of denim shorts, white V-neck shirt, and a pair of flip flops. Regardless of what she thinks, Julia has the kind of natural beauty and grace that make her always look effortlessly put together, no matter if she's in her man panties at bedtime, a chic black cocktail dress for a gala, or a simple white tee-shirt for a summertime wine festival.

On the drive into town, she finds it interesting that the nervous anticipation of seeing Matt somehow also got washed away in the monsoon of tears earlier. She's not sure if that's a good or bad thing.

Julia parks her car along the street in front of the *Messenger* office. She pauses before getting out and flips down the visor to check her reflection in the small mirror one last time. In that moment, she notices something different about her eyes. She studies a moment longer. Her eyes are smiling, and that makes her gently smile, too.

As she emerges from the rental car, the nostalgia kicks up like the dust lining the street curb. She smiles thinking of herself years ago parking along this same street, hurriedly running into the office to write up a story before she forgot a detail or looking for Dan to share some new piece of information.

She reaches over and tugs at the door handle to ensure the car is locked then chuckles to herself remembering there's really no need to lock her car in Murdoch. Pushing open that old glass door leading into the *Murdoch Messenger*, she smiles again and inhales that familiar musty scent of matted carpet and old paneling, though the cigarette smell has faded.

Back then, she made absolutely no money as a newspaper reporter but she didn't care. Every day, she arrived to this office with a sense of duty and purpose. What's funny to her now, is that the stories she covered were really mostly glorified gossip, except for the two murders. That was her first crack at actual investigative reporting. As she looks around the room, it feels smaller than she'd remembered and she's amused to find that it's almost exactly the same, except the desks and computers, which have been updated.

"Hello? Matt?" She calls loudly once inside.

"Oh hey!" Matt strides around the corner from the back workroom. "I see you remember how to get here." He laughs as he walks over to greet her.

She feels the urge to hug him but awkwardly sticks her hand out instead. He shakes it as he did the other night and that same current runs through her. She blushes and breaks his gaze.

"Yes, how could I forget? Still looks the same."

"Oh now, Julia, you really expected it to be different? You know, change is a dirty word 'round here." He laughs. "Lemme just lock up, and I'm ready to go."

Outside under the bright sun, Matt pulls on his wayfarer sunglasses and walks around to the passenger side of his burgundy Ford truck. Julia's confused about what he's doing until he yanks open the door. The feminist in her momentarily balks at the chivalrous gesture, but there's another part of her that secretly loves it. She smiles and mutters a "thank you," before hoisting herself into the passenger seat and clicks into her seat belt.

"You know, I haven't ridden in a pickup in almost twenty years." Julia laughs.

"What?" Matt fakes astonishment. "You mean, they don't have pickups in New York City?"

"Oh, they do but most of the people I know barely own a car."

"I can't even imagine how you'd function without a car." Matt glances at her. "So you like the city?"

"I do…" Julia nods, as Matt heads out of town to hit MS-533 south to Natchez. "It's home, and like anywhere, it has its good and bad."

"So are you from there originally?" Matt quizzes.

"Oh…no, I grew up outside of Chicago and then went to Ball State in Indiana." She pauses wondering how much of her story to reveal right now. "That's where I met Seth, and we ended up back here soon after he finished the police academy."

"I see…" Matt nods thoughtfully and then glances over at her.

"What about you? Do you like New York?"

"Actually, I've never been…" He shrugs.

"Really? Why not?"

"I guess I've just never had a reason to go. Honestly, I'm not sure how long I'd last with all those people." He shivers playfully. "I think I'd feel like a big 'ol country rat in a cage."

Julia belts out a laugh. "Yeah, I can certainly see that. I'd never really noticed the frantic pace of life in New York until I started traveling a lot with the book. When I'd go home, it always took me a day or two to adjust and reintegrate."

"Well, this festival will be a great reintegration to the South." Matt looks at her and smiles. "Seems the Natchez Food & Wine Festival brings everyone out of the woodwork...the rednecks and the Southern socialites."

Julia laughs. "So how long have they been doing this festival?" She didn't remember such an event, but then again, her palette for wine back then only went as far as the inexpensive varieties she and the girls could find at Salty's Liquors.

"I'm not sure, really. I've been coming the past five years or so."

Julia's voice turns playful. "So then which category do you fall in? Are you a redneck...or a socialite?"

"Oh, I don't know...depends on the day, I guess. I have learned my way around nice wines and love to cook. But since I drive a truck in live in rural Mississippi that might push me to the redneck side." He teases and smiles over at her, revealing that lone dimple in his right cheek.

Nothing about Matt's Ray Ban sunglasses, pressed red Hawaiian shirt, khaki shorts, and leather flip flops screams redneck to her. She loves his simple style and the drifts of his woodsy cologne occasionally filtering her way as the air conditioner blows full blast.

She smiles back at him. "I don't know you well enough to say for sure, but when I think about rednecks, I don't think of guys in Hawaiian shirts. I think of those hairy, pot-bellied guys who breathe heavy and think they are God's gift to the world, especially to women. You know like..." Julia's voice trails off not sure she should continue, as she hasn't determined where Matt's allegiances lie.

"Like...?" Matt quizzes.

"Like Ricky Watson."

Matt bursts into laughter. "Touché."

After a long pause, Matt steers the conversation that direction.

"Speakin' of Ricky, how's the research going?"

The question reels Julia back to last night's dinner with Paul and Marilee, the crazy phone call, and pouring over the old articles this morning. "Good, I guess. But the deeper I seem to go in all this, the less I seem to know for certain."

Matt laughs wistfully. "Yeah, I completely understand. It's why I have started and stopped about ten times by now."

"So what were you planning to do?" Julia wonders whether Matt had considered writing a book also. "With your research, I mean…"

"I honestly don't know." He shrugs. "At first, it was to just see if I could figure out what happened to Allison Mercer, but I never really intended to write about anything…just wanted to see what I figure out. I mean, it just seems strange that they never even arrested anyone for her murder. I mean, not a single person. How is that possible?" Matt sighs heavily. "After awhile of gettin' nowhere, I began wonderin' if Allison and Betty Ann's deaths weren't related. So I began down that path…"

"So did you find anything to make you think they were?" Julia interrupts, mulling over her questionable theories from this morning.

"No, not directly but clearly both women found out something they weren't supposed to know…and it got them killed." Matt looks over at her, as Julia stares intently out the front windshield in thought. "I mean, I don't think they were random murders. I think they were both premeditated. What 'bout you? You think they were related?"

"Yeah, I do…"

"Have you figured out what they might have known?" Matt quizzes her back.

"No, not really. The articles don't reveal much." Julia hesitates to share anything more, especially given Paul's warning about Matt last night. So she opts to turn the questioning back to Matt. "So have you had any big revelations?"

"Not really, but I figured out pretty quick after comin' to Murdoch that I better keep a low profile about it all."

"Why's that?"

Matt glances over at Julia. "Because George Stark still has a lot of influence about what's happenin' in that town."

Julia's taken aback. "What do you mean? He's in prison?"

Matt looks over at her. "How do you think Ricky Watson got to be chief of police? We both know he's not an upstanding citizen...or cop for that matter."

Julia's mind races wondering why George would still need Ricky's help after all these years.

"What's wrong?" Matt notices the distracted look on her face.

"Nothing. I've just never fully understood the connection between Ricky and George..." She decides to test him. "I think Ricky was involved in all of it. I just can't figure out if he killed Allison for George...or if something else happened. Maybe he came onto her and she turned him down, so he killed her for spite."

Matt abruptly turns look at her, before returning his eyes to the road. "Was Allison having an affair with Ricky?"

"No, not that I know of but from what I understand he was always flirting with her. You know she worked in city hall during the summers. My friend Kate was George's assistant. She said Ricky was always parading through the office on his way to see George. And you know...there was a rumor about a cop car being spotted around the pool about the time Allison was supposed to have been there."

"Damn, Julia. Where were you before when I was trying to sort this out?"

"I was in New York trying to pretend none of this happened." She looks over at him.

Matt smiles at her. "Well, I'm glad you are here now."

The color rises under her sunglasses. She smiles. "I am too."

"Yeah, I just don't know...I mean, I've often wondered what George and Ricky were up to. I'd heard rumors about all the drug business, but I never found anyone or anything to substantiate it. I still think Betty Ann musta found out somethin' about George...and maybe Allison did, too. What other motive would there be?" Matt's voice grows intense.

Julia thinks about Marilee's admonition about the phone call from Betty Ann the night before she died. She stares out the side window at the beautiful countryside, mind clicking through her thoughts as fast as Matt's truck passes the huge trees lining the road.

Just as she glances over at Matt, she remembers again what Paul said last night about trusting him. She studies Matt, trying to discern for herself whether he's trustworthy. "So tell me about your interview with George in prison. Did you ask him about the drugs?"

"Yeah, I did and he denied it, of course. He said that drugs were a problem in other parts of Adams County but not Murdoch."

Julia laughs. "That's ridiculous. They busted a huge heroin lab five miles south of the city limits soon after Allison died."

"Yeah, but did the Murdoch police bust it?" Matt makes a point.

Julia thinks back. "That's true. It was the county, not Murdoch PD, but still, that's ridiculous. Heroin was a huge problem back in the nineties. A few football players in Pleasant Ridge overdosed within a few months of each other. I had to write about it for the paper. It was so sad…"

Julia has more questions than she has time for right now, realizing they are just outside of Natchez. She opts for the burning one. "So what'd George have to say about his alibi on the night and morning of Betty Ann's death?" She looks over at Matt. "About that ridiculous story of the woman he apparently left the happy hour with…Sheila?"

"Well, he's convinced he was framed for the murder."

"Framed? How?" Irritation escalates in Julia's voice. "He hung himself because his story was crap. They never produced any witnesses to account for his whereabouts after he left the bar. And why would it take him nearly five hours to get from Jackson to his house on the morning Betty Ann was found dead?"

Matt looks over at her. "Five hours…really? But Jackson's just seventy miles away from Murdoch. Why'd it take him so long?"

"Exactly!" Julia's voice grows louder. "Dan and I got there before nine that morning and Peterson pronounced her death around ten. George didn't show up until nearly one-thirty that afternoon, even though they had called him around eight o'clock that morning. So where was he all that time? I mean, if you get a call that your wife had been brutally murdered, wouldn't you drive like a maniac to get home?"

Matt shakes his head dumfounded. "That's unbelievable! I never knew that. George was evasive when I pressed about the timeline. He made it sound like he rushed right there when he found out, and you know that stuff wasn't really reported in the papers. So I was left trying to connect random bits of gossip and George's interview, which was probably a huge pack of lies…"

"So then you think he was lying to you about everything?"

Matt sighs heavily. "I don't know. The thing about George is he's a charmer. He reels you in with that big personality. Makes you feel like you're his long-lost best friend, so it's easy to get sucked into his bullshit. I mean as crazy as it sounds, he's a really likeable guy." Matt looks at Julia in resignation.

She nods her head silently in agreement, understanding full well the two sides of George Stark. George could be the handsome, endearing good 'ol boy and then the angry, ruthless snake. Not the kind of snake that just bites and poisons you quickly, but the kind that wraps you into his web so slowly and tightly that he suffocates and swallows you before you know what's happened.

Julia's so engrossed in the conversation, she doesn't realize that they are already in downtown Natchez until Matt turns his truck down Jefferson Street to find parking. She proceeds anyway.

"So what about the woman…Sheila?" Julia asks again. "Did he talk about her?"

"Yeah, I asked why she wasn't produced as a witness to help confirm his story. George said he didn't know her last name, and she left his hotel room around eleven o'clock and he never talked to her again. Said he didn't have her phone number."

"It's probably because she was a figment of George's imagination." Julia's brain ticks through the chronology. *But if this Sheila woman was real, then I bet she was in the room when George called Betty Ann that night.* Her stomach turns at the thought.

"You okay?" Matt notices the expression of disgust on her face.

"Yeah, it's just all a total mind fuck…excuse the expression." Julia sighs in frustration.

Matt laughs as he pulls his truck into the parking space. "You're right, it is that…and no apology needed. You know, I've found that with a Southern accent, you can pretty much tell anyone to fuck off or go to hell…and it still sounds sweet." He turns off the ignition. "So that means you may just need to stay around a little longer to work on your Southern accent, Julia Jarvis." He says in a high-pitched exaggerated Southern twang.

Julia breaks into laughter. "Well in New York, we used to call that your free drink voice…"

"Seriously?" Matt laughs harder. "Well, in that case, ma'am, may I buy you some wine?"

Julia takes a deep breath, realizing just how wound up she'd gotten in the drive over. She smiles back at him. "Whether you're in the North or the South, you can always win me over with wine."

CHAPTER 32

Over the next four hours, Julia and Matt roam through downtown Natchez, making stops at the different venues participating in the food and wine fest. It's a delicious assortment of Southern foods with an elegant flare, paired with robust varieties of Merlot, Cab, and Zinfandel. Turns out, Matt isn't a white wine fan, either.

Through the course of the afternoon, which has now spilled into evening, Julia discovers Matt is the youngest of three. His sister, Rachel, is six years older, and brother, Derrick, four. "Though I wasn't treated like the baby." Matt offers in his own defense. Julia laughs disbelievingly. Julia also shares select stories from her childhood, and of course, he wants to know more about her writing career and *Steelhouse*.

At the final restaurant, they nibble on a melt-in-your mouth chocolate soufflé paired with a glass of Old South Winery's Natchez Rouge red wine. With their palettes and sensibilities loosened by their wine and culinary adventure, Julia's curiosity is also heightened.

"So may I ask you a personal question?"

"Of course, you can ask me anything…" Matt takes a bite of the soufflé.

"From what I gather, you must be the most eligible bachelor in

Adams County, maybe even all of Mississippi." She smiles teasingly over the candle-lit table. "How is it that you're still single?"

Matt shrugs. "I don't know…my ex-fiancé broke my heart pretty bad. Since then, I guess just haven't found anyone I really connect with for very long. I mean, I've dated women since then…and even had a few more serious relationships…"

"But none that lasted?" Julia quizzes.

"No…" Matt shakes his head.

"So why's that?" Julia realizes she may be prying too much but she's genuinely curious.

"Honestly, I don't know. I mean God knows, I'm no saint. I read too much, fish too much, and sometimes drink too much. I'm a pretty simple guy, but I guess I've just always wanted a relationship with more depth. I want someone I can have fun with and could grow old with. I know that may sound old-fashioned, but my parents have been married nearly forty years. I've always wanted what they have." Matt sighs. "I guess I just haven't found the woman who wants that same thing." Matt looks up at Julia.

Maybe it's just the wine clouding her judgment, but she senses he's searching her as if asking a question. She says nothing, just listens intently.

Matt taps his fork gently against the table. "Besides, most of the women I meet are so shallow. They have don't have gumption." He smiles.

"Gumption?" Julia laughs at his word choice.

"You know, initiative…class."

"I know what the word means, I just don't hear many men your age use it." She smiles at him, and he smiles back sheepishly.

"So do I have gumption?"

"Are you kidding? You have gumption in spades, Julia Jarvis."

She plays along. "Well, thank you for the compliment, Matt Case."

After another sip of wine, he leans across the table. "In fact…I have a confession…" His deep voice is just above a hushed whisper.

"Oh, what's that?" Julia leans in and notices the twinkle in his eyes from the candlelight.

"I was nervous as hell to meet you the other night. I mean it's not every day that I meet beautiful women who have all their teeth and a brain, but then a bestselling author on top of that? Well hell, it's a little intimidatin'…" He smiles broadly, revealing that dangerous dimple. She's not sure why she's so fixated on it, but through the course of the day, it's been like a vortex sucking her in with every chuckle and smile.

Julia laughs at his comment about her teeth again, which she begged her mom to have straightened with braces when she was fourteen. Her mom finally relented.

"Well, I have a confession also…I was, too." Julia's still leaned in, elbows across the table, and her voice matches his hushed tone.

Matt sits up in his chair. "Really? Why? What about a hack of a small-town newspaper editor could make you nervous?" He laughs with self-deprecation.

Julia pauses, unsure how to answer. She has yet to put her finger on exactly what she finds so alluring about him. In some ways, they couldn't be more opposite, but whatever it is, it's incredibly attractive to her. "I don't know. I saw your picture online when I looked up your email address and you just have this thing about you. This energy…"

"An energy, huh? I'm not sure what that means exactly…but you're sittin' here so it must not be bad." He laughs. "So you mean, you stalked me online before we met?"

Julia laughs. "Not really. My intentions were strictly business, but I have to admit that I was curious about you…"

"And now? Are you still curious? Curious enough to see me again tomorrow?" He beams in anticipation.

"Yes, I'm that curious." She smiles playfully.

"Well, first you have to satisfy my curiosity."

"That sounds dangerous…" Julia teases, reveling in every second of their flirtatious banter.

"Well, it may be dangerous for me." Matt winks. "So answer me the same question…how is it that a beautiful, smart, famous author is still eligible?" As soon as the question rolls off his tongue, his disposition changes. It occurs to him Julia admitted that she didn't have a husband, but didn't say anything about a boyfriend.

"What's wrong?" Even through her wine haze and the dimly lit restaurant, Julia notices the shift.

"Nothing…" Matt bristles slightly. "I mean…I assume you're single? I guess that's the better question."

Julia hesitates about how much to reveal. Breakups are always a buzz kill. "Yes, I'm single…"

She notices Matt lets out a little sigh and then looks her squarely in the eyes. "So why do I feel like there's a 'but' in here somewhere…"

She opts for the truth. "Honestly, I was seeing someone for awhile…*but* it's over. It had been over for a long time, and we just recently finalized it." Julia sighs. "It's for the best. He's a good guy but it wasn't working…"

"I see…" Matt's not totally satisfied with her answer, sensing there's something she's not saying, but remembers what happened the other night when he pressed too hard. He'd rather just take her at her word than know the intimate details.

"So to answer your question…I am single because I chose me." She glances down and then looks at him, realizing she has absolutely nothing to lose, and it's a realization that feels completely liberating.

"Honestly, it's been a long, hard road since losing Seth. The relationships after him were pretty much doomed from the start. The one that just ended had been the most serious relationship since my marriage, and it revealed a lot for me. I think it was even healing in some ways, and I'm really grateful for that. I just came to the realization that I'm not interested in convenience anymore. It's not enough to just have a warm body next to me taking up space. I mean I'm forty-four years old, and I'm tired of dating...especially if it's dating the wrong person." The vulnerability of the moment forces Julia to break Matt's intense stare, as she swirls the wine in her glass. "The truth is, I have spent half my life running from my past and all that happened in Murdoch. So I'm not really sure what I'm looking for next...but after everything I've been through, I do know this. I'm ready to have a hell of a lot more fun." She breaks into a broad smile.

Still lost in thought, or perhaps clouded from the wine, Matt nods in understanding. "I really appreciate your honesty...and I get it." He lets out another sigh. "Damn...sounds like we both have a tall order. " His face cracks into a smile, and he winks before taking a large gulp of his water, which has sat on the table so long, all the ice has melted.

As they finish dessert, the tone of the evening has shifted downward, and the tiredness settles over Julia from this highly charged day. The drive home is punctuated with simple conversation, and Julia wonders if Matt's interest has changed after her confession about Frank. Then, she tosses the thought out the window, like she would a banana peel, right into the warm summer evening, which is now becoming fully night. The last trace of the sun has ducked below the horizon. She smiles to herself in the realization that these are the mind games she's no longer willing to play. If Matt is interested in her, then he can step up and own that, and the same goes for her.

Back at the *Messenger* office, Julia gathers her purse from the floorboard, and Matt walks her over to the rental car. Standing on the sidewalk, a flash of nerves sparks the question as to whether he will try to kiss her.

"Well, I had a really great time today." Matt smiles at her under the street lamp. "Thanks for coming with me."

"And thank you for inviting me. I had a wonderful time...and a great reintegration to the South."

He laughs. "Good. So do you still think I'm a redneck?"

"I've never thought you were a redneck." She smiles back at him. "You were a perfect Southern gentleman, Matt Case."

"Then it won't be too forward of me to invite you over for dinner tomorrow evening?" He teases.

"I'd like that…"

"Great, I'll touch base with you tomorrow, then." With that, he leans over and kisses her on the cheek and draws her toward his chest in a brief hug. Just long enough for her to inhale the faintness of his cologne again.

The arousal tingles through her, and it takes everything in her being not to sink into his broad arms and kiss him. Instead, she gently hugs him back before pulling away.

"Have a great night, Matt. See you tomorrow."

"You too…" He waves and smiles. "Oh and hey Julia…I can give you a copy of my notes from the interview with George, if you want. I don't plan to do anything with them."

"Really? That'd be great."

"Anything I can do to help…just let me know."

"Thanks, Matt. I appreciate that."

"Bye Julia." And with that he, hops into his truck and drives away.

CHAPTER 33

Leaving Matt in downtown Murdoch and heading out the farm-to-market road toward the cottage, Julia's mind see-saws between thoughts of her evening with Matt and visions of taking a hot bubble bath. It's hard to believe she's only been in Murdoch since Tuesday, less than a week, though it feels like months since she's been gone.

It's as if the last year of her life had been in slow motion until Memorial Day weekend with Kate and Marilee. Since then time has been fast-tracked, packing months' worth of insights, memories, and emotions into mere hours and days.

Nearing nine-thirty, the bright summer sky has morphed from its clear blue to deep black, stars dotting every imaginable space. Above everything she misses while living in the city, it's the expansive sky sprinkled with stars and constellations. She slows the car along the dirt road so she can peer through the windshield, quickly spotting the Big Dipper above her. Julia rolls down her window and inhales the thick summer air. She smiles as she accelerates again, pulling up to the cottage.

The beam from her headlights illuminates a black pickup parked out front. "What the..." She murmurs aloud. She stops the car wondering if it's the same black truck from this morning.

Heart racing, she picks up her phone, not really sure who she'll call given the chief of police is now stepping around the side of the truck directly in front of her car. She clinches her phone tighter.

"Hey Julia." Ricky nonchalantly motions a wave.

She forces a smile and half waves as she opens the car door. She steps into the crevice between the open car door and the driver's seat, making a barricade of sorts between them. The car's headlights shine brightly on him producing the only source of light around the cottage. She had forgotten to leave the front porch light on before she left earlier.

"Hey Ricky. What are you doing here?" The adrenaline courses through her. She's suddenly wide awake, praying Ricky doesn't smell her fear, which escalates by the second.

"Oh I've just been waiting for you to get home..." He spits a stream of tobacco. "So we could have a chat."

His belly looks even bigger in the plain red tee-shirt hanging over the waistband of his Wrangler's, paired with dirt-covered, steel-toed boots. Beads of sweat roll down his forehead and he brushes them away with the back of his hand. She wonders how long he's been waiting out here in the pitch black.

"Chat about what?" Julia still clenches her phone in her right hand, keys in the left, and mind racing plotting an escape route.

"'Bout this book. Seems some people in town are in a tizzy 'bout you writin' it." He kicks at the dirt in front of the car. "So I told 'em I'd come have a talk with you, since we go way back and all." The way he chuckles at the last statement makes her wonder if he's been drinking.

"Well, I don't even know if I'm writing a book yet." She lies to distract him.

"Then why'd Nelda say you are?"

"Because she's old and gets confused."

"Yeah, Mrs. Dixon is gettin' up there but I know she means well. I also know she ain't a liar. You on the other hand...I've never been too sure about you." He peers angrily her direction and his voice rises. "You got some helluva nerve waltzin' back in here after all these years. You got no right tryin' to make a dollar off what happened here for yourself...or your fancy publisher in New York. Ain't that where you live now?"

"Yeah, that's right." She offers nothing more, studying Ricky's movements closely to ensure she has clearance to jump in the car if he steps toward her. She and Cheryl have taken self-defense several times over the years living in the city. Fortunately, she's never had to use it, but she's not above doing so now, even it means kicking Murdoch's chief of police square in the groin and running like hell. Staring at him now, the years of anger simmer under her skin.

"Well, then here's some friendly advice. I think it's best you pack your shit and take the next flight back...and forget all 'bout this book bidness. Ain't nuthin' here for you to write 'bout. I mean your husband's dead now, so he can't protect you." With that, he spits again.

Now, her anger reaches full boil. She chews her threatening words like the cows chew their cuds. Drawing a deep breath, she tries to soften her tone because she knows better than to fight with the devil.

"I understand, Ricky. I'll be leaving soon. Just going to see the Johnson's and Nelda one last time and then flying back." She stares at him intently.

It seems to work, as he backs down. Ricky peers at her a moment longer, the haze of the headlights streaming between them.

"Okay then...I guess I'll get goin' and let you get back to your evenin.' But you should know that everyone's watchin' you..." Ricky turns and hoists himself into the black truck, revs the engine, and then gasses it as he pulls around past her. He waves out the open window, and she lifts her left hand in a half-wave.

Just as the truck clears the back of her car, she notices it's a Dodge truck, verifying that it is, indeed, the same one from this morning. She freezes, still tucked in the space between the door and the driver's seat.

Julia doesn't budge until Ricky's halfway down the road. She grabs her purse and sprints to the front porch, fumbles for the key, and unlocks the door. She throws open the heavy door, reaches for the double light switch and flips them both, illuminating the front porch and the dining room. She quickly slams the door shut and locks it tight, hands now shaking.

She's just about to dial Kate's number, and then it clicks. *No, call Matt.*

He answers on the third ring. "Hey Julia…"

She clears her throat. "Hi Mmmatt…I'm so sorry to bother you…"

"No, not at all…what's wrong?"

"Ricky…he was here when I got back to the cottage." Her words come out choppy between labored breaths, the adrenaline cascading through her. "He started spewing…about…about…how I needed to forget about the book and go back to New York because my husband was dead and couldn't protect me." She swallows hard, choking back the fear-lined tears. She cannot stand it that Ricky Watson unnerves her so. "I'm sorry to call this late…it just freaked me out to drive up and have him standing there. I really hate that man."

"God, please don't apologize. You okay? Do you need me to come over there?" Matt's voice rises in concern.

"Yeah…I mean, no…no, it's okay." Julia stammers in confusion. "I'll be okay. I just got a little rattled." She takes a deep breath and looks around the small cottage. She isn't sure how she will sleep.

"Are you sure?" The concern is evident in Matt's voice. "I don't mind at all…I'm only ten minutes away. You're at the Peterson's cottage, right?"

"Yeah…yeah…I am. You sure you don't mind?"

"Not at all. I'd rather you not be there alone. Lock the doors, and I'll be right over."

Safely locked inside, Julia's hands still shake as she quickly showers, trying to scrub away the sight of Ricky standing in front of her. She pulls her hair into a bun and slips on a pair of black yoga pants and purple tank top. Just as Julia wanders into the kitchen, she jumps hearing a knock on the door.

"Julia, it's me...Matt." He taps softly again.

Julia cracks open the door to verify it's Matt, feeling even more exhausted and slightly embarrassed. She's never wanted to be a damsel in distress needing a man for anything.

"Hey..." She opens the door wider so he can enter. "Come in before the mosquitoes carry you away."

Not two steps into the cottage, Matt envelopes her. The stubble on his cheek grazes hers provoking that deep stirring within her.

"You okay?" He pulls away slowly, pinning her with a look of genuine concern.

"Yeah...yeah, I'm fine..." She smiles.

"Good..." Matt grins and takes the few steps toward the counter to free his hand of his wallet, phone, and keys. "Sorry you have to see me so casual." He chuckles. His Hawaiian shirt and khakis have been replaced by black athletic shorts and a navy Atlanta Braves shirt. "I didn't take time to change...but now you know that I'm a closeted Braves fan."

Julia smiles. She's never followed baseball, so isn't sure if that's a good or bad thing. "I was just making some hot tea. Want some?"

"Sure, that'd be good..." Matt wanders around taking in the cottage. "This is a great place."

"Yeah, it's really been the perfect getaway except for the unexpected phone calls and uninvited guests." She sighs. "Thanks so much for coming over..."

Matt settles into one end of the sofa, Julia crosses her legs underneath her on the other facing him.

"When I saw it was you callin', my first thought was that you couldn't wait until tomorrow to see me again…" He teases and laughs softly.

She smiles. "Now Matt…you said I had gumption." She mocks surprise, as she gingerly picks up her steaming mug of tea.

He winks then his voice turns serious. "So are you really okay? What happened? And what's this phone call you keep mentioning?"

"Oh last night, I had gotten home late from the Johnson's and was washing my face…and suddenly the home phone rang. I didn't even know there was a landline phone here. Anyway, this man called trying to warn me I needed to go home. He sounded angry and drunk, but it didn't sound like Ricky. I don't know who it was, though it's unnerving realizing strangers know I'm staying out here alone. So then tonight, I pull up and Ricky's truck was parked out here in the pitch black waiting for me. He said about the same thing…that I needed to forget about the book and go home." She pauses and looks up at Matt. "The thing that really shook me was his comment that my husband was dead and not here to protect me." Julia glances down at the hot mug and blows on the steaming liquid before taking a sip.

"Sounds like he was just being an asshole. I've come to learn Ricky is mostly all talk, except when he's really angry. Then he turns into a monster. He wasn't that angry…was he?" The concern is clearly etched across Matt's face.

"No…no he was trying to be civil, I guess. I mean as civil as a backwoods redneck cop can be."

"Well, I'm glad you called me…" Matt smiles.

"You are? I feel a little dumb now…" Julia replaces the mug onto the coffee table next to the Jesus box, which she'd left perched half open this morning. "I'm not a woman who wants to be saved."

"You mean by me or Jesus?" He points to the box sitting in the middle of the table.

Julia breaks into a laugh and Matt chimes in.

263

"So why do you have a Vacation Bible School box? Is there somethin' else I should know about you?"

"No…it's Nelda's. She used it to store all my old articles about the murders."

It takes him a second to register the irony, and then lets out a throaty laugh. "Seriously? That's hilarious…and sorta twisted don't ya think?"

Julia laughs harder thinking of Nelda's puzzled face when Julia had questioned her about the box a few days ago. "It is but totally something Nelda would do. She said everyone could use a little more Jesus."

Matt's laughter shakes his mug of tea, with a few drops spilling over onto his mesh athletic shorts. He leans forward and places the white ceramic mug on the table. He glances over at her, and their eyes catch, and the howling erupts. Julia's still not sure why she finds it so hilarious that Nelda would use that Jesus box, and perhaps she should duck in fear of a lightning bolt for being irreverent, but she cannot help it. It's just, well, so Nelda.

Matt finally regains his composure. "You know, I haven't had a chance to talk with Mrs. Dixon much but she sure seems like a character."

"Oh, you have no idea…" Julia takes a deep breath to relieve her diaphragm, which had been doubled over in amusement. "She's one of the best people I know."

Matt adjusts his position on the couch so he can turn to face her. In the motion, Julia notices he's moved a little closer. "You said the other day you haven't been back in years…so then it's been awhile since you'd seen her?"

Julia's smile drops into that pool of guilt she still carries about Nelda. "Yeah…yeah it had."

"You didn't want to come back to see her?" Matt asks softly.

"Oh, I did…I mean…I wanted to but I just couldn't. I wasn't ready to face her. She and Seth look so much alike, even the other day it was like staring at his ghost. We talked regularly after he died and then the calls were less frequent…only on his birthday." Her voice drops. "I'm sorry. Is this weird for you? I mean to talk about him."

"Not at all. I mean, it's part of your past, and clearly Nelda is important to you." He smiles. "So then, had it been that long since you'd seen the Johnson's?"

"No…I see Marilee pretty regularly for our girls' weekends with our other old Murdoch friend, Kate…but Marilee always flies out to meet us wherever we are." Julia looks up at him, the tiredness melding with that easy feeling you get after a hearty laugh.

"So has it been hard? I mean…being back? Harder than you thought?" Matt pauses and smiles, catching himself in the midst of the peppering. "Am I asking too many questions?"

Julia smiles. "You can ask me whatever you like. And yes…it's been hard. It's brought back a lot of old memories, but it's also been really good…seeing Nelda especially. I just love that woman. She's been like a mother to me."

Matt smiles. "Yeah, I've always had this soft spot for older women."

"Oh you mean like cougars?" Julia plays along.

"Noooo…gross." He laughs. "I mean the grandmotherly types who have so much wisdom. I just look at old people and wonder what their stories are…what have they seen? What do they remember? What moments changed their lives?" He runs his left hand through his wavy hair and then leans his elbow on the sofa's overstuffed backrest, knuckles curled over into a gentle fist, resting against the side of his high jawbone. "In the end…I think that's all we really have to leave behind…"

"What's that?"

"Our stories…" He pierces her with his eyes again, and Julia tries to stuff down the desire that keeps flickering up within her.

Navigating the dating scene in New York for years and then

being with Frank for so long, Julia was certain when she arrived in Murdoch four days ago that men like Matt Case were dinosaurs, extinct creatures relegated to some fairy tale you only see in the movies.

Yet, here he is right in front of her. This sexy, smart, sensitive man, who's really single (and straight) explaining to her why he loves talking to old grandmothers. She keeps waiting for some freak flag to pop up at any time, some weird idiosyncrasy, or some offending comment to just turn her off, but so far, nothing. He's an anomaly to her, but then again, she knows any man can be an exception to any rule after only a few conversations.

Surely there are ghosts in his past or some wickedly awful habits lurking that will dismantle it all. Fortunately, or perhaps unfortunately, she's leaving Tuesday and in that realization, Julia settles back into this moment to detach a little. Suddenly, it occurs to her that she has no tethers or commitments to Frank, Matt, or any man. She has no need to assume responsibility for anyone else's feelings, only to show up in the integrity of who she is and be in this moment. And that sense of freedom feels both delicious and dangerous.

"It's why I admire what you do as a writer." Matt interrupts her thoughts.

She smiles at the compliment. "What do you mean? You write, too."

"No, not like you. You aren't just a writer, Julia. You're an artist. You have this way of evoking imagination, phrasing sentences, and illuminating the best parts of humanity in your characters and the real-life people you write about. It's really sexy." He smiles mischievously. "The truth is, I have been following your writing for years."

"You have?"

"Yeah, I read your work regularly in *GQ* and in some of the other magazines. Now here you are sittin' on a couch with me in

Murdoch, Mississippi of all places...drinkin' hot tea. It's a little surreal." His soft laugh is lined with a hint of disbelief.

She blushes and glances down so he won't see her cheeks. She looks up to find him slowly scooting closer to her along the sofa. Before she can fully comprehend his movement, he's inches from her face.

"And I have another confession." He whispers looking playfully into her eyes.

Adrenaline forces her heart against her breastbone and she's certain he will hear the loud thumps. "Oh?" She whispers back. "What?"

He presses his face closer to hers. "I've wanted to kiss you since the minute I sat down at McCain's."

Julia gives him no time to say anything more, his words are the invitation to lean into the moment. As their lips graze and then fully connect, every nerve in her being strains toward him. She reaches up and folds her slender hands along his chiseled jawline, pulling him into her. His tongue dances teasingly against hers, before pulling back and playfully biting her bottom lip. It's all she can do to not throw him backward on the couch.

She pulls away briefly to draw in a deep breath and opts to follow his lead. His eyes are full of delight and his half-smile asks a question, without saying a word. Her seductive smile replies, "yes," and he leans in again, this time running his hand along the side of her face and down her neck. His lips follow, with kisses and nibbles that become more insistent. She sinks into the pleasure of his taste, touch, scent.

After a few more rounds of Matt's persistent kisses, she wants more. "Why don't we go to the bedroom?"

He leans back surprised, searching her face. "You sure?"

Julia's taken aback by her own brashness and hesitates momentarily. "Yes, but I don't have any..."

"Don't worry...I do..." He smiles and leans back to regain

composure before standing. He extends his hand to help Julia off the couch. "I'll be there in a minute."

After a trip to the bathroom to check her face and brush her teeth, Julia pulls back the duvet and sinks into the bed. Her exhaustion pales in the backdrop of the night. She crosses her legs under her and leans back against the stack of pillows. This brief pause creates space for a rumble of nerves, followed by an unwelcome pang of guilt. Just this morning she was sitting on the edge of this bed reading messages from Frank. She pushes away the thoughts of Frank and the ensuing guilt and takes a deep breath. She's startled back to the moment with a loud rattling of pots and pans in the kitchen.

"Are you looking for something?" Julia raises her voice for him to hear.

"Got it!"

A moment later Matt enters the bedroom with three pillar candles he's retrieved from the cabinet, a book of matches, and two rounds of protection (just in case). He places the candles on the side tables, switches off the overhead light, and walks around to sit by her on the edge of the bed. Julia quietly observes him.

"You okay?" He leans over and looks at her. "Did you change your mind?"

"No...did you?" She smiles.

He smiles back and shakes his head before leaning across her to softly kiss her again. "Good...I'm glad." He whispers and adjusts his position so that he's now laying beside her on the bed.

Even though they are still fully clothed, the heat between them is palpable. He leans in again and kisses her. She can feels his pleasure against her thigh, which elicits an even deeper hunger.

Matt drinks her in, as he runs his large hands gently down the sides of her bare arms. His touch is so light, it verges on a tickle.

He pauses and looks genuinely into her eyes. "You're a beautiful woman, Julia Jarvis."

Julia smiles not because of the flattery but because of the sincerity. She leans forward and presses her soft lips onto his, as his hands continue to flick and tease as they explore down her back. In a brief pause, he leans away and pulls her shirt over her head and then tosses his own on the floor.

She caresses her hands across his broad, muscular chest and barely flicks his nipple which produces a half laugh. "They're sensitive." He says in a low voice.

Julia laughs and opts to retreat from them. She closes her eyes and feels the interchange between hands and lips dancing across her breasts, neck, and the soft, sweet curves of her womanly belly. His fingers tease along her waistline. She moans with delight, trying to push away the thought that's just emerged of how unsexy yoga pants are in this intimate moment.

Julia's quickly jolted back to the present, however, as Matt slides her pants down. Then in sequence, his shorts also come off. She's never been with a man so confident, and yet so thoughtful, in the removal of her clothes. The hunger inside of her just wants him to tear into her.

But Matt takes his time, hands tracing every line, curve, scar, and freckle. Like two hands caressing a piano, he simply follows where the moment takes him.

In an equally smooth exchange, Matt prepares for the next arrangement. She arches her back and thrusts upward to receive him fully. He gently and rhythmically works his hips in concert with hers. Soon their sweetness turns sultry.

"I want you…" Julia whispers huskily in his ear breaking the relative silence between their chorus of moans and exhales, a confession that catches them both a little by surprise.

He works his hips harder and faster, seizing the heat and openness of her body occasionally looking into her eyes and kissing her.

Their bodies now glisten with dampness of the hot summer

night and the added fire of the moment. Julia moans, inhales a deep breath, and allows Matt to take her to that ecstatic high, a shudder of heat, desire, release. To her amazement, he rides that final crescendo of pleasure right alongside her.

They lay silently entwined a moment longer, deeply inhaling to catch their breaths and regain composure, before he releases her from the weight of his body. It's not long before he's enveloped her in the perfect embrace, feet nestled under hers, chest against her back and face nuzzled under the crook between her neck and her ear.

"You okay?" He asks softly.

Body and mind completely relaxed, Julia smiles in the dark. "I'm wonderful…that was amazing."

"Yes it was. I didn't expect you to…"

"What?"

"Be so passionate…"

She laughs. "Oh there's a lot you don't know about me."

"Well I'd like to know a lot more."

She smiles again. Silence falls between them.

"God I love this." He says softly.

"What?" Her voice barely above a whisper.

"Layin' here like this. I'm about as red blooded of a Southern man as they come, so clearly I love having sex. But layin' here like this is one of my favorite things." He sighs heavily and kisses her bare shoulder.

"Me too. I love spooning."

"Spoonin'?" He laughs. "What the hell is that?"

"What we're doing. You've never heard that?"

"No." Matt's mind is foggy and it takes him a moment to process why laying in this position is called spooning. When it clicks, he breaks into a laugh. "That's a stupid name but okay…I love spoonin.'"

Julia echoes his laugh and in their post-sex euphoria, this interchange is funnier than it should be. Their belly laughter produces coughs and tears until finally they both relax back onto their pillows, where they swap stories of distant memories and old dreams.

It's after two o'clock in the morning when they fall asleep entangled in each other's arms.

CHAPTER 34

Julia stirs and kicks the white sheet off her naked body. It's too hot for covers. She blinks her eyes open, and the lingering peace of last night's delights produce a sleepy smile, until her eyes flutter fully open.

What time is it? Oh my God...Matt. Julia glances over and sighs with slight relief that he's not in bed. She's not quite sure she's ready face to him in the daylight. Julia has never been prudish, but she's never considered herself one to swing from the chandeliers, either. Last night's encounter was a first for her, sleeping with a man she barely knows on the heels of breaking up with a man she once loved.

Did he go home? With every passing second, her mind wakes to full attention and regret over last night slowly seeps into her thoughts, quickly intensifying to full-strength guilt. Guilt over allowing herself to take it that far and enjoy it that much. She recalls the conversation with Frank and hears his hurt ringing in her ears, and that was just yesterday morning.

As Julia rubs her sleepy eyes, a deeper truth settles over her. The guilt amplifying to the point it forces a gasp. She had sex with another man in her husband's hometown, and that man wasn't her husband. Her heart was aflutter last night after that passionate exchange, but now, in the light of day, that emotion verges on recoiling fear. Lingering a bit longer in the soft bed, Julia finally regains her composure.

As she sits up and plops her feet onto the hardwood floor, she inhales deeply the smell of bacon now wafting back to the room. She glances at the closed bedroom door, unsure whether to feel relief or regret that Matt hasn't left.

Standing upright in the mirror brushing her teeth, the merry-go-round of thoughts take hold. *Didn't I just tell Frank yesterday that I couldn't do the long-distance thing anymore? That I wanted something more? Matt lives here, and I live in New York, so what else could this be but a one-night stand? Damn'it, what did I do?*

She retrieves her yoga pants and tank top, and pulls her hair into a loose bun before wandering barefooted into the small kitchen. Matt stands with his back toward her, bent over the stove in his athletic shorts and Braves shirt, quietly whistling.

"Good morning." Julia's voice makes him jump.

"Well, hello…" Matt turns on his heels, feet bare, with that dimple beaming along with his smile. "I didn't wake you, did I?"

"No…but I thought you'd left until I smelled the bacon." She smiles.

"Well, I left for a bit but I came back." He grins even wider striding over to her, pulling her into his arms. She slightly stiffens at the intimacy of the embrace. He kisses her forehead before grazing her lips and then peers into her eyes. "Seems you only have rabbit food 'round here and we needed a real breakfast. So I ran into the store."

"I see that. So vegetables aren't real food for you?" She smiles again.

"Well, yeah but not for breakfast. I woke up starving." He winks, softly pecking her lips again and returns to the stove.

Julia's no doubt impressed with the spread of scrambled eggs, bacon, and those canned biscuits you pop open and bake. The kind Seth always cooked when he'd make breakfast for dinner. She's always loved lathering butter and jelly on those big, flaky biscuits, but given her mostly organic diet, she never allows herself to buy them, only eyes them from time to time in the market.

She smiles at his effort and heads to the pot of freshly brewed coffee. "This looks amazing. Thank you for doing all of this."

"Happy to. I love making breakfast. I used to wake up early when I was a kid and help my MawMaw. She made the best homemade biscuits and gravy. But I decided I had to save a few tricks, so you get the store-bought ones."

Julia smiles, though her heart dips again, as she takes a sip of coffee. The scene is far too reminiscent of mornings with Seth. "Well, you didn't have to do this."

Matt interrupts. "It's okay. I wanted to."

He pulls the biscuits out of the oven, while Julia wanders over to the coffee table and then to her purse. "Have you seen my phone?"

"Yeah, it's over on the edge of cabinet near my wallet. I moved everything to set the table." He looks over at her. "It's been goin' off all morning."

Julia retrieves her phone and looks down to see a missed call from Kate and three missed texts from Frank. The first message from Frank was sent somewhere in the wee hours of the morning, almost as if he knew she was with Matt. It simply read:

I miss you Julia.

She tries to hide the added layer of guilt in her face. Then, just an hour ago, Frank had sent the other two texts.

I wish you were here so we could talk in person.

Are you getting these? I know there's nothing more to say, really. I feel like I screwed everything up. I know you deserve more, Julia. Just wish I could be the one to give it to you. I love you, baby.

As if things weren't complicated enough in her arriving at the decision to end things with Frank, now she's convoluted everything further by sleeping with a man she really likes, but who lives thirteen-hundred miles away. Her cheeks flush as she feels Matt's intent stare.

"Everything okay?" His voice brings her back to the moment.

"Yeah, yeah...I'm fine. It's fine." She deletes Frank's messages and returns her phone to the counter.

Matt stands with two plates in hand. "Okay...well breakfast is ready." He smiles, still studying her face and detecting her shift in mood, but doesn't ask anything more. And she doesn't offer.

At the cottage table, they quietly eat, though she feels Matt's eyes on her every few bites.

"You okay this mornin'? I mean, you don't have any regrets about last night?" Matt's brow furrows awaiting her reply.

Julia tries to sidestep her true feelings, secretly wishing she could relax and just let it be whatever it was. "Well, no...I guess not. I had a wonderful time with you...but..."

"Uh oh, there's another but..." Matt interrupts trying to lighten the intensity clearly evident on Julia's face. "But what?" He smiles.

"It just feels more complicated this morning."

"What's complicated?" He shrugs.

"This..." Julia waves across the table.

"Breakfast is complicated?" Matt teases.

"No...breakfast after sex is complicated. I mean, one-night stands don't usually include a meal afterward." Julia realizes the barb in her words, but they fly out anyway. Matt sits back in his chair.

"Oh, is that what it was? Just a one-night stand?"

"No, I didn't mean...I'm sorry...it's just more confusing now, that's all." Julia tries to backpedal. She sighs heavily. "I guess I'm just not sure where this can go. I mean, I'm leaving in a few days..."

"Look, Julia I don't have any expectations here. I just enjoy being with you." Matt looks over at her. He takes a sip of coffee as she quietly scoots her scrambled eggs around her plate. A few awkward moments hang over the table before Matt breaks the silence.

"Maybe a little good Southern barbecue and beer would help simplify things. I'm hopin' you'll still come over this evenin' so I could make you dinner." Matt smiles hopefully.

Julia sighs. Honestly, she'd love to see him again, but also knows her time is limited. And the more time she spends with Matt, the more confusing things could become. "Well, I'd love to, but I am meeting Dan later and not sure how long that will take."

"Well, maybe tomorrow then?"

"I'm not sure. I have a few more people to see tomorrow and need to get packed. I have to leave early for Jackson Tuesday morning to fly back home."

"I see…" Matt looks over at her. "I was sorta hopin' you'd extend your stay…"

Julia pushes back her half-eaten plate, as suddenly exhaustion and overwhelm fill her belly. "Matt, I had a really great time yesterday, but I have to be honest…I just recently ended a long-distance relationship. I'm not looking for another one." Julia realizes her statement may be presumptuous but she also knows she cannot get entangled again so soon after Frank and at the start of this book.

"Oh…I see…well I didn't say I was looking for one, either." Matt's tone turns defensive. "I just thought we might spend a little more time together, that's all…"

"I know and under different circumstances, I'd love that." She smiles honestly at him. "I just realize that I have to stay focused on what's in front of me and that's going home and writing this book."

Matt nods. "I understand…and certainly don't want to get in the way of that." He stands abruptly and marches to the sink with his plate. He quietly runs water over it, looking out the window in thought. Finally, he breaks the silence and turns to her with a smile.

"But I do have one condition…"

"What's that?" Julia looks up at him.

"If you come back to Murdoch, you have to look me up again."

"You got it." Julia smiles back.

Matt offers to help Julia clean the kitchen, but now with their honest exchange still laid out on the table, every passing minute grows a bit more uncomfortable. She assures Matt she can handle the clean up. After a long hug on the front porch, Julia waves him good-bye with a heavy heart. She truly does wish the circumstances were different. Arms crossed over her chest, she stares as Matt's truck lumbers down the dirt road. The late morning sun blazes down on her. *Why does the Universe always bring what I want when I'm not ready for it?*

Julia returns to the cottage to finish cleaning the remaining dishes and then grabs her phone and falls heavily into the couch. She scans through her email and social media accounts before resting the phone on the coffee table.

She's not sure how long she's been asleep when the phone jars her awake. Julia abruptly sits up and retrieves the phone, smiling to see who's on the other end.

"Hey…"

"Hey gurl! Whatcha doin'?" Kate's bright voice is contagious.

Julia clears her throat. "Nothing, just resting a minute. I laid down on the couch and guess I fell asleep."

"Yeah, you sound a little groggy…what's goin' on? Late night?" Kate chuckles.

"Actually…yeah it was a very late night." Julia's yawn punctuates her sentence.

"Ohhh dawg! What happened? Were you with Matt?" Kate cackles into the phone. "You better spill it!"

"Uhhh…why do I always get myself into these messes?" Julia moans, legs outstretched on the sofa with one hand cradling her phone and the other palm resting on her forehead.

"What mess? Gurl, you gotta tell me what happened!" Kate's voice rises in excitement then she gasps. "Wait a minute…you slept with him?"

277

Julia hesitates. "Something like that, but we didn't do much sleeping."

"Hoooo, Lawd! I knew it!" Kate cackles louder into the phone. "Good for you, gurl. You needed some fireworks. You were wound up tighter than a snare drum." Kate laughs harder.

Now Julia chimes into the laughter. "Well, there was definitely fireworks…." Then lowers her voice. "Honestly, it was the best sex I've had in years."

Kate scoffs. "I wouldn't know anything 'bout that. Lately, I haven't even had time to think 'bout sex. I've been as busy as a cat tryin' to bury its shit in a marble floor."

Julia doubles over in laughter with her friend on the other end of the phone, her spirit momentarily lightening until the pang of guilt returns.

"Well, it was fun but now it's just made things more complicated." Julia sighs heavily staring up at the eggshell-colored ceiling.

"What's complicated about two consenting adults having some fun?"

Julia sighs. "I know…and Matt's a really great guy, but I just woke up feeling so guilty today."

"Because of Frank?"

"Yeah, we finally talked yesterday morning and I broke it off with him. I think he understands, at least I hope he does. He's been the only man I've slept with in over six years. So there's that…and then…well then there's Seth." Julia's voice clouds saying his name.

"Well I'm glad you talked to Frank and told him the truth. I'm sure that was hard for you but we both know it was beyond time. He'll be okay. So I get that part, but what I don't understand is why you'd feel guilty 'bout Seth?"

"It probably sounds stupid…" Julia sighs. "But I just feel guilty about sleeping with another man in his hometown. I mean, this is where we began our life together, and my whole purpose in coming here was to make peace with that. Now, I've just created a bigger mess. Matt's great and we have a lot of fun together. He wanted to see me today but I just don't know if that's a good idea…" Julia rubs her forehead, the confused thoughts swirling.

"Jules look, your purpose in goin' to Murdoch wasn't just about Seth. It was about Allison and Betty Ann. It sounds like to me you've just let yourself get distracted from that purpose. So you had a little rendezvous…good! You needed to cut loose a little. But gurl, you don't owe Frank…or Seth…or Matt anything. You gotta get your head straight and refocus on *you*. You went there to get those articles from Nelda and figure out your next steps. That's it. Don't try to make this all harder than it really is…"

"I know…you're right." Julia sighs and swallows back the lump in her throat. She knows deep down that Kate is right and maybe her real frustration this morning is realizing she let herself get sidetracked. In coming back to Murdoch, she has blurred the boundaries of past, present, and future.

Julia clears her throat. "I know it's time to get back to my life in New York." She pauses remembering nasty Ricky Watson hulking over her last night. "Besides I think I've worn out my welcome here, anyway."

"Whaddya mean?" Kate quizzes. "What happened?"

"When I got back to the cottage from the wine festival with Matt, Ricky was out here waiting for me. I don't know how long he'd sat out here in the dark, but he told me I needed to go back home and forget about the book." Julia pauses in thought, the anger seeping back to the surface. "He also said I needed to be careful because my husband wasn't here to protect me. I don't hate many people but I can honestly say I hate that son-of-a-bitch."

Kate gasps. "Oh shit, are you okay? What nerve that man has to say that after all you've been through…and especially when we both know his hands are dirty in all of this!"

"Exactly…why else would he be so threatened by me being here and writing the book?" Julia's anger morphs to vindication. "I may go home…but I'm not giving up on this."

"Good gurl, you shouldn't."

After a few more minutes of hearing about Kate's case and her upcoming vacation with Jerry and Jennifer, the two exchange good-byes. Julia promises to touch base with Kate when she's back in New York later in the week.

Before returning her phone to the coffee table, Julia texts Marilee to see about having lunch on Monday. She yawns heartily and stretches to the full length of the sofa, relieved to see she can get in another thirty-minute nap before visiting Dan. The cool air of the ceiling fan creates the perfect gentle breeze to send Julia lazily off to sleep.

CHAPTER 35

Julia finds it amusing to use a navigation system in Murdoch. Years ago, she'd just stop at a gas station and ask for directions because everyone knew where everyone else lived. Now she's relieved for the technology, as it leads her easily toward 4211 Magnolia Place.

The Murphy residence is in a newer subdivision outside of Murdoch, which was just a thicket of trees and native Kudzu when she lived here. She'd never heard of Kudzu before arriving in Murdoch.

"They say it's the vine that ate the South," Seth had laughed one day while trying to explain the wild green vine, "because it will overtake everything in it's path, including you if you stand still too long."

Turning onto Magnolia Place and pulling up in front of the Murphy's two-story brick home, Julia finds it modest in stature compared to some of the other houses lining the street. The Murphy's front lawn is well manicured with rich Saint Augustine grass, and the rose bushes lining the front of the home brilliantly show their red summer blooms. Julia inhales a deep breath, nerves beginning to rumble as she retrieves her purse, leather notebook, and phone from the passenger seat.

Dan answers soon after she rings the doorbell. She hopes her gasp isn't audible but it's one of those involuntary responses that happens when you see someone from your past that looks so drastically different. Dan's round belly is completely gone behind his blue, buttoned-down shirt tucked neatly into his khaki shorts. The shorts are clearly too big and held in place by a brown leather belt. His face is perhaps the most striking, with his signature beard now completely white, though it fails to hide his sunken cheeks and ashen skin.

Julia finally regains her composure to speak. "Hi Dan." She smiles at her former mentor genuinely happy to see him after so many years.

"Julia!" He beams upon opening the door fully. "I'm so glad to see you. Come on in." He gingerly takes a step back to allow her room to enter and they exchange a quick hug. Though she's careful to not tip him over or squeeze too hard. She's afraid of hurting him.

Maybe this wasn't such a good idea. Julia's still unsure what's really going on with his health, but it's clearly taken a toll on him. He shuffles in front of her towards the living room. Dan settles into an overstuffed recliner, asking between gasps if she found the house okay, then pulls on a nasal cannula attached to a portable oxygen pack sitting on the end table.

"Sorry but it's the way things are now." Dan smiles sadly.

Julia tries not to stare but she's never been around someone so frail. Her maternal grandparents both died suddenly, and she never knew her paternal ones. So aging and illness are both somewhat foreign to her.

"No, no it's okay. Please do whatever you need." Julia smiles back.

Dan's wife greets them with cold lemonade and after exchanging pleasantries, Alice returns down the hallway to whatever she was doing.

After taking a long sip, Dan's curiosity can no longer wait. "So, tell me 'bout this book. I've been intrigued since we talked yesterday. You know, I read *Steelhouse* about ten times I think." He chuckles.

Julia blushes. "I'm glad to know there's another man who enjoyed it." She and Priscilla had gone around and around during editing, as Julia worried it would be too much of a chick book.

Dan laughs. "Well, some men are smart enough to know good writin' is good writin,' whatever the story, and that was damn good writin'."

"Thank you. I had a great mentor." Perched adjacent to Dan on the couch, Julia crosses her long legs and smiles over at him.

Now it's Dan who blushes. "Aww, hell. You had the talent. You just needed a little guiding at times, that's all." He wags a long finger her direction. "But deep down, you always knew what to do." He smiles.

It's evident time and illness have softened him, and Julia's flattered by the exchange. She had always admired Dan's tenacity, and that's what feels sad about seeing him like this. His zeal has faded. Pushing seventy, Dan certainly isn't old by number, but by appearances, it's clear that the years have taken their toll.

"So the book…I mean what the hell are you doin' in Murdoch, anyway?" He smiles.

Julia shifts the cross of her legs again. "Well, if you'd asked me a few days ago I would say I'm here to retrieve my old *Messenger* articles to write about Allison Mercer and Betty Ann Stark's untimely deaths…"

"And now? Now, what would you say?" Dan peers over at her.

Julia sighs. "Now I'm not sure. It seems I have more questions than answers. It also seems there are a few people who'd rather I forget everything again and just go back to New York."

Dan nods his head and laughs under his breath. "Well, it sounds like you're at about the right spot then."

Julia's look of confusion makes Dan laugh harder. She's slightly unnerved by his evasiveness and wonders again if perhaps this was a good idea. *Maybe Dan's loyalties have shifted over the years from independent editor to compliant citizen? Maybe he's like Paul and Marilee and so many others in Murdoch who would rather this all just be left alone?*

Julia finally tastes the sweet lemonade and welcomes the cold liquid against her dry throat. She glances around the cozy living room, simply decorated with family photos and trinkets.

"Look Julia, I'm not laughin' at you. I know exactly where you are...and how frustrating it is. I spent the better part of the last twenty years asking myself the same questions you are now. I'd try to forget them and focus on something else, but then I'd be off coverin' a story or talkin' to someone and somethin' would trigger me. All of a sudden those questions would come floodin' back. I'd get so angry 'bout what happened to those women...and to Seth too, for that matter. So I'd quietly research on my own again for awhile." Dan pauses and sighs. "At first I was convinced I could put it all together. I even thought about writin' a book myself. Hell, I even went to the prison a few times to talk to George. But I'd always end up back at the same place..."

"And where's that?"

"Stuck...and scared." Dan says flatly.

Julia's taken aback by his honesty. "Scared of what?"

"Not what...but whom. I haven't told many people 'bout this..." Dan leans forward slightly and lowers his voice. "I got more death threats than I could count. But when Alice started gettin' them too, I had to stop."

Julia gasps. "Death threats? Who sent them?" Her face flushes deeper remembering the anonymous phone call and Ricky's impromptu visit last night.

Dan shrugs. "I don't really know. They coulda been bullshit, but it didn't matter because I obliged. It wasn't worth risking our safety. My family always comes first." Dan peers over at Julia, his voice laced with concern. "Who knows you're here? I mean who knows about this book?"

"Well, I've talked with Paul and Marilee of course. Marilee and I are still good friends." Julia takes another sip of lemonade. "I've also met with Matt Case. The one that bothers me most is Ricky...he also knows. I saw him at Nine Ed's the other day."

Dan's face grimaces at the sound of Ricky's name. "Aww hell, that's the last person you want knowin' your business."

Julia refrains from offering anything more about Ricky's visit last night. She doesn't want to worry Dan more. Instead, she shifts directions. "So are you willing to talk to me about what you've uncovered?"

A half smile returns to Dan's face. "Julia in case you can't tell, I'm a dyin' man. I got cancer and it's spreadin' fast. I fought it as best I could but I don't have much fight left in me. I'd never, ever want anything to come back to hurt Alice or my family...or you for that matter. So you have to watch your back." Dan looks at her sternly and sips his lemonade before returning his glass to the coaster on the table. "But I've got nothing to lose, and I believe this is a story that needs to be told. It's why I'm glad you're doin' this. So where do you wanna start?"

Before arriving Julia had jotted down the most important questions on her legal pad but now sitting with Dan, she opts to simply converse, leaving her notepad closed beside her.

"Well, let's start with Allison. Why would someone murder a kid? And so ruthlessly? What I really don't understand is why we had to stop investigating and writing about it?"

"You always had this way of asking four questions at a time. I see that hasn't changed." Dan chuckles and then smiles over at her. "Well, let's back up. Allison Mercer was a good kid. Smart, pretty, ambitious. She had everything goin' for her, but she was an unfortunate casualty of a larger web of greed and deceit." Dan pauses in thought and swallows hard before continuing. "It was her death that really haunted me for years. My youngest son Jake was in her class, you know, and he was really messed up about it for a long time. It just didn't seem right that a kid would die and no one would do anything 'bout it."

Julia nods her head. "Well then why didn't we keep going at the paper? We just stopped, and I never understood that."

Dan sighs heavily. "Trust me. It went against every ounce of journalistic integrity in me to stop that investigation. That day George came in, he made it clear in not so many words that if we didn't stop then he'd make sure we did. So I let it be for a few years. Then after he went to prison, I started working with the Mercers to investigate. They had moved to Kansas City by then, but people 'round here slowly starting figurin' out what we were up to…"

Julia jumps into the pause of Dan's slow speech. "So what was Allison a casualty of?"

"Of George and Ricky's side businesses." Dan takes a sip of lemonade.

"You mean the drugs?" Julia quizzes.

"Yeah, drugs were big business for them…"

"What kind?" Julia pries further.

"Mostly pot but also some heroin and meth. Anything to keep the customers comin' back." Dan scoffs. "I'm not sure what all went on but my sense is that things were startin' to spiral out of control. Ricky couldn't cover for George anymore…"

"Wait…" Julia interrupts. "I thought it was the other way around? I thought George was covering for Ricky."

Dan coughs deeply. "Sorry." He takes a deep breath before continuing. "Nope, George Stark was the ring leader, but he started gettin' scared that he was in over his head. So he wanted to switch gears and move in a different direction."

"What kind of direction? And how did that involve Allison?" Julia's confusion grows.

"So if you remember, Allison was a student worker at city hall for a few summers. Well, she was there in June of ninety-six. Let's see, I guess it was 'round the twenty-seventh or twenty-eighth...ahh...doesn't matter. Anyway, at the end of June she was workin' late one day and overheard Ricky and George talkin.' George was puttin' the pressure on Ricky to slow down on the drugs and move into prostitution..."

Julia gasps. "What? Are you serious?! The good Baptist George Stark?" Julia laughs to herself that Marilee was right. He would stick it into anything with a pulse.

Dan nods his head. "That's right. Good 'ol George. So Ricky gets pissed and tells George he's been coverin' for him on the drugs...and you better believe Ricky was in deep on that. But Ricky said the prostitution was takin' it too far, and he couldn't cover for George anymore. They got in a big argument and Ricky storms outta George's office not realizin' Allison's sittin' there, and he tells her to forget she heard anything."

"Holy shit...so..." Julia pauses and lowers her voice, unsure about whether to ask the next question.

As frail as Dan is physically, his mind is still sharp and he answers without her having to ask. "I know what you're gonna ask and that's the piece I still don't know. I still haven't figured out if Ricky actually killed her. Whoever did knew what they were doing because there was no DNA trail."

Dan wipes away beads of sweat forming on his forehead.

"Is this too much for you? I don't want to upset you..." Julia hands him a tissue from the box next to her on the side table.

"No, no it's okay. It actually feels good to be talkin' about this again." Dan's eyes twinkle a bit brighter.

"So how did you find out all of this?" Julia looks puzzled.

Dan leans forward, his tone hushed. "The Mercers."

"Seriously? How did they know? Did Allison tell them before she died?"

Dan shakes his head. "No. Well, not in so many words. Do you remember the rumor about the diary?"

Julia nods. "Yes, of course. That was one of the biggest rumors going around."

"It wasn't just a rumor. There was a diary but it never saw the light of day. Allison had gone to the Mercers that same night in June and told them she wanted to quit her job at city hall. She wouldn't give them a straight answer as to why. She just said it wasn't working out and she wanted to focus her last summer of high school and on studying for the SAT and having fun with her friends. It seemed logical to the Mercers, so they agreed."

The rush of adrenaline rises up Julia's neck, as she wonders why Kate never told her this. This is the first she's heard about Allison quitting, but then again, as Julia quickly scans her mental timeline, she remembers Kate was off work that whole week leading up to July Fourth because they had all gone to the lake. So if Allison had quit that Friday or following Monday, Kate wouldn't have known until after the holiday, which was the week Allison died.

Julia collects her thoughts. "So Allison wrote about all of this in her diary?"

Dan shakes his head gently. "Not in detail, but yeah, according to the Mercers, Allison wrote that things were going on in town and that she knew something she wasn't supposed to, and she was scared to talk about it. Her last journal entry was from that Friday before she went missing on Sunday."

Julia's quietly lost in thought trying to place these pieces of information together, wondering if Seth knew about all of this. Did he know about the depth of George and Ricky's involvement in the drugs? Did he know about Allison and the diary?

"So did the Mercers take this diary to the police?"

Dan shakes his head. "No…"

Julia's taken aback. "Why not? Couldn't it have helped with the investigation? I mean for God's sake's no one was ever even arrested!"

"I advised them not to…advised them to let me work on things behind the scenes to see what I could find out. I mean, at the time I didn't know everything I do now, but I knew there was something fishy goin' on. I'd been suspecting Ricky and George were up to something for years. I just didn't know what." Dan coughs and leans his head back on his recliner. "I knew that diary wouldn't have gone anywhere because the police weren't going to do anything. To tell the truth, I don't think they wanted there to be a motive. They'd have rather kept folks believin' Allison randomly died because of some sick outsider."

"So then was it George who had Allison killed?"

Dan shrugs. "I don't know, but I do know George was adamant we not write about her death. He said it was too upsettin' and at the time, I could see that. Hell, as a parent, I was upset and terrified somethin' like that could happen to an innocent kid." Dan looks down at his hands in thought and then finally up at Julia. "Honestly, I have so many regrets 'bout it all. I wish I could have done more."

Julia quietly absorbs the information, understanding completely the angst of wishing you could do more. Dan's explanation sounds familiar because it's exactly why she never pushed any harder on finding the true cause of Seth's death. Deep down she knew something was horribly wrong about it all, and yet she knew having the Murdoch police investigate would have been a complete joke.

Julia sips the lemonade to steady the emotion in her throat. "It sounds like you did what you knew to do at the time. I understand what that's like…carrying regret, I mean."

Dan nods, his eyes cloud as he peers over at her. "I'm sure you do. I'm so sorry all that happened, Julia. You were so young…"

Already on the verge of tears, Julia interrupts Dan's sentiments to refocus the conversation back to Allison. "Did you go to Seth with what you knew about Allison? Maybe he could have helped you…"

"Julia, Seth didn't have any power to do anything. He was completely hamstrung…"

"How so?" Julia's emotion morphs into frustration.

"As far as I know, and want to believe, Seth was one of the only good guys in that police department. I'm not sure he knew what was happenin' but I think before he died, he started figurin' some things out."

Julia's brain quickly sorts and shuffles memories and snippets of conversations trying to land on anything solid about what Seth might have known. He was so withdrawn by the time he died, their conversations rarely entailed anything other than grocery lists and quick run-downs of weekend plans. Her eyes begin to glisten as she thinks of the burdens he must have been carrying about all of this, and most of all, the feeling of helplessness to do anything about it.

She sighs heavily in resignation. "Yeah, I think he did, too. I questioned him often, but he never would share much with me."

Dan nods in thought. "Well and he couldn't talk about it, especially if he was trying to protect you. There were just so many layers to all this, and it was hard. I mean, no one wanted to believe all this could be happenin' in Murdoch, Mississippi of all places. So I think folks just began to bury their heads about Allison. George had everyone fooled, so they followed his lead and trusted that it must have been an outsider. But then Betty Ann was so brutally killed...and so soon after Allison. Well, it shook this town to the very core."

Dan's musings stir Julia's questions once again. "So then how does Betty Ann fit into all of this? Did Allison tell her about the conversation she heard between George and Ricky? Or did Betty Ann figure it out? Is that why she was killed, too?"

Dan shakes his head. "I honestly don't know...and this is where it gets really complicated. I do know George had been going to Jackson a lot over that summer. So I suspected that Sheila woman was a prostitute and workin' for George, but I wasn't ever able to prove that. I mean she was clearly nowhere to be found after Betty Ann died, and I'm pretty sure Sheila wasn't her real name."

Julia's still taken aback about how the clean-cut, Bible thumping

George Stark could be a pimp. The deceit of it all angers her, especially for Betty Ann.

"So did Betty Ann find out about the prostitution? I mean, maybe she threatened to go public?" Julia recalls the conversation with Marilee and how upset Betty Ann was the night before she died. She obviously knew something.

"I can't say for sure, but yeah, I think so." Dan finishes his lemonade. "George is a smart man, and those smarts were backed by good looks and a heap of old Southern money. On top of all that, he was as slick as oil and could charm the pants off anyone. And that's a dangerous combination when you're convinced you can do whatever you want, whenever you want. So he would've rather gone to prison than lose face over being seen as a sinner peddlin' sex and drugs. I think Betty Ann became another casualty to his ego…and his greed."

"So that's why the defense would have never put that Sheila woman on the stand. It would have cleared George of the murder but would have pointed back to the larger web of scandal he was involved in…and implicated Ricky and whoever else in Murdoch was involved."

"Yep. Exactly." Dan nods. "So that's why George had no choice but to take the fall."

"But what about the evidence they had against George from the murder? Didn't that prove his guilt for killing Betty Ann?" Julia crosses her legs again, which are getting stiff from sitting so long. She glances at the clock and realizes she's been engrossed in conversation for well over an hour and should probably let Dan rest, but she can't tear away now.

"Well, yes and no. That whole investigation was a damn waste of time. Don't you remember how mad I got the day they found Betty Ann? I'm certainly no police officer but I'd been on enough crime scenes to know protocol, and nothing about that investigation was right…or with Allison's investigation for that matter. I think they had George pinned for Betty Ann's murder before he ever stepped foot back in Murdoch." Dan leans forward and lowers his voice. "I think it was Ricky's way of takin' care of things for good."

"So you really think they framed George for the murder? But then who really killed Betty Ann?"

Dan sighs heavily and shrugs his slender shoulders once again. "I don't know, Julia. I honestly don't. It seems plausible that based on the timeline George could have driven back to Murdoch some time that night and done it. It also seems plausible that it could have been Ricky, but once again whoever did it knew what they were doin' because there was no real conclusive DNA evidence. But the kicker to me was that the prosecution didn't ever really produce a motive, at least not a public one."

Julia nods her head slowly. "Yeah, I never understood that, either. So what did George have to say when you visited him? Did he admit that he was framed?" Julia cringes at the thought of sitting across from George in his prison-issued jumpsuit and at how she, too, was reeled in by him. Clearly, George Stark had everyone fooled.

"Of course not. He wouldn't admit to anything, especially not to me." Dan chuckles. "It was all bullshit, and honestly I have picked this all apart every which way I could for years. I've spent years searchin' for some solid evidence to find Allison's murderer and to link her death to Betty Ann's. But once George went to prison, no one cared anymore about finding who killed Allison. Honestly, I think everyone was just so tired of being afraid."

"So wait, you don't think George killed them both? Or had them both killed?" Julia peers at Dan.

"I'm honestly not sure but the more I investigated, the more I've come to believe George didn't have it in him to actually kill those women himself. Ricky, well he certainly has a temper, but even still, I don't think he's dumb enough to commit murder in his hometown as an officer on the police force. He had too much to lose. So this is where I always got stuck. I don't think Ricky or George were the ones to commit the murders, but are they innocent? Hell no. Allison and Betty Ann's blood are all over their hands." Dan hesitates before continuing on. "And honestly, I've often wondered if Seth's isn't also."

Julia sucks in a quick breath, stomach lurching at the memory of Ricky peering over her last night. She swallows hard before speaking. "Yeah, I have spent the past twenty years thinking the same thing."

Dan's voice softens and lowers. "I can't even imagine what you went through being so young and losing him like that." He pauses and looks at her. "Can I ask you something?"

"Sure…"

"Are you writin' about Seth's death in your book, too?"

Julia sighs. "No. It's overwhelming enough to rehash all of this about Allison and Betty Ann…and you've been so helpful, Dan. This is what I needed to really get going, but as for Seth, no I'm not writing him in. Mostly because I'm not ready but also because it's so unbelievable all that happened as it is." Julia inhales a deep breath before continuing.

"Honestly, after Betty Ann's death and George's indictment, he just kept spiraling downward. At first, I thought it was because of their family relationship with the Starks. I mean, Seth had known George since he was a kid." She swallows back the emotion once again. "I would try to get him to talk about it because I knew things were getting more stressful for him at work. But he would just withdraw more, so whatever was going on obviously had to do with what he knew…or didn't know…about Allison and Betty Ann's murders. The more he withdrew, the more he drank. There were nights he'd just sit on the couch sipping whiskey and blankly staring at the TV. I'd go in the next morning to find him passed out on the couch. I was so worried about him but felt completely helpless. I didn't know what to do to help him…"

Lost in the trail of thought, it's Dan's cough that brings her back to the moment. She blushes at the confession, as she'd never talked about Seth's drinking before to anyone except her therapist. She'd always felt it would have been a betrayal to Seth and perhaps somehow indicted him for his own death.

She sighs and looks up at Dan, the tears now fully present. "I never thought Seth would kill himself, even as low as he was. I knew he loved me and would never do anything to hurt me, but then the thought of someone killing him…and it going unsolved like with Allison…was equally abhorrent. I just had to keep focusing on what I could control and that was somehow finding a way to move on in my life. But yes, it was really hard, and still is sometimes."

Dan smiles softly, graciously receiving Julia's confession. "And you've done very well for yourself, Julia. I know it must have been painful to start over like that, but I'm so proud of all your success." He beams at her. "I know all that happened in Murdoch has the makings for a great book, but I have to say I'm worried 'bout you. Are you sure you're really ready to write 'bout all this?"

Julia glances at Dan, his brows furrowed in concern. She sighs heavily. "I've been asked that a lot and I've thought about it a lot, too. I know this is my book to write. In some ways, I feel like this book is taking on a life of its own. I just feel like it wants to come through me, even though I'm not quite sure why yet. I guess partly I feel like in knowing what really happened with Allison and Betty Ann, I could also understand what happened to Seth. I could understand why he felt so burdened by their deaths…and maybe really figure out why…and how he died. Looking back and knowing what I do now, it's almost as if he felt responsible."

Dan swirls the melted ice in his glass, before taking a sip of the watery lemonade mixture. "I wish I could give you answers 'bout what really happened to him…hell to Allison and Betty Ann, too. But all I can give you is what I've cobbled together and my gut feelin' on it all. I think all three of them were killed for similar reasons. I just don't know exactly why or who did it."

Dan pauses and returns his glass to the coaster. "So then can I ask you another question? Are you tryin' to solve all of this?"

Julia shakes her head and smiles sadly. "How can I? I mean no one seems to know conclusively what happened, except for probably Ricky and George. And I'm certainly not involving them…especially after last night."

Dan looks confused. "What happened last night?"

"Ricky showed up at the cottage where I'm staying. He'd been waiting for me to get back, and he told me I was upsetting people. He said I needed to pack up and go home."

Dan groans. "Well, and as much as I hate to say it, I think he's right. I learned a long time ago that Ricky isn't someone you wanna mess with. I don't believe in livin' in fear, but I also don't believe in being stupid. I'm not sure how you will write this book…or if I'll even live long enough to read it. But if you want an old man's advice, then don't try to write this book based on a true story. You just can't do it, Julia, and it's too dangerous. Ricky and George still have their pulse on everything happenin' in this town."

Julia's taken aback by Dan's warning, certain he would want her to push forward to finish what he began years ago to unveil the truth. "I understand…but I can't stand the thought of them getting away with this. It's just not right!"

"No…it isn't right. They have both been paradin' around this town for too long. But if there's one thing I've learned in all this…" Dan motions his hands toward his frail body. "It's that you gotta enjoy your life for you. You can't change the past, and trust me, Ricky and George will get what's comin' to them, either in this life or the next. I don't know if I've ever told a writer to take liberty with the facts, but I'm tellin' you. Just go write a good 'ol story, and most of all take care of yourself. Promise me you'll do that…" Dan smiles broadly at her. "And I really do hope I'm around when that book is done, because I know it will be great. Either way, I'll be proud."

Julia smiles at the thought of adding Dan to the list of people she's promised to be careful. Mostly, she wistfully smiles at the idea of having so many people concerned with her well-being, when for so many years, she was convinced she had to shoulder life alone.

"I promise, Dan. I'll be careful."

After wrapping up their conversation, Julia profusely thanks Dan for his time and hugs him slowly good-bye, for they both know this may very well be the last time they see each other.

Julia drives back to the cottage with the car windows down. Despite the heat, which swirls through the car and brushes her skin, she heeds Dan's words to live her life on her terms. Maybe she cannot fill in every detail of what happened or solve anything, as she has so desperately wanted to do.

As she sighs heavily into the dense summer air, she notices a sense of peace underlying the lingering cloud of questions. Maybe Dan is right, and she'll never be able to unearth the facts of what really happened years ago. But her editor has given her permission to write the story, anyway. And something in her knows it's the biggest assignment of her life.

CHAPTER 36

A hue of gray light permeates the cottage in those minutes just before the sun fully greets the day. Julia's head feels equally gray and hazy after little sleep. She stares at the ceiling fan, making it's rhythmic rotations, much like the rounds of thoughts swirling through her mind. From wondering whether to see Matt again to the new nuggets of insight Dan revealed yesterday, Julia had tossed and turned much of the night.

The only conclusion she's drawn is that coming back to Murdoch has been like shaking a snow globe. All the emotions, memories, and dreams that had once settled into the crevices of her life suddenly got turned upside down. Now as she thinks of leaving, she feels tossed and confused in the aftermath. In some ways, she's leaving with closure and in others, more open-ended questions. Her brain and heart play tug of war in particular around one question. Is she walking away from a potentially good thing with Matt?

Julia rolls to her side and hugs the fluffy down pillow close. She lets out a heavy sigh knowing deep down she needs time to process all that's happened. She also reflects on Kate's advice to go home, refocus on her life, and start writing. With another heavy sigh of tired frustration, Julia realizes sleep is not returning.

After her usual routine of pulling up her hair and brushing her teeth, Julia wanders into the kitchen to brew a strong pot of coffee. Despite the quickly escalating heat, she carries her mug to the front porch. From the white rocking chair, she can see a squirrel playing along the river's edge, darting from tree to tree.

Suddenly, a flash of red catches her eye as a brilliant red cardinal swoops in and perches on the edge of the cast iron fence, interrupting her line of sight between where she sits and the riverbank. She smiles and thinks back to only a short month ago when she sat on the porch at the Johnson's cabin at Lake Burton. The bird flaps his wings clamoring even more attention, which makes Julia laugh aloud.

"I see you." She murmurs aloud as she sips her now lukewarm coffee. The bird turns and abruptly flies away. Her heart sinks as she realizes there's one more thing she must do on her final day in Murdoch.

◆ ◆ ◆

While showering and getting dressed, a random summer thunderstorm had rolled through the area. The dusty road now kicks up thick clumps of mud from her car tires as she heads toward the Murdoch Memorial Cemetery. Clouds still threaten overhead, much like the feeling of dread that looms over her.

Julia had often wondered about facing this moment. What would she say? How would she feel? What purpose would it really serve to stand there talking to Seth's tombstone? She still isn't sure.

Resting her left elbow in that crevice between the door panel and window, she slowly rubs her temple as she steers with her right hand. As cynical and pragmatic as Julia is about believing in signs or synchronicities, on some level she knows the cardinal was Seth's way of reminding her that there's one final piece of unfinished business.

The day Seth was buried, it took every ounce of self-restraint to not throw up or rip off her black pumps and run away. Julia recalls little about the day except sitting on a cold metal folding chair in a black dress next to Nelda, with Kate and Marilee right behind her occasionally taking turns leaning forward to rub her back. For some reason, she also remembers a huge oak tree standing watch over the Dixon family plot.

Julia navigates slowly down the cemetery's worn chipsealed road, which is now broken in areas leaving big pot holes. She draws closer to the tree noticing that grass threatens to overtake the areas between plots, with thick sprigs shooting up. In other places, the ground is almost bare to the dirt. Time has inevitably left its mark on the once lush grounds overseen by the city.

She parks at the edge of the road, sucking in a nervous breath. The car door feels exponentially heavy, and she's greeted by an oppressive wall of sultry air. Julia's sunglasses fog in the contrast of temperatures, even though she doesn't need them with the overcast skies. She wipes the lenses on her shirt before returning them to her face.

Julia tiptoes between the dozen or so gravesites on her way toward the tree, careful not to step squarely on anyone's plot. If not for the tree, Julia might not have found Seth's gravesite. She sucks in an audible breath as she reads his name. It's her first time seeing his tombstone as it was placed a few weeks after the funeral. It resembles Doc's, though both of the thick, marble slabs are now a few shades darker after weathering years of Mississippi's unrelenting heat, pounding thunderstorms, and that rare occasion of snow.

Something about standing here in front of the etched stone punctuates the reality of it all and produces a deep, guttural response. She moans as the tears freely tumble and quickly escalate to sobs. For in this moment, she realizes this is what she had tried so hard to avoid.

The finale.

If she never returned to Murdoch, never stood here as a widow, and never saw the grass covering her husband's grave, Seth remained alive. Year after year on the anniversary of his death, she had replayed the last time she saw him. It's been as etched in her senses as his name in this cold, hard slab.

It was the Friday after Christmas in 1996, just a few months after Betty Ann's murder. Seth's high school friend Scott Turner was throwing a holiday party with all of their old friends who were home visiting their families. Julia didn't want to go but Seth insisted they make an appearance for a little while. She was still silently angry at him for getting so drunk on Christmas Day. He had lashed out at her that night in a drunken stupor, and then profusely apologized for it the following morning, though he admitted that he remembered little of the incident.

She told him that he needed to get a handle on the drinking, and he justified it as stress at work and the fun of the holiday season. He promised to get back to being healthy after the New Year. Above all, he begged her not to say anything to Nelda, and Julia reluctantly agreed. Though they had made up, Julia wasn't convinced of Seth's promise, given the frequency of his drinking bouts the past few months.

That frustration was sparked again as soon as they arrived at Scott's party. Seth had started on the Jack and Coke. Then a few hours later, he wandered over to kiss her.

"I'm gonna run home and grab our domino set so we can get a game going. I'll be right back." He smiled down at her.

"Are you okay to drive?" Julia looked worried, scanning his eyes.

"Yeah, baby, I'm fine. It's just down the street. It won't take me ten minutes."

"Why don't you take Paul with you?" Julia encouraged.

"Oh, he's out back by the fire telling some hunting story. I'll be fine, baby. It'll just take a few minutes. Be back soon..." Seth had pecked Julia on the lips before turning to head out the door.

Julia relented but Seth was right in that their house was, at most, five minutes from Scott's and the route was all backstreets. Plus, as an officer, Seth knew better than to overindulge and drive. But when an hour passed and he still wasn't back, Julia's frustration turned to anger and then morphed into sheer panic. Something wasn't right, and she knew it in her bones.

It's at that point the story becomes hazy. Like how you wake up after a night of intense dreaming, remembering only flashes of colors and frames of scenes. She remembered Scott and Paul leaving the party to look for Seth, and she remembered Paul's voice on the other end of the receiver. Paul's voice cracked through his tears as he relayed to Julia that there had been an accident. Seth was dead.

It wasn't until much later that she learned that Seth never made it inside the house. He must have been walking from their carport behind the house because his body was found in the backyard. Their next door neighbor had called the cops when she heard the gunshot, which pierced Seth through his right temple. The gun found next to him was his police-issued pistol, which he carried in his truck when off duty.

Given that the cops could find no indication of foul play and Seth's prints were on the gun, they immediately ruled Seth's death a suicide without further investigation.

The days that followed Seth's death were all blurred together. Numb from the shock, the funeral was a haze of faces and apologies, though for some reason she remembered this huge tree. At the time of Seth's service, the limbs were bare, stripped of the lush green leaves that now billow from the tree's thick trunk.

Julia glances up at the huge oak, even larger in stature than before. The swirl of memories, conversations with Nelda and Dan, and now the visual image of Seth's grave cascade upon her, shoulders visibly shaking under the weight of it all. She blinks through her tears as she stares again at his name, Seth Allen Dixon, and then down at the dates: November 7, 1969— December 27, 1996.

So much life lived in that single dash, and yet not enough. Not nearly enough time, certainly not enough shared memories.

"How could you leave me?" Julia screams in anger. "Why Seth? Why did you leave me?" She drops her hands to her knees, sobs seizing her strength to stand. Completely overcome, Julia falls the rest of the way to the ground, knees burrowing in the grass still damp from the rain earlier this morning. She gently rocks back and forth like a small child on a blanket. "Why Seth...why?" She groans quietly over and over.

Why would Seth tell her he would be right back if he planned to kill himself? That's the part she never understood, and it's what made the conversation with Dan yesterday even harder to comprehend.

Julia's not sure how much time passes when the sobs finally relinquish. She inhales as best she can to catch her breath. The tears still catching in her throat. "I loved you so much. I just don't understand...I don't think I will ever understand."

Overhead, the sun darts between patches of clouds beginning to dissipate. She pulls off her sunglasses again to wipe her eyes with her slender fingers, and then uses her shirt to remove the smudges from the lenses. When she returns the glasses to her face, she glances up and notices a large rainbow appears to be shooting straight out of a grove of trees at the edge of the cemetery.

Julia half-smiles in spite of herself, takes another deep breath, and stands up. She brushes away the damp grass from her bare legs, then dusts her hands lightly on the back pockets of her shorts. Her throat feels tight as she softly speaks again.

"I just miss you so much, Seth. I don't understand why you died...or how. Was it Ricky? Did he kill you? Or was it someone else?" She shakes her head gently. "I never believed you took your own life...never. I knew you wouldn't leave me...and especially not Nelda. No, not like that...so suddenly with no note or clue as to why. It's just never made sense." The tears silently course down her cheeks.

"I'm just so sorry..." Her voice catches again. "I didn't know what to do back then. After Doc and then Allison and Betty Ann, I just couldn't face any more death. So I just left. I packed up what I could and tried to run as far away as possible. But it didn't work. Clearly, it didn't work. It's been years, and I still think about you all the time. I can't imagine what you were carrying...what all you knew. I just wish you would have come to me. I wish you would have let me into your world. Maybe I could have helped. Maybe you would still be here..." She smiles wistfully. "I have often wondered what our lives would have become if you hadn't died."

Julia looks up into the tree and takes a deep breath, remembering the conversation with Dan yesterday. Her eyes settle back at the tombstone. "I'm so sorry, Seth. I didn't have the strength back then to fight. I didn't have the strength to find out the truth..." She inhales a deep breath of resilience. "But I do now...so somehow...in some way I am going to find out what happened to you, Seth. I promise you that."

The clouds have now made their final departure as the sun beams full force. Julia brushes the sweat now forming along her brow. After a few more quiet moments, she turns to leave. In the car, she finds a tissue in her purse to wipe away the streaks of mascara.

Unsure what to do with herself, Julia begins aimlessly driving toward town. She lands at the one place that Seth used to take her that always made her feel better. Straight to the Dairy Queen for a dipped cone. She also orders an extra hot fudge sundae and heads for the Dixon farm.

CHAPTER 37

By the time Julia arrives at the farm, the ice cream has softened even more, quickly becoming a soupy mixture. She retrieves it from the cup holder and wanders to the front door. Nelda answers on the third knock.

"Oh Julia!" Nelda smiles. "What a surprise! Come'on in."

Julia steps in and envelopes Nelda into a tight hug.

"I brought you some ice cream but I'm afraid it's mostly melted." Julia laughs in spite of herself, feeling like a kid visiting her grandmother. "Did I catch you at a bad time?"

"Oh no honey…" Nelda slowly moves toward the kitchen with her ice cream and places it in the freezer. "It's wonderful to see you, but did you tell me you were coming over?" Nelda turns and looks at her in thought. "I don't remember if you did. Then again, I'm gettin' so forgetful these days I could hide my own Easter eggs."

Julia laughs, feeling the wave of deep tiredness that surfaces in the aftermath of such an emotional release. Her voice is tight upon speaking. "No, I didn't. I just thought I'd stop by and see you…I'm leaving tomorrow morning. I'm sorry I didn't call first."

Nelda retrieves a frosted glass from the cabinet and fills it with iced tea. "Oh you don't ever need to apologize for that. I love that you just came on by, and thanks for the ice cream. You remembered my favorite." Nelda smiles broadly and hands Julia the cold glass. "Here, let's sit down…" She points toward the living room.

"Well, I couldn't leave town without a dipped cone." Julia laughs. "And seeing you again…"

Nelda settles into her wooden glider and studies Julia's face, which is free of mascara but obviously not of emotion.

"You okay, honey?" Nelda asks quietly.

Julia shifts uneasy on the couch and places her glass on the ceramic coaster on the coffee table. "Yeah, I'm okay." She swallows hard and bargains with the tears to keep them at bay. She cannot cry anymore. "I just went to the cemetery. It was the first time I'd been since the funeral."

Nelda nods pensively. "I see. Well, guess it was time for you to do that."

Julia loses the negotiation, as tears once again emerge. She quickly brushes them away. "Yeah, I guess it was. I was sitting on the porch this morning at the cottage and this cardinal showed up." She smiles. "I felt like it was Seth's way of telling me to go."

"Oh heavens, he sure loved those damned birds, didn't he?" Nelda laughs. "I'll never forget that he came home one day from school…oh I guess he was somewhere 'round third or fourth grade. He had checked out a book from the school library all about birds. I think he memorized that book and then walked around looking for every type of bird he could find." She shakes her head. "'Bout drove us crazy…"

Julia laughs. "Oh I remember, he still did that in college. I never understood it, either." She pauses and looks down at her hands. "Every time I see cardinals though I feel like he's talking to me. I didn't want to go today but I'm glad I did."

"Well, it's good for you to have some closure, honey. At least it was for me. I went a few times too, but haven't been back in years…"

Julia's a bit surprised. "Really? Why not?"

"Because they aren't there, and it never made sense to me to stand 'round talkin' to some tombstone. Besides, my life's out here." Nelda waves her hand around her. "Pamela and the kids need me, and as hard as it was, I had to figure out how to move on...just like you."

Julia sighs. For as many conversations as she and Nelda have shared over the years, never did they venture down the path of discussing how Seth died. At first, Julia didn't know how to talk about it, and then over time, it just seemed futile. The only thing that mattered was he was no longer here. Now, however, those memories simmer at the surface, and Julia isn't sure how to shake this feeling of certainty that Seth's death was actually the third murder in Murdoch. The thought of Ricky and George getting away with it all seers her from the inside, out.

"But aren't you angry? His death made absolutely no sense. If he killed himself, why didn't he leave a note? And if it didn't pull the trigger, then who did?" Julia's voice raises as she peers at Nelda. "Don't you want to know why?"

Nelda nods. "Of course I do, honey. I spent years tryin' to figure out what happened...tryin' to understand why and how he died. Honestly, I spent years really pissed off. Finally, I just came to the realization that life's ultimately about being thankful for what God's given you, not angry at what you didn't get...or what was taken away. Really, the harshest truth is realizin' it wasn't yours in the first place. We don't know when someone will arrive in this crazy world or when he'll leave. I'm just so glad Seth was here for as long as he was." Nelda smiles sadly. "Of course it wasn't long enough. Parents aren't supposed to outlive their kids. It's just not right. Ultimately though, I had to remember we're here to serve God and we don't know His timetable. Once the anger passed I remembered that." Nelda smiles again softly. "I think sometimes the real lesson is learnin' how to play with the cards God deals us, especially when we feel like we got dealt a shitty hand."

Julia nods, though she doesn't buy the whole line people would tell her of "it was God's plan." That's one thing she never could wrap her head around...why God would make some people suffer when others got to be happy. She'd spent years trying to come to peace with that and finally stopped trying. So she shoved that unresolved issue down with all the others.

"Well, I don't know about all of that God stuff. I do know I'm glad I made this trip. It's been really hard, but also really good to come back." Julia sighs again as she mentally ticks through all that's happened, though flushes when it comes to Matt. She guiltily looks down at her hands again before taking a sip of tea.

"So can I ask you somethin'?" Nelda's voice turns pensive.

"Of course..." Julia nods.

"In all this, I'm just wonderin' if you've forgiven yourself yet?"

Julia looks up surprised. Nelda's gaze makes her uneasy and she breaks it to stare at the ice cubes she's swirling in her glass. "I don't really know." Julia shrugs. "I'm not sure it's really about forgiveness as much as it is regret. I just feel like I should have done more...like I should have known...and then maybe I could have..."

Nelda interrupts her. "That's what I'm talking 'bout, honey. That line of thinkin' right there. You can coulda-woulda-shoulda yourself until you're plum crazy but you gotta stop that." Nelda's voice turns into a gentle scolding. "You gotta stop thinkin' this is your fault because it's not."

The tears flow freely now. "I know, Nelda. I just loved him so much..."

"I know, honey...and he knows that...but forgiveness doesn't need a line-item recount. It's the unforgiveness that keeps you stuck and livin' in the past." Nelda gently wags her finger at Julia. "I understand where you are though because I did that for awhile, too. I kept goin' over what happened thinkin' the ending would change. But it didn't, honey. The outcome was always the same. So what you have to trust is the love, and know love's always enough."

Julia wipes her eyes again, though she's sure by now there's absolutely no makeup left. "Then how did you let go? How did you forgive?"

Nelda clears the emotion in her throat. "I realized one day it was a choice. Forgiveness was a choice I could make, like choosing what shirt to put on. I had to put on my forgiveness. Eventually, it began to be a habit and then somehow...one day I was just free. I don't know when it happened, exactly. I just know it felt like the burden of unforgiveness...and all the anger that came with it...had lifted. So you gotta decide, honey. Are you willing to *choose* to forgive?"

Julia smiles at the wisdom packed in that small body across from her. She nods in thought. "Yeah, I think I am..."

The two chat for a bit longer about simpler topics before the exhaustion fully overtakes Julia completely. She bids Nelda farewell, hugging her tight and promising to call soon. As Julia heads toward the cabin, she smiles realizing the one thing she's been reminded of above all else on this trip. You have to make time for the people you love and enjoy them every minute they're here.

◆ ◆ ◆

After nearly an hour nap and a cup of hot tea, Julia's sense of balance feels restored. She didn't want to sleep too long, as she needs to sleep tonight. She has to be up early in the morning to head to the airport. Packing her bags, her mind also sorts and folds all the events of the past week.

Overwhelmed by it all, she turns on the clock radio in the bedroom to the local classic rock station to distract herself. She loudly sings to The Eurythmics' "Sweet Dreams," as she plops on the edge of the bed and picks up her phone. Julia responds to a few emails and then texts Jeff to remind him that she'll be home tomorrow afternoon. Just as she's engrossed in some random video on her Facebook page, she jumps abruptly.

BAM, BAM. Julia's heart lurches and she jumps to her feet, mind in overdrive looking for an escape route. *What if it's Ricky? Or that crazy man from the phone? Shit.*

BAM, BAM, BAM. The second round of knocks are more persistent.

Why didn't I hear them drive up? Adrenaline rushes through every nerve. She pulls back the white curtain framing the window and through the pane she's relieved to see the familiar truck parked next to her rental car.

Matt's just turning to step off the porch when she opens the door.

"Leaving so soon?" Julia hopes he doesn't detect the nerves in her voice.

Matt spins back around on the heels of his flip flops. "Oh hey! I thought maybe you were tryin' to avoid me." He flashes that smile and points to her car. "I mean, your car is here."

She smiles and leans against the door frame in an attempt to tame the adrenaline still coursing through her. "I was just packing."

Matt nods. "That's right, early flight, huh?"

"Yeah…" Julia smiles again. "Want to come in?"

"Of course I do, but that's probably not a good idea." He winks and she blushes.

"No, probably not." She glances down at her bare feet.

"I just came by to give you this." Matt steps toward her and hands over a manila folder packed with paper. "It's a few more articles from the *Messenger* and notes from my conversation with George. I'm not sure how much of it you can actually use, but I thought you might want it."

Julia flips through the copies. "Yes, this is great. Thanks so much. You didn't have to…"

"Yeah I did…" Matt interrupts. "I needed an excuse to see you again since you wouldn't come over for dinner last night." He teases.

"Matt, I'm sorry…" Julia's voice turns serious.

Matt holds up his hand. "You don't need to apologize for anything, Julia." He peers at her. "I'm the one who jumped in a little too quickly. I just got excited because it's not every day that I meet successful, beautiful women like you."

"You mean ones who have all their teeth?" Now it's Julia's turn to tease him.

He nervously pushes back his hair and lets out a hearty laugh. "Yeah, that too."

An awkward silence follows, and it's all Julia can do to restrain herself from taking that final step toward him. She pushes her shoulder harder into the door frame, remembering yesterday's bout with guilt and the many miles between them. Something about his playful smile just begs her to forget reality and forget consequences, and yet she knows she cannot cross that threshold again.

"Well, I guess I should let you get back to packing." Matt waves toward his truck. "I hope you have a great trip back, and good luck with the book."

"Thank you…" She changes her mind and quickly steps toward him with outstretched arms. Matt receives the embrace and hugs her close.

"I had a great time." He says softly.

Julia inhales his scent once more. "Me too." She forbids herself from lingering and pulls away before the hug turns to a kiss and that kiss turns to a replay of the other night.

"Take care, Julia." Matt smiles and spins around once more to leave.

Julia returns to her post at the door and watches him walk away. Just as he's about to open the gate, she yells louder. "Hey Matt!"

"Yeah?" He turns eagerly to look at her.

"If you ever make it to New York to see the rats, give me a call, okay?" Julia smiles.

He laughs loudly. "You got it!"

With that, Matt drives away and Julia returns to her suitcase on the bed, a little more flustered and more convinced it's really time to go home.

CHAPTER 38

The nervous anticipation that Julia experienced last week flying to Murdoch is replaced with a sense of nervous exhaustion on the way home. Fortunately, the four-and-a-half-hour flight isn't at capacity so she escapes sitting next to any chatty passengers. Though it wouldn't matter, as sleep evades her.

As soon as she closes her eyes, Julia's mind and body rhythmically hum with the airplane's engines, vibrating from the inside out with emotional exhaustion, tumbling thoughts, and a whole new set of questions. So she spends the rest of the flight listening to music and thumbing through the articles and notes Matt gave her yesterday. Turns out, the articles and notes don't reveal much of anything new that she hasn't already heard or figured out.

It's nearly two o'clock by the time she retrieves her checked bag, secures a cab, and completes the last leg between the airport and home. Over the years, Julia's traveled this same path dozens upon dozens of times between LaGuardia Airport and her apartment. Yet, she's never noticed how frantic the energy feels. It's as if everyone in the airport, cab stand, and sidewalk is on fast forward, huffing and moving quickly. Most are talking or typing on a cell phone with complete disregard for anyone or anything around them.

Matt's right. Everyone does look like a rat scurrying around. She smiles thinking of his assessment and marvels at the contrast between Manhattan and Murdoch.

Julia's not sure what to expect when she opens her front door. She hopes Mr. Pickles hasn't destroyed the place and that Jeff actually upheld his cat-watching duties as promised. But true to her friend's word, the place is just as she left it, with a clean litter box, watered plants, and mail stacked neatly on her breakfast table. She parks her large purple suitcase and drops her leather purse and computer bag on a chair. She shuffles through the mail and alongside it discovers a scribbled note:

Jules ~
Hope your trip was great and you're ready to write! I know it's going to be fabulous. Call me when you can.
Love,
Jeff

Julia smiles at his sweetness and wanders into her bedroom to find Mr. Pickles lying sleepily on her bed sunning himself in the afternoon rays. She lays down to cuddle him, and within minutes, she's sound asleep.

◆ ◆ ◆

Julia awakens confused, uncertain for a moment where she is and then smiles sleepily remembering she's home. Her body must have needed that sigh of relief as well, as she never naps for hours in the afternoon. In fact, she'd stopped taking naps all together before she arrived in Murdoch last week.

"Oh Mr. Pickles, did you miss me?" She rubs his thick coat and he purrs even louder. He must have because he seldom sleeps alongside her, usually preferring the eggplant-colored armchair in the corner of her bedroom.

As she sits up, Julia's stomach lets out an audible rumble, reminding her it's well past lunch and now almost dinnertime. After changing into her yoga pants and favorite tee-shirt, she wanders to the fridge and surveys the scene, which sadly amounts to a carton of spoiled organic milk, two apples, and an assortment of condiments. She grabs the container of Todaro Bros. olives she'd picked up a few weeks ago at her favorite little Italian shop on 2nd Street. Still groggy from her nap, she nibbles on a few as she leans against the kitchen counter. Her stomach growls again and she obliges by ordering Chinese takeout.

After her edamame and Chengdu Chili Chicken arrive, Julia opens a bottle of her favorite Merlot and at last settles into her overstuffed armchair. She enjoys the familiar routine of eating dinner, sipping wine, and watching a few hours of mindless television. By eight o'clock, however, she grows bored and flips off the TV to turn on her favorite jazz station.

She sends a few texts to Kate and Jeff to let them know she made it home, and for a split second, she flirts with the idea of messaging Matt as well. Something in her stops short, and instead, she heads to the kitchen to pour another glass of wine and gather her journal from her messenger bag.

Nestled back in her chair, Julia stares at the blank page and chuckles to herself. *Where should I even start?*

Tuesday, June 28

As I sit here, I don't even know where to begin. So much has happened in such a short time.

Now that I'm home, Murdoch feels so far away. Given the many miles and vastly different rhythms that separate the two, it's easy to see how I could distance myself from Murdoch for so long. It's easy to see how I could get swallowed up in this pace of the city. Here, I could just mindlessly move through my days without much regard to anyone around me.

Dropping myself back in the middle of Murdoch, however, created a ripple effect. Perhaps it's because everything in a small town has its own cadence, one that's intertwined with everyone else's. I had forgotten how intrinsically connected everyone and everything is in Murdoch. It's that connection that I both loved, and the one that I feared, for it can create a stranglehold on your perspective.

As I sit here now, with the frantic city all around me, it's clear to see how I could judge everything that happened. What's most evident now is just how much I had both demonized and romanticized my past.

For years as a writer, I have been driven by questions, and in some ways, I have often found myself more intrigued by the questions than the answers. I realize it's what led me to Murdoch and what's propelling me forward in this book. I still have so many questions. Though some were answered around Allison and Betty Ann, many new ones opened around Seth.

In going back to Murdoch and revisiting my past, my heart broke open all over again. Yet, even through the grief and through all of these questions that still remain unanswered, I feel more at peace than I have in years. For what I realize now is that it's living in the midst of the questions that eventually you live your way into the answers. Curiosity is the essential fuel to keep moving ahead, moving through the uncertainty and fear.

In returning to Murdoch, finalizing the relationship with Frank, and meeting Matt, I discovered, or perhaps was reminded, that I don't have to know. The key to writing this new book will be remaining open, remaining curious, remaining in the mystery, and hopefully I will live my way into the answers of how it all unfolds.

In my conversations with Nelda, I also came to see just how much I had been trying to squelch that curiosity. It felt unsafe to allow my heart to wander through those unknown spaces without a very detailed, very orchestrated road map. For years, I had convinced myself that certainty was my safety blanket, and so I had to calculate every move and feeling to remain safe. Then, in meeting Matt and sleeping with him, it's as if the window broke wide open and the map flew right out. It's no wonder it scared the hell out of me! Matt shook up my very predictable life.

Julia halts her pen, and looks up from her page. She smiles thinking of that night of ecstasy with him, and for the first time since, simply allows herself to enjoy the memory without guilt. She swirls the wine in her glass and takes a sip before picking up her pen to continue.

As I look around my house and hear the city's chaos outside in the distance, I remember that life is always a balancing act of duality, of contrast. Up and down, black and white, happy and sad. For so long, I pushed and struggled to make sense of that duality, of how could I be both sad about the past and happy in the present. I lived as though my happiness was either/or, not both/and. In other words, I never allowed myself to consider that I could mourn the past, while enjoying my life now.

Maybe then I wouldn't have gotten so stuck. Maybe then I could have allowed myself to enjoy my success and even enjoy love. I realize now just how much time I spent looking over my shoulder at the past and invested so much energy trying to change what happened. Then, when I couldn't change it, I just shut down and tried to ignore it.

I finally understand that I cannot rewrite the story of my past. That's what really clicked in my conversations with my sweet Nelda. In hindsight, I see that going to Murdoch wasn't about solving the mystery of Allison and Betty Ann...or even Seth. It wasn't about collecting material for a book.

Going back to Murdoch was about coming home to myself. However, I didn't fully grasp that coming home to myself meant forgiving myself. It meant letting go and relating to my life not as a widow, but as a woman with a story. Perhaps it's not the story I envisioned would happen in my life. It's certainly not the story I would have chosen to write for myself. But what I have finally come to understand is that there's no room for judgment anymore in my story, for it's made me who I am.

For the first time in my life, I am starting to understand that mine isn't just a story I lived. My story is a story worth telling.

EPILOGUE

Julia digs in the back of her closet and pulls out her favorite red sweater. Over the past week, the unusual heat wave finally released its grip and fall has tumbled into the city. She's always loved the first smell of fall in New York and wandering through the collection of golden leaves in Central Park.

The sweater is probably overkill, as she's just stepping out to the market to clear her head. She hasn't left home much over the past four months. When she has ventured out, it's only been for a quick dinner or happy hour with her inner circle of friends.

Of course, she'd also made time to keep up with Kate, Marilee, and Nelda. Over the months, she had graciously declined the countless other invitations for happy hours, lunches, and guest talks, and even backed out of teaching this semester.

Julia's time and attention has been singularly focused on writing. She hadn't really planned it that way, but after she returned from her trip, *Murder in Murdoch* spilled out of her, and a few weeks after Labor Day she delivered the first manuscript draft to her editor, who absolutely loved it.

Now, she's been working on edits to get the next version to Priscilla by Thanksgiving. Even for Julia, it's been a truncated writing schedule, but after returning from Murdoch, she found the inspiration she needed to finally sit down, listen to her inner muse, and write.

On this crisp Friday afternoon, however, she's feeling antsy, wondering what she might do this evening to celebrate the arrival of fall. She roams into her living room in search of her phone and finds it on the coffee table. Just as she picks it up to call Cheryl, she hears a soft tap at the front door. *That's weird. No one buzzed me, so how did they get in?*

Julia squints her right eye to peer out the peephole and quickly steps back. She blinks, heart now racing. *What the...*

TAP, TAP, TAP. The quiet knock returns.

Julia takes a deep breath and opens the door. Standing across the threshold is the last person she'd expect at three o'clock on a random Friday afternoon.

Matt peers at her, wearing that brilliant smile, and cradling a bottle of the red wine they'd shared in Natchez months before.

"Matt! What are you doing here?" Julia smiles completely dumbfounded. She's thought about him so often over these months but would quickly push the thoughts aside. She'd even picked up the phone a dozen or so times to text him but never sent a single one. Reason told her it was better to leave Matt in his world so she could focus on hers.

"I figured if you weren't coming back to Murdoch, I might as well come to you. Besides, you told me if I ever made it to New York to give you a call. It took a lot of convincing over the last few months, but Marilee finally gave me your address. She wouldn't give it to me until she knew you were in a good spot with the book." Matt smiles again broadly. "So I figured I'd surprise you with a bottle of wine to celebrate."

Julia laughs, flattered by his patience and determination. She peers into his bright eyes, which sends that jolt surging through her. "Well, I can't say I've ever been hand delivered a bottle of wine from across the country."

She steps to the side and opens the door wider. Matt moves toward her and before she can speak again, he envelopes her in a hug.

"I wasn't even sure you'd be home." He says softly. "But I'm so glad to see you."

She inhales his familiar scent and smiles with excitement. "I'm really glad to see you too, Matt."

ABOUT THE AUTHOR

J.L. Bass is the creative pen name of the mother-daughter team of award-winning writer, Lara Zuehlke, and her mother, Jan Zuehlke. Hailing from a Southern community similar to the fictitious town of Murdoch, they found inspiration from various true-life events to craft *No Motive in Murdoch*.

For fans and book clubs, be sure to check out the website for fun insights and information.

www.JLBassBooks.com

38209283R00191

Made in the USA
Middletown, DE
07 March 2019